For Roy Erw

H

Sword Of Peace

Cover design by Roseanna White Designs
Model images from Shutterstock
Background painting by Abraham Beerstraaten, public domain

Unless otherwise noted, Scripture is from The Holy Bible, Revised Standard Version

While the events described and some of the characters in this book may be based on actual historical events and real people, Anna is a fictional character, created by the author, and is a work of fiction. A list of actual and fictional characters is at the back of the book.

Disclaimer: The religious views held in this book are typical of the views held at this time in history, and are not intended to disparage or commend any religious denomination.

ISBN: 978-1-7752328-1-0 (digital)
ISBN: 978-1-7752328-0-3 (print)

Sword Of Peace

By Louisa Bauman

Chapter One

November 1531, Amsterdam

These are only a shadow of what is to come...Col 2:17

Anna sighed as she kneaded the bread dough with both fists, punching it into a misshapen brown ball. With work-roughened fingers, she lifted the wad close to her nose, trying to inhale comfort from its yeasty smell. It didn't work. Frowning, she flung the dough back in the wooden bowl where it landed with a satisfying smack. She slapped a cloth over it all, then set the dough on the mantel to rise. Now it should be good for an hour or more.

I'll just slip over to the market to buy butter until the bread is ready to bake. That way I don't have to go see Maeyken's baby right away. Anna grabbed up a wooden spoon and gave the mutton stew a vigorous stir, scraping the sides of the iron pot. The stew burbled over the hearth fire, and she hoped it wouldn't burn while she was gone. Her elderly employer, Simon van Kramer, would never complain if she served him burnt food, but he deserved better.

She tossed aside the flour-dusted apron that covered her floor-length red kirtle and tucked a few unruly dark curls under her white headdress. Swinging her hooded woollen cloak around her narrow shoulders, she headed out the door. The wooden *trijps* on her feet clunked on the worn cobblestones as her easy strides carried her along the narrow streets of Amsterdam. Tall houses loomed on each side, with their street-level shops already open for morning business. Passing them, she crossed the wooden bridge spanning the Amstel river, joining many other market-goers on their way to Dam Square in the heart of the city. As always, she tilted her head to admire the stained-glass windows of the *Oude Kerk,* sparkling like rainbows in the morning sunshine.

A cacophony of voices in Dutch, and in a hodge-podge of foreign accents assailed her ears as she entered the busy marketplace, where dozens of vendors haggled and hawked their goods. Out in the harbor beyond the square, hundreds of ships swayed on the water while merchants from the Baltics, Denmark, England, and other lands, traded their wheat and their wool for the famous Flanders cloth of the Low Countries.

Above the din, sudden angry shouts erupted from the vendors' area, and Anna craned her neck and pushed forward. Who was fighting? Anna sidled closer, slipping between some well-dressed foreigners wearing curly wigs and rich fur cloaks. Near the bookseller's stall, a crowd of curious market-goers surged forward, surrounding two men engaged in a furious argument.

"Just leave us alone and go back to Spain with your senseless orders from Charles!" The red-faced bookseller shouted, clenching his fists. He stood nose to nose with a furious Spanish official, who was trying to show the bookseller some legal document. "We have been running our city for hundreds of years without the interference of Charles V, and it's none of his business what we read, or what we believe!"

"And I command, by the decree of Charles V, Holy Roman Emperor, that you destroy all Bibles, all religious books and all tracts immediately." The officer's lips pulled back from his long, white teeth in an ugly grimace. "They are forbidden, heretical writings and will not be tolerated."

Anna didn't wait around to hear more. She had witnessed firsthand the results of Charles V's uncompromising discipline back in Germany, and she had moved to Amsterdam to escape all that. His imperious decrees did not endear him to all his subjects in the Netherlands or elsewhere, though he was their sovereign, and the ruler of a vast empire "on which the sun never set".

Anna hurried over to the dairymaid's stall, the best place to go for information. As she approached, Helga beckoned her closer, her round blue eyes and red lips nearly bursting with eagerness to relate whatever gossip she knew.

"Did you hear about the new mandate the Emperor has sent out?"

"No. Pray tell me about it." Anna leaned forward, as the noise and bustle of the morning shoppers swirled around her.

"The Emperor is determined to get rid of heresy in all his lands, and has ordered the council to ferret out and arrest every heretic in the city. Which to Charles is everyone who doesn't attend the Catholic church." Helga lowered her voice. "It annoys the *burghers* when Charles sends orders, you know. They have run the town their own way for generations, and they resent being told how to run their affairs." Helga tossed her head, as if nobody should dare to annoy these top citizens of the city. Anna remembered that Helga's father served on the city council.

"Yes," Anna said. "But everyone has to obey the Emperor. God will punish us if we do not."

"Oh Anna!" Helga said. "You're such a loyal saint, bless your heart. But personally, I do not believe God will punish us for not bowing to every decree of that *ondraagkijke man.*

Just because he controls most of Christendom doesn't mean he has to stick his nose everywhere. Charles has never liked Amsterdam, and I think it's because the *burghers* here are better dressed than he is, and they're wealthier too. The Emperor is running out of money with all the wars he's fighting."

Anna frowned. In her experience, the consequences of disobedience were too severe to take the risk. "So, do you think the council will obey?"

"They will have to. Charles set up the Council of Holland at The Hague, and he's going to remove every councillor in Amsterdam who doesn't agree with him. That Spanish man over there, arguing with Bert the bookseller, has been sent here to clear the city of this 'nest of heresy'." Helga looked around before continuing. "The founders of this country had a mighty struggle raising the place out of the marshes and turning it into a rich land. Charles will have a fight on his hands if he means to take away the privileges the citizens have worked so hard to get."

Anna shivered involuntarily. Would there be bloodshed here, as well?

"Helga!" she warned, "Do be careful to whom you talk like this. Your loose tongue is going to get you in trouble." Anna selected a pound of butter, suddenly ready to leave Dam square.

"You won't tell anyone, will you, Anna?" Helga wrung her hands.

"No, not if you keep your disloyal thoughts to yourself from now on. Now I really must get home to bake my bread." Anna paid for the butter, then hurried away.

She was a loyal Catholic for good reason. The Emperor was only one step beneath God Himself, and it would be a sin to oppose someone this close to Heaven. It would mean torment forever in purgatory after death. Anna walked faster, already feeling the demons chasing her. Adhering to the state church was the only way to survive, now or in the afterlife.

She wound her way out of the crowded Dam square, dodging groups of strutting foreign merchants and swaggering Dutch *burghers*. They clutched purses full of coin in their hands, oblivious to the unwelcome tidings; tidings which would affect numerous of the wealthy in Amsterdam. Anna had to get home and tell her best friend, Maeyken, about this disturbing news. At least her best friend was loyal to the crown, and to the Catholic faith.

Anna was halfway home before she remembered the new baby. Drawing in a sharp breath, she slowed her steps. Why did she let it bother her? In a day or two she would recover. She would say her catechism and pray to Mary to help her. She would go to Father Hendricks at the cathedral, and on her knees, confess to the sin of envy. Maeyken was her friend, and just because Anna was a spinster at age twenty, didn't mean she had the right to be jealous.

Straightening her shoulders, she decided she had better get it off her mind and see the baby now. Popping into Simon's house, she dropped off the butter, and took a quick peek at her rising bread dough. It would be good for a little while longer.

Forcing a cheerful smile onto her narrow face, she walked the few steps to her neighbor's house, which was crowded beside Simon's home on the Langestraat, the street of the goldsmiths and jewelers. As usual, she let herself in her friend's back half-door and entered a high, square kitchen, which was lit only by a tall window on the south wall. Maeyken's young maidservant, Janneken, was cutting up cabbages beside a trestle table. She smiled shyly, nodding towards the bedroom.

"*Vrouw* Maeyken is expecting you."

Anna peered into the dim bedroom. Its firmly closed shutters spared the baby from any draughts of unhealthy air, but also made it a little difficult to see anything. A low-burning fire in the fireplace on one wall saved the place from total gloom.

From the rumpled bed in the corner, her friend Maeyken greeted her with a glowing smile. "Anna! Come in, it's so good to see you. The birth seems complete now that you've come to see the babe."

Anna moved to the bedside, swallowing her unworthy thoughts. She tried hard not to feel covetous, but Maeyken seemed to have everything she wanted for herself, everything Anna would never have – a new baby; three other children; a handsome and kind, well-to-do husband; a beautiful face; a lovely home; even a maid.

"How are you doing?" Anna asked. The new mother looked pale as milk, though maybe it was just the lack of light. Longingly, Anna gazed at the tiny sleeping bundle lying on the bed beside Maeyken.

"Well, I don't think I've ever been so tired in my life, but then, I hardly got any sleep last night." Maeyken grinned ruefully.

Anna couldn't take her eyes off the baby. A deep, longing ache reached into her heart and clenched it.

"Would you like to hold her?"

"Of course, I would love to. She's so beautiful." Anna reached out and picked up the tiny, swaddled infant and hugged her tenderly to her breast. *Babies ... they are such sweet little angels.* She sat on the nursing chair beside the bed with the precious armful.

"We named our third little daughter Anna, after you."

Anna jerked her head up, surprised and pleased. "You did? That's an honor I don't feel I deserve. *Maar ik dank u.*" Guiltily, she remembered her thoughts of a few minutes ago. "So Dirk didn't get a little brother. Oh well, maybe next time." She inhaled the sweet, clean baby scent and touched the downy fuzz of hair. "She looks like Adriaen. The dark hair and the wide forehead." Anna's smile and her voice both wavered the tiniest little bit. Maeyken's husband was an example of perfect manhood, the most adoring family man Anna knew, not to mention the handsomest one. He ruled his household firmly, but lovingly, and she had never heard him raise his voice to Maeyken or to the children. In fact, he was as gentle as her own father had been...but she must not think of her father now, or she would end up weeping.

"You would be such a fine mother, Anna," Maeyken whispered.

Anna winced and looked down at the babe as her eyes filled with tears. She was glad for the dimness of the room just then; it was childish and silly to cry because she wanted something she couldn't have.

"You know as well as I do that I will never marry."

"Anna, I know no such thing. There's still lots of time for that. You are only twenty, you know. Not eighty." Maeyken reached out with a languid hand and touched her arm. "You would make some man a good *vrouw*."

"No, I'm too ugly. Every man wants a beautiful wife, or at least a charming one. I am neither."

Maeyken snorted. She could afford to, with her golden hair, smooth complexion, and eyes as blue as a summer sky. She must have been sought after by every panting lad in the

Netherlands if not in all of Christendom. At sixteen, she had married Adriaen, the son of a master goldsmith, and would never be in want for anything.

Maeyken had married exactly the kind of man Anna longed to have for a husband. There had been a man once, but that painful experience only made it plain that it was foolish of her to expect any man to marry her, when there was such an abundance of beautiful women to choose from. Through cruel words, Anna had learned how unattractive she was. Besides, she had coarse country manners, and she was too strong-willed and opinionated. Why should any marriage-minded man look at her twice? As if that were not enough, she was nearly penniless. It had not always been so.

Anna gave herself a mental shake and resolved to stop dwelling on it. She still had plenty to be grateful for. She had a roof over her head, regular meals, and employment with a wonderful old gentleman who always treated her courteously. As if she were a lady, and not just a servant. Best of all, she had found a friend in Maeyken, a friend who would never be so shallow as to judge by appearance, but gladly shared her heart and her little family with Anna.

"I've known you for a couple of months now, and you haven't convinced me there's anything undesirable about you. Somewhere there must be a good man for you. Maybe closer than you think," Maeyken assured her. Anna wanted to plug her ears. Everyone said that, though it was simply not true. The best men were all taken, including Maeyken's husband Adriaen.

Anna abruptly changed the subject. "When are you planning to have her baptized?" she asked, stroking the perfectly smooth baby cheek with a tender fingertip.

Maeyken shifted and the bed creaked on its ropes. "Anna,

she will not be baptized."

Anna looked up sharply. "Maeyken! What are you saying? Babies are always baptized. The only ones who are not baptized are..." Anna's jaw dropped. "Surely you cannot mean...?" She felt cold, as if someone had thrown a bucket of icy water down her back. She stared at the innocent child on her lap, then to the white-faced mother on the bed.

It could mean only one inconceivable thing. An inconceivable thing which Anna had heard too much about at home, something which divided the faithful and the damned. Anna stared at Maeyken as if she had never seen her before. "But you must! You know you must! It's the law!" Anna's raised voice caused her friend to cower into her pillows and clutch the covers. Even the sleeping baby on Anna's lap trembled and blinked in distress.

"Listen! Maeyken, you just listen to me! I heard at the market today that Charles has sent another mandate, and he is putting severe pressure on the council to root out heresy. All the heretics will be punished, and you know what that means. You can't be thinking of joining them."

"Anna, please calm down, and try to understand! It is not heresy to read the Bible and follow Jesus. Let me explain..."

"If you're not baptizing your baby, it's heresy, it's as simple as that." Anna thrust the baby back into Maeyken's bed. "I must go home now and bake my bread." She spun around and hurried towards the door.

"Anna, don't go like this. I can't bear it. Please say this won't change our friendship." Maeyken stretched out her hands, as if she could prevent her friend from fleeing.

"You changed it. I can't believe you allowed yourself to be deceived by heretics. I can't listen to this." Anna shook her head and hastened home as fast as she could go.

Back at Simon's house, she sank down on a stool beside the fireside, the bread forgotten, and stared sightlessly into the dying coals. Her limbs wouldn't stop shaking. She realized that at some point, she would have to go back to Maeyken and apologize for her rude departure, but first she needed time to think.

Thoughts slugged through her mind like the muddy waters swishing through the rivers and canals of Amsterdam. Anna had come to the Netherlands to get away from the persecutions in her homeland, away from the haunting memories. She thought the Lowlands were untouched by the Reformation going on in Germany. It appeared she was mistaken. The heretics were as thick here in Amsterdam as anywhere else, but up until now, the authorities hadn't challenged them. Things were bound to be straightened out now that Charles V's officers had arrived, and Anna's heart filled with a nameless dread. The storm clouds were hanging heavy on the horizon, and there was no safe haven for any one disagreeing with the Holy Roman Emperor.

Father Hendricks, in his services at the *Oude Kerk*, had repeatedly warned his dwindling congregation about these false prophets, to no avail. Anna noticed that each Catholic service she went to, fewer and fewer members attended. By the hundreds, Amsterdam's citizens abandoned the Catholic church and flocked to hear the seditious upstart preachers. These men falsely fancied themselves prophets, said Father Hendricks, claiming that Jesus would be returning soon, and the world was about to end. They blasphemed the pope, calling him the Anti-Christ, and they denounced the Catholic church by naming it the whore of Babylon. But now, their game was over.

Charles V had found out.

Anna jumped up, remembering the bread. She fed twigs into the round-topped oven, heating it to the perfect temperature for baking. The dough had risen too long and was likely to be full of holes - as full of holes as the ideas of the *Anabaptists*, the name given to the new religionists by their adversaries. When the oven was hot enough, she scraped out the coals, throwing them into the hearth fire, then set the dough inside.

Anna stirred the coals with the iron poker until they glowed and sparked, then added more wood. Fire was such a terrible thing; it destroyed and left nothing behind except ashes. Heretics died by burning if they refused to recant, at the stake or even in their own houses. The nightmare was real, and the memory returned to haunt her once more.

On New Year's Day, shouting officers on their horses had chased everyone into the house in Mantelhof, Germany—her parents, her brothers, her younger sister, the neighbors who tried to run away from the shouting officers and their dogs. Then the officers locked the house and set it on fire. Anna should have burned with them. But she had been out on the hills, gathering firewood, and they hadn't found her. The smoke she had seen through the trees had been her first warning, and when darkness fell, only red-hot coals and ashes remained of her home and her family.

In a near panic, she stepped outside, away from the heat of the oven. According to the priests, heretics would continue to burn in hell forever, and so it would never end. She stood on the stone step of the house and leaned back against the door frame. The neat rows of buildings on Langestraat looked deceptively innocent as she stood there. Which buildings housed Anabaptists, and which held adherents to the true Catholic church? Lifting her face to the sky, she prayed to

Mary to intervene for her soul. Back in Germany, she would go and buy indulgences to cleanse herself from sin. Here in the Netherlands such things were not allowed.

Buying indulgences from priests, who had special permission from the Pope, reduced the time the soul spent in purgatory, and she used to buy them as often as she could. The religious Reformers protested vigorously against this act, denouncing the indulgences as useless bits of paper, and insisted that only through forgiveness of one's sins through the death of Jesus Christ could one go to Heaven. They thought the money would be better spent on the poor. They also attacked the Sacraments of infant baptism, extreme unction, and the mass; and condemned the relics of the saints and the use of images, among other things.

The long-standing traditions of the Roman Catholic church had been honored for centuries. Why were people stirring up trouble now? If a person obeyed the commandments of the church, went to communion and mass regularly, and confessed all sins to the priests, they were an obedient subject. There was nothing wrong with that.

She alone of her family had refused to listen to the Anabaptist hedge-preachers in Germany, must she listen to them now? Her parents and siblings had begged her to go with them to the secret 'meetings', but she loved the old familiar chants of the Catholic priests, the beautiful cathedral with its stained-glass windows, the paintings of Jesus, the golden images of Mary, the smell of incense and the air of holiness. Images of her family burning in hell forever tormented Anna's dreams. No priest had administered the last rites to them, they had not been anointed with the holy oil. It seemed cruel and unfair, the worst thing that could happen. She could not bear to witness the death of loved ones again, not without the comfort of knowing that their souls were winging up to Heaven.

Maeyken an Anabaptist? It was impossible. Anna had thought nothing of it when her friend no longer attended mass, assuming it was because of her increasing girth, and then her confinement. With difficulty, Anna controlled the urge to go back to Maeyken's and beg her on her knees to come to her senses. Somehow, she must convince her friend to forget this nonsense. She simply could not know what she was letting herself in for. Was Adriaen involved? With a sinking feeling, she knew he must be. Maeyken would never do such a thing without her husband's approval.

Anna shuddered. Maeyken and Adriaen had no idea what she had suffered already because of heresy. She must warn them, only she could not tell them her story without reliving the terrible memories. It seemed she had not run far enough away from home. The nightmare had found her here.

As Anna had found out in Germany, a sure sign of Anabaptism was the refusal to have their children baptized. They claimed it was unscriptural. This idea was absurd, and Anna was glad the Emperor was stepping in, lest the land become populated by little devils in the form of children. By not reporting this new baby, Anna realized with a start that she would be regarded as a sympathizer, and therefore a criminal, and worst of all, she would be accused of consorting with the devil. But Maeyken and her family were not evil!

She clenched her fists. How could Maeyken put her in this position? She could at least have kept it a secret. Why, oh why, didn't they just have the baby baptized and be done with it? Why oppose the powerful state church about a minor thing like this? Were their beliefs worth imprisonment, or execution? Did they not believe that they were risking their souls, and that it was a sin to disobey the ordinances of the church?

Anna shook her head as she went back inside. She must stop dwelling on it. There was work to be done. Simon would soon be home from the market, and he would be hungry. Perhaps with the wisdom of his age he could tell her what to do. It would be impossible to report her friend, and impossible not to. However, she was not ready to lay her neck under the sword, die at the stake, or be buried alive.

She rubbed her neck. Distractedly, she set some cheese and wine on the table and removed the golden-brown bread from the oven, scraping the charcoal flecked bottom. The pigs would get the bottom crust for their supper. As she was scooping the hearty stew into a pottery bowl, Simon arrived for his midday meal.

"Smells wonderful in here, Anna. You can sure cook." Simon greeted her with his usual words of praise as he lowered himself into his chair.

To Anna the food was tasteless, and she picked at it as she tried to find the words to share her predicament. But would speaking her mind condemn her gentle, elderly employer as well as herself? If she told him, he would become as guilty as she. What if he then made it his duty to report Maeyken's baby? No, it would not do. She would have to think some more. Though God would surely punish her if she didn't do her duty, she thought, crossing herself. Simon glanced at her fleetingly.

"Anything the matter?" he asked, concern in his faded blue eyes.

Anna shook her head. "Nothing at all."

She decided it would not be fair to involve him. So, in the end, she said nothing.

In the evening, Simon informed her he was planning to visit a friend some distance away and he would be home late, possibly staying until tomorrow.

"Perhaps you might stay with Maeyken for the night?" he suggested, fastening his good velvet cloak. "Adriaen is going with me, and I know Maeyken would appreciate having you there."

Anna stared at him in dismay. Ordinarily, she would have rejoiced at the offer. But now...how could she possibly go back there so soon? She crumpled a corner of her apron with restless hands.

"I shall think about it. Though I do not fear staying here by myself."

Simon peered at her with keen, old eyes as he stroked the wispy white beard adorning his wrinkled face.

"You decide what you want to do. You are free until tomorrow morning." Simon clapped his plumed hat on his head. Anna nodded, her head spinning. With another inquisitive glance he left, leaving her standing in the middle of the swiftly dimming kitchen. Evening shadows crept all around her and still she didn't know what to do.

Would Adriaen tell Simon about his newborn daughter? Would he take the risk of Simon reporting it? Anna didn't think the kindly old man would do such a thing, but the alternative was disobedience to God and to the government.

Finally, deciding she was too worn-out to see her friend that night, Anna crept up the stairs to her small room and climbed into her straw-mattress bed. Pulling the woollen blanket around her ears, she tried to block the voices warring in her head, as well as the images of red and gold flames that insisted on twisting through her dreams. Guilt pricked at her conscience for not doing her duty to the church by reporting

Maeyken. The bells on the church chimed the midnight hour by the time Anna made up her mind to deal with it first thing in the morning.

Chapter Two

Amsterdam, November 1531

I have no one like him, who will be genuinely anxious for your welfare...Phil 2:20

After tossing and turning all night, Anna was ready to get to work. It was too early to visit Maeyken, so she grabbed a bucket of water and got down on her knees on the doorstep. She scrubbed until it was clean enough to use as a trencher. If only her conscience were this clean.

Maeyken's house was quiet and still as Anna slipped inside the unlatched back door a little later. She tiptoed across the checkered tile floor, as pale morning sunlight slanted into the shadowy kitchen. In the adjoining bedroom, Maeyken snored, with the tiny infant snuggled against her cheek. The frilly night cap on Maeyken's tousled head rested askew, and with gentle fingers Anna touched the golden strands of her friend's hair.

She stood back, both admiring and coveting the picture of new motherhood. If she did her duty to the church and the state, this too-perfect little world would be destroyed. All she needed to do was go to the town hall right now with her story, and the constable would arrive before Maeyken awoke. But how could it be right to arrest Maeyken? She hadn't done anything wrong, except missing church and refusing to baptize the baby. But wouldn't God punish Maeyken for these omissions? The priests claimed so, and who was Anna to think otherwise? He was a God that would not be scorned, and His wrath was terrible. Anna crossed herself.

An image formed in her mind of the rough constable arriving with his sharp steel sword and his chains and his voice of doom, and then poor Maeyken quivering in chains. She should not have come here, sympathy for her friend was preventing her from doing the right thing. But right for who? There could be no justice in arresting a new mother, especially not Maeyken. Anna remembered there had been a woman back in Germany who had been chained to the table leg, making her a prisoner in her own home, while allowing her to continue with her household duties. Maybe this would be the only punishment for Maeyken if she reported her. Still, Anna could not do it. Why should her friend be dragged from the childbed and put in chains for refusing to baptize her baby? Anna didn't agree with the actions of her friend, yet she found she didn't have the heart to destroy this little family, rules or no rules.

But what if Anna was arrested for her part in this deception? Was it worth the risk to herself? There was no answer and no way out, but still, she could never forgive herself if she caused the execution of her only real friend in the world. No matter how strongly she felt about the rightness of the Catholic church, or how dire the punishment to herself, this was where she put her foot down.

There was only one thing left to do. Maeyken must be persuaded to forget her fanatical new ideas. Didn't she realize the baby would also be cast into purgatory if it died before receiving baptism? Anna shivered as she remembered seeing those unhappy graves set apart in a place reserved for the damned. Of course, the damned could not be buried alongside the blessed. Imagine those poor infants sharing a spot in unconsecrated ground with criminals and witches.

No, her little namesake must never rest there.

Maeyken stirred, and gave a start to see Anna standing at her bedside. Her eyes flew open. "Anna! What a surprise!" Maeyken croaked. "I didn't think you were coming back."

"I had to come back, Maeyken, for good or for ill."

A troubled look flitted across Maeyken's face. "I can trust you, can I not?" She struggled to sit up, and Anna extended a hand to help. She ignored the question for the moment.

"Should I make you some bread soup? Or some ginger tea?" Anna offered. "Then we can talk while you eat."

Maeyken nodded as she picked up her infant daughter and held her close to feed. "Be sure to make some for yourself."

When Anna returned with a steaming bowl of bread and hot milk, Maeyken was lying down again, with the baby struggling against its firmly bound cocoon. Baby Anneken put her head back as far as she could, wailing with her tiny pink-gummed mouth wide open.

"I've had another tiring night," Maeyken admitted, with fatigue in her voice. "This baby is a hungry little thing, and with Adriaen gone, I hardly slept at all."

Anna started guiltily. "You should have sent the maid over to fetch me. I could have rocked the baby for you."

Maeyken frowned as she spooned the soup into her mouth with a thin, white hand. "Anna, you must understand why I could not do that." She took another spoonful and leaned back on her pillows. Maeyken had never looked this ill before. The usual sparkle in her blue eyes was gone, and her fair hair tangled limply around her head, a fact not hidden by her cap. The dingy gray woollen robe did nothing to improve her color.

"Maeyken, I want to apologize for my actions yesterday.

Forgive me, I did not handle the shock very well." There, it was out.

"I do forgive you, from the bottom of my heart. These trying times will test many friendships, I am sure. I just couldn't keep this secret from you any longer. I trust you to do the right thing."

A heavy burden slipped off Anna's shoulders, although she was certainly not worthy of any trust Maeyken put in her. At least Maeyken was not angry with her. She picked up the squalling baby. Anneken was surprisingly strong and protested noisily as Anna quickly changed her and bundled her up in linen swaddling.

"This one will be strong-willed, I do believe." She walked the floor, murmuring to the baby. "She will need lots of love." Anneken stopped crying, and with contented little sighs she slowly fell asleep.

"Oh Anna. I often think you should be the one to have babies instead of me. You have a real touch with them." Anna quickly turned her face away from Maeyken and blinked away a tear. "I don't want to have babies instead of you," she said, "I want us both to have a husband and children."

With a touch of bitterness, Anna shook her head. She was more likely to be drowned as a witch than bear children. So far, no man had offered for her hand and she couldn't blame them. One glance at her reflection in the looking-glass told her why. Her face was narrow and long, with large, murky gray eyes and a nose that was too long by an inch. Ugly, even if Maeyken didn't think so. To her sorrow, she had long ago realized that she possessed none of the coyness that men seemed to adore. She was just a stiff old spinster whom nobody would ever love. Every day she must struggle against self-pity, bitterness and envy, something she failed at far too often, and which brought her continually to her knees confessing to Father Hendricks.

"Don't despair," Maeyken said. "I believe the day will come when you have your own family."

"I hope you're right." With a sigh, Anna settled into the woven-straw nursing chair at Maeyken's bedside, the sleeping babe in her arms. She swayed gently, reveling in the feel of the soft body next to hers, imagining it was her own child. What if it was hers and Adriaen's? Anna jerked her head up. Where had that shameful thought come from? Her face grew hot, and she was glad Maeyken had dozed off again.

A short time later, the trill of children's voices trickled down the stairs. The maid, Janneken, got them dressed and fed, while the happy chatter of children's voices filled the kitchen. Janneken had been clattering around since had Anna arrived at the house, and now the aroma of baking bread wafted into the bedroom. When Maeyken awoke, Anna opened the door to the kitchen and let the children in to see their mother and the baby.

"Is *Vater* home now?" Trijntgen inquired, skipping to her mother's side. Shy Bettke, just three, stayed in the doorway of the bedroom, while Dirk crawled in on all fours and pulled himself up at Anna's knees. With their fair hair and blue eyes, and dressed in white gowns, the children resembled little angels. Only the baby had inherited Adriaen's dark hair and eyes.

Maeyken glanced to the window, unable to hide her concern. Adriaen should have been home before dawn or shortly after, and it was mid-morning already. "No, he's not back yet. Why don't you go sit on the doorstep and watch for him? I am certain he will be home soon." After taking an adoring peek at the new addition to the family, Trijntgen did as her mother asked, and went to play a game with pebbles on the doorstep.

"Now we must talk," Anna said, though Maeyken was rubbing her eyes which were still heavy with sleep. Anna rocked faster. "How did you and Adriaen come by your misguided beliefs? Surely you do not intend to stick with this fanatical sect."

Maeyken sighed deeply. "Anna, I am but a simple housewife, but I know this is not a fanatical sect. The *Doopgesind*e desire only to live by the Scriptures. If only I could read, I would show you exactly what the Bible says," Maeyken glanced at a shelf on the wall, and Anna noticed for the first time the thick volume resting there. Anna could read a little, but she didn't offer to hand the Book to her friend and read to her. Reading the Bible was the sacred duty of the clergy, who were consecrated by God to do so, not for laymen and women.

"At the meetings when the Brethren read," Maeyken continued softly, "my heart becomes filled with peace and I know it is the truth. No matter what happens, I am ready to lay down my life if need be, and suffer, as Jesus did for my sake."

Anna stared at her friend. *Doopgesinde.* 'Baptism-minded'. She remembered that her own family hadn't liked being called Anabaptists, or Re-baptizers. Their baptism as babies they had called worthless, as if it had never been, so they could not be *re*-baptized. Their baptism as adult believers was their first true baptism. Even then it was only a symbol of the blood of Jesus washing away their sins, the water itself having no power. The disturbing thing about it was that it did somewhat ring true, and Anna did not want it to ring true. She wanted everyone to stop the upheaval and live in peace, as before.

A strong premonition came to Anna that she was too late to prevent her friend from continuing her course towards a certain early death at the hands of the Court officers. After Maeyken faced the wrath of the officers, she would then have to face the wrath of God.

"Who gave you these ideas? And when did you see these people without telling me?" She frowned, not comprehending how Maeyken reached this life-changing decision without Anna hearing about it.

"You remember when Adriaen's brother, Joachim, was here for a few days, about a month ago?"

Anna remembered well enough, but she was shy of strange men and had made herself scarce at Maeyken's house during that time. She had made the mistake of falling in love once, and it had been a mistake. By now, she knew better, and there was no point in battling against the inevitable. After the first brief glimpse of Adriaen's handsome brother, she ran into her own house and hid there until he left.

"What about him?"

"He is one of the preachers for the Brethren, and he goes from place to place spreading the word. We melted many a candle in the night while he taught us from the New Testament. One night, the believers even met in our barn." Her eyes turned soft in remembrance. "That's the night Adriaen and I were baptized."

Anna nearly dropped the baby. "You mean you have already been baptized by the Anabaptists? Is this not a bit sudden? Maeyken, did you even think about what you were doing?" Her feet hit the floor with a noisy thump. "I should not even be here talking to you! My life and my freedom are in danger as much as your own. What if you are arrested? What about the children? What if you are executed? I do not understand."

A couple of tears slid down Maeyken's cheeks. "I know you don't understand. You are as solidly Catholic as a priest." She sniffled, and Anna handed her a clean cloth. "And yet, more than one priest has left his papist beliefs and joined the new religion. A monk in Germany and a priest in Switzerland awakened the world to the need for change."

"Oh yes. My parents were full of Martin Luther and Ulrich Zwingli, and those two are bad enough. But even *they* don't tolerate adult baptism or the refusal to use the sword." Anna looked at Maeyken hopefully. "If you're not happy with the Roman Catholic church, couldn't you join the Lutherans, or the Reformed? This group you've joined is so radical!"

"No, Anna," Maeyken answered. "The clergy are more concerned with their earthly lives than anyone's spiritual life. They spend their time gambling and drinking and worse. Also, the true Christian cannot kill, and neither Luther nor Zwingli wants to stop fighting wars or stop executing those who oppose them. Maybe when I'm stronger, you could consider going with me to a meeting of the Brethren and see the difference for yourself?"

"Me?" Anna's head jerked up. Her startled voice woke the baby, who started fussing again. "Me? Go to a heretic meeting? If I did what I should, I would race to the town hall and bring the bailiff!"

"What is stopping you?" Maeyken's voice was quiet and sad. "If you really believe that, I am ready to bear whatever God allows. As it stands, the law demands of you that you do it."

"Oh Maeyken..." Anna joggled the whimpering baby.

"No, I could never report you. I know the law, but report you, my best friend? No. I cannot be the cause of your arrest, and much less of your death." Anna rose from the chair with the baby in her arms and walked the floor again. "But what will you do? I cannot stomach the thought of causing your arrest, but someone else may well do it for me." A frown creased her forehead. "You can't hide a baby forever. Can't you just have her baptized and save your life?"

Maeyken sank weakly onto her pillows. "No, Anna. Adriaen and I have turned our lives over to the wisdom of God and wish to do only what is written in the Scriptures. Nowhere does Jesus desire infants to be baptized. He said, 'Suffer the little children to come unto me.' They are innocent. Baptism is for believers. Jesus also said, 'If any man would come after me, let him deny himself and take up his cross daily and follow me.'"

Anna opened her mouth, but words refused to come. She had never heard of this. Few people she knew were good at denying themselves. For some reason, Father Hendricks came to mind. She wondered if he had ever denied himself anything in his life. Quickly she crossed herself. Where did that unholy thought come from? She swept the picture of his bejeweled and fleshy person out of her mind.

Maeyken held out her arms for the fretting baby. "She must still be hungry." Anna handed her over and kept on pacing the floor. "Who taught your so-called preachers all this? Why would your group of merchants and burghers better understand the Scriptures than the universities, or even the pope? They must be interpreting the Scriptures wrongly."

Maeyken sighed, her voice a mere whisper. "God teaches us through the Scriptures, and He alone is the authority. It is a simple faith. Many of the priests have never read the Bible, you know. We can't really trust them to teach us the truth."

Anna's jaw dropped. She twisted her head from left to right, as if checking for the devil crouching in a corner. What terrible curse might fall upon her for listening to this sacrilege? She backed towards the door.

"I'm tiring you out. Why don't I take Anneken to the kitchen when you've finished with her, and you get some rest?" Maeyken nodded wearily.

The maid was chopping onions near the kitchen window, and the strong odor brought tears to Anna's eyes. Or were the tears for something else?

It was mid-morning and she ought to be at home doing her own housework. However, if Adriaen wasn't home yet, chances were, neither was Simon. Why had they not returned? Simon had told her they might stay the night, but she assumed they would be back early in the morning. Something must have happened to delay them, and she had dark suspicions about where they had gone.

She darted a quick look outside. The three children were playing in the dirt yard, waiting patiently for their father to come home. Trijntgen was leading her younger siblings in a game of hide-and-go-seek. Their childish voices and pattering feet brought a pang of sorrow to her heart. What was their future?

When the sun was high in the sky, the men had still not returned. Anna stayed for the main meal of soup and fresh brown bread, and carried a tray of food to Maeyken, who needed a few more days before she could get out of bed. Her face was even whiter than it had been in the morning. She kept tilting her head to listen, clearly desperate to hear her husband's footsteps on the stone path.

It became obvious, yet unspoken, that Simon and Adriaen had gone to a secret Anabaptist meeting, and Maeyken had good reason to be worried. If Anna's capacity for shock weren't already full, she would be shocked about Simon. As it was, it all fit together. The evening was a strange time to go visiting, unless there was a secret, forbidden nocturnal meeting. Had the two men been discovered?

Anna was not surprised to see that Maeyken ate very little. She managed a few sips of soup, then laid down her spoon. For the first time, there was an awkward silence between the two young women, and the only reason Anna stayed was because Maeyken seemed to be too tired to care for her baby.

As the afternoon wore on, the anxious mother alternated between taking short restless naps, listlessly feeding Anneken, and straining her ears for the sound of footsteps. Maeyken's lips moved in prayer, her face pinched and gray, 'Father, Thy will be done.'

Towards evening, the sound of horse's hoofs striking on stone struck terror into their hearts, and they looked at each other with eyes as large as saucers. The only people who travelled with horses were the officers. Should they flee? There was nowhere to go, even if Maeyken had the strength.

Chapter Three

Amsterdam, November 1531

...the Gospel for which I am suffering and wearing fetters like a criminal. But the word of God is not fettered...2 Tim 2:9

A swarthy officer with a drooping, red under-lip barged into the house, clanging a chain, without so much as a knock or a shout of warning. Anna gasped, recognizing him as the same man who had been arguing with the bookseller at the marketplace. The overpowering reek of sweat trailed in after him and dampened the under-arms of his blue and yellow slash-sleeved doublet. The smell mingled with that of horse manure, which was spattered on the striped hose stretching valiantly over his flabby legs. The officer was followed by his long-nosed little servant, who in contrast was clad in plain brown doublet and hose.

The terrified children quivered in the corner beside the hearth with Janneken the maid. Her face was as white, and her eyes as huge, as any of the children's.

The heavy boots clomped straight to the bedroom, where their wisp of a victim lay pale and resigned in her bed. For a second the big man paused, his hairy hands opening and closing on the chain. He drew together his formidable eyebrows above cruel, hard eyes. "In the name of the Holy Roman Emperor, I hereby place you under arrest for heresy. Get dressed immediately."

Anna rose like a great brown hawk from the chair beside

the bed. "What do you think you are doing? This woman is weak from childbirth! She will die if you drag her off to prison!" Her whole body shook with rage and indignation. "Leave us in peace. This woman has done no wrong!" She clenched her fists as if ready to attack both men single-handedly.

The slap of a powerful palm smacked into her face. "Quiet, you ugly witch! We take no orders from women. Especially not those who defend heretics. Pieter, fetch another chain. This one's going too."

Anna clutched her swelling face with trembling hands, dazed and bewildered. "But I'm not a heretic. You can't arrest me!" She glared at the constable's unyielding face.

His flint gray eyes glittered like shards of granite. "Chain her hands too, Pieter."

The servant was down on his knees attaching the cold chain to her ankle as the officer spoke. The burly constable was doing the same to Maeyken, having changed his mind about allowing her to dress. Anna watched helplessly as Maeyken submitted without protest to the man's rough treatment. Not for Maeyken the heated protests of her indignant friend. Maeyken grabbed the baby and some extra swaddling from the bed as she was being prodded across the room. The pair of chains clanked loudly across the tile floor.

The children! Anna hoped Janneken had enough sense to take them out of sight, so they wouldn't have to see this — though the girl was probably too scared and inexperienced to think of such measures. Sure enough, they were still clinging to each other in the corner by the hearthplace as they passed through the kitchen.

"Can you keep them safe until we come back?" Anna hissed, peering into the quailing maid's eyes. Janneken nodded. A terrible wailing and crying arose from the corner, which chilled Anna to the bone. What would happen with the children? She knew she ought to direct them somewhere safe, but her mind was in a whirl and she could not think.

Outside, she searched the street with stricken eyes, desperate for rescue of some kind. Surely Adriaen and Simon would come along any minute. Yet inwardly she knew they would not come.

Up and down the street there was silence. All the inhabitants had vanished into their houses, though she sensed them peeking out from behind their curtains. Cowards! Did the cobbler then have no boots to mend today, and had the goldsmith perhaps run out of gold to work with? Anna clamped her teeth together so hard they could have bent out of shape.

Why didn't someone come out and put a stop to this indignity? She knew as she fumed that it would only serve to the constable's advantage if he could find more victims. Doubtless, the horse's saddlebags held more sets of chains.

Anna kept anxious eyes on Maeyken as she stumbled along the street. Would she be able to keep up until they reached the town hall? If she had the freedom of her own hands, she could at least carry the baby. She opened her mouth to demand the bailiff to let her do this, then clamped her lips together. The quieter she stayed, the better for them both. She feared she had said too much already.

Fortunately, the *Stadthaus* was only two blocks away. A couple of times Maeyken nearly fell, and Anna worried she would drop the baby. The chains jangled and banged along behind them, the iron fetters chafing her ankles as she trudged along. The horse huffed along beside them, not understanding why he must keep to the slow pace of women.

The sharp hooves landed far too close for comfort, Anna thought. And must the servant keep brandishing that mean-looking whip?

The sad procession kept on going past the shops. Anna looked straight ahead with her neck stiff and her back straight. She might be ugly Anna who had no husband, but a criminal she certainly was not. This constable must know that he had no business arresting her just because she happened to be in Maeyken's house. On the other hand, Maeyken needed someone to care for her where they were going.

The twilight sun beamed into the town of Amsterdam this evening as the bell on top of the *Stadthaus* tower tolled the hour of vespers. The last chime still vibrated through the air when they stumbled onto the cobblestoned court of the *Stadthaus*. A stable boy came running up to collect the snorting horse, and the officer dismounted. Using the whip in his hand, he pointed the way past massive ornate columns supporting five imposing arches, above which the second-storey mullioned windows seemed to frown in disapproval. The square-faced tower loomed over the surrounding buildings, and high up on its square sides peeked several tiny windows.

The officer prodded the two women through the double oak doors, marched them down an arched stone corridor, and up a winding open stairway, passing several landings. Maeyken climbed slower with every step, white-faced and hollow-eyed. When they reached a small landing almost at the top of the tower, they were pushed through a plank door into a small austere room.

Maeyken staggered over to the bed and sank onto it, hanging her head as she panted and swayed with fatigue. Anna hurried to her side, grabbing the baby before the child fell to the stone floor. She wrapped her free arm around her friend while the officer stood in the doorway twitching the whip and glowering at his victims. The servant removed their chains and hung them on a peg on the wall.

The cell held one narrow, filthy-looking cot and not much else. Anna wrinkled her nose; the odor of the previous tenants hung heavily in the air, making her wish she could open the tiny window. But it was barred with iron rods, and too dirty from the dust of many years to let in much light.

"If you want to be present at your husband's trial tomorrow," the officer said, looking at Maeyken, as if he enjoyed passing on this cruel message, "tell the jailkeeper when he brings your bread in the morning."

Maeyken fainted in Anna's arms, and Anna laid her back on the bed as gently as she could. "Go away!" she cried, no longer caring what they might do to her. "Don't you see you've done enough to this poor weak woman? And mind that you bring some warm blankets and some decent food tonight! She needs nourishment for the poor babe's sake. Or do you mean to kill the baby too?" Anna trembled with rage and fear.

The two men took a step back and looked at each other in disbelief. "Let us depart," the servant said, clutching at the officer's sleeve. "This may be a witch."

The officer jerked his arm away from the servant, and the two men hastened to leave, closing the heavy door behind them with a thud. The key turned in the lock with finality and doom.

Hours later, a bowl of steaming soup was thrust into the room along with a woollen blanket and a jug of stale water, the door opening only a crack, so they couldn't see who brought it. Maeyken lay still and pale on the cot, shivering under the thin blanket. The baby's thin wails echoed hollowly in the stony-walled room. Anna laid her down beside Maeyken, but she got little nourishment. She managed to feed her friend a few sips of the tasteless soup, ate a little of it herself, then decided she had better save the rest for the morning.

During the night, Maeyken tossed and turned and mumbled incoherently. Anna wet a corner of the baby's extra swaddling and wiped her friend's feverish face. Little Anneken fussed herself to sleep in Anna's arms, frequently waking through the long night, her crying becoming gradually weaker. Anna fumbled in the dark and offered her little finger to the searching mouth, but this only worked for a minute or two. Frowning, Anna laid her down beside her feverish mother, then shook Maeyken awake.

"Maeyken!" She moaned and rolled over. Anna grabbed the baby and set her beside her mother on the other side. Hungrily the infant tried to feed, but soon she put her head back and wailed in shrill frustration. "Maeyken! Wake up!" Anna shook her again, more than a little uneasy when she touched her friend's hot body. Holding the squalling baby in one arm, she managed to wet the cloth and wash her friend's face.

If only she were at home she would send for the doctor, or at least brew some herbal tea. It was the longest night Anna had ever lived through, and she prayed without ceasing to Mary and every other saint she could think of, until morning came at last. She had not slept at all and Maeyken was clearly delirious. Folding some of the swaddling and laying it on the filthy floor, she made a nest of sorts for the baby, who now merely whimpered in her sleep.

Much as she dreaded seeing her captor again, it was the

only hope she had of doing anything for Maeyken other than wiping her face with tepid water, and that too, was running low. For a long time, she held her best friend, whispering, "Maeyken, wake up! We love you. We need you. Your baby loves you. Adriaen loves you and so do Trijntgen and Bettke and Dirk." Maeyken rolled her blue eyes as if trying to struggle out of the delirium that held her fast. She moaned, then slumped forward, her weight resting on Anna's shoulder.

Anna tried not to think about the reason they were trapped in here at all. If Maeyken and Adriaen had not so foolishly let themselves be drawn to the treasonous Anabaptists they might all be at home, safe and comfortable. Now God was punishing them, and Anna wasn't surprised. People who had to sneak about at night to preach must be hiding something.

She gazed down at the tiny bit of life, about the size of Adriaen's two hands, and thought it extremely unjust that this tiny person must suffer because of her parents' erroneous beliefs. If Anneken died, Anna crossed herself, no one would grieve more than she would. Why had she let herself become so attached to this innocent little one? She hugged the little bundle to her breast, and tears fell unheeded. She tried to rid herself of the thought that the devil had not yet been baptized out of the babe.

Sitting up straight, Anna eyed the jug of water on the floor. A little bit of water remained, and she could baptize the infant herself! If midwives could baptize in dire situations when no priest was available, she reasoned, then so could she. What would Maeyken say to that? Was it more important to obey the priests, or laymen? The answer was clear. It would be her secret. Anna bent and lifted the jug, sloshing the water inside. There was enough.

She held Anneken out in front of her, and three times

she sprinkled a few drops of water on the infant's head. It would have to do. "Anneken, I baptize you in the name of the Father, and of the Son, and of the Holy Spirit. Amen." Anneken blinked her eyes, but continued to sleep. Anna held her close, satisfied that the baby was now blessed if the worst happened. Sitting on the edge of the cot at Maeyken's feet, she bowed her head and prayed for Maeyken, for the baby and for herself. She vowed that if they all got out of this place alive, she would stop wishing for a husband and serve God only, all her remaining days. It seemed a small sacrifice to make.

Opening her eyes, she couldn't decide whether the sun was shining or whether it was a grey day. It was hard to tell through the dingy window. Anna's stomach growled. Eyeing the soup from the night before, she considered feeding some of it to Maeyken, except it had a grayish scum floating on top. Anna couldn't feed her that, and she decided she wasn't hungry either; moreover, fasting was good for the soul, and this was an excellent time to do so.

After what seemed like hours past sunrise, she heard the tread of heavy footsteps coming up the stairway. Anna didn't know whether to be relieved or terrified. The key rattled in the lock. She shrank back onto the cot when the officer stepped through the door, wearing the same smelly clothes of the day before. He stared with hard eyes at the tiny form in Anna's arms, then at the crumpled, limp figure on the cot.

"Get her up. You're going for questioning now."

Anna stared at him, her eyes bulging. "Get her up?" she sputtered. "I've been trying most of the night to wake her up! Don't you know a deathly ill woman when you see her?"

The man narrowed his granite eyes. "You're mighty bold for a witch, aren't you? We'll see how well you can defend yourself at the trial."

Anna shivered involuntarily. The officer marched over to the cot and gave Maeyken a rough shake. He must have been convinced by her hot body and small moan that she truly was sick.

"Leave her, and come along now." He reached for the ankle chain hanging from a peg and shook it, the sound sending another shiver down her back. She did not fancy being fettered like some animal going for slaughter, though that was possibly what she was.

"I don't need to be chained. I won't run away, I promise." But the cold metal was already squeezing her ankle.

The chain clattered along behind her as she descended the long, winding stairway with difficulty, the officer tight at her back. He led her along the arched corridor, and into the main hall, a large square room with windows on three sides. A row of stern-faced, black-robed councillors sat on benches, and the clerk sat at a desk with a heavy book in front of him, his quill poised to record every word of the trial. The judge rose, rustling some official-looking papers. What was written on there to condemn her? Anna, with a guard on either side of her, held her head high as she stood facing the row of intimidating faces, determined to prove her innocence.

"Have you been re-baptized?" the hook-nosed, heavy-set judge asked her severely.

"No, Your Honor, I have not, nor do I intend to be." He gave a small start of disbelief. His dark eyes bored into hers.

"Then kindly explain why you were keeping company with this seditious Anabaptist sect." His eyes never left her face as she stammered out that she had been unaware until that very day that her neighbors had joined the Anabaptists, and she had gone to help with the new baby.

"A likely story. I think you know more you are telling." He studied her face shrewdly. "So you won't mind if we go ahead and bury alive your friend back in the cell who is feigning illness, trying to elude justice?"

Anna cried out, "NO, Your Honor! You can't do that! She is truly ill and very weak. She needs to be at home in her own warm bed with wholesome food!" Her whole body shook. "I doubt the baby will live much longer. Is this what you intend to do...murder babies?" The judge's face darkened. She had angered him with her outburst.

"Just tell us the name of the man who re-baptized her, who else was there and where they meet. Then you can all go home." Anna stood there in shocked silence. Her head began to spin until she thought she would faint. Though she certainly was no Anabaptist, her stomach roiled at the thought of betraying anyone to a certain death.

"You must tell us what you know," the judge ordered. "Unless you're one of them, you will give us this information. Justice shall be served. You are already guilty because you did not report the baby." He coughed delicately into his black sleeve. "We will get the information out of you one way or the other. Perhaps you would like to visit the questioning room?" Anna shook her head in horror. How had she gotten into this mess?

The judge spoke in a soft, wheedling voice. "You do want your friend to be able to go home today, don't you? Do as we ask, and you shall be on your way within the hour."

Anna trembled from head to foot in mighty temptation and anger. How dare they put her in such a trap? She considered what she knew and wished she knew nothing. Maeyken, with her trusting nature, had told Anna things which could end up costing them both their lives, as well as the life of her husband.

If Anna gave the judge Joachim's name and the information that he was a leader, they would probably let her and Maeyken go. She thought of Maeyken lying feverish in the cold cell, and the poor babe, her namesake, who would die if she didn't receive milk within an hour or two. She weighed this against the sure knowledge that Adriaen's brother would be hounded to every corner of Christendom once they found out he was an Anabaptist preacher. And when—not if—they found him, he would be made to suffer cruelly and be executed painfully. But maybe Joachim could evade them for a little while longer.

"Wha...what do you want to know?" The councillors looked at each other, a glint of triumph in their eyes. The clerk bent to his black book, moving the quill in rapid strokes. A deep despair filled Anna's heart. These men were ordained by God to administer justice to criminals, but this verdict wasn't fair. Maeyken and Adriaen and his brother never hurt anyone, even if they did read the Bible and preach without the authority to do so. By his cunning, the judge had her in a trap, exactly where he wanted her to be.

"I will tell you, but only if you promise to take Maeyken home...on horseback, not walking," Anna said, lifting her chin a trifle.

"So, you think to negotiate. Very well, you have my word." The judge waited, like a dog expecting a juicy bone. Of course, Anna thought bitterly, releasing a dying woman was an easy trade for an Anabaptist preacher.

Anna tried to get the image of Adriaen's handsome brother out of her head. Her mind froze. *Mary, sweet Mother of Jesus, help me.* Adriaen would hate her if she betrayed his brother. She would hate herself. Would God ever forgive her?

She prayed Joachim was well on his way to another part of the country by now.

"Tell us who baptized Adriaen and Maeyken Geerts. And where this man is now," the judge insisted.

Humiliated by their pleasure, she told them what she knew, which wasn't much, but quite enough to set the hounds on the trail of someone she barely knew and had nothing against. She sagged, and the guards prodded her upright again. When they were satisfied that she knew no more they took her back to the cell and removed her chains.

Maeyken was still thrashing around on her cot. Anna wrapped her in the woollen blanket, not caring who it belonged to. She motioned to the guard who had escorted her back to the cell and he picked up Maeyken, slinging her over his shoulder like a bag of wheat. Anna winced. Picking up the featherlight bundle from the floor where she had left her, she frowned and followed him out. The baby's veins showed bluish through the translucent skin, and her eyes looked sunken. She barely stirred as Anna settled her in her arms.

Outside in the sunshine, Anna blinked and took a deep breath of sweet, free air. A stable boy brought a saddled horse, leading him beneath the arched portico. Anna hovered nearby as the guard swung up Maeyken, then mounted the horse behind her.

"Do you know where she lives?" Anna ventured. The guard nodded curtly. Maeyken mumbled some unintelligible words, but she didn't wake up. Anna stood in the shadows beside one of the ornately carved pillars, the babe in her arms, and watched Maeyken leave, wracked in indecision. Would the guard treat her friend with compassion? Anyone was better than that horrible officer, Anna thought. She needed to follow Maeyken home and take care of her, yet the baby would die if she didn't get milk very soon. She strode to the corner and looked left and right. Which way? Maeyken or the baby? Who needed help the most? Breaking into a half-run, Anna made up her mind.

Elizabeth's house was only a block away, and much as she hated abandoning Maeyken right now, she had to save the baby. She slipped down a narrow side alley between rows of tall, looming buildings and arrived shortly at a tidy little house tucked between two taller ones. She pushed open the door without knocking. A pleasant-faced young woman looked up from her work in surprise. Elizabeth sat in a chair by the window, knitting, and at her side on the floor was a woven basket with a small form inside. Anna had met Elizabeth only once before, a few weeks ago, when she had come here with Maeyken to see the new baby boy.

"Anna!" she gasped. She tossed her knitting aside and rose, holding out her arms. "What is this?" Anna's tears fell, clouding her vision, as she crossed the room.

"Maeyken's baby. She is...she was...!" Panting, she handed the infant to Elizabeth. "Help her!"

"Of course. You can tell me later." Gently she unwrapped the fragile bundle and shook her head when she saw the wrinkled little face. "It may be too late, but I'll do what I can." She sat in her chair and held the baby close. Anneken sucked weakly, trying to draw forth nourishment, then fell asleep again.

"Elizabeth, do you know where Adriaen's brother went after he left Amsterdam?" Anna asked in a strangled voice. Elizabeth raised an eyebrow.

"Why?"

"His life is in danger! I must send word to him. Could

you ask your husband to find out where the Anabaptists hide and send them a message?" Anna crumpled the corner of her apron in agitation. Elizabeth shrugged, her brow furrowed. Anna couldn't keep still another moment, and she turned to leave.

"I can't stay. I must see to Maeyken, she's very ill. Will you do what you can for the baby? I will come back later to check on her."

Elizabeth nodded. "You do that. I want to hear what happened."

Racing along the cobbled street, Anna hastened back to Maeyken's side, stopping only at the apothecary for some Angelica root to help get the fever down.

Her friend lay dishevelled in her bed where the officer had deposited her, with the children and the maid gathered around her, crying and frightened. Anna sent the children and Janneken outside with kind but firm words, asking them to search for more firewood. They were not to worry. Anna would take care of their mother, and she would be fine in no time. She doubted her own words, but there was no need to alarm the children now.

Anna plumped Maeyken's pillow, smoothed the sheets, and shifted her into a more comfortable position. She combed her friend's tangled golden hair and placed a clean cap on her head, straightened her gown, and tucked the blankets around her. She crossed to the kitchen hearth and checked the stew pot. Thankfully, Janneken had some pea soup cooking above the fire. With a wooden spoon, Anna dipped out some of the fragrant liquid.

One spoonful at a time, she fed tiny sips into Maeyken's mouth, and managed to give her some of the powdered Angelica root. When she had done everything she could think of to make her friend comfortable, Anna finally took the time to eat some soup herself. She tried not to gulp down the food.

And, she tried not to think about Adriaen and Simon lying in prison and what they might be enduring. She wondered how it happened that the two men became captives, though she presumed they had been surprised at an Anabaptist meeting. Gentle Simon with the Anabaptists? Why?

What was it that caused these people to gather in obscure hiding places to hear someone speak about the Bible? Did their preachers know something that the Catholic church didn't? How could that be? The pope, the bishops and all clergy were ordained of God, and were these commoners saying that God made mistakes? Anna wished she had asked more questions of her parents, God bless them, but she had not wanted to hear a word about it. And she didn't now, she only wanted to know what was so special about their meetings. Nothing, she told herself, could induce her to risk being arrested out in a field somewhere, and she hoped never to see the inside of a prison cell again.

Still, she wished these people no harm, even though she had been coerced into betraying one of them. At this very moment officers were out there, scouring the country, hunting for Joachim, intending to execute him, not for murder or theft, but for preaching against the doctrine of the state church. Of course, he was disobedient, but still she hoped they never found him. She was all for law and order, but she couldn't help but feel the church was taking things to an extreme. First, they took her family in the most horrible way, and now they were after her only friends.

Was this another sin to confess, that she was questioning the actions of the church? Did that make her a heretic as well? She supposed not, since she regularly attended mass and confession. This covered a multitude of sins and was something she could do to prove that she was faithful. She would pray like never before, confess her sins to Father Hendricks, and do her penance for doubting the Holy Church. But could she walk away from her Anabaptist friends in their time of need?

She looked at Maeyken, who tossed and turned in her sleep, her cheeks flushed and hot. Tenderly, Anna arranged the blankets around her friend once more. She managed to coax a few more sips of broth between her lips, although most of it dribbled out again. Anna frowned. Was this her penance and her punishment from God for being jealous of Maeyken and her new baby? And her adorable husband, she admitted with shame. Must she lose her only friend, who had welcomed Anna so warmly to the neighborhood when she was alone and friendless? Perish the thought. Maeyken could not die on her.

"I'm so sorry, Maeyken," she whispered. She smoothed Maeyken's damp and tangled hair, alarmed at her increasingly hot skin. Should she fetch the doctor? Or the midwife? Anna dreaded bringing in someone who might ask too many questions, someone who would be obliged to report the situation. She filled the basin on the washstand with cool water and wiped Maeyken's face and neck. The washcloth came away practically steaming.

She had promised to check on the baby, and she must go soon, or she would be out after dark. Sighing, she left the bedside. Inspecting the herbs hanging from the ceiling in the kitchen, she selected a bunch of mint leaves and crushed them, inhaling the refreshing fragrance. She made a poultice and wrapped it up in a cloth. The children stared at her, their eyes huge with worry. Anna's heart melted at their innocent little faces.

"Janneken, can you sit with Maeyken for a minute?" The maid nodded timidly. "Take this poultice and hold it onto her forehead. It might help break the fever." Anna took the two youngest children on her lap, snuggling their trusting little bodies close. Trijntgen huddled against her side.

"Where's *Vader*? And the baby?" demanded Trijntgen, looking at Anna with worried blue eyes.

"*Vader* has gone away for a little while, and the baby is with Elizabeth and her baby, Jorg," Anna said. "Do you remember going to see them?"

Trijntgen nodded. "A bad man brought Mama home." After a long pause, she asked the question Anna did not want to think about. "Will Mama die?"

Anna hesitated. She wished she knew the answer, and that she could truthfully say she would not. But there was so little anyone could do for childbed fever. And with the terrible happenings of the day before, it only added to her troubles.

"Trijntgen, only God knows this. You must be very brave and play quietly with your brother and sister. Perhaps when your mother is feeling better, you can see her. For now, Anna will be here to take care of you, no matter what happens." The little girl seemed satisfied for the moment. Anna realized she was committing herself, but she felt she had no choice. The maid was young and inexperienced and there was no one else. She would do this for Maeyken, and because she loved the little family like her own. Even the father was a prince among men in her opinion, and she wished he were there to comfort them all.

"And now I must go and check on your baby sister.

Elizabeth is looking after her while your mother is sick. Come, here is some bread for you to eat while I'm gone."

Before Anna could change her mind, she checked on Maeyken once more, then sped down the street, racing against the gathering darkness. She was in a blur from lack of sleep, and fervently hoped the baby had revived. The houses loomed over her, shoulder to shoulder, with their jagged rooflines silhouetted against the purpling sky. The windows reflected the gloomy clouds, and shutters were being closed for the night. Anna arrived at Elizabeth's house, out of breath and uneasy.

Elizabeth let her in with a smile, and showed her the two little bundles sharing the woven straw basket. Anna's spirits lifted, and she was gratified to see Anneken alive and looking much better.

"How is she doing?"

"When she realized she was actually getting food, she perked up," Elizabeth smiled. "She's a strong baby." Anna nearly sagged with relief, and she breathed a silent prayer of thankfulness to God for sparing the innocent child thus far. It was a miracle. She had been so afraid she might come to a scene of grief, and she would have dreaded going back to Maeyken's with sad tidings.

"Can she stay a while longer?"

"Of course. Now, sit down on this stool by the fire and have some of this meat. You look like you're ready to drop on the floor yourself." Elizabeth handed Anna a plate of chicken wings, which she accepted with thanks. "Now, tell me what this is all about. What happened to Maeyken?"

Anna picked at the meat as she related the story, and Elizabeth's brown eyes grew wider and wider. "So Adriaen and Simon are in prison, you say?" she asked, a ripple of concern on her forehead.

Anna nodded. "They haven't come home yet. The magistrates were threatening to 'question' them. We know what that means." The thought of Adriaen and Simon on the rack tore at her heart.

"Oh Elizabeth, I betrayed Adriaen's brother! I wish I had never known about him being an Anabaptist." She put her hands to her face and wept, tears dripping through her fingers. Elizabeth laid a comforting hand on Anna's shaking shoulder.

"Yes. But then they may have tortured you if they didn't believe you don't know anything. Thank God you were spared that." She stood at Anna's side, deep in thought. "When Claes comes home I will ask him what to do. Thanks to you, Joachim had a head start. If it be *Gods wil* for him to escape, he will. Do not fear."

"Well then, I will ask Mary, the mother of Jesus, to pray for me and for Joachim, in the hope that it is *Gods wil* to spare him." Anna wiped away the tears with the back of her hand, and bent over the two sleeping babes. Elizabeth's healthy boy looked twice as large as tiny Anneken. She smiled, her maternal, protective instincts coming to the fore as she studied her little namesake. It was incredible how much better the baby looked, with pink color in her soft rounded cheeks. Anna stood to leave, satisfied that Anneken was well taken care of. Elizabeth's kitchen was fast becoming dark and Elizabeth was lighting candles by the time Anna left for home in the hastening twilight.

Maeyken was no better. Her breath came shallow and faint, and at first Anna thought she was not breathing at all. She tucked in the blankets and washed her face. Anxiety overwhelmed her, and she wished Adriaen was home. What else should she be doing to save his wife's life? Would he want her to send for the doctor? The priest? Probably not a priest. Should she go light a candle in the church or ask the Virgin Mary to intercede? Somehow, she didn't think it was what they would want. She had no idea what Anabaptists did when someone was deathly ill, but she'd bet it wasn't that.

Anna was so tired, and she dropped in the chair by Maeyken's bedside, folded her hands and laid her head beside her friend. Throughout the day she had prayed to Mary and to the saints to intercede for her, and now she also tried praying to God directly, just in case the Anabaptists were right, and He could hear her desperate prayers.

Chapter Four

Amsterdam, November 1531

For here we have no lasting city, but we seek the city which is to come... Heb 13:14

When Anna woke up, she was shocked to see thin rays of sunlight poking through the slits in the shutters. Morning already! How long had she slept? She jumped to her feet, and her hand shook badly as she reached out to touch a much-too-quiet Maeyken. Panic rose within her. Why was Maeyken so cold? She placed a hand on the unmoving lips. *Dear Father in Heaven, let there be breath!* But no flutter of breath warmed Anna's fingers. She probed her friend's neck, desperate to find a pulse, while her own very-alive heart thudded in her chest.

"Maeyken! Wake up!"

It could not be true. Maeyken's life could not have faded away while Anna was sleeping. Anna couldn't move, couldn't speak. As the truth sank in, a heavy stone seemed to settle in her stomach. She had failed to stay awake during her friend's last moments. She steadied herself on the bedframe with one hand, and gazed at the white face, the peaceful smile, the bluish, translucent eyelids. Finally, she leaned forward and covered Maeyken with the sheets.

The tears froze in Anna's eyes and refused to fall, and through the pain, a numbing despair took over. All those prayers she had said asking Mary and the saints to help her had done no good, neither had it availed anything to pray like an Anabaptist. God had seen fit to remove Maeyken from her life, and she must accept it as *Gods wil.* Why hadn't God taken her instead of this much-loved, much-needed young mother?

There was a chill in the air, and Anna walked over to the window and opened the shutters wide, desperate for warm sunshine and fresh air. A couple of chickens pecked around in the dirt yard, and a bird sang its morning greeting from the boughs of the apple tree. Anna looked left and right, up and down the street, and saw only a young shepherd boy on his way to the pasture to guard the village sheep, with his crook over his shoulder and his meagre lunch in a bundle swinging on the end of it. She longed to join him in his carefree day, to whistle on her way without a care in the world like he was doing.

Sighing heavily, Anna turned around and dragged herself back to face the still body of her friend. What now? Was Maeyken's soul in Heaven, and had she won her crown as she had believed she would, or the other...but she would not think of that. Of course, sweet Maeyken would not go where the fiends dwelled. Even if a hundred Father Hendricks said so, she refused to believe it. She crossed herself and shivered. Would the bells on the church toll for Maeyken, or would the clergy refuse to do her friend this last honor because she was Anabaptist? With a start she wondered whether she could even be buried in the churchyard. And if she was, would she be in the part where the witches and murderers were buried, in unconsecrated ground? *Please, God, no! Maeyken deserves better than that.*

She must tell the children. Anna wiped her eyes with her apron, and splashed some cool water on her face from the basin beside the bed. The dreadful task must be done, and there was no way around it.

They were chattering away to Janneken as she prepared her daily bread dough. As soon as she stepped into the kitchen, the babbling stopped, as if the children sensed that something terrible had happened. Trijntgen blanched and stared at Anna, while Bettke put her thumb in her mouth and backed into Janneken, whose hands ceased their kneading. Alarm filled the maid's face as the truth sank in without a word being spoken.

Anna sat on the bench close to Janneken and gathered the children around her. She picked up Dirk, who at only one year old would never remember his mother, and held him to her breast. "*Kinder...*" she began, but before she got another word out, Trijntgen and Bettke burst out in sobs, and there was nothing for it but to weep along with them. Janneken resumed her kneading with tears running down her cheeks, and kept on kneading long after the dough was done.

"*Kinder*, I am so sorry," Anna tried again. "Yes, dear *Moeder* has died, *God zegene haar ziel*." Maeyken's love of God had been clear, and it must be true that He blessed her soul. But what would she do about a burial? It was not in her place to arrange this, it was Adriaen's duty. He should be home to take care of everything instead of lying in prison. Would the officers allow him to come home for his wife's funeral, or were they too hard-hearted?

Without giving it more thought, she picked up Dirk, and taking one of Bettke's hands and Trijntgen the other, she strode towards the door. "Come with me, *kinder*. We're going to find *Vader*." Three teary-eyed, forlorn faces looked at her with awe.

"And bring him home?" Trijntgen asked hopefully,

wiping her nose and her eyes with her apron. Anna fished a cloth out of her bodice and cleaned everyone's face.

"Let us hope so." Losing one's parents was hard, and having their father home would surely assuage some of the grief the children were suffering.

"And Janneken, you come too."

"Thank you, miss. I...I'm a-feared to stay here alone with... with her."

"Of course."

Anna settled the little boy comfortably on her hip and headed for the *Stadthaus*, her chin in the air. The children needed their father now that they no longer had a mother. Surely, the authorities could not be cruel enough to deny this to Adriaen and to his children, at least long enough to bury his wife. The Court officer was probably still lolling in bed this early in the morning. Or so she hoped. Housewives threw open their shutters, and stared with round eyes at Anna, the maid and the children as they passed beneath their windows. The stench of their just-emptied slop pails crowded out the clean scent of the fresh morning breezes, and Anna wrinkled her nose.

"Anna, where are you going? Out to the sea, to wait for a handsome prince to come sailing in and carry you away?" The housewives smirked at each other, then turned away laughing. Anna clenched her jaw and looked straight ahead. If only it were so simple. Why couldn't they just go hide in their houses again? Should she tell them that Maeyken had died? Would they care?

The guard looked up drowsily from his post outside the door of the *Stadthaus* when she arrived, unfolding his head from his large black beard, bleary from his drinking the night before. He straightened up when he saw who had arrived, and he narrowed his small and piggish eyes. His meaty hand clutched the hilt of his sword, and he puffed out his wine-splattered, satin-slashed doublet.

"Where are you going this morning, *mijn lieve heks?"*

I'm not your dear witch, Anna thought, but said nothing. The guard eyed the children as if they had just crawled from beneath a pile of dung. "And the lovely children." His smile didn't reach his eyes, but revealed his uneven yellow teeth.

"I've come to take Adriaen Geerts home." She stared the man in the eye, giving him a look that used to terrify the village bullies when they had pushed her too far.

He laughed incredulously. "My, my! Aren't we brave this morning!"

Anna glared at him, not giving an inch. Surmising that he was half-drunk, she pushed past him, the children in tow, shoving open the heavy oak door of the town hall. The guard swore and followed her for a few steps, thought better of it, and returned to his post. She marched her little procession along a stony arched hallway, dim with age and tears. She surprised the young jailkeeper, who was loafing in the study with his feet on the desk, a jug of wine in his hand.

Stiffening her resolve, Anna collected every shred of conviction within her, and took a deep breath. "I need you to unlock the cell of Adriaen Geerts. These are his children. His wife passed away last night, and he needs to go home and bury her. He will make sure you are well paid."

The jailkeeper eyed her up and down, then raked his gaze over the young maid. "How do I know that's true?"

"Have you ever known Adriaen Geerts to not honor his commitments? I know his family means more to him than his money." She glared at him. "A fact you cannot fathom, I'm sure."

The jailer narrowed his eyes, "Watch your mouth, *je heks.* I could lock you in the dungeon as easy as not, so be respectful." He appraised her once more, a cunning look in his eyes, then stood. "I don't know why I'm helping you out, except I know Adriaen has the money, and as you said, he will honor this unauthorized charge you are casting upon him. In any case, I will make sure he does. I may as well take a share of the money before the Court confiscates it. I will need 10 florins."

Anna gulped, but tried not to show her dismay. This was more than her father had made in a year on the farm but, of course, a master goldsmith like Adriaen probably earned much more. She shoved away her guilt about promising Adriaen's money to this crooked jailer, deciding Adriaen would want to get out even if he lost some money. His wealth wouldn't do him any good if he were executed.

"Of course. Now show us the way."

Jangling his keys nonchalantly, the jailkeeper sauntered down the hallway and opened the door that led to the cells downstairs. Anna shivered. This was no place for wide-eyed children and cowering maids, but what was done, was done. She ought to have left them all at home, but with their poor dead mother lying there? No, it wouldn't do. She could still turn around and go home, only there might never be another chance to rescue Adriaen. And she wanted him out! Shifting Dirk to her other hip, she stepped down the crumbling stone stairway, with the others hanging onto her skirt as they followed her downwards.

Someone was groaning down there, and another cursing, but above and between all that, Anna heard a soft, clear tone. Someone was singing! Adriaen. She would know his voice anywhere.

"My God I am thine, what a refuge divine..."

His ardent baritone floated through the squalid quarters, masking the cursing voice, almost letting her forget, for a moment, that this was a dungeon. Almost, but not quite. This area was much worse than the place where Anna and Maeyken had been kept. A pervading dampness clung to the skin, and the eye-watering stench alone was enough to be called torture. The odor of unwashed bodies, human waste and the decay of ages was sickening.

Anna reached down to bring her apron to her nose, but then thought better of it. She refused to show any weakness in front of this contemptible man. He must never know how hard her heart was beating.

The children clung to her long skirts, pressing their little noses into the folds. The jailkeeper fiddled with his keys, then looked at her maliciously.

"I don't think I have the right key with me. I guess you better go home."

As if on cue, the children all began crying at once. Their barely restrained terror had been contained long enough. Janneken had a fierce grip on Anna's elbow, and even she was sniffling.

The singing stopped. "Maeyken, is that you?" Adriaen's muffled voice came through the rough board wall. Now she would have to tell him about Maeyken, and a lump formed in her throat.

She raised her voice through the din of the children's cries. "Tis only me, Anna, and I..." She could not tell Adriaen about his wife's death through this commotion. What an impulsive, half-witted idea it had been to bring the little ones to this place. But now, she wasn't leaving without seeing Adriaen. Not when she was this close. She swung around to face the jailkeeper. The keys dangled in his bony hand and she had half a mind to snatch them away and unlock the cell herself.

The jailkeeper, disgusted with the noise, hollered. "Go, go home! You can't visit today."

Anna jerked towards him in a passion and shook her finger in front of his nose. "I have come to take him home! The Court cannot be so cruel as to forbid a man to see to his wife's funeral. I'm not leaving without him!"

The jailkeeper took a step backwards, his eyes stretched out in surprise, and something else. Fear? He *had* called her a witch. Grudging admiration? Undoubtedly not.

"Well, don't say I didn't warn you." He got out his iron keys and found the correct one without any trouble. "But he can't go home today. You'll see."

He sounded altogether too ominous for comfort.

At first, Anna thought the jailkeeper must have opened the wrong door. The man lying in the straw on the stone floor was limp as a rag, his dark hair disheveled and caked with dried blood. He tried to raise an arm in greeting, but it fell back, and a grimace of pain crossed his filthy face. The place smelled worse than a rotted dung heap. Only the eyes looked familiar, those honey-tinted brown eyes which held a look of grateful welcome. With an effort, Anna held back her tears. She must be strong for Adriaen.

"Adriaen! What did they do to you?" She crossed the cell to kneel beside him, and he made no attempt to rise. The jailkeeper stood smirking in the doorway. The children shrank against the stone walls, not recognizing their strong father, who was reduced to little more than a shrunken heap of useless limbs.

"The questioning, Anna. Didn't Maeyken tell you we have

been baptized?" Anna nodded. "The judge wanted to know who the leaders are. But let's talk about something else." He nodded towards the children, then at the man standing just inside the cell. "How is Maeyken? And the babe?"

Anna did not want to be the one telling him the grievous news. She cleared her throat, but words wouldn't come. The man on the floor stiffened.

"Anna, what is it?" He looked at her pleadingly. "Is...is she sick?"

Anna shook her head. "Worse than that." The tears refused to be held back any longer, and she dabbed at them with her sleeve. A shadow crossed Adriaen's weary face as he digested the cruel truth, and he closed his eyes in a mute prayer, his lips working. Finally, he brightened with an effort.

"So, the Lord has called her home and she has obtained the crown. Let us not weep too long for her, for she has entered the City of Gold, where joy and peace abide. Oh, that I could join her there."

Anna was startled. "But the *kinder...*" Did Adriaen wish to die? She, too, wanted to believe Maeyken was in Heaven, and she supposed Adriaen longed to be there with her. But how could Maeyken be truly reconciled to God since she hadn't had extreme unction administered by a priest? Anna had baptized Anneken, so why had she stopped short of sending for the priest when Maeyken was dying? She squirmed. Something had held her back.

"Ah yes, the children." He smiled at them. "*Mijn lieveling kinderen*, don't you remember your *liefdevolle Vader*? Finally, they acknowledged this man lying on the floor as their father. They shuffled up to him, still sniffling a little, and sat down beside Adriaen in the straw, staring at their broken *vader*. Janneken went to sit beside Anna.

Dirk was the first to reach out and touch his *vader's* stubbly cheek. Dirk giggled, and drew back, then did it again. Bettke stuck out a tentative finger and poked Adriaen's chin, then bent closer to examine why it felt so scratchy. Trijntgen pushed the matted hair back from the wide forehead, smoothing it into place the best she could. Adriaen's eyes dampened at their innocent caresses, and wincing a little, he moved his arm to encircle them.

The jailkeeper cleared his throat. "Tell her where you hid the money, then they must leave. Officer Stein will be back soon, and you better be out of sight before he comes, or you won't see the prisoner again." There was so much more Anna wanted to say.

"I promised you would give him money if he let me in to see you," Anna confessed, looking at the floor. "I was going to take you home..."

Adriaen didn't seem surprised that she'd had to bribe the jailer. He whispered, "In the cellar...." Anna nodded. She would find it. It was horrible to have to pay such an outrageous amount of money for a visit of such short duration. "Will you promise that if something happens to me, you will take care of them?" Adriaen asked, nodding towards the children. They were scrambling up from the dirty floor, ready to leave this disturbing place where their *vade*r was so weak.

Anna stared at him in alarm. "You must not speak so. Of course you will come home."

Adriaen shrugged. "Only God knows."

"I must leave, but is there anything I can do for you?"

"You are very kind, Anna. I don't need much, but I have longed to read from the Bible, lest I falter in the faith." In a low whisper he told her where to find it. "Besides that, only paper and ink to keep in touch with the Brethren."

"I'll do what I can." *What you really need is someone who can put your limbs back in their sockets.*

Their time was up, and she still hadn't asked him what to do about Maeyken's body. And Simon! Where was he?

The jailer prodded Anna and the children out of the cell, and up the damp stairs. She called over her shoulder, "Simon, are you down here?"

Was that a groan? Simon's groan? "Simon! Have courage!" She was nearly at the top of the stairs, and soon she would be pushed out of Simon's hearing. "I will try to get help for you!"

"Quiet!" hissed the jailer. "Don't get me in trouble, or you shall regret it." Anna closed her mouth and hastened with her little tribe down the arched corridor, averting her eyes from the winding staircase, which a few days ago she had been forced to climb in chains.

The jailer escorted them as far as the oaken doors, then hastened back to his study, presumably to reunite with the wine jug. Anna hurried the children out the door, past the guard who scowled when they passed by him, and hastened through the massive arches and down the cobbled street.

She took a detour to Elizabeth's house, though her back was bent with fatigue from carrying the one-year-old. The children plodded along beside her, too overwhelmed to say anything. Janneken the maid held the two little girls' hands as they followed wherever Anna led them. The full weight of her responsibility burdened her heart and her shoulders. What if she were arrested and the children taken away? What if the plague came and took the children? What if some other illness sent them to an early grave? Losing this little family would break her heart, though her heart had never healed since the violent deaths of her own family. However, with all

Christendom floundering in a dark storm of religious strife, no person could be immune to loss.

She must faithfully attend to her prayers and confession so that God would look favorably upon her. Anna had envied her friend's perfect and happy life, and now she was gone. Maeyken's death was the punishment she got for thinking those unworthy thoughts. Anna's guilt multiplied. Not only had she been covetous of her friend's blessings, she had been cowardly, and a man was being hunted because of her. She deserved to be chastened, but why must her loved ones suffer instead of herself?

Anna shook her head wearily. She had involved herself with the affairs of the Anabaptists, and maybe God was displeased with her. But how could she stay uninvolved when it included her dearest friends? Would God want her to betray those who had shown her kindness? And would He ask it of her to deposit the children at an orphanage, or a monastery, where nobody would love them? This was something she must ask Father Hendricks about, at the earliest opportunity. But would she agree with his answers?

She tried to stifle the anger that surged within her when she thought of everything Adriaen and Maeyken had risked by joining the Anabaptists. Not only were their own lives in peril, but also their children's security, and worst of all their souls, although obviously they would not agree with that.

To be sure, the Anabaptists she had met were nothing like the violent German peasants she had seen at home, even though the authorities judged them all the same. Either you agreed with the government, or you were a heretic. Peace-loving citizens who wanted to worship God in their own way were just as treasonous as those who attacked nobles and ruined church images.

Couldn't they be content with the old traditions of the Holy Roman Catholic Church? She had heard the gossip about the corruption of the priests and bishops, but Anna doubted they all drank and gambled and cavorted with women. Did Father Hendricks?

Was it blasphemous for the priests to chant masses in Latin, just because nobody understood a word they were saying? Nobody needed to know what they were saying. If everyone paid the tithes, and went to communion and mass, the priests took care of the soul. That's what their job was, making sure everyone got to Heaven. Who would intercede for Maeyken's soul?

Elizabeth was feeding Anneken when Anna arrived at her house with her adopted family. Jorg, Elizabeth's little boy, cooed happily in his basket, not worried about having to share his food. Anna dragged her weary body to a stool and Dirk slithered off her lap and crawled over to the baby's basket.

"You look terrible, Anna," Elizabeth said. "When did you last sleep?" Her kind, brown eyes were full of sympathy.

Anna yawned. "I can't remember." There hadn't been time for sleep.

"What have you been up to? You look right *uitkeput.* The children look haggard and unhappy too."

Anna buried her face in her hands. Bringing news of death to people was an unpleasant task, she had discovered, and she fidgeted on her stool, wondering how to break the news of Maeyken's death to Elizabeth. She knew Elizabeth was Maeyken's friend, but Anna really didn't know Elizabeth that well. How would she take the news? Finally, she blurted it out.

"Elizabeth, Maeyken died."

"Oh no! She succumbed to the fever?" Elizabeth gasped, and her eyes widened in distress. "I didn't realize she was quite that sick."

"Yes," Anna said through gathering tears, "I did everything I could think of, but it wasn't enough."

"Oh, Anna. Don't feel that way. Nobody can cure childbed fever once it sets in. Knowing you, I'm certain Maeyken was in good hands." Elizabeth bowed her head, and moisture shimmered in her eyes. "Maeyken gone. It doesn't seem possible, and I'm going to miss her so much."

"I know. She was very kind to me when I moved here, and she opened her heart and her home the very first day." Anna twisted her hands in her lap. "I need someone to look after her. She had joined the Anabaptists, and I don't know what to do." Elizabeth gave a small start. "Someone needs to come. Who will bury her and where? I was hoping Adriaen would be allowed to leave prison long enough to see to her, but he's in no condition to do so."

"How do you know that?"

"I went to see him in the dungeon." Now that she was safely away from the prison, she couldn't believe she'd had the nerve to do what she did.

"You what? Anna! Did you talk to him? How did that come about?"

Between sighs and tears, she related what she'd seen and heard in the dungeon. "And Adriaen is asking for his Bible and some paper and ink. And I need money to pay the jailkeeper. I bribed him, so I could see Adriaen." Anna couldn't bear to dwell on Adriaen's suffering. Did Simon share the same fate, or worse? That parting groan haunted her; what had they done to the elderly, harmless man?

"Elizabeth, what is it that gives the Anabaptists the strength to endure torture without revealing anything? Adriaen was even singing. And then when I saw him, my heart broke. I'm afraid he'll never walk again." There, she had said it. She was glad Maeyken would never need to know what tortures they had inflicted on him.

Elizabeth put her hand on Anna's shoulder. "Anna, souls are much more precious than bodies. Nobody can take that away, even when everything else is gone."

"Of course, the soul is precious. So why would anyone throw it away to join the seditious Anabaptists?"

Elizabeth shook her head. "I shall pray you find an answer to that someday. Will you be looking after Maeyken's children?"

"I wouldn't dream of parting with them." Anna glanced at the infant dozing peacefully on Elizabeth's lap. "Are you able to keep the baby a little longer?"

"Of course. I love Anneken just as much as I love Jorg. Would you like to hold her now?" Anna held out her arms and Elizabeth gave Anneken to her.

"About Maeyken..."

"Don't you worry. I'll find someone to take care of her, as soon as I've fed Jorg. You just stay here and rest until I come back. Janneken, will you come and assist me?" The maid agreed, half fearfully, as if she would like to object but didn't dare. Elizabeth put Jorg in his basket, then disappeared into the bedroom and changed into her black mourning gown, and put on a black bonnet and shawl. She carried a satchel in her hand and Anna didn't even want to know what was in there. With a reassuring smile, Elizabeth left with Janneken.

After they left, Anna stayed on her stool, holding the tiny girl in her arms, the children gathered around her in subdued silence. They sat on the floor within the warm circle of the fire, and Anna wished she could think of something comforting to say. To lose their mother and see their father laid low all in one day was a tragedy they should never have had to go through. She ached for them, and berated herself once more for taking the children to the prison. How thoughtless she had been!

"Anna," the normally exuberant Trijntgen asked in a quivering voice, "Will *Vader* die too?"

Anna stroked the little girl's golden hair and swallowed hard. "No, Trijntgen. Your father will not die." Anabaptist men were often executed by the sword, and sometimes burned, but not Adriaen! He had found the strength to sing in his affliction, and she would have to find the strength to help get him out of there, along with Simon. She had promised to send help, and she must get her mind off her grief and do something.

Chapter Five

Amsterdam November 1531

He who doubts is like the wave of the sea that is ...tossed by the wind... James 1:6

Anna's head drooped, and she shook her head trying clear the fog in her mind. She must stay awake or she would drop the baby. Perhaps she should put her back in the basket, beside young Jorg who now slept peacefully, his tummy satisfied, and with no cares in the world. Anna wondered with a start whether *he* was baptized. Somehow, she didn't think so.

She gazed at the infant in her arms with awe and pleasure. How could anyone be so small? Everything was there, but it was all in miniature. The tiny fingers, curled into fists on either side of her delicate face, the perfectly formed nose, the innocent pink mouth out of which no evil word had yet been spoken, were all a miracle.

It crossed her mind to wonder how the devil could enter an innocent child like this. Was it even possible that he dwelled in a newborn baby? It did make more sense that baptism was for believers of Christ who desired to follow Him. She crossed herself; she should not think such unfaithful thoughts. She was thinking like a heretic.

She found some furs for the children to sleep on; they were too tired to sit up any longer. Like puppies, they cuddled together haphazardly, drawing comfort from each other's bodies. Anna laid down too, finally giving in to fatigue, and was asleep on the hard floor within seconds.

Anna wasn't sure how long she had slept when she was startled awake by someone walking around in the room. She stiffened but pretended to be still asleep. By the way the man made himself at home, Anna realized this must be Claes, Elizabeth's husband. He paused a moment by the fireside, looking amazed at the assorted bodies lying in front of his fire. Anna held her breath as he stepped around her. He must be wondering why a strange woman was sleeping on his floor. Should she let him know she was awake? But she was so cozy and sleepy, and too tired to deal with introductions this time of night. Claes added some small pieces of driftwood to the dying fire. He lit a candle and sat by the table to read a letter that he pulled out of his coat pocket. He unfolded the fragile pages carefully; they must have been folded and unfolded many times.

Elizabeth returned just then, closing the door quietly behind her. Tiptoeing across the room, so as not to awaken the sleeping ones, she joined him and bowed her head as well. Claes said, in a voice just above a whisper. "Hans Bauer sent these precious words from the Tyrol. There is much suffering there as well, and he has now exchanged his earthly body for a heavenly one. He wrote this letter the day before he departed this world. Let me read it to you.

"Dearly beloved Brethren and Sisters, to you be peace and love from above. I, your brother in the Lord, do now beseech you with my heart and pray to God, that you build your foundation on the Lord, where no storms may destroy or fire devour, for no one shall enter Heaven except His chosen ones who love Him and obey Him in every thing. Be not distressed on my behalf, though flesh must suffer and the soul be tempted for I have put

my faith in God, and He will reward me with a crown when I bid this life farewell. Pray for me and repent of your sins that we may meet again on the golden shore..."

For a long time, Elizabeth and Claes sat by the table. With tears in his eyes, Claes bowed his head in repentance, and prayed to be free of sin. He asked God for strength to serve Him for as long as his life should last, to spread the truth wherever a willing heart might be found. Anna was astounded and strangely moved. With every word, her heart beat faster. Elizabeth and Claes Anabaptists? Why was she surprised? But of course. It all made sense. Elizabeth's willingness to take Maeyken's baby, and to see to Maeyken's burial, and Claes being out late in the evening. And she had unwittingly taken refuge with Anabaptists!

She thought of Father Hendricks and his pompous incantations, and it seemed like sacrilege to even think of him in this holy moment. She wouldn't be surprised if she could reach into the darkness and touch God Himself, so near did He seem.

Elizabeth broke the spell when she murmured in a low tone, "Maeyken died of the fever. Daniel and Arents are taking her away to be buried in Friesland." She motioned to the bodies on the floor. "These are Maeyken's children and Adriaen is in prison." Claes looked up, startled.

"And the woman?"

"Anna, Maeyken's Catholic neighbor who works for Simon den Kramer. I'm not sure how much she is involved or whether we can trust her, yet I believe we can. She dared go to the prison to see Adriaen. It's a miracle of God that she got out of there safely, and I can't imagine how she did it."

Anna eventually went back to sleep while the couple was still talking softly, to be awakened some time later by a sound, she knew not what. It took her a few heartbeats to remember where she was, then she lay there stiff as a board, listening. Singing? Why was she hearing singing from upstairs? She sat up, her eyes staring wildly into the darkness. A faint light shone from up there and she scuttled closer to the children when she heard someone creeping down the steps. Where were Elizabeth and Claes, and why was someone on their stairs? Their bed was downstairs and nobody else lived in the house.

"Wh..who goes there?" Anna failed to achieve the authoritative tone she hoped for.

"Anna? It's only me."

"Elizabeth! I thought you were a thief!" Anna released a huge sigh of relief. But what was Elizabeth doing upstairs in the middle of the night? Anna had been frightened half out of her wits, as if she'd seen a ghost.

Elizabeth glided over to the fireplace and peered into the baby's basket.

"No thief," Elizabeth smiled, "Just me, coming to check on my *schatjes*." She lifted her son and commenced feeding him. "Did you have a good sleep?"

"Yes, but what's going on upstairs?"

"Why don't you go and see?"

"Me? Are you sure it's safe? I heard singing..." Unless she had dreamed it, which was quite possible in her unsettled state. Elizabeth said nothing. And then she heard it again; a slow, solemn tune, reverently sung. What could it mean? People singing in the middle of the night, upstairs? She *must* be dreaming. "Elizabeth...?" And then finally it dawned on her. She was sheltering in a house where a secret meeting was being held. Her mind spun in dizzy circles as she tried to make all the pieces fit.

"Elizabeth..." Really, it was too much. No matter where one went, there were the Anabaptists. Were they taking over the whole town? Did they have constant meetings all day and night, and when did these people sleep? And the most nagging question of all; what was it that made instant converts of so many people? People who knew their days were numbered once they joined the forbidden sect.

How did they manage with Charles V's officers hot on their scent? The spies...they were everywhere, following unwary travellers to their secret destinations, their empty money bags gaping, begging to be filled with the rewards doled out by officials determined to purge their territory of the insurrectionists. Wheedling their way into clandestine meetings with ingratiating smiles, pretending to have a desire to learn about the Scriptures and learning their secret greetings; they were the thugs who would do anything for money. The Anabaptists might have the wrong idea, but Anna had no sympathy at all for these scoundrels.

Was it worth the risk to stay here, or should she gather up the children and take her chances out in the night and go back to Maeyken's house? No, the children had enough excitement for one day. They would be terrified if she forced them to travel home in the dark.

But what if the authorities were lurking about tonight and discovered this forbidden meeting going on upstairs? Would she be spared then? Who would believe she wasn't one of them since she was practically sleeping on their doorstep? She was rapidly being caught up in their spell, whatever magic or witchcraft they were using to mislead her. The only way she could prove herself loyal without a doubt, and without further tainting her reputation, was to get out of here and report these people. Yes, that was exactly what she must do.

She steeled herself to venture out into the night by herself, determined to do her duty to law and order. It was high time she made a clean cut, and left these people behind while she still could. On to a different place, where no Anabaptists lived to disturb her peace of mind. Maybe she could go to France, or Italy. She reached for her cloak which hung from a peg in the wall.

Elizabeth's face was a white moon in the flickering candlelight, but she didn't say a word. Anna turned towards the doorway, and made the mistake of looking to the fireplace, where the children slept cuddled together on the furs. She stopped short. What was she thinking? Abandon Maeyken's children? After she had promised Adriaen to care for them? Impossible. Time passed as she stood staring at the children, while the low hum of muted voices wafted down the stairs. Somebody would take the children if she left, and at this age, they would soon forget their parents, and herself even sooner. With the resilience of children, they would only mourn for a brief time, then adjust to whatever life they were taken to. But would Anna survive this? She pondered on this for a moment, and finally concluded that wherever she went, trouble would follow. She could never outrun it. With a sigh, she removed her cloak and hung it back up on the peg.

Elizabeth silently exchanged babies and began to feed Anneken. Anna watched her, wracked in indecision. Since she was in the house, and would be implicated if the officers came, would it be so much worse to investigate this meeting upstairs? Surely her Catholic faith was strong enough that she could preserve it, in case she did hear things she somewhat agreed with. Crossing herself, and breathing a brief prayer to Mary, she made up her mind.

This was a chance too good to pass up. She would go and satisfy her curiosity, despite the danger. The risk was not as great as it could be; the bailiff was probably asleep over his cups and this house was small and located in an out of the way street where it was not very noticeable. She simply would not think about spies.

On soundless feet, she crept up the stairs, the children being too worn out to notice her leaving. Upstairs, she followed the yellow glow of candlelight to the doorway of a small room. From the hallway, she peeked into the room, which was packed with people, perhaps two dozen. She was embarrassed that they had seen her when they arrived, sleeping like a lazy dog in front of the fire. Of course, they were used to quietly sneaking about, so it wasn't surprising she stayed asleep.

A tall, bearded man was reading from a book—the Bible, she supposed. Everyone listened hungrily in rapt attention to every word. She looked around the room at the assembled persons, surprised by who she saw.

There was the cobbler with his worn coat, who talked little, but bent his large head to his work from morn till night whenever she saw him in his shop. A couple of weavers, combing their fingers through their wiry beards. Two young men who could be fisherman, judging by their patched coats. The burly village blacksmith towered a head above the others. Half a dozen women, with their hair swept neatly out of sight under their large white headdresses. And in the far corner, a small man scholarly in appearance, his hair and beard neatly clipped, his hands clean and smooth.

Here were the common tradesmen who took it upon themselves to read the Bible, then spread their interpretation of the Gospel, in such a way that people flocked to them from far and near to hear their message. Anna had seen it all in Germany, and what had happened to her family? How could these people sit there, so peaceful and content, their eyes glowing with some strong emotion? Anna stood outside the door, unobserved, yet unable to tear herself away, while the words read by the tall man lodged themselves in her mind.

"Love your enemies, do good to those who hate you...." This was preposterous. Enemies needed to be destroyed, not loved. And why would you do good to someone who hated you? These people must have a different Bible than the Pope's.

In the middle of the room, a rough board table held the remains of a loaf of bread, and an empty wine jug lay on its side. Anna's eyes widened. They must have held their own communion, with no priest present. She drew in a sharp breath. What sacrilege. Of course, strangely, they didn't believe the bread and wine was changed into Christ's body and His blood. This much she had gathered from conversations around the dinner table at home. Anna shuddered to think of the judgment God would send upon these sinners. How had He judged her family? She dashed the thought from her mind.

After the sermon, they cleared a space in the middle of the room, and the two young fishermen kneeled. Anna stared in amazement as the preacher took a pitcher of water; chanted a few words; poured a bit of water on their heads, then gave them his hand as they rose, and kissed the kiss of peace. A simple ceremony to be sure, and even mystical. She guessed that she had just witnessed an adult baptism.

She slipped downstairs before anyone noticed her and met Elizabeth on the way up.

"I just fed them both," Elizabeth said. "You're not staying

upstairs?"

"Uh...no, I'll stay with the children."

Feeling suffocated, Anna stepped outside into the crisp night. The stars winked at her as if they too were keeping the same secret she was. How long were these people staying? She had lost track of the time, but it must be well after midnight. The houses pressed their tall dark shadows against the moonlit sky. Across the flat land, a wolf's howl echoed in a hollow song, answered by the barking of a dog somewhere in the town.

What was that? She jumped a foot into the air. Something or someone rustled from behind her, and she nearly lost her skin. Spies! She rushed inside and barred the door. Blankets covered the windows in the room upstairs; had someone still seen cracks of light? She stood trembling against the door, not daring to move. Holding her breath, she expected an intruder to break in at any moment.

If the bailiff had been alerted, she would be held as guilty as anyone, even though she was a Catholic. Nobody was allowed to help the Anabaptists in any way, not by giving them food or shelter or anything else, much less open up one's house for a meeting. It was an effective way to get the house demolished. If Anna was found consorting with Anabaptists a second time, she could expect a harsher punishment to be imposed, if not death.

She leaned against the door, trying to slow down her panicked breathing. Just then, the meeting began to break up. In twos and threes or individually, the furtive guests tiptoed down the stairs and gathered around the table. Elizabeth had set out bread, cheese and wine. After a quiet prayer, the men and women ate in silence, while Anna stood in the shadows close to the door. Should she warn them about the sounds she had heard outside, or had that rustle been harmless? It could have been an animal, after all. Remembering that she was unlikely to escape trial if these secret worshippers were caught, she finally ventured closer to the group. She touched the tall preacher's elbow. He looked at her and she cleared her throat. "Sir, I was outside just a moment ago, and I heard a rustling near the house. Someone could be spying on you."

"How kind of you to warn us," the tall man said. "We shall be extra careful as we leave, only one or two at a time, and we will scatter in different directions. Apart from that, nobody can harm us unless God allows it." He smiled, glanced at her curiously, then put on his black hat and stepped outside. He would be the one treated the worst if they were betrayed. Preachers were valuable prizes because they were the ones who led everyone astray. Anna was wise enough not to ask anyone's name this time. She couldn't tell what she didn't know.

When the last person had left, Anna barred the door for the night. There it was again! That rustling! She motioned for Claes to come listen, and he pressed his ear to the wood. Anna and Elizabeth held onto each other, tense and hardly daring to breathe. Was there a spy out there? What if even now, someone was racing to the sheriff with names of all the Anabaptists who had been here, and the location of this house?

Claes turned around, a grin on his face. "It's only one of the town's pigs. I heard it snort." The two women released their breaths and chuckled. "That's a relief!" Elizabeth said.

"*Ja*, that it is." Anna sighed. "Now, I'm tired. I think I will go back to my nest until morning." The last thing she needed was Claes and Elizabeth questioning her about what she had witnessed that night. She was much too confused to explain how she felt about the secret meeting.

Anna snuggled down near the children on the warm bearskin. But she could not sleep, even after praying all the prayers she knew. So many thoughts circled through her mind, over and over, like churning butter.

Where had they taken Maeyken? She hadn't heard the death bells tolling, so that meant they had stolen away her remains, to some hidden place. She was grateful to Elizabeth for seeing to Maeyken, and for taking on the little baby girl, Anneken. At least she might be able to save Adriaen's children for him if he ever got out alive.

Would Adriaen survive to visit his wife's grave, or must he soon follow her there? The memory of her muscular neighbor reduced to a broken heap on the floor would haunt her for a long time, adding to the image in her mind of Maeyken dying, as well as the horrendous fire which had taken her family. How Adriaen would hate her when he found out she betrayed his brother, and slept while his wife died. Where was Joachim now? Had he found a safe hiding place somewhere? She grimaced, picturing him being chased like a rabbit. She didn't want him to end up broken and bleeding like Adriaen.

How could she send aid to Simon, and get him out of the dungeon, along with Adriaen? The kindly old man needed a comfortable place to sleep, not a cold prison floor with only a thin layer of filthy straw. She hoped to persuade Claes to smuggle the two men out of there; it was no job for a woman. If the jailkeeper could be bribed once, he could be bribed again. Adriaen had told her where he hid his money, and she hoped it would be enough.

In the morning, Claes assured her that he would do what he could to rescue Adriaen and Simon. She was not to worry about the money, that's what the Brethren stood for, to help each other out. Anna sighed with relief and thanked him from her heart. They all avoided talking about the subject uppermost in their minds; the night meeting. Anna kept herself busy in the kitchen and avoided meeting Elizabeth's eyes. She needed to sort things out in her mind before she was ready to discuss it. Elizabeth didn't push it, either. Did she sense Anna's reluctance? After the children were awake and fed, Anna decided it was time to take them back home. When the sun's pink rays flooded the horizon, Anna was on her way, the children and Janneken stumbling along beside her, and the youngest on her hip.

The house stood empty, cold, and silent as they approached it, and Anna squared her shoulders. This was home for the children, and she would do her best to make it warm and welcoming for them, and for Adriaen, if the rescue attempt succeeded. She found a few live coals left and got the fire going, setting the maid to baking bread. The children played listlessly in the yard, and Anna's heart ached for them.

By mid-afternoon, she had the house all straightened up and clean, with fresh bread to eat and the fire glowing with a simmering pot of pea soup above it. She stepped outside for an armful of firewood, admiring the beautiful autumn morning…and heard the dreaded clattering of hooves on cobblestones, headed her way. She turned her head left and right. Where to hide? She threw the wood on the ground and ran to collect the children. They raced for the cover of the woods beyond the house, but it was too late. They had been seen.

The same rough pair who had come the other day had

returned. The officer waved some papers. "You have one hour to leave this house. It now belongs to the state and has been confiscated because of heresy. Leave everything here, including the money. Adriaen told us exactly how much there is, so don't take one farthing. I will be back." Anna didn't want to think about the methods they had used to pry that information out of Adriaen.

The two men rode away, leaving Anna standing, open-mouthed with shock, in front of the house. She hadn't thought of this possibility. In a frenzy, she gathered the bread the maid had baked and some other food. They would move to Simon's house.

Except they had confiscated his house as well. Anna stood on the doorstep with the children, reading the notice, shaking with fury. This was too cruel.

"Can you hold Dirk for a minute?" She handed the little boy to the maid. The state had no right to her personal belongings. In a daze, she gathered her things, which didn't amount to much, and her small stash of money, which was hardly worth mentioning.

Putting on a brave smile, she said to the children, "How about we go for a picnic? It's a beautiful day, and perhaps we can find some hickory nuts."

The little faces brightened, and they headed for the forest, though the trees of November were bare of leaves. Anna knew of the perfect spot, not far from the house, with a little stream they could sit beside and watch the water. It would help to lift everyone's spirits. While the sun was sinking to the horizon, they ate some of the bread and drank water from a clear spring. While the children napped beneath a large willow tree, Anna searched her mind for a solution.

They could probably go back to Elizabeth for the night,

but they could not stay there for long. It was not safe enough. If the authorities were bent on ridding the town of the unwanted sect, it would only be a matter of time before they were discovered. The last resort would be the orphanage, but Anna vowed to try everything else before she left them there. Amsterdam, like every other town, supported an abbey and a beguinage, and she could go to them for temporary shelter and food. The beguinage in the middle of town was probably the best place to go for sanctuary, and the nuns would care for the children. Still, Anna was reluctant to take her little brood to one of these establishments, and she told herself it was out of respect for Maeyken and Adriaen's new beliefs. But if she were honest, the idea did not appeal to her, and she wondered why. If only Adriaen were free to take care of his family. Reluctantly, Anna decided there was nothing for it but to go back to Elizabeth's house, at least for the night.

Elizabeth welcomed them back upon their return, a worried little frown creasing her forehead. "Make yourselves comfortable in front of the fire." She arranged the skins on the floor and the children rolled happily into them. Elizabeth took Anna aside.

"Claes has gone with a few others to try and get Adriaen and Simon out. We're hoping the same guard is still there and can be bribed."

"I'm so thankful to leave that job for the men," Anna said. "I would have done all within my power to get them out, but somehow, men seem to be more successful at rescues. But what will the court do when they find out Adriaen's gone? Won't they search for him?"

"We must leave that in God's hands," Elizabeth said. "But yes, they may come here searching for Adriaen when the

Court finds out he is missing. Ideally, the jailer won't report it right away, so we have a chance to hide him. It wouldn't be the first time one of the Brethren has mysteriously escaped from prison."

"I don't trust that jailer one bit. He treated me like I was nothing more than a stray dog."

"Yes." Elizabeth sighed. "That's how much some men value a woman, and especially an Anabaptist woman. They think we are only good for bearing children and serving men. In times like this, I try to give my burdens over to the Lord. We need never be alone in our troubles."

Anna stared at Elizabeth, not comprehending her words. "You make it sound like you can just ask God, like he's in the room with you."

"God is everywhere, Anna. In this room and wherever you go, always listening to those who call on Him."

"God wasn't listening when I asked Him to spare Maeyken. I prayed to the saints, and also to God the way Anabaptists do, without calling on the saints, and she still died."

"Just because He did not answer your prayers doesn't mean He isn't real, or that He doesn't love you. God knows the bigger picture, and He works in mysterious ways His wonders to perform. As to the saints, they have no power to speak to God on your behalf. Nor do the priests have the power to forgive sins. Only Christ, through dying on the cross, can take away our sin."

Anna turned away, uncomfortable with this peculiar view and with the disregard for the holy saints. Many people went on long pilgrimages to Rome and to other shrines to worship the relics of the saints, and thus to rid themselves of their sins.

She picked up Anneken, and cuddled her close. There were so many conflicting ideas churning around. How could she know what was right in the eyes of God?

She concentrated on the infant in her arms, who was looking more like Adriaen every day. Her face was beginning to fill out, and the dark eyes were open more often. Adriaen had seen her only once, Anna realized. Once right after she was born, and then he had left for the secret meeting and never returned home. He would not recognize his little daughter if he got to see her again.

For this moment, she would pretend this was *her* baby and that Adriaen was coming home from prison to *her*. She shook her head in disgust and shame. Where had that sinful thought come from? Her dearest friend's body was being carried to a distant unhallowed grave, and already she was fantasizing about her widowed husband. She must cease these thoughts and never allow them to surface again. It was a terrible sin and she didn't doubt God would send some severe punishment down on her. She crossed herself but found little comfort in the familiar gesture.

That night, sleep was impossible. It seemed like an eternity before she heard Elizabeth's outside door creaking open. She held her breath. Were they back? Had they been successful? In the dim shadows, two wide-shouldered men came inside, carrying a litter between them. Adriaen! Anna sprang to her feet to see for herself. They laid him carefully on a bed prepared in the corner, and Elizabeth came tiptoeing down the stairs. A third man entered, carrying a large bag. The doctor, Anna thought. So, the Anabaptists did have a doctor among them.

The three men worked over the man on the bed; he

groaned feebly, and Anna's insides roiled. She hovered in the background, too tense to lie down again, yet not daring to get in the men's way. Elizabeth prepared hot cider for everyone, and the men worked silently, trying not to disturb the sleeping children. It seemed like an eternity before the moaning and groaning stopped and the men stepped back from the bed.

"We've bled him and reset his bones, so all he needs now is time to heal," the doctor said in a low tone. "I'll visit him tomorrow." He and the other man slipped through the door into the dark night. Their patient lay motionless on his bed, with Claes keeping watch beside him.

"I can take a turn in two hours," Elizabeth whispered. Anna wanted to offer but the words wouldn't come. She wanted to be near Adriaen more than anything in the world, but that was a secret she kept to herself. She had absolutely no right to think of him as anything more than a friendly neighbor. If they asked her to help, she would not refuse, and she would do whatever she could to help him recover, the same as she would help anyone else who was in need. That was all.

The next morning, Adriaen was awake, and he motioned Anna over to the bed. Slowly she approached him, afraid her eyes would betray their desire to do that very thing. His brown eyes were dull, and his dark hair was tangled, but he was alive. Anna's hands itched to smooth the dark hair away from the wide forehead, and she wondered if it would be appropriate for her to wash his grimy face. It would only be nursing a sick man, and nobody need read anything more into her actions. And neither would she. He needed to be washed and she would do it, with no more emotion than if she were washing one of his children. She couldn't stop herself. A basin of tepid water sat on a small stand beside the bed, with a clean cloth beside it. Elizabeth must have intended to wash him, but something or other prevented her from doing it. Anna dipped the cloth in the water and wrung it out.

"Mind if I clean your face a little?"

"Go ahead. I'm sure I look a fright." Anna shook her head and gently wiped his wide forehead, smoothing the straight-cut hair out of the way. With careful strokes, she removed the dirt around his gold-tinted brown eyes, noting the short straight lashes. Around and over the bridge of his straight nose she swished the cloth, rinsed it and rubbed at his stubbly cheeks and firm chin, being careful not to get too close to the bruised lips. The rest of him looked no better than his face had, but she laid down the cloth. At least his face was clean.

"Anna, I need to tell you some sad news. Simon passed away in prison. He stayed true till death, singing as long as he had the strength." Anna stared at him, shocked, not only because her employer was dead, but because in her concern for Adriaen, she had practically forgotten about Simon. "He left the house to you."

"To me? How can he leave the house to me?" Anna's eyes grew round in surprise. "Women can't inherit property, can they?"

"Fortunately, here in the Netherlands women can indeed inherit property. This is the only place in the Empire where it's allowed, and the house is now yours. Claes can help you with the legal procedures."

"But why me? This is too generous of Simon, yet so like him to do this."

"He thought the world of you, and he had no family left. It was his wish to provide for you, his faithful housekeeper."

Anna had never dreamed of such a possibility. Her heart leaped with joy. God did indeed provide. How else could one explain the house falling into her lap at the very time she so desperately needed a place to go?

"But I thought the government confiscated it."

"Yes, but now that Simon has died so shortly afterwards, they are honoring his will, because it is passing into Catholic hands."

This was the perfect reason to stay Catholic, Anna thought. She had never dreamed of owning a house, and the idea gave her immense pleasure. She would be independent, almost equal to the men! Uttering a whispered prayer of thankfulness, she vowed to be more faithful. The first thing she must do when things settled down, was to go to the cathedral, and give proper thanks to all the saints for helping her. She would attend mass twice a week from now on; she had been very lax lately.

Adriaen smiled, and his gentle brown eyes melted her heart. "I'm glad you have a place to live. And maybe some day you will decide to join us."

"Oh...I...I can't do that." It was one thing to help keep them out of the claws of their persecutors, quite another to join this perplexing group.

Chapter Six

Amsterdam November 1531

For there is one God, and there is one mediator between God and men, the man Jesus Christ, who gave himself as a ransom for all...Timothy 2:5

After the children had eaten, Anna gathered them up and prepared to leave. She sent the maid back to her own home, she really could do all the work by herself and she had enough mouths to feed. She cuddled the baby once more; she was becoming almost too attached to the sweet little thing. After all, she couldn't keep Anneken now that Adriaen was back, and she might as well stop pretending right now. The children would live with their father once he recovered and she'd have no excuse to keep hanging around.

Anna put the house in order, and the children followed her everywhere, asking countless questions, their spirits higher now that they had seen their father so greatly improved. Life settled into a routine. Maeyken's house was empty and forlorn, and Anna tried not to think about it. More than once she caught Trijntgen gazing over to her old home, her blue eyes full of unshed tears.

With the work all caught up, Anna no longer had an excuse to absent herself from the church, Father Hendricks, and confession. Christmas was coming, the time for the faithful to repent of their sins and do penance, in preparation for Christmas mass. It would be a relief to rid herself of the burden of the mortal sin she carried for deliberately consorting with the Anabaptists. Not only did she knowingly aid them, but she had watched and listened to a part of their sermons. Did this truly offend God? It had never been her intention to offend God, and perhaps she had only committed the venial sin of being too curious. When Maeyken had first told her about the Anabaptists, Anna had been upset, but the more she saw of the Anabaptists, the more questions she had. She would do any penance Father Hendricks required of her, if only her pathway would then become clear.

She postponed going for two more days, telling herself she didn't know what to do with the children while she was gone. But then she thought of Janneken. The maid lived on the other end of town, although Anna wasn't quite sure where. No doubt, anyone on the street could direct her to the right house. Wearing a clean black kirtle and apron, a freshly laundered white cap, and her good cloak, she finally set out with the children in tow. The brisk walk and fresh air would do them all good.

They tramped along the narrow streets, where tall, narrow buildings leaned towards them, and clunked across the wooden bridge. Beneath it, the surface of the water rippled slightly, stirred by puffs of wind. A couple of blocks later, they arrived at an older part of Amsterdam. Here, shutters drooped, waste collected in piles along the street, and tattered hosen and worn linens hung from the windows to dry. Skinny, barefoot children sniffled and coughed as they trailed after Anna and her tribe. Anna gathered her little ones close, wondering where in this rundown place Janneken lived. She didn't know any other name for the maid, and there were probably a hundred Jannekens in this town.

"Do you know where Janneken lives?" Anna asked,

turning to a ragged boy, "The maid?"

"*Wil je oude Janneken, wilde Janneken, Janneken met de houten poot, of Dirk Janneken?*"

"Oh, dear. The Janneken I'm looking for is not old, or wild, and she doesn't have a wooden leg. Can you show me where Dirk's Janneken lives?"

"*Ja ik kan. Ga met me me.*" The boy wiped his runny nose with a threadbare sleeve and motioned for Anna to follow. "*Mijn naam is Balthasar.*"

"Thank you, Balthasar. My name is Anna." The boy seemed bright enough, and Anna followed him to a back alley to the bottom of a rickety set of outside stairs. Here she stopped and could not bring herself to go further. She had taken the children to enough dangerous places lately, and she simply could not schlepp them up these stairs to unknown dangers.

Balthasar looked at her in confusion for a moment, then understanding brightened his face.

"*Wil je dat ik op zoek naar Janneken?*"

Anna sighed in relief. "Could you, Balthasar? I don't want to take the children up there." The boy nodded and sprang up the steps, disappearing through an open doorway on the second floor. Anna kept her eyes on the doorway, feeling guilty all of a sudden that she had let the lad go up there when she was too afraid to go herself. She would feel even worse if he didn't come down again right away. She released her pent-up breath when Balthasar grinned down at her from the doorway, with a familiar figure beside him.

"Janneken!" Anna exclaimed. "There you are! Can you come down here for a moment?"

The girl smiled shyly and descended the steps behind Balthasar. "Janneken," Anna said, "Could you come with me to the church and help with the children while I see Father

Hendricks?"

Janneken nodded. "I'd love to. *Ik laat moeder weten.*"

"Yes, let your mother know. Will she mind your leaving now?" Janneken shook her head as she returned upstairs, then joined Anna down on the street. Trijntgen and Bettke ran to Janneken and each grabbed one of her hands, full of chatter as they skipped along beside their former maid. Janneken smiled and answered with her eyes shining, pleased to see the children again.

Anna fished in her bag to find a coin for Balthasar, and though he hesitated to take it, Anna insisted he take the silver pfenning. He held it in his palm for a moment before closing his grimy fingers around it, then with a smile and a wave, he hurried away in the opposite direction.

At the Dam Square, the stone Oude Kerk stood resplendent, as it had for centuries. Five multi-colored stained-glass windows formed a half circle, and above each one, a sharp gable pierced the heavens, while the watchtower rose into the sky and guarded the surrounding city. Inside the watchtower were the bells, which tolled a different chime for every occasion, be it announcing the hour of the day, prayer time, weddings, death, attack or fire.

With a sigh, Anna turned towards the solid oak door of the Oude Kerk. She had come here to confess to Father Hendricks, and now she must see the thing through. Was God offended that she had listened to the Anabaptists? Heresy was a mortal sin, which sent the soul straight to hell if one died without confessing, yet Maeyken had explained why Anabaptism wasn't heresy. Father Hendricks might not see it that way though. Confessing to the priest would not absolve her sins unless she was exceedingly penitent and vowed never to commit this sin again. She swallowed and squirmed, wishing she hadn't come. Once again, she hadn't thought things through. And yet, coming here would assure her safety somewhat. It was those who hadn't gone to church in years who would be scrutinized the most for signs of heresy.

Reminding herself to breathe normally, Anna held the door for the others. Inside, at the west end of the nave, they all stood and admired the cavernous interior, as Anna did every time she came here. The wooden ceiling, covered with painted masterpieces, arched high above her. To the right and the left, high, graceful arches curved upwards between massive columns hung with banners, plaques and heraldic shields. Straight ahead, the altar was set in a backdrop of exquisite painted altarpieces depicting Mary, the mother of Jesus, and other Biblical figures.

The mysterious scent of incense pervaded the church, and Anna couldn't help but compare this place to the crowded upstairs room in Elizabeth's house. Anna led her party across the dark grey stone slabs on the floor, beneath which the dead were buried. It always seemed strange to be treading on their tombs, but the church had been built on top of a burial ground centuries ago, for it was the most solid location in marshy Amsterdam. Anna passed the wooden pews, where a young mother rested with a sleeping child in her arms.

"Can you watch them for me, now?" Anna said to Janneken.

"*Ja, ik kan dat doen.*"

"Thank you, I won't be long." Anna handed Dirk to Janneken. Her arm had become numb awhile ago, and her back ached. Dirk needed to start walking; he was becoming too heavy to carry everywhere.

"You may play here quietly until I come back," Anna

said to the children. Trijntgen and Bettke lost no time in clambering up on the pews, and Janneken sat down with Dirk. Anna continued on her way, passing two elderly gentlemen in animated conversation, who were leaning on spades, and peering into an open vault in the floor. A skinny dog followed her for a few steps, then detoured into a dim corner, perhaps he was on the scent of a mouse.

And then, she reached the altar, where Father Hendricks waited out of sight for the penitent souls of his parish, and Anna gathered her resolve. She had offended God long enough, and it was time to make a clean breast of her sins. Taking a deep breath, she ascended a couple of scrupulously clean steps, but Father Hendricks was nowhere to be seen. There was a door off to one side, and she wondered whether the priest was in the room beyond it. She paused, uncertain. Was the priest even here at the church? He ought to be. Then her mouth dropped open, as she heard the titter of a woman's giggle. What could it mean? Why was a woman back there? Uneasily, she thought of the rumors of priestly corruption, and she admitted she could not altogether dismiss the idea.

There was still time to leave, and Anna turned on the steps, ready to do just that. But just then, the door opened, and Father Hendricks appeared, a little flushed, in his flowing, white cassock. He adjusted the cincture around his waist, as if he had just finished dressing. The ends of his stole, which he always wore precise and even, today hung lopsided. Reaching up to straighten the black merlino biretta on his tonsured head, he finally acknowledged Anna with a nod.

"What is it you need today, sister?"

Anna hung her head, "I have come to confess my sins, Father Hendricks."

As the priest came closer, Anna smelled wine on his

breath, but surely Father Hendricks had not been imbibing. He beckoned her to follow him to the shriving pew in the chancel, where he seated himself.

Together, Anna and Father Hendricks prayed the sign of the cross, then Anna got down on her knees in front of the priest, while the murmurs of the children echoed in the nave. Anybody who walked in could see her there, and she felt more ashamed than ever.

"Father, it has been six months since I last confessed," Anna said, then paused. "I have sinned by keeping company with Anabaptists, and listening to one of their sermons, for which I am truly repentant, for I am afraid I have offended God. Also, I have been envious of the good fortune of my friend Maeyken, and now that she is dead, I do wish her husband were mine own. For these and all past sins, I do repent." Anna waited for relief, for absolution and forgiveness.

"Your sins are grievous, and border on heresy," Father Hendricks slurred his words. "As penance, I prescribe your attendance at a heretic burning, as well as three 'Our Father's and three 'Hail Mary's, besides your act of contrition." Anna fought for self-control. This was all for her own good, yes, for the good of her soul. On her knees, she repeated the 'Our Father's' and 'Hail Marys' three times, ignoring the discomfort of the cold stone floor on her knees. Mortifying the flesh was a necessary thing.

Finally, she was ready for the act of contrition. "O my God, I do heartily regret offending Thee, and I detest all my sins, because I dread the loss of Heaven, and the pains of hell, but most of all because they offend Thee, my God, Who are all good and deserving of all my love. I firmly resolve, with the help of Thy grace, to confess my sins, to do penance, and to amend my life. Amen."

Anna kept her head bowed in humility while Father Hendricks prayed in Latin. "God the Father of mercies, through the death and resurrection of your son, you have reconciled the world to yourself and sent the Holy Spirit among us for the forgiveness of sins. Through the ministry of the church, may God grant you pardon and peace. And I absolve you of your sins, in the name of the Father, and of the Son and of the Holy Spirit. Amen."

Anna crossed herself once more, and Father Hendricks said, "Your sins have been forgiven, now go in peace." He bid her to rise. "You will be summoned tomorrow morning to do the rest of your penance. Jan Jansen of Haarlem will be burned at the stake for heresy, and you will watch the proceeding to the end, as a warning of what happens to those who oppose God and country."

"Yes, Father Hendricks." She staggered down the aisle in a daze to collect the children. The woman who had been sitting on a pew with her child was gone, and so were the two elderly gentlemen. Only the gaping hole remained uncovered, ready to swallow the remains of some deceased body. Jan Jansen's? No, a heretic would never be buried inside the church. Anna shuddered and avoided looking at the hole as she passed. The children were reluctant to leave their play on the pews, but Anna hustled them outside. She thanked Janneken and gave her two silver pfennings for her trouble. With a heavy stomach, Anna asked Janneken to come to Simon's house the next morning to stay with the children. She needed to go to the marketplace. Janneken agreed, and the children jumped up and down for joy.

On the way home, Anna wondered why she didn't feel more unburdened and forgiven. Father Hendricks had absolved her in the name of God, so her soul should be purified for a long while. Except she kept hearing Maeyken's voice in her head. "Only through the blood of Jesus can our sins be forgiven. The Pope, and let alone the priests, have no power to forgive anyone's sins." Anna blamed the Anabaptists for spoiling her faith in the Catholic church, and for raising questions that she never would have thought of by herself. It had been hard enough to steel her heart against the Protestant talk of her own family--she crossed herself--and instead of escaping those sentiments, she had run headlong into the same kind of trouble in the Netherlands. What was God trying to tell her?

Tomorrow loomed ahead in a cloud of horror, and her stomach heaved when she thought of her penance. Did Father Hendricks know what a terror she had of fire, what torture he was inflicting on her? At this moment, she could not see how she could endure the next day's events. Back at the house, she distractedly fed the children and put them to bed. Brooding in front of the fire, she wracked her brain trying to find a solution, but there was nothing she could do. If she didn't go by herself, she would be dragged there by the officers, something she wanted to avoid at all costs.

Morning came too soon, after a night of little sleep for Anna. Janneken arrived with a smiling face before the children were awake, and Anna gave the maid her instructions for the day. Wearing her black kirtle, a bonnet and shawl, Anna let herself outside and wiped away a few tears as she trudged along the cobbled street. Was Jan Jansen an Anabaptist, or some other type of so-called heresy? Whoever he was, she did not want to see him burn, not even if he was the vilest criminal ever born. And to think that some people enjoyed the spectacle of another human suffering in indescribable agony. She smelled the smoke before she saw it and cringed.

Father Hendricks and another priest were walking around the Dam square, and Father Hendricks nodded to her and smiled slightly, acknowledging her obedience in appearing this morning. He made sure the executioner did everything right, the faggots piled just so, and the scaffold built to the proper height. In the middle of the smoking faggots, a post had been installed and chains hung at the ready. All they needed was the prisoner, and too soon, Anna heard the clank of chains being dragged across the cobblestones. She hardly dared look. Who was Jan Jansen?

She clapped a hand to her mouth when she saw him. He was young, in his early teens, and he reminded her too much of her younger brother. She stifled a scream behind her hand and vomit threatened to rise into her throat. A mere boy. The authorities were going to execute a handsome, innocent-looking boy, and they were going to think it great entertainment. Anna hoped she wouldn't faint, but when she caught Father Hendricks' narrowed eyes on her, she made an effort to hide her terror at the proceedings. Like a board, she walked to the edge of the gathering crowd, as far away from the scaffold as she dared, without Father Hendricks having to come and force her publicly to a better vantage point.

She glanced at the youth and was surprised at his calmness. He gazed at the assembled people with serene blue eyes, then closed his eyes. Only his lips moved. He was praying. Up onto the scaffold he was prodded, and his charges of heresy read to him. He answered respectfully, but refused to recant his faith.

'Just say it,' Anna pleaded silently. *'Just tell them you'll go to church once a year, then you will be free.'* But he would not. Jan Jansen shook his head and waved away the holy oil with which Father Hendricks wanted to anoint him before

his death. Father Hendricks looked annoyed and ordered the faggots to be piled onto the smoldering fire. Two guards led Jan Jansen to the post in the middle and tied the boy to it with the chains. Some of the bystanders, with sympathetic looks, heaped the fire even higher, hoping to hasten the painful end instead of prolonging it.

Afterwards, Anna never knew how she managed to stay upright, but she dared not fall, not with Father Hendricks watching her. Surely this would purge her soul of any remaining sin she still had hidden in her soul, which she was unaware of, and therefore had neglected to confess.

As soon as she dared, she left for home, dizzy and sick to her stomach. She asked Janneken to stay a little longer, she needed to rest a little, and recover from her ordeal. Janneken happily agreed.

Anna knew she ought to stay away from Elizabeth's house, and she had fully intended to do so after she went to Confession, but as days went by, she almost regretted having gone to see Father Hendricks, God help her. The truth of the matter was, she had great difficulty in avoiding the Anabaptists. Contrary to what Father Hendricks had hoped to accomplish by forcing her to watch the burning, it had only put more questions into her mind. Such as, how could the priest be serving God by meting out a horrible death to a young man who was obviously not a hardened criminal? Rather, the boy had the aura of a saint, which made those around him seem coarse and evil by their despicable actions.

A week later, she found she could resist no longer. She had to know how Adriaen was doing, and whether the family was still safe in their home. If she had made more friends since moving here to Amsterdam, she could console herself with them, but as it was, the only friends she had happened to be Anabaptists. Her parents and siblings would rejoice if they could see her now, wavering in her Catholic faith, and considering the Anabaptists her friends.

She put clean clothes on the children and combed their blonde heads till they shone. Grabbing a clean apron for herself, she inspected her little party and decided they passed muster.

Adriaen's brown eyes lit up when he his little family arrived. He sat on the edge of the bed with one blue woolen blanket wrapped around his shoulders and another one tucked securely around his lap. The children raced to his side, all chattering at once, then climbed on the bed and strangled him with hugs. Anna wished she could do the same.

He looked much better, though still quite feeble. A look of deep suffering haunted his eyes, along with a certain resignation. The tousled, dark hair and haggard shoulders made him seem older, and he was a long way from being the energetic, ambitious man he had been. Anna wondered whether he would ever completely recover his vitality, and yet he appeared to be calm and even content. She noticed the Bible beside him on a stand and imagined him drawing comfort from the Word of God.

Elizabeth took the opportunity to run to the market while Anna supervised Jorg and the children, and then Anna was alone with Adriaen and the children. Anna didn't know how to act. She snatched up the baby and held her close, wishing for the thousandth time she could stop being so flustered around handsome men. No wonder she was a spinster.

"I thought you'd never come," Adriaen chided her. "I haven't thanked you for your hand in my rescue." He rummaged in his leather pack, and fished out a stained piece of paper.

"A friend sent me a copy of this song in prison, and it comforted me in my darkest hours. I sang it until it is planted in my mind until death. Can you read?"

"Yes, a little bit." Her father had taught her brother, a long time ago, but she had been the one most interested. She blinked back tears. Those sweet, happy days were past, torn from her in one terror-filled day which she longed to forget.

"I'd like you to have it. I have few possessions left to give, but perhaps this hymn will comfort you in some way." Adriaen held it out to her.

She accepted it with trembling fingers, touched to the soul. "Is this what you were singing in prison?"

Adriaen nodded. "It kept me from despair in my darkest hours."

Anna unfolded it carefully and began to read.

"Can you hand me my little Anneken while you read? Seems I can't get enough of her to make up for lost time."

She passed the baby to him, being careful not to brush against his wide hands. Pulling up a stool, she continued reading. What she would really like was for Adriaen to sing the hymn for her—but of course she couldn't ask for that.

Oh God, do Thou sustain me, in grief and sore duress...
Pride counter which disdains Thee, and comfort my distress.
Oh Lord, let me find mercy in bonds and prison bed.
Men would seek to devour me with guile and controversy
Save me from danger dread!

Thou wilt never forsake me, this firmly I believe
Thy blood thou hast shed freely, and with it washed me.

Therein my trust is resting, in Christ, God's only Son
On Him I am now building, in tribulation trusting
God will me not disown.

To die and to be living until my end I see
To Thee my trust I'm giving, Thou wilt my helper be
Soul, body, child, companion, herewith commit I Thee.
Come soon, Lord, come and take me, from ruthless men do save me
Be honor e'er to Thee. Amen.

Anna was moved by the words, and she did understand how Adriaen would have been strengthened by this song, but she didn't think she should be digging too deeply into Anabaptist prayers and beliefs. She crossed herself, and Adriaen glanced at her.

A shadow of some emotion flickered in his eyes briefly; was it disappointment? She tucked the paper into her bodice, aware that it could be a condemning piece of evidence depending on who saw it. But nobody would. She would keep it close to her heart, because it came from Adriaen.

"It's...it's beautiful," she murmured. And it was. If she didn't quite trust the message of the hymn, it was still precious because it meant so much to Adriaen.

"The more often you read it, the better you will understand it." He smoothed the baby's hair with gentle fingers. "It's well that you came to see me now, and I hope you come again before I depart. As soon as I can walk, I will be leaving. The truth needs to be spread to every corner of the Netherlands."

Anna's mind reeled. He was leaving? Why?

"It is no longer safe in this town," he answered, responding to the unasked question. "When I find a safe place to live I will come back for the children."

Anna's heart sank. Her unattainable dreams shattered around her feet. If he left there was no one left to light her life, no one to live for. But no—why was she even thinking these thoughts? Without a doubt, it was for the best that he was leaving. Then she would have to forget her ridiculous spinsterish daydreams, and when he came back he would be flaunting a new bride on his arm. Irrational disappointment washed over her. Even though Adriaen would never see her as a future wife, even after he was out of mourning, she still liked having him nearby. Him just being there brought a certain guilty pleasure to her life. Nobody must suspect her feelings, and she would do everything she could to hide this embarrassing secret.

He cleared his throat and gazed at her uncertainly. "I know this is asking a great deal of you, but I have a rather weighty request to make." Anna nodded, though she couldn't imagine what he was thinking.

"Would you consider keeping the children with you for the time being? I know I can trust you, and they would be in good hands with you. Money would be sent to you for their care, so you need not worry on that score."

Anna didn't hesitate. They already seemed like her own. Her heart leaped. In that case, Adriaen would come back, if he could.

"I would love to have the children. I will care for them as if they were my own." Never mind the pain of these little reminders of Adriaen around her every day.

"I knew I could count on you. You have been such a faithful friend to Maeyken and me." A small shadow of pain crossed his face. Little had he known when he left for the secret meeting several miles away in a forest a few nights ago, that he would never see his wife again. Now he must continue without her the best he could.

"If you are ever in need, let Elizabeth know. She will know where to find me."

Anna nodded. "We will be fine."

His loving glance fell on little Anneken in his arms. "I'm glad we named her after you. She has much to live up to."

His fingers brushed against hers as he passed the baby to Anna, her skin tingling where they touched. Their eyes met momentarily, confused, then they both looked quickly away.

Chapter Seven

Amsterdam December 1531

All those who desire to live a godly life in Christ Jesus will be persecuted... 2 Timothy 3:12

After Adriaen had been recuperating for over a month, he was done with being coddled. He and Claes arrived at Anna's house one day in mid December and chopped piles of wood for her fireplace, repaired windows, and plastered cracks in the stone walls, ensuring the house was as snug for the winter as possible. Anna bundled up in her warm cloak and hood and went outside into a crisp early winter day.

"Can I help pile wood?"

"This is men's work," Adriaen said. "You just leave it to us and stay inside where it's warm."

"I want to help." She might be a woman, but she was strong enough to handle wood. Out of the corner of her eyes, she watched him work. Sweat beaded on his wide forehead as he chopped wood, and he rested frequently, leaning on his axe until he caught his breath.

Anna turned worried eyes towards the street. "Are you sure it's safe for you to be outside in public?"

"In God, we are always safe," Adriaen replied gently. His brown eyes sparkled almost like they had before his arrest, and only a few fine lines etching his forehead betrayed what he'd been through. His shoulders were as wide as ever and his back still straight. Anna tried not to stare at him. He was a recent widower, she reminded herself, and would be in mourning for a year. She had no right to be admiring him in this way. Not now, and probably never.

She helped pile the fragrant hickory wood until her back ached, and then some. Her hands were chafed and cold from handling the rough wood, but it was well worth it. By evening she had a pile of wood almost as high as the house, surely enough to keep the house warm for two winters.

She thanked the men with cups of hot cider and regretted seeing them leave. Had Adriaen minded being so close to his former home? It must have been painful to see the house he had shared with his beloved wife for five years, now confiscated and owned by the Court. The house stood empty and lonely, as if it too could not understand why love and laughter had been torn from it's bosom. Anna missed Maeyken's company dreadfully, and she could well imagine how sad Adriaen and the children must feel. Anna shook away the melancholy thoughts and forced herself to think of happier things.

In one more week, Christmas would be here. Anna baked a special nut cake to give to Elizabeth and Claes; the mulled wine she had added should keep it nice and moist. Spending a few of her diminishing store of coins, she bought some candied fruit for the children. She had saved a bit of money for candles for the church as well.

One evening, after darkness had fallen, with the kitchen lighted by the glow of candles, Anna gathered the children around the fire. "*Kinder*, have you ever heard the story of St. Nicholas?" she asked, smiling.

Trijntgen shook her head, her eyes shining. "Tell us a story, Anna!"

"Story! Story!" Bettke clapped her hands. Dirk looked from one to the other, then clapped and babbled in a tongue of his own.

"Tomorrow is the last Saturday of November," Anna began, holding Dirk on her lap. The girls sat on stools at her feet. "It's a special day, when a much-loved visitor will sail across the water in a boat to Amsterdam. His name is St. Nicholas, and he lives far away in Spain with his helper, *Zwarte Pete*, and his white horse. When he steps off the boat at the harbor, everyone will stop working and run to greet him."

"Can we go?" Trijntgen interrupted.

"We shall see. St. Nicholas will ask all the children, 'Have you been good little boys and girls this year?' If they have been good, St. Nicholas will give them presents a few days later. If they have been bad, Zwarte Pete will put them in a sack and take them home to Spain for a year and teach them how to behave." Anna smiled at the wide-eyed children. "But you will not have to worry about that. You are the best little children I have ever seen. So, in the evening, you shall set your shoes by the fireplace, or on the windowsill, and fill them with hay and carrots for St. Nicholas' horse. Then I'll help you sing some songs about *Sinterklaas*, as he is also called. In the night, *Sinterklaas* will ride his horse on the roofs of the houses. Zwarte Pete will climb down the chimney, or through the window, and leave presents for all the good children."

"Oooh!" Trijntgen said. "Will Sinterklaas come here?"

"I am certain he will. On December the fifth, which is still seven sleeps away, we will set out your shoes at bedtime, and in the morning, we shall see what he has brought you." The little girls giggled in anticipation, and Dirk joined them although he had no clue what they were giggling about.

The next morning, there was nothing for it but to bundle everyone up and go to the harbor to wait for St. Nicholas to arrive. Everyone else in the city must have had the same idea, since Dam Square was packed like salted herrings in a barrel. Spirits were high, and snatches of *Sinterklaas* songs wafted through the air. There was no sign of religious animosities today, which was a blessing. All eyes were glued to the sea, and finally, a white sail appeared on the horizon. Cheers and songs broke out, and continued until St. Nicholas stepped ashore, leading his white horse, waving and smiling to the crowd. His long red robe flowed down to his boots and fluttered in the wind as he made his way towards the inn. He asked every child he met along the street the usual question, "Have you been good this year?" Without fail, each one of them claimed they had been good. Zwarte Pete did not have to stuff any child into his sack.

When *Sinterklaas* on his white horse came prancing up merrily to Anna and the three children, he leaned over and asked Trijntgen, "Now, little maid, have you been a good child?"

Rosy-cheeked and sparkly-eyed, Trijntgen answered "*Ja!*" Anna forgot her anxieties, and her heart lifted to see the children so animated. It would give them something cheerful to think about for a long time to come.

On the eve of December the fifth, Anna helped the three of them set out their wooden shoes in a row on the windowsill. They found some hay and a handful of carrots and filled their shoes, although half of their offerings landed beside the shoes. With giggles of anticipation, they snuggled down in front of the fire, hoping to catch Zwarte Pete in the act of exchanging their generous offerings for presents.

Anna smiled a bittersweet smile, and a lump formed in her throat. It had been so long since she was a happy child looking forward to Christmas, back when her family was still together in body and in spirit, before the Anabaptist messengers had filled her family's heads with their heretical faith, which then led to their fiery deaths.

When the excited children finally settled down and went to sleep, Anna cleaned out the little shoes and placed the candied fruit inside. With a sigh, she climbed into her own bed, but for a long time she lay awake, too lonely to go to sleep.

During the night, the east wind dropped clouds of snow over the city, and in the morning, her citizens awoke to a glistening white landscape. After the glee of the children had subsided somewhat, and they had eaten a bit of candy, Anna bundled them up and took them outside to play in the snow. Afterwards, they gathered by the fireplace to drink warm milk and eat the *Oliebollen* she had made. The children asked for stories, and she obliged, over and over again. Anna did her best to make the children's Christmas a happy one.

On the chilly morning of the seventh day of December, two days after Amsterdam's Christmas, Anna again dressed the children in warm hooded cloaks, and they went to the busy marketplace to buy fresh vegetables for the stew. As always, it was crowded and noisy there, and she had difficulty keeping the children from being trampled.

What was all the commotion about today? Everyone streamed to the centre of the Dam square in great excitement. Curious, she allowed herself to be pushed along. When she got there, she desperately wished she had fought against the tide of people and gone home.

But it was too late now. Vomit rose in Anna's throat. Thankfully the children were too short to see. She wanted to look away, but the grim spectre claimed her attention, just as it claimed that of everyone assembled. Mounted on poles around the square were heads. Heads with no bodies. Real human heads that had recently been attached to human bodies. A scream curdled in her throat as she counted nine of them. Nine heretics. A few even looked vaguely familiar. This is what happened to people for disobeying Charles V. When would people learn?

She must leave. Pushing and scratching, she fought her way through until people moved out of the way, dragging the children along as she inched her way through. Why did so many people want to see the horrible display? The whole city must have come out to see. It was the worst sort of entertainment one could ever hope for, though she knew even worse things had been done to traitors. Jan Jansen's execution, for example. What had those nine men done to deserve their fate? Amsterdam was becoming just as frightening as Germany had been.

At long last she was on the outskirts of the crowd, panting and panicking. Her breath came in short gasps as she hurried across the bridge and along the deserted street. Elizabeth's house was just around the corner, and she burst in the door without a knock. She pulled the children in after her and shut and bolted the door. Sagging against it, she tried to calm down.

"Anna! Have you seen a ghost?" Adriaen struggled to sit up in his rope bed in the corner. Nobody else was around.

"Father!" Trijntgen ran to her father's side and climbed on the bed for a hug.

Anna stood against the door in mortification. Her feet

had brought her here, as to a haven of comfort, but she hadn't reckoned on Elizabeth's absence.

"Something even worse." Her voice came out in a croak. She looked meaningfully at the children. After they each claimed hugs from Adriaen, he sent them upstairs to play.

"Come and sit in the chair, Anna." She complied, though her discomfiture made her feet heavy.

"Now, what happened?" he asked. He waited patiently while she tried to untangle her tongue.

"In the square..." Her voice trembled as bad as the rest of her, and she couldn't continue.

"Just take your time. You will feel better if you tell me." It was just as well he didn't know that half the shivers came from sitting so close to him.

"There were heads..."

"Heads?"

"Yes. Nine heads on poles."

Adriaen blanched. "And you saw them?"

Anna nodded, unable to utter another word, as sobs shook her body. Somebody rattled at the door, and Anna jumped up.

"Who's there?" she asked in a choked voice.

"The master of this house!" Claes said, obviously wondering who dared lock him out of his own home.

Anna unbolted the door with a bang, and Elizabeth and Claes entered with the two babies. Claes' shoulders sagged, and his haggard face told Anna he had seen the same thing she had at the market. Elizabeth looked red-eyed and resigned.

"Jan Trypmaker and eight Brethren have been executed," Claes reported. "Their heads are on display in the Dam square."

"So it begins." Adriaen said quietly. "Charles V means

business." Anna didn't say anything about the other execution she had witnessed. It made her too dizzy and sick to even think about it.

"They won't be the last, I'm sure. When Charles is on the rampage, the blood flows like rivers." The two men sat quietly as they digested this news.

"None of us will be safe anymore in Amsterdam." Claes' face was sober. "And it's not because of our city officials. It's Charles' men at the Court of Holland who are making trouble. Jan Hubrechts, one of our magistrates, even sent his maid to warn the Brethren when the Court officers were on their way here, giving us time to hide."

"I'm not surprised. The councillors who are *Sacramenten* are in just as much danger from the Court as we are, even though they don't have believer's baptism."

"Sacramenten?" Anna looked up, surprised. "You mean there's more than one group of you heretics in Amsterdam?"

Adriaen winced. "We don't think of ourselves as heretics, Anna. Jan Trypmaker, our leader, always urged us to peace and obedience to the government. We want to be obedient subjects as long as it doesn't go against Scripture."

"But you don't like to be called Anabaptists either, do you?"

"That's what the Catholics and the Reformers call us. But that's not accurate. Our baptism as infants was no real baptism, so Anabaptist, or Re-baptiser, is an insult to us. We call ourselves the Brethren, *the Doopsgesinde* or the *Bundsgenote*."

"How confusing. So how did Trypmaker get caught?" Her stomach churned when she recalled the gruesome warning of the blackening heads on those poles.

Claes stroked his ginger-colored beard with short, thick fingers. "He turned himself in to the authorities, probably because he wanted to spare the rest of us. He knew the Council would have no rest until they found him because he was a leader. They 'questioned' him until he revealed the names of eight others."

"You mean they executed them right here in Amsterdam?" Anna shivered.

"No, our magistrates refused to do it, so the Court men took the prisoners back to The Hague and executed them there. But they brought the heads back to Amsterdam and put them on display as a warning."

Tears pooled in his dark blue eyes. "Who will become our leader now?"

"We still have Jacob van Campen. Too bad Melchior Hoffman went back to Strasburg." Adriaen said.

"Melchior Hoffman?" Claes scratched his head. "Sometimes I'm not sure what to think of his prophesies and revelations."

Anna's eyes widened. Surely these people would agree that true prophets should be listened to, and respected. "What kind of prophesies and revelations did he reveal?" Anna asked.

"He claims to have visions about the world ending in 1533. I wonder whether he really is the second Elijah?" Claes said. Anna shivered. She might as well have died with her family in the fire.

Adriaen shrugged. "Only God knows."

Elizabeth returned from feeding the two babies in the bedroom. "Won't you and the children stay and eat with us?"

"If it's not too much trouble." Anna was relieved not to be returning home alone right now. Her head was spinning with the implications of this incident, and spending time with Elizabeth was much more appealing. How much longer would they be safe in Amsterdam?

Chapter Eight

Amsterdam December 1531

For you had compassion on the prisoners, and you joyfully accepted the plundering of your property, since you knew that you yourselves had a better possession, and an abiding one...Heb 10:34

A few days later, Anna found an old sled standing against the back of the house, and she piled the three little ones onto it. With the well-wrapped nut cake tucked under her arm, she tramped through the snow towards Elizabeth's house. She hadn't delivered the cake before Christmas because Elizabeth had gone to visit her family for a few days, but the longer the cake cured, the better it would taste. On the arched, wooden bridge, she paused and showed the children the merry skaters flitting like colorful butterflies on the ice below. The children clapped and laughed, and begged to go on the ice.

"Maybe another day. Today we're going to see your father, your little sister, and the others." She packed the blankets around them and continued on her way. If Elizabeth didn't mind, Anna might leave the children with her, and attend communion at the Oude Kerk. Elizabeth, of course, would not be going. If she had planned on going anywhere, it would be to a clandestine Anabaptist meeting.

As soon as she rounded the corner to Elizabeth's house, something felt wrong. The shutters were closed in the middle of the day. The path in front of the door was untrampled--

not so much as one boot-print marred the newly fallen snow. Anna stood staring at the wooden door, and a feeling of dread turned her feet to stone.

She peered up and down the street, but nobody was in sight. Putting one heavy foot in front of the other, she reached for the latch and found it unlocked. Shivering, she turned around. The children clambered off the sled in happy anticipation. Maybe Elizabeth and Claes had gone visiting friends and stayed for the night. The snow had covered their tracks. Yes, that's exactly what had happened. The couple had many friends in the city, of course. And the meetings. They attended secret meetings with the Brethren, and often these were held at night. At night, as well as in the daytime, in hidden places.

The door opened with a creak loud enough to alert the whole street. Anna opened it part way, enough to stick her head inside. A choked scream escaped her throat. The house was completely upside down. The bed in the corner where Adriaen slept had been ripped apart, the straw strewn across the room. Pieces of pottery and ashes were scattered into every corner. And the baby's basket! It was tipped onto its side as if someone had dumped the contents into the fire. At the bottom of the stairs, the table lay in splintered ruins.

Anna couldn't shut the door fast enough. She swept up the children, deposited them on the sled, threw the blanket over them, and ran. Their bewildered little faces tore at her heart.

"*Vader*!" Trijntgen cried.

"Sorry, *shatje*, *Vader* isn't home. Want to go on the ice now?"

"No! I want to see *Vader*!" Bettke and Dirk joined in with a chorus of wails. Anna's tears froze on her cheeks. She staggered back the way she had come, pulling the sled-full of crying children behind her.

What had happened to her friends? Who ruined their house? Why would anyone destroy the inside of it? Even as she asked herself these questions, the answer was clear. Anna's veins turned to ice, as the haunting nightmare returned. Red-hot flames burned through her mind. She tried to calm her racing heart, consoling herself that there were no flames, her friends and the babies had not burned. Not yet, anyways. But such senseless destruction. And for what? Anna no longer felt secure in this town, but was there anyplace to go that was safer? Running away from scenes of destruction didn't last very long; trouble followed wherever she went.

By the time they came to the bridge, the children had changed their minds and clamored to watch the skaters. Anna wanted to go home and hide under the bed. Everyone she saw on the street could have betrayed her friends and helped wreck their house, yet nobody paid any attention to her.

She left the sled at the edge of the canal and helped the children dismount. Lifting Dirk onto her hip and asking the little girls to follow, they made their way down the steps and sat on a snowbank beside the ice. The steel blades of the skaters flashed by with dazzling speed, and Anna almost wished to join them. Though she'd probably end up flattened on the ice, like the young boy who slid to a stop in front of them. As the boy got up, he quickly checked up and down the ice. Nobody else was within hearing distance.

"Anna?"

"Balthasar!" Anna exclaimed. "How are you doing?" She noted with concern the lad's pinched face and thin body.

"I can't stay long, but I have a message for you." He

scanned the ice again. "Adriaen, Claes and Elizabeth got away with the babies. Someone reported them, but the family was warned in time for them to grab all they could carry and run. The Court officers tore the house apart looking for any forbidden writings."

A heavy weight lifted from Anna's shoulders. Her friends had gotten away. Just then, a small man in drab brown doublet and hose came gliding in their direction. A flicker of fear crossed the boy's face and he dashed away.

"Wait!" Anna called after him. "You forgot this parcel for your *moeder*!" She didn't even know if he had a mother. In a swoop he circled back, and she thrust it into his hands. The nut cake would taste better to him than it would to her. He grinned and waved, then sped away after taking another backwards look at the approaching man.

It was Pieter, the servant of the officer that had arrested her and Maeyken! She gasped and buried her face in Dirk's hood. *Go away! Go away!*

"Well, well. Who do I see here enjoying the view?" His raspy voice grated on her ears. She smelled sweat and horse manure before he even got within speaking distance. Did she have to answer?

"Adriaen and Claes are in prison," the pointy-chinned man said with a smirk. "This time they will die."

Before Anna could gather her wits to respond, the furtive little man skated away, the steel blades on his shoes slashing and scraping the ice, just as his words had slashed and scraped at her heart.

It was time to get home; she was too much of a public spectacle sitting there beside the ice. Anna collected the children, who protested at leaving so soon, but she soothed them by promising them more sweets when they got home. She needed to get away, now, out of sight of those who wished her harm. She wanted to believe Balthasar, but she was so confused. If he truly knew anything about the matter, he must be one of the Anabaptists.

Who was telling the truth? And which of the two even knew the truth?

Chapter Nine

Amsterdam, January 1532

Today when you hear his voice, do not harden your heart... Heb 2:7

In the first month of 1532, the children all came down with coughs and fevers, and Anna got little sleep for days at a time. The wind intruded with its frozen breath through every little crack in the house--the men must not have found them all-- and only the circle around the fire was warm. Half-starved dogs roamed the streets, creeping up to houses and sniffing around the door in search of some tidbit of food. Keeping the fire going was hard work. Adriaen had made sure there was wood for the fire, but it had to be dragged in from outside, and every time the door opened it took a long time for the kitchen to regain the heat.

The children wore layers of woolen clothing to stay warm and spent their days playing games by the fire. Anna hoped that Elizabeth and Claes were safe and warm somewhere with little Anneken. She missed the baby, and absurd as it was, she missed Adriaen.

She had received no letter, no news of any kind. Day after day, the children were her only company, and much as she adored them, she did crave adult conversation. Spring could not come soon enough. On rare occasions when the sun came out, she bundled up her little trio and took them outside to play in the snow, desperate to see something other than the four walls of the kitchen.

A few times when she went outside, she thought she saw a figure slinking away around the corner—but it had to be her imagination. She tried not to think of Pieter, the officer's servant. He had no business spying on her. She had gone to church, done her penance-- harrowing as it had been-- and what more could he be watching for? Unless, she shivered, he was snooping around, waiting for Adriaen to come to see the children. It was all too possible, though she tried to dismiss these thoughts as a result of overwrought nerves and loneliness.

The children were daily reminders of Adriaen and Maeyken. Every sacrifice she made for them—the sleepless nights, the struggle to stay warm in the winter, the sharp eye on the food supply, the loneliness of the winter, the loss of her freedom to go out whenever she wished—was all done for them. Sometimes, she reached into her bodice and pulled out the song Adriaen had given her, and reading it brought him painfully near. The words were strangely comforting even though she didn't fully understand their meaning.

Oh God, do Thou sustain me...

One late afternoon, near the end of January, Anna was sitting by the window with her distaff under her arm, spinning wool for little garments, when a sound distracted her from her half-sleep. She stiffened and listened again. There was a tap-tapping on the bedroom window. Her skin prickled. Waves of hot, then cold sensations engulfed her body. The spy! There it was again. It was not her imagination.

She turned terrified eyes towards the children, who were rolling about aimlessly in front of the hearth. With gray eyes even larger than usual, she got up from her chair and stood there for a minute. Surely, her mind was playing tricks. The tapping came again, louder this time. With leaden feet she walked towards the downstairs bedroom, where Simon used to sleep. Why would someone be tapping the window back there behind the house? There must be knee-high drifts of snow back there. A whiff of freezing air enveloped her when she opened the bedroom door, which she kept closed to conserve the heat.

"Anna, where are you going?" Trijntgen asked, shivering. The little kitchen was losing more of its precious warmth.

"Ssshhh, *schatje*, just stay there. I'll be right back." Trijntgen, Bettke and Dirk, in true childlike fashion, took this as an invitation to follow her. She let them. They were small, but she needed an escort of some kind as she undid the shutter and opened it a crack. A man was out there, and he turned to face her. Could it be?

"Adriaen!" she cried. He was bundled from head to toe in a heavy coat, fur hat, and a thick scarf, but his figure was unmistakable.

Her rigid body relaxed when he grinned. This was the last person she guessed would be intruding. She assisted him as he climbed in the bedroom window, dropping clods of snow on the floor as he entered. A miniature flurry descended as he shook the freezing white flakes from his coat. The bedroom was so cold that the snow didn't even melt on the floor.

"I hope you're not startled too badly. I didn't dare come in the front, because I have a suspicion the house is being watched."

"I am startled, but you can't think how relieved I am. I thought you were an intruder, bent on mischief. At least you aren't languishing in some cold, damp dungeon, like before."

"Not this time, God be praised," Adriaen said.

Anna led the way to the fireplace, with the children hopping and dancing in glee around their father. "*Vader's* home! *Vader's* home!"

"Va-va..." Dirk imitated his sisters.

Anna laughed. "Looks like you're home just in time to hear Dirk speak his first word."

Adriaen shucked his overcoat and lifted his son into his arms. Moisture glittered in his eyes. "Well done, my boy."

The two girls clung to his legs, laughing and crying at once. Anna would have liked to leap into his arms as well, if propriety had admitted. Never had she been so happy to see anyone. She reminded herself this was because Adriaen was the first adult she'd seen in a month, nothing more. The absolute joy in her heart would have been there for any friendly adult, of course.

Anna led Adriaen to the fire, and everyone huddled close to its circle of warmth. Anna added another log and heated some apple cider as a treat for all of them. She held back the questions she longed to ask. Where had he been? What had he been doing? And most important of all, how long could he stay?

Adriaen spent the last hour before dark playing with the children, while Anna prepared the evening meal of pickled herring, bread and cheese. Adriaen ate hungrily, as if he hadn't eaten in a long time. As Anna served him his supper, she noticed the tiny lines webbing from his dulled brown eyes-- eyes almost hidden by lids drooping with fatigue. Wrinkles furrowed his wide forehead, and his wide shoulders were bent forward as if he had no energy left to straighten them.

Anna's heart contracted at this evidence of the hardship and sorrow he undoubtedly suffered. Yet his voice was kinder than ever, and he seemed to possess a depth of inner peace which Anna marvelled at. Adriaen had not become bitter, even though he had lost so much; his wife; his home; his livelihood; the presence of his children. What did he have instead that surrounded him with this aura of contentment? How could he accept so calmly everything that had happened to him?

It could not be said that Adriaen, or any of the Anabaptists Anna knew, were anything but humble, helpful, and forgiving. But these were all traits they could put to beneficial use in the official church, Anna thought. There was no need to separate themselves and disobey the authorities.

When the kitchen began to dim, Anna spread the thick, black bearskins on the floor for the children to sleep on. It was too cold for them to sleep upstairs, and she had grappled with her own mattress to get it downstairs where it was warmer. There she could keep the fire going and watch the children.

Would Adriaen be staying for the night? The thought tickled her spinsterish heart, even though it would be scandalous for a single man and woman to be alone for the night. But where else could Adriaen go that was safe? Besides, the children were there, which would make it a trifle more respectable. Anna took down Simon's big, black overcoat from a peg in the wall.

"Anna! Are you leaving?" Adriaen asked, alarm in his voice.

"Not unless you want me to," she said, with a small frown. Should she leave? But where would she go? "I was just going to carry in logs to last the night. It's getting dark outside, so I better see to it now." It was a chore that didn't get any easier the more often she did it.

Adriaen jumped to his feet. "Let me do that, Anna." He held out his hands for the overcoat. His own coat was dripping wet and hanging from a peg near the fireplace to dry.

"But you're so tired. And someone might see you."

"I've had a rest now, and some food. It's dark enough that nobody will know it's not you wearing Simon's overcoat."

Anna bit her lips; she would much rather do the job herself than risk Adriaen going out there. "As you wish," she said, handing over the overcoat. "If you see anyone, will you come inside right away?"

Adriaen nodded. "Don't fret. I will be fine."

Anna whispered a prayer to Saint Michael for his safety as he went out the door, though it rang hollow to her ears. What power did Saint Michael have, after all, compared to God Himself? The Anabaptists did not believe in venerating the saints, and she decided it could do no harm to say a prayer directly to God. For Adriaen's sake, she fumbled an awkward little prayer to God as well.

The children couldn't bear it if anything happened to their father, now that he was finally back. She was mostly concerned for them, Anna assured herself. And she would be just as anxious for anyone's safety, not only because this was Adriaen. He came to see the children, and she happened to be their caregiver. She meant nothing more to him.

When Adriaen came back inside, out of breath and shaking snow from his shoulders, Anna breathed another prayer of thankfulness. Together, they piled the logs neatly beside the fireplace. By the time the task was finished, the children were sleeping soundly.

Adriaen turned to Anna. "Now, how have things been going, really?" He spoke in the same tone she imagined he might use when speaking to his grandparents or an aged aunt.

Anna fumbled to get a candle lit. What did she expect? A sultry lover's voice? She burnt her finger and shook it in disgust. "We have been managing better than I could have imagined. The children all got sick with coughs, but mustard plaster and onions on their chests worked wonders, and they were up and about in no time."

The two of them sat down by the fire as far apart as possible, while remaining within the circle of warmth. Adriaen looked at her with keen eyes. "And you're not too lonely?"

She shook her head. "I don't mind living here with the children in the least." Well, not anymore, now that he had returned.

"I had to come back to see the children," he said. Had he missed her too? No, of course not, the thought had probably never entered his mind. "I searched all over for a safe place for them to live, but there is no such place. The Brethren recommended that I leave them here. That is, if you agree. You must tell me if it is too much of a burden."

"Of course not."

"Moravia is relatively safe, if the authorities don't capture you on the way there. But travelling that distance with three small children is too perilous, I fear."

"They will be fine here with me." And he was welcome to stay as well. For always. For a moment she allowed herself to dwell on the picture of herself as Adriaen's wife, then sadly set the idea aside. For one, he would never marry a woman outside of his faith, never mind how much he admired her, and how convenient it might be. It would be unbelievable if Adriaen entertained any such ideas. Besides, how could she even consider being so disloyal to Maeyken? A few months ago, Maeyken had been alive and happy, and it was much too soon for Anna to be pining after her husband. But oh! He was so handsome, she thought, studying his profile by the flickering light of the flames in the fireplace. His thick brown hair was cut straight across his forehead and around the back of his neck. His nose was straight, his chin firm, and his lips wide and generous.

She compared him to the man back in Germany, whom she thought was in love with her. He was handsome too, in a loose-jointed way, but he had turned around and married someone else, just as Anna was finishing up her hope chest. The chest was gone now, burned to ashes, along with everything and everyone else she had loved. She was an outcast, a lonely, poor, and altogether plain spinster, who clung to her papist faith. With so many beautiful women in the world, why would he choose her if he ever did re-marry? Would he even live long enough for that?

"You know that Claes and Elizabeth have gone into hiding with the two babies?" Adriaen asked.

Anna nodded. "What happened to all of you?"

Adriaen cleared his throat. "It was close, I must say. We had a few minutes to grab our things and run. Claes and I each carried our own infant, and a pack of whatever we could think to toss inside; a bit of food, candles, knives, a small amount of gold and some blankets. Elizabeth remembered our Bibles, and all the religious tracts we had in the house, which was fortunate. I glanced inside Claes' house before I came here, and the officers tore the place apart."

"Yes, I saw that. I was going to take them a nut cake at Christmas but ended up giving it to a boy on the ice." Her heart beat faster as she remembered her shock.

"Claes and Elizabeth are in Harlingen; it's somewhat safer there. With Jan Trypmaker and some of the leaders executed now, along with so many other men and women, the remaining people are scattered all over like sheep without a shepherd. I heard there's a man, Jan van Geelen, who is gathering followers, and he will be our leader." Adriaen shook his head. "I'm afraid his life will be short too."

Anna wrinkled her brow. "So why doesn't everyone go back to the Church? Then you could all live in peace again."

"Anna, we would have no peace. Perhaps we would no longer be persecuted in the flesh, but our souls would have no peace. Do you not know how corrupt the priests are, with their drinking and gambling and fornication? How could we, as disciples of Christ, call them our brothers?" He reached into his pocket and pulled out a small booklet. "Would you like to read this?"

Anna sucked in her breath. "What is it about?" Chances were, whatever it said, Charles V would call it heresy. Especially if the writing came from the press of the Anabaptists.

"It tells us where in the Scriptures we find the basis for our beliefs. The Pope, and the state church, claim their Sacraments and ordinances are commanded by God, but in fact they are mere human inventions. Please read it. Perhaps you will gain a better understanding of our faith. But hide it well. You don't want the Court officers to see you with it."

He held out the tract and Anna accepted it by its very edge, making sure she didn't touch his fingers. She felt distinctly uncomfortable with Anabaptist writings in her house, but she didn't want to hurt his feelings. She would probably burn it in the morning. Why risk the wrong pair of eyes finding it? The officers did a thorough search for evidence when they suspected someone, as she had witnessed at Elizabeth's house. Besides, most likely she wouldn't be able to understand the words, even if she did read the tract.

Adriaen got up to leave. "I had better go now. I will find a place to sleep, for I cannot put you in danger by staying here. I've seen the children and thanks to you, they seem happy and healthy."

There was no use in being disappointed. What he said made perfect sense. He was only thinking of his children's safety, and hers.

"Will you visit again? For the children," Anna added hastily. She blushed, grateful for the darkness of the kitchen hiding her warm face. What if he saw right through her and caught on that she was asking for herself as much as for the children?

"I will come when I can. I will try to find work, perhaps on a ship. They don't usually ask many questions. They need able-bodied men to sail a ship, and if a man is hardworking they don't care much what religion he is."

Anna groaned inwardly. Sailing was a dangerous job this time of year, and he might not be back for months, or even at all. But what did it really matter? Whether he was at home or a thousand miles away, he was just as out of reach for her. Taking care of his children was as close as she would ever get to him, and his occasional visits to see them would be all she could hope for.

"I wish you well," Anna said, sincerely, yet with a heavy weight in the pit of her stomach.

Adriaen rose to his feet. "It's time I left." He looked into her eyes for several long moments, and much as she wished to, Anna could not look away. "I will be praying for you." Adriaen said.

"For me? The priests pray for my soul. Why should you do so?" Anna asked.

"Because I desire for you to find peace in your soul." He paused. "Come with me to the meeting tomorrow night. Jan van Geelen, the man I told you about, is going to be there, and you could hear first-hand what we believe in. Also, I don't want you to live in seclusion with my children. You need to get out sometimes."

Anna jerked her head up. Did he seriously believe she would be interested in attending an Anabaptist meeting? "You're just like my parents, who were always trying to lure me to secret meetings," Anna burst out. "And what happened to them?" She clenched her fists, and tears began to roll down her cheeks. "They were burned, unshriven, along with my siblings and our home. And now, I'm afraid they will be tormented in purgatory forever. In this land I can't even buy indulgences to free them, and my prayers, and lighting candles in the church may not be enough."

"Anna, Anna." Adriaen laid his hands on her shoulders. "I am so sorry. I did not know. So your family had joined the Brethren?" Anna nodded, shaking with silent sobs.

"Are you the only one of your family who survived?" Again, she nodded. "I believe," Adriaen cleared his throat, then continued, "that God has a very special reason for sparing you. You may not know at this time what His purpose is, but we do know He never makes mistakes. You must believe that, instead of suffering, your family is singing for joy in their heavenly home. Everything works out for good, if we trust God."

Now the silent sobs turned into a noisy torrent of weeping. Did God really care about her, and her family? Could it be true that He had some divine purpose in sparing her life? To Anna, it seemed as though she was no more than a piece of driftwood, washed up on the shore, having little value to anyone.

"I simply must go now, it's getting late," Adriaen said. "I will let you think about it until tomorrow night, then I will come back. If you decide to come with me, I will be very much pleased. If not, I understand, and I will not hold it against you."

"But the children...I couldn't take them, could I?"

"I'll send Janneken over. If you decide not to go, she can either go back home, or stay here and keep you company. Does that meet with your approval?" Anna nodded, wiping away the tears.

"Good. Now I really must be on my way. *Goedenacht*."

Anna stared at the door long after he had gone. The tract he had given her lay on her lap. She picked it up and held it in her hands without opening it. She read the title, which was written in German: '*Von einem wahrhaften Ritter Christi, und womit er gewappnet muss sein, damit er uberwinden moge die Welt, das Fleisch, und den Teufel.*' Anna stared at the words for a long time. 'Concerning a True Soldier of Christ...' Much as she admired Adriaen, and would gladly do anything to protect him from the cruel officers, she could not bring herself to turn the page. Was she a True Soldier of Christ, or was she marching to her own tune? Or to the tune of a church that had lost its glory? After a while, she got up and tucked the booklet under her mattress.

Chapter Ten

Amsterdam, January 1532

Preach the word...be unfailing in patience and in teaching...2 Tim 4:2

The following night was crisp, clear and moonlit, and not too severely cold, considering it was January. It had been a long day of agonizing indecision for Anna, and evening brought Janneken, but no relief. She longed to spend more time with Adriaen before he sailed out of her life. The temptation to go out with him, away from the same, endless four walls with only children for company, was overwhelming. But she must not let her heart rule her reason, nor loneliness her common sense. 'A true soldier of Christ, a true soldier of Christ.' The words twisted and circled through her mind all day, and the pamphlet under her mattress kept luring her gaze in that direction. She steadfastly ignored it.

Just in case she decided to go to the meeting with Adriaen, she changed into a clean kirtle and apron, then laced up her bodice with trembling fingers. She brushed her dark, unruly hair until it was as glossy as it ever had been in her life. A crisply starched white cap, and soft leather boots completed her outfit. But would she go? She bit her fingernails, and straightened the kitchen, which was already neat as a pin. Janneken and the children had a happy reunion, and they giggled and chattered as they played games in front of the fire.

Finally, after dusk descended on Amsterdam, Adriaen arrived. His cheeks were ruddy with cold, and his ears were well-covered by his flat woollen cap, but his eyes sparkled beneath it like diamonds on snow. Though his bulky overcoat covered his muscular frame, Anna noted that the tired stoop was gone from his wide shoulders.

"Are you coming with me?" Adriaen asked, smiling.

"Yes, I will go." Anna could hardly believe she had agreed. It must be a sign of her desperation to be near a man who saw her only as a nursemaid to his children. It was not because she was the least bit curious about the meeting. In fact, she was taking her life in her hands by attending. But tonight, she would try to figure out what being a 'true soldier of Christ' was all about.

Anna wrapped herself in her fur-lined cloak and wound a fleecy scarf around her head. In spite of herself, her spirits lifted as she stepped outside into the night with Adriaen. As they walked in the shadows of the tall houses, she savoured the freedom of being outdoors without the responsibility of watching out for small children. Adriaen led the way to the woods, striding easily on the snow-packed trail.

A meeting in the forest...it was strange, and her nerves tingled with the danger of it. She couldn't help looking over her shoulder frequently. She was sure she heard someone following them, and her heart almost beat out of her chest. Adriaen listened too, then shrugged.

"Maybe an animal, or others coming to the meeting." Of course, Anna thought, feeling foolish for her alarm. Others would be going too. Just because someone was following them didn't mean there was a spy. It was just that sneaking about at night like this made her shiver. Every sound could be the officers coming to arrest them all. And to get rid of them all.

After a brisk walk, they arrived at a small clearing surrounded by cedar trees. Half a dozen men and women were already assembled there, the men already deep in some discussion. They greeted the newcomers warmly and indicated a couple of logs for them to sit on. Nobody introduced themselves or asked for Anna and Adriaen's names. But then Anna remembered-- you can't betray someone unless you know their name. It was rather comforting, this feeling of anonymity. Nobody would know who she was either.

A clean-shaven man of medium height and shoulder-length hair seemed to be the leader. Was this Jan van Geelen? Or Jacob van Campen, who was the bishop of the Amsterdam Anabaptists? Every time another person came brushing through the snowy cedar branches, she froze, certain that this time it was a spy, or the officers, come to betray or arrest them all.

What was she doing here? What would these people think if they realized she had already betrayed one of their number? Adriaen had told her that his brother had arrived safely in Moravia, but now that the authorities knew Joachim to be a leader, it would never be safe for him to return to his native home in the Netherlands.

Besides Anna, there were two other women there that night, one an older woman and the other appeared to be her granddaughter. They greeted her with smiles and motioned her over to sit with them on a large log. Anna never did find out their names.

Eventually, when the *Dienaar* were satisfied that no more people were coming, they asked everyone to gather round. The assembled believers formed a half-moon in front of the three *Deinaar*. The night was beautiful, the stars winked above, and though the air was brisk, the spot was sheltered by the cedars and quite comfortable. Anna thought of the rich decorations in the Oude Kerk, with its colorful stained-glass windows and statues of gold, the altar with its burning candles of incense, the ancient relics and the gold-laced tapestries.

But in this lovely place in the wintry woods, where she knew only one person by name, she felt like she could almost belong to them. Somehow, God seemed much closer here than He ever had anywhere else. She could almost feel His presence here in the woods He had created. She felt closer to these humble people upon meeting them once, than she had in the entire Catholic congregation where she'd been attending all her life.

She didn't know exactly what it was that made them different. Their voices were kind, yes. It was hard to know who the leaders were, since several of them took turns speaking, and none of them seemed to be the head of the others. Nobody wore expensive clothes, only the simple, unadorned garments of the layman.

The clean-shaven man had opened the service by reading from Scripture in a strong voice, as if he were a 'True Soldier' marching in the spiritual army of Christ. "As my Brethren have desired it, I will read from the sixth chapter of the letter of Paul to the Ephesians: 'Finally, be strong in the Lord and in the strength of his might. Put on the whole armor of God, that you may be able to stand against the wiles of the devil. For we are not contending against flesh and blood, but against the principalities, against the powers, against the world rulers of this present darkness, against the spiritual hosts of wickedness in the heavenly places...'"

A slight stir of alarm filled Anna's heart, and she wondered whether these people viewed the state church as the devil, the ruler of darkness. The assembled ones bent forward in rapt attention, the light of the moon shining on their eager upturned faces. The next *Dienaar am Wort* to speak was a large man wearing a long black robe and a beard. He spoke on *gelassenheit*, a total surrender to the will of God. At the end, he asked anyone desiring baptism to come forward. His eyes seemed to linger on Anna, but she shrunk into the shadows. Did she appear so interested in his words that he thought she might join the Anabaptists? True, she was curious, and she longed to experience the closeness of these people, not the least because Adriaen belonged here, but she was not ready to become one of them.

The young girl came forward to be baptized, as well as a middle-aged man, who was wearing the tunic and hose of a farmer. Her father? They knelt in front of the preacher, and he baptized them in the name of the Father, of the Son, and of the Holy Spirit, sprinkling a few drops of water on their heads. He gave the man his hand, and the farmer stood while the preacher blessed him, and welcomed him to the brotherhood with a holy kiss of peace. He repeated this with the girl but omitted the kiss. At the end of the service, Anna looked around in bewilderment when everyone kneeled on the snow to pray. When she noticed she was the only one sitting, she hastened to get down on her knees, her cheeks burning. In the Catholic church, most of the people stood during the whole service, including the prayers, and only the priest prayed.

The sermons over, the Anabaptists began to discuss practical matters. Their faith was so new, and they were so scattered by persecution, that it must be difficult for the leaders to get together to debate and adopt unified practices. Anna got up and walked around the edges of the little clearing, alert for any unusual sound, as the men discussed their doctrine long into the night. One loud-voiced, outspoken man seemed to be pushing some sort of scheme which included using force, and he kept quoting violent parts of the Old Testament. The others speedily convinced him to drop that idea. The only sword they would use was the sword of God's word --the sword of peace and love.

Anna stiffened in alarm when they began discussing the need for more 'apostles' to spread the Truth to the world, and then she heard Adriaen's name. Just like that, and before her very eyes, Adriaen knelt in front of the tall preacher. The preacher laid his hands on Adriaen's head, asked him a couple of questions which Adriaen answered with '*ja*'. Adriaen was pronounced *Dienaar am Wort,* an evangelist who would spread the Gospel, wherever in Christendom God led him to wander. Adriaen stood, bowing his head in humility.

No! Not Adriaen as a preacher! Anna gaped at him. Adriaen was standing tall and straight in the moonlight. He was the perfect image of a True Soldier of Christ. A lump formed in her throat. How could he look so untroubled and undismayed, yet strong, standing beside the other preachers? Did he truly believe that the Anabaptist view of salvation was the correct one? Anna shook her head. What made him agree to go on a mission that promised to make his life very short? If he lived another year or two, it would be a miracle of God.

He would be in ten times as much danger. Any weak adherent to the Anabaptists who was caught could be tortured until they broke down and betrayed Adriaen's whereabouts. Then the Court officers would send the *tauferjager* after him; these rough hooligans would do anything, even hunt human beings, for money. They would chase him until they found him, then after they were done tormenting him, he would be executed by some barbarous method. They would burn down his house, take everything he owned, including his children.

Anna took a step forward, then stopped. Who was she to protest God's will? She had no right to interfere with Adriaen's life, nor with what God called him to do. But in that moment, she realized how much she cared for him, how much she wanted him to stay alive, and she might as well admit she loved him. Yet now, more than ever, he was out of her reach. He would not marry anyone who wasn't an Anabaptist, and Anna was no Anabaptist, though it did seem she was being pulled in that direction. Otherwise, why would she be here?

In the shadow of a sheltering cedar, she prayed for the salvation of Adriaen's soul, for his safety, and for the steadfastness of any unfortunate soul the authorities caught. She prayed to the Virgin Mary, to every saint she could think of, and to God Himself.

A short time later, Adriaen was ready to leave. Neither of them spoke much on the way home. Anna's heart was so full she didn't know what to say, and Adriaen walked as if in a trance. Was it sinking in for him what he had committed himself to do? Instead of sailing away on a ship, he would have to tramp over the whole of the Netherlands and beyond, hiding in forests and swamps wherever he could, and scavenge for food like an animal. The Anabaptists convinced Adriaen that God required him to do this, and he accepted the mission without question.

She feared she would never see him again. In a few weeks, a few months, or a few years at the most, she would hear that he was dead, long after it happened. Perhaps she would hear that he was languishing in some damp dungeon and suffering...

"Adriaen," Anna faced him in the shimmering moonlight. "Don't go away!"

Adriaen stopped in the middle of the path and stared at her, a puzzled look in his eyes. "Go away where? Are you saying you don't want the truth of the Gospel to be pronounced to all Christendom? Because you believe your gambling, drinking, Latin-chanting priest is telling the truth?"

Anna clapped her hands to her mouth. "But that's blasphemy! You cannot speak like this and go unpunished!"

"I will let God decide who will be punished." Adriaen's eyes held concern. "Am I asking too much of you to take care of the children? If so, I will find someone else to look after them."

Anna shook her head. That was not what she meant at all when she asked Adriaen not to go away. But how could she tell him what she did mean? That she would miss him too much, and that she was afraid for his safety, and if anything happened to him, she would be devastated? Or that she feared he would die unshriven in some castle dungeon, and would suffer eternally? She couldn't tell him. He must not find out how much he mattered to her. He would be disgusted.

"I...I...just don't want them to lose their father as well as their mother." Their footsteps crunched on the snow-packed path as they continued wending their way homewards. A deep fatigue settled on Anna's mind. Maybe it would be best to just stop caring and worrying so much about her loved ones; let a numbness creep into her mind, like the numbness of her toes from the cold.

"I wish the same, Anna," Adriaen said. "I will be constantly praying that the children can live with me again, but in the end, I must also pray 'Not my will, but Thine, O Lord.'" He paused, but Anna didn't answer. She was so tired. "Will you send messages when I'm gone, and tell me how you and the children are doing?"

"Yes, but how?"

"The baker, Geryt, can be trusted to deliver any letters. I will also send messages as I am able, and I will send money through him as well. I hope to have the children brought up in the true teaching of God when they are a little older, but in the meantime, you must do what seems proper to you." He looked intently into her face; what was he searching for? "I will pray also that you come to a knowledge of the Truth and give your heart and your will to God."

Anna let the numbness creep into her soul. That's what she thought she had been doing all her life. What mortal could know God's will?

"I will arrange something for them in case I perish," he continued. "But I may still live a long time, you know. With God, all things are possible."

If all things are possible, Anna thought, she wished that the world could agree on their religious views, so everyday life could settle down. And if all things were possible, she wanted to settle down with Adriaen as her husband. Was it sinful to wish this? It seemed reasonable to her mind. She would have to ask Father Hendricks about it, but of course, the way things stood, he would not recommend her marrying an Anabaptist preacher. Still, here she was, on the way home from a forbidden meeting, an Anabaptist preacher at her side. She ought to confess it, but she decided Father Hendricks didn't need to know about it, at least not for now. The confessor's zeal for eradicating the Anabaptists might stop Adriaen in his tracks. If Father Hendricks found out Adriaen was back in town, the newly-ordained preacher would never take a single footstep across Europe. Anna would not be the one to inform on him.

"Adriaen, now that you're a *Dienaar*, might I ask you a question?"

"Certainly. I will do my best to answer, although I am not as learned as some men, you know." He smiled. The moon shone down in silvery rays through the branches of the snow-dusted trees, while the night breezes carried the clean scent of cedar.

"How is it that the Anabaptists are not afraid to die?" There. It was out.

Adriaen bowed his head, in almost a prayerful attitude. Perhaps he was praying. Praying for the right answer to give her, so that her interest in his beliefs would not float away like the down off a thistle.

"God loves those who follow His will, accept Jesus as His son, and believe that He died for our sins. Only through Jesus dying on the cross can our sins be forgiven, not through any earthly priest," he said gently. "Nothing stands between us and God except our own sins. Jesus suffered and died for us, and if we obey His commands, he will prepare a place for us in Heaven where great joy and a crown awaits us."

Anna walked on, trying to make sense of it all. It was difficult for her to imagine a life where there was just a man and his God, without calling on the saints to intercede, and without confessing to any priest. It was quite a leap from the grand cathedrals of the Roman Catholic church to a secret meeting spot in the woods. And a great contrast between the chanting of the richly robed priests before their holy altars, and a discussion in the middle of the night between a dozen men in the woods.

Adriaen walked with Anna to the door of her house, and she turned to bid him good-night. An inscrutable look lingered in his gentle brown eyes.

"Sleep well, my friend," he said.

"I will try. And I hope you have a nice warm bed to sleep in."

Feeling shy all of a sudden, Anna stepped into the doorway of the house, her pulse racing, and with legs that felt as wobbly as a pickled herring.

"I shall be fine." His tender gaze penetrated her soul. "May God be with you and grant you his peace." Then he vanished into the crystal night. Anna remained on the doorstep, her heart aching and throbbing like a drum.

She'd have to go find herself a respectable widower somewhere, with ten children who wouldn't care who or what she was, as long as he had someone to care for his children. Maybe that would cure her of this ridiculous fantasizing whenever she was around Adriaen. It was intolerable to pine after him like this. He was an Anabaptist preacher, she was Catholic. It would never work. Not now, and not when he was done mourning. Not even if she was the most beautiful woman on earth.

Inside, she tore off her scarf and tossed it on the trestle table, followed by her heavy cloak. She sat beside the fireplace in brooding silence. The children and Janneken lay sprawled at her feet, sleeping, and she sighed. The spell of peace she had experienced in the forest had disappeared along with Adriaen. If she had as much faith as Adriaen did, it would be easier to trust her future and eternity to God.

Chapter Eleven

Amsterdam, January – February 1532

Do not neglect to show hospitality to strangers, for thereby some have entertained angels unawares...Heb 13:2

Just as suddenly as Adriaen had come, he was gone. He had arrived unexpectedly, like a ray of sunshine on a cloudy day; and now loneliness returned. The winter hours grew long, her thoughts kept going in circles; from Adriaen, to the fanatical faith he lived for, to scrutinizing the Roman Catholic religion, to her future, to her past, then back again. The children became increasingly bored, and often annoying, with their whining and petty quarreling. None of the little daily household tasks she did lifted her spirits. Day after day passed the same as the one before, and she wished for some diversion to break the monotony.

It was nearing the end of January, with at least two more months of winter before she could take the little ones outside on a regular basis. She hadn't lived in Amsterdam long enough to make many friends, even if she had been more outgoing. Nobody ever visited.

She often found herself praying to God for stronger faith, almost as much as to the saints. She had no idea whether or not God even heard her. No heavenly vision came to her with an answer. Her soul didn't feel any different. She prayed for Adriaen's safety and for his return to her, and she prayed for strength to any captured Anabaptists to hold their tongues and not to betray him. She prayed that he was warm and had enough to eat, and she prayed to accept God's will for her life and for Adriaen's. Maybe he only needed his faith to live for and had no room in his heart for another woman.

Her attendance at the Catholic church grew gradually further and further apart. When she did go, her thoughts kept wandering to that gathering in the moonlit forest and how enchanting that experience had been. She wanted to know more about Adriaen's faith, and she wanted him to tell her about it. Out of habit she went sometimes to Mass, and to avoid coming under suspicion by the Court officers, not because it brought her any peace.

She did not need the sharp-eyed Father Hendricks asking questions and casting doubts on her faithfulness. The Catholic clergy were on a sharp lookout for signs of heresy as the number of their congregation dwindled, and they spared no efforts to drag unfaithful ones back to their church.

Anna asked herself what the church wanted most -- to save the souls of their congregation, or collect their money with their tithes. Quickly, she stifled the traitorous thought. The church needed tithes for the glory of God, to build shrines and honor the relics of the saints. As a symbol of homage, God's cathedral must be made magnificent with costly ornaments. No expense should be spared, and since the soul was more important than the body, members must be willing to sacrifice everything to maintain the splendor of their cathedral. If the peasants lived in squalor, yet paid the tithes, their place in heaven was assured.

Anna drove herself nearly insane as she compared these extravagant ideas to the simple piety she had witnessed at Anabaptist meetings. The radicals owned next to nothing when it came to worldly goods, let alone a building for holding services, yet she had seen them worship the Lord with grateful hearts and rapturous faces. She searched for the answers in prayers to every saint she could think of, and to God as well. All to no avail; peace would not come. Her thoughts kept spinning along the same paths, like the wool she was spinning into cloth. Trijntgen was fast outgrowing her clothes, and soon they could be passed down to Bettke.

After one particularly long day, she decided her melancholy came from her lack of faithful church attendance. The sun was out the following Sunday morning, and the wind had stopped its incessant blowing, so a stroll in the fresh air would work wonders for her and the children. Hopefully the little ones would be absorbed with the church and the congregation, and stay quiet. She sponged their hands and faces and put clean clothes on them. She put a shiny coin into each little palm, to put in the collection box. Teaching them to give to the church would not do any harm, regardless which church they ended up joining. After bundling everyone in cloaks and blankets, she hustled them out the door and packed them in the sled. Dirk was finally walking, though not outdoors in the snow.

Anna felt better already. The children's eyes glowed with pleasure, and Anna breathed in the glorious crisp air. Along the street, over the bridge to the Dam square she strode, pulling the sled, and squinting in the bright sunshine. Only a few other people were out who were heading in the same direction. Father Hendricks would draw his brows together in displeasure and no doubt report his faithless members to the Court officers.

At least they would be so busy with those not present, that they would pay no attention to Anna. The unfinished *Nieuwe Kerk* on the square might never need to be completed if too many people turned Anabaptist. She shivered as she walked past the Stadthaus, a place she hoped never to visit again. She reached the door of the Church of St. Nicholas, or the *Oude Kerk*, in time to see the sneaky little Court servant slip inside. Pleasant company, Anna thought, hunching into her cloak.

She was struck anew by the opulence of the church's interior. Instead of the awe and holiness she was used to feeling there, the exquisitely painted scenes on the altarpiece seemed a little vulgar, with nearly nude men and women swirling in a vision of red, blue and gold. The stained-glass scenes of the Last Supper on the windows were lovely today, with the sun shining through. But Anna could not admire them as much as she usually did, though she tried hard. The picture of a snowy clearing in the cedars kept intruding into her mind. The high stone arches were as impressive as ever, hung as they were with all kinds of banners and coats-of-arms. Still, it irritated Anna that she could only see them as pretentious, while remembering the fragrant arches of cedar branches beside a path through the woods.

The churchgoers seemed more distant, and their devotion more contrived than ever before. Anna held Dirk, and Trijntgen and Bettke clung to her skirts, thumbs in mouth. If Anna was less than entranced, the children made up for it. Their eyes were blue circles of amazement when the priest began his chants, though they understand not a word of the Latin he spoke. The hair on the back of Anna's neck rose when she noticed the sneaky little servant standing nearby, partly hidden by a column. He stared at her with narrowed eyes. Maybe she wasn't as secure here as she'd hoped, even though she was obediently attending the Catholic church.

Afterwards, on the way home, Anna couldn't shake the

feeling of being followed. When she glanced back over her shoulder, she saw no one, yet out of the corner of her eyes, she kept seeing a flitting shadow in the doorways. With some relief, she reached home without incident, content to stay indoors once more.

About a week later, on a freezing cold February night, after Anna and the children were all tucked in their beds, Anna suddenly bolted upright. What was that sound? Those bumps and thumps against her door? Thank goodness it was bolted. Was it only a half-frozen stray dog trying to find shelter, or something else? Goosebumps formed on her body and she hugged herself. Did she hear a faint shout or was it only the wind? When she heard the sound again, she got out of bed, shivering, and wrapped a blanket around her body. She lit a candle with shaking fingers and trembled from head to toe as she walked to the door.

The floor was icy cold for her stockinged feet as she fumbled with the latch. The fierce wind pelted a billow of snow into the kitchen as it blew inwards, nearly ripping the door out of her hands and instantly extinguishing the candle's flame. Something large fell onto the floor in front of her with a hard thump and a groan. She stifled a scream. She felt, rather than saw, another figure enter the room. It too fell on the floor. She struggled mightily with the door until finally she was able to re-fasten the latch.

The blanket lay somewhere on the floor behind her. Anna shook violently with cold and fear. Stepping carefully around the bodies on the floor, she felt her way to the fireplace to relight her candle. She put more wood on the fire and got a roaring blaze going before she found the courage to turn around and see what the wind blew in.

By flickering candlelight, she crept over to the still figures on the floor. She felt dizzy. Adriaen? Two nearly frozen men lay there, one mumbling incoherently, the other too far gone for that. After a quick check, she was both disappointed and relieved. No Adriaen. She grabbed one of the men under the arms, and, with much effort, dragged him closer to the fire. He groaned and shifted himself onto his side. At least he was alive.

She was panting and shaking, but she had to get the other one over to the fire too. Somehow, she managed it. This one was only a young boy, certainly smaller and lighter than the other. He made no stir. Now what? She found her blanket and wrapped it tightly around the boy. By rummaging in a chest, she found another blanket for the man. She removed their boots and rubbed their icy feet with her hands. There was sure to be frostbite.

Who were these men? What were they doing here? And most important, were they friend or foe? She'd find out when they revived enough to talk. She warmed some water in the kettle above the fire until it was no longer ice cold, then filled a bowl and placed their hands in the water, one freezing blue hand at a time. After what seemed like hours, but might have been minutes, the heavy-set man finally came around and looked about with wondering eyes.

"Is this the right place? You are Anna?" Anna started in surprise. How did this stranger know her name? She hugged her arms around herself.

"Yes, I am. How do you know my name?"

"Adriaen sent us with a letter," he replied. "Can you lodge us until the weather allows us to travel farther?" He winced, rubbing his hands together. "That blizzard is terrible. We almost didn't make it."

Anna was speechless. Happy as she was to find out

Adriaen was alive, she was alarmed that these men asked to stay here. They must be quite desperate for shelter. Had they run out of safe homes to hide in?

"My name is Willem, by the way. Sorry for intruding."

Anna just shivered. Willem peered with concern at the young man who was finally beginning to show some signs of life. "Poor fellow, he's about done in." Anna kneeled beside the boy, alternately rubbing his feet, then his hands. She was worried about him, but she wanted Adriaen's message, and she wanted it now.

"How is Adriaen doing?" She tried not to sound too eager. Really, the important thing was reviving this young man; supposedly, the message could wait.

"He was at Antwerp when last I saw him. There is quite a large following there. However," Willem continued, "persecution is becoming quite severe. The dungeons are full, and so are all the other places the authorities use to confine them. I fear they will soon execute large numbers to make room for others."

Anna's chest constricted. This man could not know what unbearable pain he was inflicting on her. She clenched her fists and her temple throbbed. The smoke of the fire brought tears to her eyes.

"But...but...Adriaen? He is safe?" She did not want to hear that he had been captured, now or ever.

"As safe as a *Dienaar* can be. He was thinking of going to spread the word in Germany, which is safer than Antwerp. Not that any place is safe for the Brethren, mind you." Anna was well aware of that. It was only a matter of time, she knew. Somehow the authorities always seemed to figure out who the leaders were, usually by unsavoury methods.

But Germany! To Anna, it seemed like an ill omen. It was

a place she had left behind gladly, and she hoped Adriaen wouldn't be staying there for long.

"Oh, where is the letter he sent...?" Willem sat up and patted his pockets. "Now, where did it go?" He reached inside his right coat pocket, then his left, and his brow furrowed. "I know I put it in here somewhere." He checked every pocket but found nothing. Anna stared at him, her eyes narrowed. He had better find it.

"It musta fallen out when I had my hands in my pockets to warm 'em. I'm so sorry." He looked stricken. "I hope there was nothing important in it, lest it fall into the wrong hands."

Yes, just produce it and put it into the right hands; mine! Anna was crushed. How dare the man lose something so important? For an instant, she was so angry she wished he had froze to death—a thought, she realized, she would need to confess to Father Hendricks. Or would she? The Anabaptists wouldn't. They confessed their sins to God only.

"Can you check just one more time?" The result was the same. He didn't have it.

"Perhaps your friend has it?" Anna knew it was a useless question, but it was beyond aggravating that this man had lost something so precious. They searched the younger man's pockets and found a collection of items, but no letter. For over a month, Anna had been watching and waiting every day for some word of Adriaen, and to have it snatched away like this was too much. She fought back tears of rage and disappointment as she continued to work over the boy, and tried to forgive the man.

When dawn arrived, the storm had abated, and the sun shone its weak rays through the storm-blown window. Anna got a better look at her guests, and guessed the younger man to be about twenty, though he was so small and slim it was no wonder she thought he was only a boy. His cheeks were sunken and pale, and he looked exhausted. He had a small beard and reddish hair in an unkempt tangle above his high, white forehead. His eyes had to be green to match, but he hadn't opened them yet.

The other man was tall and probably in his forties, with the wide shoulders and muscular appearance of someone used to heavy labor. His dark hair was streaked with gray, and his dark blue eyes were wide-set above a rather large nose. He wore the rough clothes of a peasant farmer, while the other looked as though he had stepped out of a university hall, with smooth hands and well-made clothing. An odd-looking pair to be sure.

Willem huddled in the blanket and shivered, but his concern for his companion was obvious. He kneeled beside the man on the opposite side of Anna.

"Jan, my friend, wake up." He shook him gently, but only the blue eyelids fluttered to indicate life. Anna found another blanket for him and added more wood to the fire.

When the children woke up, Trijntgen jumped up from the furs near the fireplace. "Father!" she cried. But she stopped short when she saw the strangers, and slowly backed away. She ran sobbing to Anna and buried her face in her apron. "I want my Father!"

"I know, *schatje,* I know. We all do." She smoothed the little girl's hair with her gentle, work-worn hands. "Would you like to give the man some bread and cheese?" Trijntgen shook her head. She was having none of this man who was not her father.

"No?" Anna handed the food to Willem, which she had prepared along with some ale. "You must be very hungry."

He nodded and nearly grabbed the food out of her hands,

before gobbling it down, smacking his lips and slurping his ale. Anna watched him warily. She chewed on some bread herself and gave some to the children. They crowded to her side with solemn blue eyes staring at the newcomers, fascinated. At least they forgot their quibbling since they had some entertainment.

As the morning went on, Willem became increasingly restless. His companion was taking a long time to come around. He opened his eyes a few times, looked around with a glassy stare, then went back to sleep.

"Poor boy, he's had a rough time of it. He ain't used to bein' out in the cold like me. I'm afraid I pushed him too far last night, even if I did carry him on my back for the last few miles."

"How long have you been travelling?"

"I've lost track of time, but it must have been a couple weeks since we left Antwerp."

"Have you been out in the cold all that time?"

"We slept at an inn the first two nights, but the second night we almost got caught. The innkeeper kept looking at us, suspicious-like, and Jan saw him whispering to his servant, then he slipped out the back door. We left right away, but had a difficult time escaping them soldiers. We hid in a barn for the rest of the night, and since then we haven't risked an inn. We slept in forests during the day, and travelled by night." He looked at her questioningly. "Do you know where the Brethren are to be found in this town? We have been sent to gather them and strengthen them in the truth."

Anna could tell him very little. She had not learned the names of the people she'd seen in the forest that night so long ago with Adriaen. She mentioned the baker as a man who could be trusted; other than that, she could give no information.

"I'll go see him if you don't mind me leaving Jan with you."

Anna nodded. The children gathered around the sleeping man, whispering and wondering. She smiled as they crept closer and closer, their curiosity overcoming their shyness.

"Barbli? Is that you, Barbli?" They were all startled when he started mumbling in confusion. The children's chatter must have awakened him. Anna laid down the wool she had picked up to wind and rushed to his side.

"Jan! Wake up!" She smoothed the reddish hair away from his forehead with a cool hand and washed his face with a cloth dipped in warm water. He mumbled something that sounded like "mother." She fed him a bit of warm water with a spoon, which he managed to swallow. He opened his eyes, they *were* green, and looked around in bewilderment and dismay.

"Where am I? And where is Willem?"

"Don't worry. You are safe here." Anna hoped this was true. The more she was involved with these people, the less safe they all became.

"I thought I heard my little sister talking." His voice was weak and hoarse, but he was alive. He spotted Trijntgen, Bettke and Dirk staring at him with awestruck faces, and smiled sadly. "I thought I was in Heaven with my little sister Barbli."

Anna swallowed. He did look almost angelic, with his sweet, sad smile and perfect features. She helped him sit up, bundled in the two blankets. The wind was still howling outside, though not as fiercely as the night before. She wondered if Willem found his way to the baker. He seemed to be a man who could never keep still.

"Are you in any pain?"

He wiggled his toes. "The feeling is coming back, and it hurts. There might be frostbite." He smiled ruefully, which brightened his pale face. "I'm not sure how I came to be here, or where I am. The last thing I remember is Willem slinging me over his shoulder like a sack of wheat, and the terrible cold and the wind. How he managed to find you is a miracle of God. We could not see a foot in front of our face." His eyes closed again, and he laid himself back on the floor and fell back to sleep.

Frenzied thoughts began rushing through Anna's mind as she plucked at her wool winding. She was fast reaching the point of no return. In the eyes of the law, she would already be a condemned heretic for the meeting she had attended—her presence in church notwithstanding-- and now she was sheltering fugitives. They were Anabaptist leaders actively seeking converts, no less. If she didn't take her information to the authorities before they found out about her, her life was over.

She looked at the children playing quietly on the floor near the sleeping man. She had them to think about, not only herself. If anything happened to her, where would they go? The authorities would be gratified and pay a good reward for reporting these two. Not only could she use the money, but reporting these so-called heretics would safeguard her own future, and that of the children, for a long time to come. The thought made her feel sick inside. It would be like betraying her own family.

On the other hand, neither did she want to be caught giving refuge to outlaws, and suffer imprisonment and a cruel death. In fact, she didn't want to think of death at all, not for a long time. It was a mystery to her how the Anabaptists went to their fiery and watery deaths with joyfulness and song, as she had already witnessed in Germany. They must be expecting a great reward in Heaven, and she wanted that assurance for herself. She was beginning to doubt that she would burn eternally if she turned to the Anabaptists. Her parents would be amazed and pleased if they knew their papist daughter was softening her stance against the Anabaptists.

The more Anabaptists she saw, including Adriaen and Maeyken, Elizabeth and Claes, the more Anna became convinced that they held a secret she wanted to know for herself. No amount of deprivation or danger seemed to shake their precious peace. They put all their trust in God, and in the saving blood of Jesus, and would hear nothing of the pompous priest's or the venerable saints' intervention for them. They refused to accept the Scriptures the way the Catholic church taught them, and insisted their own interpretation was the right one and the only one that mattered.

Little did they care for the rules and decrees of popes, kings or magistrates if they interfered with their beliefs. They would rather suffer cruel deaths than stray one step from the path of what they read in the Gospel. In one thing Anna agreed with the authorities- these people were obstinate, no doubt about that. Whatever else they were, they were still human beings, and if she betrayed them, she would be no better than a murderer. Whatever she became for defying authority, nothing could compel her to send innocent people to slaughter.

Anna didn't know how much longer she could keep up the charade of being a faithful Catholic. She wanted to know more about these Brethren, who seemed so much more real and approachable than any priest. They dressed simply and talked plainly. It was incredible how they could have their sins forgiven just by praying to God. Probably their sins were not very great to begin with. Not like those who were filled with unholy rage when someone lost a letter.

Anger bubbled up in her heart again, just by thinking about such rank carelessness. Besides the bitter disappointment, there was the danger of the wrong person getting it into their hands, which would betray Adriaen, and probably herself. She knew that she would have guarded such a letter with her life.

And where was Willem anyway? He had shown such concern for his friend before, and now he had vanished. She hoped he hadn't been caught.

Jan stayed awake in the afternoon for a few hours. He was quite attracted to the children, and they to him, after they got over their shyness. He explained to Anna that he had several younger brothers and sisters at home in Switzerland, besides Barbli who had died in the fall, and he was also a schoolteacher. So, she had guessed correctly when she thought he looked like he came out of a university hall.

He entertained the children with stories and even some songs in a beautiful tenor voice. The children were disappointed when Anna made him sleep some more, but he still looked so tired. Anna smiled to see how the children kept leaning over and peeking into his face, hoping he wouldn't sleep too long. She loved this young man like a brother already; his loving nature just shone through. He awoke in time for the evening meal, though he didn't eat much.

Jan got up and started pacing the floor afterwards, stopping frequently to gaze out the window, where he looked left, then right, shook his head and sighed. Anna hoped Willem would come back before dark; she had no desire for another fright tonight.

Twilight fell, and the man had not returned. Black night descended and still he had not returned.

In the morning, Jan straightened his shoulders and announced that he was going to find out what happened. He swayed a little as he bundled himself up and headed for the door, steadying himself as he opened it.

"Please wait until you're a little stronger," Anna entreated, but he wouldn't listen. This young man had already come to feel like a brother to her, the brother she had lost. Tears welled in her eyes. Nobody could ever take the place of Heinrich, but this lad came close. He was just one of those people who instantly won the hearts of everyone with his cheerful outlook and easy smile.

"I must go."

"Be careful!" Anna warned him, wringing her apron. "Please don't get caught."

Chapter Twelve

Amsterdam, February 1532

The Lord is my helper, I will not be afraid, what can man do to me?
Heb 13:6

In an hour Jan was back, wild-eyed and panting. "Anna, grab your warmest clothes and come with me!" he gasped. "Now!" He swung an anguished look towards the children. They stared back at him in bewilderment. Three innocent faces turned to Anna, wordlessly asking for an explanation.

"No! I will not leave the children." Anna put her hands on her hips and refused to move. "How can you even suggest such a thing?"

"You must trust me! It won't be for long. We will come back in an hour or so, when the officers give up hunting for us," Jan insisted, his green eyes flashing as he shifted from one foot to the other in agitation. "They arrested Willem and the baker, and when they've got those two locked up, they're coming here! We have a head start of a few minutes, and we must be out of sight. Please. I'm asking this for your own safety."

"Well!" Anna said, not moving an inch. "What about the children's safety?"

Jan wrung his hands and searched the room with his eyes. Spotting her cloak hanging from a peg, he grabbed it and held it out to Anna. "Put on your cloak, I beg you. I assure you, the officers do not harm children. The worst they will do is take them to some Catholic home. We can find out where they are later." He shook Anna's cloak, as if his desperation alone could make her put it on. "You have two choices--come with me for a chance to escape, or stay here and be arrested. You must see that by staying here, you are risking the children's future more than if you flee."

Anna's body seemed to be turned to stone as she allowed Jan to help her with the cloak. The children cried and so did Anna. "Be brave, my *schatjes.* I will come back as soon as ever I can." Jan hustled her to the door, while Anna's heart broke in two. Outside, he took her arm and hurried her along in the direction of the forest where the Anabaptist meeting had been held. He must have found a reserve of strength somewhere; it was hard to believe he had lain at death's door the day before.

"They're coming!" Jan gasped as they ran. Anna did not ask who was coming. She knew.

They plunged through the snow, their footprints filling in with drifting snow seconds after they left them behind. It was to their advantage.

"Do you... know... a place... to hide... in the forest?" he asked, panting. She knew of a place, but not how to get there. She had only been there once, about a month ago, but there had been a path. Now there was only snow and it all looked the same. They found a sheltered spot under the low-hanging branches of a cedar hedge and rested briefly. Jan's breath rattled noisily. If anyone was trailing them, they need only follow the sound of his wheezing.

Anna peeked through the snowy boughs of cedar. She felt as tense and stiff as an iron poker.

"Tell me about it," she said.

"I went... to the baker's house," Jan said, between puffs,

"but he... wasn't there. His wife... hissed at me to begone, ... that it wasn't safe... there anymore. Her... husband and Willem... have been... arrested, and they are going to... arrest the heretic... who had given him shelter. You!... We have to... keep running or hide..."

Anna stood up in alarm. "But the children! We can't just abandon them." She wished she had stood her ground and stayed home. Yet if she'd stayed, it was true she'd be on her way to prison and execution, or banishment at the very least. She groaned. These men should never have come to her house seeking shelter. They had lost the letter they were supposed to deliver into her hands, and they brought serious trouble down upon her head.

She prayed the officers would treat the children kindly, and she had to admit she had never heard of them harming children. The worst they would do was baptize them and teach them papist beliefs, which might be the best thing for them anyways. It had been an easy to thing to become engrossed with the Anabaptists and their humble kindness while no one was chasing her. But now, a safe place in a Catholic home seemed very attractive. No doubt, Anabaptists parents thought this a fate worse than death.

"Do you know anyone who could... take them in?" Jan asked, still out of breath. "If we manage to shake... our pursuers, we could go back in the night... and take them somewhere. Or find someone... to go to them."

"They are like my own children. I *must* go back myself and make sure they are unharmed."

"I understand. I will ...come with you." They were plunging through deep snow, a biting wind nipping at their cheeks. "But I don't want you... to be captured."

"I may not get caught." She burrowed her face into her

cloak. Jan had seemed to care for the children, so why was he even implying she should leave them behind? To hide in the woods for an hour or two was one thing, but she refused to abandon them to an unknown fate. Their mother was dead, and their father was in great danger. That was more than enough tragedy for little children to bear.

"You *will* be caught, Anna. Once the magistrates are on someone's trail, they do not give up easily. They will be guarding the house, expecting you to go back to the children. Don't do it."

"But I promised Adriaen I'll take care of them. I can't break my promise to him."

"Adriaen knows that if you go to prison or die, you can't care for them either. God will take care of them. And I promise to help you find a way to have them looked after."

Anna's tears ran in frozen rivulets down her cheeks. It wasn't good enough. They were not just any children. They were Adriaen's children, and Maeyken's children. There had to be another way.

The two of them floundered in the snow for a long time, deeper and deeper into the forest. Anna was nearly collapsing with exhaustion, and Jan's hoarse breathing would give them away if the officers got close enough. Jan was bent nearly double; he didn't have the energy to walk upright any longer. Anna held on to his arm, afraid he'd pitch headfirst into the snow. They tried to stay in the denser part of the forest, and soon they would have to stop.

Just when Anna thought they would perish of cold, they stumbled into a small clearing surrounded by cedars. She didn't think it was the same one; it seemed smaller. It was almost like entering a house. Here the freezing, driving wind could not enter, and the two fugitives huddled together under a cedar tree, their breaths coming in short, frosty puffs.

"Do you think they will come after us here?" Anna asked bleakly. It would be awful if after all the struggling in the deep snow, they were discovered and forced to march back the way they had come.

Jan shrugged, his chest heaving. "They... might. It depends... how bloodthirsty... they are tonight." His green eyes were like emeralds in his white face. Laying down in the snow, he curled up in a ball, pulling some branches over himself for warmth. Anna stared at him in alarm. She didn't want to be stranded here with a sick man. Why bother running, only to freeze to death?

"Jan! I hear something!" She shook him violently. Something was crashing through the trees. Voices? She shivered uncontrollably. So, was this what an Anabaptist's life was like? To live in constant fear of every sound? She felt like a cornered fox. More than ever, she wished she had refused to flee earlier, and gone to the authorities. Then she could live in peace with the children in the little house Simon had so thoughtfully left her. She would rather be safe and warm in church listening to a priest's chant than lying out here in the bush, freezing to death. Especially with a dying man, waiting for the hunters to find their prey.

"Probably some animal," he mumbled, already half asleep.

"It's not an animal! I hear voices!" she whispered hoarsely. She grabbed his coat and shook and shook him with all her might until his teeth rattled, forcing him to wake up. He looked at her, bewildered and confused.

"Why are you shaking me?"

"The *tauferjager* are coming! You can't sleep now."

"The *tauferjager?*" He blinked. "Why are the *tauferjager* coming?"

"They are coming for us! Wake up! Wake up!" He merely closed his bleary green eyes, and then she could not wake him again. The shouts were coming closer. Would they be able to see the tracks? She pushed Jan over against the tree trunk, then slid next to him, making herself as small as possible. She tugged at the branches, pulling the fragrant cedar down lower to hide the two of them as well as possible.

Holding her breath, Anna listened to the snorting of the horses, the clacking of the bits in their mouths. There were two riders. She placed her hand over Jan's mouth, in case he made some sound in his sleep. She heard the clanging of a chain and her ankles tingled, already feeling the cold metal. Silently she sent a desperate prayer to Heaven, praying like she had seldom prayed before. She didn't think there was enough time for the Virgin Mary and the saints to intercede for her, but perhaps God would hear. Unless He was punishing her for complaining about her monotonous winter.

"Dear God, I know I have hidden myself from You, but please forgive me, and hide us from these terrible men who thirst for our blood. Hide us, dear God, especially this man who is needed to spread Your word. Amen."

Let's go home. I'm cold," one of the officers complained. Amen to that, Anna thought. She could see the horse's hoofs through the branches. These men were bundled up to their ears and were hiding behind their high collars, otherwise they would certainly have spotted their prey.

"Oh, all right. I don't like hunting in the winter either. Let's get back to the inn and warm up with some of Herman's ale. The fox has got away this time, but we'll find him yet." They turned their horses around, so close that Anna could have reached out and touched a hoof. If they had their ears uncovered, they would have heard her sharp, short breaths and hammering heart.

The early evening shadows were upon them by now, and soon it would be dark. Anna wondered if any death the authorities might inflict on them could be worse than freezing to death. The temperature dropped as the sun went down, and Anna had to snuggle up to Jan to stay warm.

But she dared not sleep. The man must not be allowed to freeze. She kept waking him and forcing him to move his arms and legs. Dozens of times in the night, she got up and stamped her feet and clapped her hands to keep her blood moving. She didn't allow herself to think about what she would do when morning came. If it ever did.

In the distance, she heard the wolves howling. She hoped they were far, far away and not too hungry. There were rustlings of smaller creatures, and once she heard the squeal of an animal that had become a meal for someone. The wind had died down and sounds echoed across the still and frozen countryside. A lonely cow bellowed from miles away; she couldn't tell from which direction. She had no idea which way home was or how she would get there with Jan.

Home. There was no longer a home. By now, the children had undoubtedly been divided up and sent to devout Catholic homes. Maybe Father Hendricks had already baptized them, but surely it couldn't do the children any harm. Why did the Anabaptists reject this sacrament so utterly? Even if they were right, and infant baptism was no baptism, would it make any difference to the salvation of their souls?

As the endless, freezing night went on, Anna's mind began to get fuzzy. She longed to lay her head down and go to sleep, but she dared not. Again and again she got up, walked around for a minute or two, shook Jan until he groaned, then sat down tightly beside him to keep him warm. When that wasn't enough, she grabbed some branches of a nearby cedar tree, tearing at them until they broke away. She covered Jan with a pile of the fragrant cedar boughs, then sat down, exhausted, tucking her numb hands under her arms to thaw them.

Would morning never come? And what would she do when it did? Was there anything she *could* do, besides walk into a trap and die? She simply could not think. If only Jan would wake up. She despaired of his life.

She wrapped her arms around her knees and tried to arrange her cloak around her body so that the icy air couldn't penetrate. And then, finally, she gave in to the urge to sleep.

Chapter Thirteen

The Woods, February 1532

Have I then become your enemy, by telling you the truth? ... Gal 4:16

Anna woke up shivering in a strange hut. She was lying on a pile of smelly animal skins in a smoky room, which didn't feel warm at all.

"So you decided to wake up, you lazy girl, when it's high noon?" The ancient toothless crone's voice crackled, as if it hadn't been unlocked in many years. Her wrinkled face and sour breath came too close for comfort. "If you think to eat of my small provisions, you hustle outside and help your husband chop wood."

"Wha...what?" Anna snapped out of her lethargy and staggered to her feet. "Who are you and where am I?" At first, her limbs were so stiff they refused to straighten. Her stomach rumbled and her mouth seemed dry as ashes. She swayed and caught at a nearby chair to stay upright, panicking when memory returned. The children! She had to get to the children!

The old woman chortled in glee. "I'm Cornelia the witch, don't you know, and I can turn myself into a wolf. Or grow two heads at will. And that's not all. I make all the crops fail and curse the cattle so they die. And I go around curdling all the cream so it won't turn into butter." She sounded bitter. "They tried to drown me but I swam away, proving that I am truly a witch. Don't stare at me! Go outside and chop wood!"

Anna obeyed. She found Jan outside leaning on the axe, his eyes glazed and vacant. He hadn't managed to chop any wood. Anna took the axe, helping him to sit on a fallen log to rest.

"Jan! Where are we? Do you know?" He shook his head vaguely. "You should not be out here in the cold. Here's my cloak." She wrapped it around his shoulders, concern wrinkling her brow. Jan nearly shook himself off the log. How dared that hag send the poor man out here?

Anna lifted the axe and glared at the log in front of her. She swung the axe awkwardly and no more than a small chip flew off. The witch must be inside cursing the axe, or perhaps the log. Another swing and she hit a different spot; another chip went flying. Outraged by her failure, she gathered all her strength and let fly again, pretending the log was the witch. A long, narrow strip of bark split off the log. After many more tries, her arms ached, and she had made very little progress.

She itched to get away from this place and back to the children. Too much time had already passed, and the longer she waited, the harder it might be to get them back. But Jan was in no condition to tramp through the snowy woods. Could she abandon him? It would be no worse than abandoning the children. And besides, it had been Jan's idea to run to the bush, so he should be the one to suffer the consequences.

She heard the door of the hut creak and whipped around. The witch was coming out, her face dark. "Have you never chopped wood before?" she asked, snatching the axe.

"No. No, I haven't."

The axe slashed downwards, hitting the log with a clean stroke, and the wood split along its length. Anna stood there staring, and the axe kept swinging. It looked so easy that she became more and more convinced that Cornelia *was* an actual witch who *had* cursed her own attempts. In a matter of minutes, the wiry, old woman had chopped a sizable pile of wood.

Finally, Cornelia stuck the axe into an un-chopped log, and swung around to face Anna, barely out of breath. "Now you know. Next time I expect you to do it." Next time? There would be a next time? Anna's plans had been to get out of there before nightfall.

"Have you ever carried wood?"

"Of course." Anna bent to pick up an armful. The old woman took Jan's arm and alternated between pushing and pulling him back to the hut. Anna staggered along behind them, burdened with as much firewood as she could carry. The weathered gray hut appeared to be nearly collapsing on the side of a low hill; its poorly thatched roof could hardly be tight anymore, and the posts holding a tumbledown porch would surely fall over soon. Boards were nailed in a haphazard fashion onto the sides, in a vain attempt to close gaps in the poorly constructed shack. No wonder it wasn't warm inside.

Snow was beginning to fall, and the heavy clouds on the horizon foretold of much more snow to come. The cedar trees, already burdened with cloaks of snow, huddled around the little dwelling, as if protecting the miserable hut from the disdain it deserved.

Anna stepped onto the rickety porch and passed through the sagging door, then deposited her load beside the smoking fireplace. She coughed. There must be a bird's nest in the chimney. Jan was lying on a lumpy cot, the witch bending over him with a vial of some dark liquid.

"Stop it! What are you giving him?" Anna ran over and grabbed the woman's arm. How bony and thin it was! The woman turned around and glared at Anna with beady black eyes above a hawk nose. Her lower lip trembled, revealing toothless gums. Then she laughed her haunting, cackly laugh.

"What do you think? I was about to turn him into something good to eat, and I hate when people interrupt my spells." She narrowed her eyes. "Do you object?" The woman was insane, no doubt about it.

"Can't you just go out and hunt or something?"

"Do I look like a hunter?" she snarled. "Go and hunt yourself, you lazy thing." Anna took a step backwards at the venomous look on her face. "I will give you one hour to catch something. After that, we eat him."

"Never!" A thought struck her. "He is a man of God, and if you harm him, God will certainly punish you severely."

Cornelia laughed bitterly. "A man of God? I've seen enough men of God to last me forever. If this one is like the rest, I should turn myself into a wolf and devour him."

"No, no you don't understand. This is a good man. He is ill, yes. Help me make him well, then you will see how good he is. He does not deserve to die."

"That's what I was doing when you attacked me; I was trying to make him well." She poured some dark liquid down his throat, and Anna stood by anxiously, her fists clenched and her heart thudding. She didn't exactly believe in witch powers, but if this lady managed to heal Jan, she might change her mind. If Cornelia could cure him fast, they could make their escape that day. If not, Jan might find himself left behind. Anna didn't wish him any harm, but the children came first.

Anna did feel sorry for what happened to Cornelia. If

the Court hunted Anabaptists like wild beasts, not taking the time to find out whether they were good or evil, justice seemed even more unlikely while they figured out who was a witch. Maybe this woman felt secure here, hidden in the trees in her rundown shack. But the loneliness! It would drive anyone insane, as Anna could attest.

A few minutes later, Jan sat up and his green-eyed gaze swept the hut. "What happened? I feel so much better!" Anna unclenched her fists, and her shoulders lowered to their usual position. He was indeed looking brighter. Whatever concoction Cornelia fed him had worked like a charm.

"Old Cornelia, the witch, made you well," the old woman said, "I've got my potions, you know, to use for good or ill!"

Anna shivered. She didn't want to know what this strange woman might do for ill, but somehow, she had managed to save their lives. "How did you find us, Cornelia?" Anna asked.

"My magic powers told me there were two foolish mortals in distress close by, and so, hoping for a good meal, I took my sled out and found you two sleeping on Samion's grave."

Anna stepped closer to Jan, while her mind spun, trying to find the nerve and the heart to leave the place immediately. Witch or not, the woman was crazy. But she didn't know the way back, for one thing, and Jan was too weak to help, for another. *But the children,* she agonized. *Where were they now?*

"Could I borrow your sled for my brother Jan to ride on, and go back to the city?" Anna asked.

Cornelia frowned darkly, her dark eyes snapping. "So, is my abode too humble for you?" Her bottom lip worked over the blackened and broken stumps where teeth had been.

"No, no, not at all. It's just that I have to get back to the children."

"Children, eh?" She tugged at the hairs on her sagging

chin. "And what do you mean, your *brother* Jan? Isn't he your husband?" She looked doubtfully from one to the other.

Anna glanced at Jan, embarrassed beyond words. The twinkle in his green eyes nearly undid her composure. He thought it was funny?

"Uh…no. We got lost when we…" She stopped, aghast that she had been ready to tell a bare-faced lie. What punishment would God send for that?

"I saw the hoofprints. Who are you running from?" The keen old eyes bored into hers, until Anna was forced to tell the truth.

"It was the Court officers."

"What have you done?" Cornelia narrowed her eyes. "I have poison here, and I'll use it on you if you don't tell me the truth." She took a step towards a rundown shelf on the wall.

"We are messengers from God, and we have come to spread the Gospel throughout the land." Jan said. "God sent us to you."

"Hmph! I would say God sent *me* to *you.* Otherwise, you would be two frozen chunks of ice by now," Cornelia said.

Anna shivered. This was true enough. "We are very grateful to you, Cornelia. How did you manage? And who was Samion?"

"I told you, with my sled. I went out to find wood, and there you were. I thought you had frozen to death on my old dog's grave."

It had been close, Anna realized. But who knew there was anyone living in these woods?

"I hope you two aren't too hungry, because I don't have much to offer you," Cornelia announced, as she set out a small, hard loaf of dark bread and some wine.

Anna stared. She felt too guilty to eat any of Cornelia's meagre rations, though her stomach rumbled. Jan claimed he wasn't feeling well enough to eat.

"Nonsense. I'll cut this loaf in three. Everyone will eat." She handed them both a share as they sat on the bed, then began sucking on her own crust. Anna chewed slowly, and made the bread last as long as possible. The coarse bread tasted better than it looked, though it was grainy and chewy. The wine warmed her insides, and it tasted surprisingly mellow.

"Now I must go back and look for the children." Anna got up from the bed, and reached for her cloak, which smelled of wood smoke and cedar.

"Have you looked out the window?" Jan asked.

Anna shook her head as she glanced outside. "It wasn't bad when we came indoors. I will be fine."

"Anna, tell me," Jan said. "What will you do with the children if you find them? You can't go back to the house, or you will be caught."

"You don't know that." What right did he have, telling her what to do? It was he and Willem that got her into this plight, and Jan was in no condition to help her out of it, Willem even less. She was the only one to do it.

"Please, Anna. Don't go out there by yourself. You will get lost." Jan got up from the bed and unsteadily walked over to face her, placing his hand on her arm. She shook it off.

"No, I won't. Besides, you can pray to God to keep me safe. I'm sure He will hear you better than He hears me."

"Anna! God hears you too! That doesn't mean you should be foolish enough to head back into danger."

Tears blinded Anna's eyes. "They are not your children, and I know you don't care about them like I do. I am the one that promised Adriaen to keep them safe, but because of you..." She stopped short of accusing him, but he still looked wounded. He clenched his hands at his sides, and looked at the rush-strewn earthen floor.

"Forgive me, Anna. We should never have come to your house." He looked up, his green eyes dark with pain. "What can I do to help?"

"Nothing! Just let me go find my children." Anna fastened her hooded cloak and wound the scarf around her face. Jan watched her leave, looking as if she had thrust a dagger through his heart. She pulled the door shut after herself and tramped through the drifts of snow in the direction she hoped Amsterdam lay.

In a few minutes, she was surrounded by a world of falling snow, and it became impossible to tell in which direction she was heading. The wind flung freezing white crystals against the uncovered section of her face, and snow sifted into her boots. Bewildered, she stopped and held out her arms.

"Stop the snow!" she howled into the wind, frustrated and angry at this blinding white curtain. Didn't God want her to find the children? He had sent them into her care, and now she needed some help to do so. Despite Jan's assurances, she didn't quite trust the authorities to take care of her charges.

Through the thick white cloud, someone called her name. "Aaannnaaa! Come back!"

"Noooo!" She hollered back, stamping her foot. Soon, it must stop snowing. She muttered to herself, angry at God and the saints, and most of all at Jan and Willem for getting her into this predicament. And now Jan had the nerve to try and prevent her from getting back to rescue the children. Anna hoped Jan was praying hard, because she was too upset to do so. In the meantime, she would just start walking straight ahead until she emerged from this godforsaken forest. She ignored the shouts, ever fainter, calling her back to the miserable hut.

Hours seemed to go by, and every time the storm let up, Anna could see nothing but more trees. She constantly bumped her head and scratched her face on low-hanging branches. Her leather boots were stuffed with snow, and the hem of her skirt was frozen all the way around and rigid with ice. Snow crusted her eyelashes and her eyebrows, and fluid froze in her nostrils.

When daylight grew dim, the storm had not let up. There was nothing to see but swirling snow and endless trees. And there was nothing to do but admit defeat. It was cold, so very cold. Her teeth chattered, and her hands and feet were numb. She had been stubborn, and she had not listened to honest advice, and now she must freeze out here in the woods. *'Oh God, I'm so sorry. Forgive me, I have sinned. I have not trusted you. I have been self-willed and impatient. Help me, oh God.'*

Cornelia and Jan had no way of knowing where she was, and besides, they probably figured she had found her way back to Amsterdam. But Anna wouldn't give up without a fight. "Heeelllp!" she shouted. "Heeelp!" She kept walking, lifting one heavy foot out of the knee-high snow, then the other. She was tired, so very tired. Her voice grew weaker. The wind snatched her wavering cries out of her mouth and flung them far away. If anyone answered, the thick white flakes muffled the sound.

When she hit something solid, she sank to the ground. Another tree, she thought in resignation. She lifted a weary arm to hold onto the trunk. She must get back up. Instead of the roundness and rough bark of a tree, she felt, unbelievably, a wall. A building of some kind.

Gathering fresh energy, she got back onto her feet, and felt her way along the wall. What was it? A barn? A robber's hideout? An empty shack in the woods? She turned a corner and continued. Somewhere, there had to be a door or an opening. There! There it was! She felt for the latch, thumping and moving her hands over the rough boards. The door gave way, and she fell inside the building. Rough hands grabbed her arms, pulling her inside. Anna used her last shred of strength to scream like a demon from the deeps.

Chapter Fourteen

Cornelia's Hut, February 1532

As we have been approved by God to be entrusted with the Gospel, so we speak, not to please men, but to please God...1 Thess 2:4

Anna shook her head. And again. Was she dreaming? Why were Jan and Cornelia here? Once the snow had melted from her eyelashes, she looked around the dimly-lit interior of the room. Her eyes widened. There was Cornelia's smoking fireplace and the rickety table, with a candle flickering on its rough surface. Anna was lying on a bed near the fire—Cornelia's bed.

"Welcome back, Anna," Jan said quietly. "I'm so glad you're safe." Cornelia said nothing, but her face wore a black look.

"How can I possibly have come back here?" Anna asked. "I was walking ever since I left-- for hours, it seemed. Did I just go around in circles?"

"Of course you did, you foolish girl. What did you expect?" Cornelia had her witch-face back on. Anna had to agree that she had been very foolish, and it was a miracle she hadn't frozen to death in the storm. Her cloak hung dripping near the fire, and she was wrapped in every blanket Cornelia owned.

Jan's red hair stuck out from his head in every direction, as if he had ben running his hands through it. The dark circles under his eyes made his narrow face look paler than ever, and worry lines furrowed his forehead. Anna felt guilty just looking at him. Did he care what happened to her? It was a new thought. She hadn't stopped to consider anyone's feelings except her own. But on the other hand, who else would search for the children? Even though she might not be able to rescue them, she wanted to know in which house they were. What kind of people had taken them. Whether they were treated kindly.

Maybe they had been taken over the bridge to the *Begijnhof* in the heart of Amsterdam, to the nuns. Wherever they were, Anna needed to *know*. When Adriaen came back, he would be devastated to find his children gone. Anna glanced to the window. It was pitch dark outside, and she could do nothing more that night.

For over a week, the weather conspired to keep the three of them in the house most of the time. When the snowstorm finally stopped after three days, the freezing rain began. Day after day, the sun refused to shine, and despair gripped Anna's soul. How much longer would they be holed up here in this dark, smoky, and draughty hut, cut off from the children and civilization?

Every morning, Anna got up as soon as dawn began to break and checked the weather. Jan and Cornelia had made her promise that she would not attempt to leave the hut again until they all agreed it was safe. And every morning looked as formidable as the one before. There was very little food, but what Cornelia had, she shared. Jan slipped out of the house one afternoon, and returned much later, chilled and soaking wet, with a couple of snow geese slung over his shoulder.

"Today we shall feast," Jan declared.

"Ooh! How did you catch them?" Anna asked.

"First with prayer, then with patience, then with speed," Jan grinned.

Everyone helped to prepare the birds, and soon the geese were bubbling in the pot, filling the air with a tantalizing aroma. That night, for once, they slept without their stomachs grumbling. They saved every shred of leftover meat, making it last for a few more days.

To get their minds off their hunger and discomfort, they told each other stories. Cornelia eventually lost her crustiness and related to them the tragic story of how she had been accused of witchcraft ten years before in a nearby village. Crops were failing on the farms, and many cattle died. To add to the misery, the plague hit the province and a number of people died. Cornelia had not become sick herself, which was determined to be one sign of witchcraft. Then the village baker, not liking her competing with his baking business, unjustly accused her of being a witch. She never married and had no man to stand up for her rights, so the authorities believed the baker's tale. They tried to execute her by drowning. But she escaped the bag they had put her in, swam away, and escaped--further proof of sorcery. She never dared go back to civilization.

Anna wept for the lonely woman. She noticed Jan's eyes were damp as well.

"When we leave here, you're coming with us," he told her. "There has to be a more comfortable place for you to spend your twilight years."

Cornelia's eyes gleamed. "If you say so."

Out here in the lonely woods, crowded into a small space together for days at a time, they had all the time in the world for conversation. But always, in the back of Anna's mind, the children lurked. Only by Jan's repeated assurances that God looked after His own, and especially innocent children, could she tolerate the confining walls of the hut. Even so, she went outside for a while every day to let the cold air calm her frazzled nerves. Cornelia and Jan claimed to want to leave just as much as Anna did, but sometimes she wondered. Cornelia was used to this life, and Jan was about as well hidden as he could possibly be as an Anabaptist, only he wasn't converting many people.

Sometimes Anna caught Jan gazing at her with a look in his eyes she didn't understand, a look that made her feel almost special, and even admired, but why would that be? Did he see her as a desirable woman? Anna quickly cleared her mind of such nonsense, ignoring the pleasant possibility of a man seeing her in that light.

Jan treated Cornelia and herself with the utmost respect, and hardly let either of the women do any work after he was recovered. He regained enough strength to chop wood, and taught Anna how to do it, because she insisted. Chopping wood helped ease the frustration of being trapped in the woods. The color never did come back into Jan's cheeks, no matter how often he was outside in the cold.

Jan was also a master story-teller and a patient teacher. There was no paper of any kind to be had, but he scratched words on the frosty walls with a stick, expanding Anna's humble amount of education. Cornelia even learned to read a little bit.

Cornelia had been away from civilization for so long that she had never heard about the Lutheran protests against the corruption of the Roman Catholic church. She never heard any news, so Jan told her everything about the state of Europe in the last several years. He told her about Martin

Luther, a former monk from Germany, who stood up to the Pope with his thoughts on church corruption, even though it put his life in danger.

"I don't doubt for a minute the wickedness and corruption of the bishops and priests," Cornelia said. "I think it's high time someone had enough courage to bring it into the open. Thanks be to God." Of course, Anna thought, Cornelia had first-hand experience of overzealous judgments.

"Martin Luther doesn't believe that the pope has the power to forgive people's sin or save them from purgatory. The common people of Germany are very poor, because they must pay all kinds of taxes and tithes. The German Dominican friar, Johann Tetzel, got permission from the pope to sell letters of indulgence, and now they are being cheated out of their money with these indulgences."

Anna had bought indulgences from that very man, and thought herself safe from purgatory as long as she sacrificed the pittance she had scraped together, to buy them.

"Letters of indulgence? What is that?" Cornelia leaned forward with enraptured dark eyes. Was she glad that the ones who caused her exile were now being challenged?

"It's a piece of paper that people are induced to buy. Albert of Hohenberg came up with the idea of selling indulgences to pay for building Saint Peter's grand basilica in Rome. He promises the poor peasants that their sins will all be forgiven if they buy these indulgences. They can even buy indulgences for their friends who have died, to save their souls from purgatory. He assures them that 'as soon as the money clinks in the chest, the soul is released'."

Anna shifted uncomfortably. Jan was talking about the church she had been loyal to all her life, and hearing about these abuses made her cringe. If everything Jan said was true, she was surprised anyone still went to the Church.

"How is the Church reacting to all the opposition?" Cornelia asked.

"They are outraged that their subjects dispute their authority, which is why there is so much persecution. Charles V, as Holy Roman Emperor, has ordered his militia to use force to make people attend his state-approved churches, and they're arresting everyone they can find who doesn't obey. Communion is held three times a year, and those not present are sought out for questioning."

Anna got up and put on her cloak. "I'm going out to get more wood."

Jan watched her go with puzzled, almost hurt, green eyes. "There's still quite a pile here."

She ignored him and went outside, where cold drizzly rain was falling. Would this wretched weather never end? The weather was as miserable as she felt. Her heart was torn all to pieces like chunks of Cornelia's hard bread, and she felt pulled to bits trying to make up her mind which was the actual True Church. The old or the new, which one was right?

Was the Catholic church wrong? Anna wanted to be safe on earth, and she also wanted to go to Heaven when she died. Was it possible to have both, or must one choose? Or what if one joined the wrong religion, and ended up having to suffer for it after death? Had the choice already been made for her when she ran away with Jan?

Carrying an armful of logs, Anna staggered back into the hut. This wet wood would probably burn badly, and they'd have to endure a smoky fire. But they were all used to that. She plunked the wood on the floor and hung up her cloak. Jan welcomed her back with a smile which showed his even white teeth. "You're just in time to hear about the birth of Anabaptism."

Anna groaned inwardly. Did she have to hear more of this? She couldn't think of anything more to do outside, so she resigned herself to listening to more about his religious views.

"First of all, Ulrich Zwingli, who lives in Switzerland, came to the same conclusions Martin Luther did. What the clergy is teaching to their congregations is not from Scripture. No human being has the power to forgive sins, not even the Pope. Tithing and taxing the poorest people, and not the wealthy, is wrong. There is nothing in Scripture requiring the celibacy of priests or any other of the clergy, and forced celibacy leads to fornication. Neither are there any rules in the New Testament about not eating meat during Lent. Zwingli, a pastor, even attended a sausage supper at his printer's house during Lent and let the printer and his workers eat sausages. There was a public outcry and the printer was arrested."

Jan leaned forward and stirred the coals, then added a log to the fire. Cornelia was wrapped in layers of shawls and blankets, and Anna tucked her skirt around her feet, trying in vain to warm them. She could have eaten several pounds of sausages right now.

"In the beginning, Zwingli, who is also a teacher, taught his young students to live according to the Scriptures." Jan continued. "He taught that it is wrong to worship statues of Mary, saints or their ancient relics. Costly displays of decorations and paintings in the church are works of the devil."

But they are so beautiful. And someone spent a lot of time making them.

"Zwingli does not believe that Mary or any other saint is able to intercede for people's souls, because there is no such thing written in the Scriptures. Only through Christ dying on the cross can our sins be forgiven. He teaches that the bread and wine of the sacraments is not actually Christ's body and blood because Christ is in Heaven, sitting at the right hand of God. The bread and wine are symbols of the covenant made with Christ."

Cornelia gazed at Jan with adoration. "This all makes perfect sense to me. When I was a child long ago, my parents, who came from the Waldenses, had a faith very similar to this. But they had to keep it a secret because the authorities would have killed them."

Jan nodded. "Yes, the Romans have monopolized Christendom for centuries. The corruption has become so bad that they will have to change. Even the church admits that it has problems. Martin Luther hoped to reform the Catholic church but ended up founding a new one.

"There was a civil war between Lutherans and Catholics, and afterwards they agreed to allow two religions; Lutheran and Catholic. Not Anabaptists, resulting in both parties persecuting us. The subjects must attend the same church as their rulers, but people are allowed to move if they don't agree with their local religion. Which brings us to the persecution here in the Netherlands. Charles is Catholic, so we all must be Catholic. If we don't go to church or leave the country, we will be punished and executed or banned."

Cornelia's grizzled gray head nodded constantly as he spoke; it was all clear to her, and she hung on Jan's every word. "So who was the leader of reform here in the Netherlands?"

"Different groups formed and separated from the church, then refugees came from Germany, Switzerland and elsewhere, bringing ideas for reform with them. Charles V was busy fighting the Turks and didn't notice what was happening here, so the movement was quite advanced by the time he found out about it."

Cornelia cackled. "And now he'll never get rid of all those he calls heretics. There are too many to destroy all of them, right?"

"I would think so," Jan said. "They say there are thousands of Anabaptists in Amsterdam, including some of the city councillors. But that is beginning to change now that Charles has set up his council at The Hague, to search for and get rid of heresy in the Netherlands. All the officials who aren't loyal to Charles are being replaced."

It was getting late in the day, and lurking shadows closed around them. Anna got up to serve their portion of bread, wine and a few dried apple pieces. They all gnawed at their food slowly, appeasing their raging hunger.

"Tomorrow, if the weather is better, I will go and search for some more wild game," Jan declared. "The food supply won't last us until spring."

Until spring? I'm leaving the first day of decent weather, and maybe before if it takes too long, Anna thought. It was still the middle of February.

"I hadn't planned on having guests,' Cornelia defended herself, "but I'm glad you came. If I don't have much food for my body, at least I am getting plenty for my soul."

"Is that enough for today, or do you want to hear about the Anabaptists now?"

"Do go on!" Cornelia exclaimed. "I'm not tired enough to sleep yet."

"Anna?" Jan asked kindly, "Is this agreeable to you?"

Anna loved hearing Jan's soothing male voice; and for

that, and because Cornelia desired it, she decided she could listen to more of his story. She couldn't deny being curious, and the only way to find out the Truth was to hear every viewpoint.

In the nearly dark hut, with only the sputtering fire for a light of, Jan continued. "As I've already told you, Zwingli lives in Zurich, Switzerland, and is a pastor at Grossmunster cathedral. About ten years ago, in 1522, he was also teaching a group of young men interested in learning to read Latin and Greek classics, but especially the Bible.

"Hardly anybody read the Bible then, because it was written in Latin and Greek. Zwingli hired someone to translate the Bible from the original Hebrew. He was going to dig until he uncovered the truth; and what he found, he preached. Zwingli is a smooth talker, and he convinced the Council of Zurich to let him preach from the Scriptures instead of following Catholic protocol.

"So, in this class he taught, there were several young men, in their twenties, who were quite interested in reading the Bible for themselves, and they read into it even more deeply than did Zwingli. "Conrad Grebel, Felix Manz and George Blaurock thought the Scriptures should be followed exactly, and must be the only authority, without deferring to the council about how to run their church services. They discovered that the early church, in the time of Christ, had been composed of heartfelt believers only, and was not united with the state. Also, they found that the true church must always be persecuted, despised and rejected, as Jesus was. They wanted Zwingli to abolish the mass right away, as well as infant baptism.

When Zwingli refused to do so, wanting to make changes gradually and only by consent of the council, there was a division. Disputes were arranged, but the honey-tongued Zwingli had the council on his side. His students were ordered to submit to authority, and to have their children baptized within eight days, or they would be banned from the city.

"On January 21, 1525, on the evening after the dispute, Grebel and his friends gathered to pray, and called on God to show them what to do. Suddenly, George Blaurock, a fiery black-haired young man, stood up and asked to be baptized. Nobody objected, so Grebel grabbed a bowl of water from the table and baptized George with a bit of water on his head. After that, Blaurock baptized the rest of them and a new church was born. Persecution began immediately.

"That was nearly ten years ago, and by now, the Brethren are spread over the whole of Christendom, and despised almost everywhere by the authorities. Is it because the Brethren are bad people? No. They have gained many followers because of their honest characters and high morals, and they go singing joyfully to their cruel deaths, in hopes of an eternal happy home in Heaven. The Brethren are persecuted because they refuse to change their beliefs at the whim of the authorities, but continue to worship God in their own way."

Cornelia sighed. "It is a beautiful story. If I were not so old, I would find one of the Brethren and be baptized. I want to be a member of this group."

Anna could hear the tears in Cornelia's quivery voice.

Jan said, "I am only a teacher, so I cannot do it. But if that is what you desire I can instruct you in the doctrine, then if you decide to go ahead I will help you find a preacher. You do realize that from that moment on your life is in danger, though it is in God's hands to use you as He will."

Cornelia snorted. "What is life worth to me? I desire to

serve Him in any way I can, and if God is with me I no longer fear death."

"I didn't think so. Anna?"

She squirmed and mumbled, "I need more time."

Back in Germany, she had heard a similar version of Anabaptism from her parents, and how it came to be, and she hadn't minded hearing it again, in Jan's words. Even if she did come to accept this new doctrine, the Anabaptists might not accept her when they found out what a sinner she was. She coveted her best friend's husband and had let his wife die, betrayed his brother and abandoned his children. She did not belong with these saintly people.

"My sin is too great," she added, looking down at her fingers twisting in her lap.

"Everyone's sins are great. Why, even Conrad Grebel was disowned by his father for his misbehavior at school; by brawling, cavorting with women, and there were even rumors he helped murder a fellow student while drunk. To God, no sin is too great. Jesus shed enough blood to wash away everyone's sins, even yours."

"And you trust a church with a drunken murderer as a founder?"

"Jesus is the founder, and by his grace and mercy, Grebel's sins are as if they had never been, washed as white as snow, because he has been forgiven by God. And so can ours be. I will be praying that you find peace," Jan said softly.

"Me too," Cornelia said.

A few lone tears dripped onto Anna's bearskin bed. "Yes, pray for me."

Chapter Fifteen

Amsterdam, February 1532

May our Lord Jesus Christ ...who loved us...comfort your hearts...
Thess 2:16

Much of their time was spent sitting around the fire; talking, dozing, adding logs to the fire and occasionally eating. Anna wondered how Cornelia could have survived alone all these years. She was half-crazy herself after a week of this life. If she knew where the children were, it would be much more tolerable. The children were always on Anna's mind; as soon as she awoke in the morning, she anguished about their fate. The pain never lessened. A few times she had pleaded with Jan and Cornelia to allow her to leave, but they always shook their heads.

'It's not worth the risk. Remember your last attempt? There is nothing you can do for the children except pray.' Anna could only try to resign herself, as well as her charges, to God's care, and yes, pray. She kept on praying to Mary, mother of Jesus. As a mother, Mary would know what Anna was going through, better than Jan or Cornelia.

One evening at bedtime, Anna made up her mind to leave the next morning, regardless of the weather or lack of permission. Then, when morning came, it was so quiet that it took her a minute to identify what was missing. She listened. The wind! It was gone! She leaped out of her bearskin and skittered to the door. The freezing rain had stopped, and the sun was coming up through the trees.

"Jan! Cornelia!" she shouted, "Wake up!" Cornelia was on her feet in a flash, and Jan only a moment later.

"What's the matter?" Cornelia asked, her shawls falling around her feet.

Jan blinked, his red hair sprouting every which way. "Is the house on fire?"

"Don't you see? The sun is out! Today I am leaving, whether you two come or not." Anna brushed her unruly hair with Cornelia's ancient comb, and put on her cap. After smoothing her dress and apron, she reached for her cloak. "Are you coming?"

"You mean right now?" Cornelia looked bewildered. "What about my things?"

"What do you want to take?" Anna didn't see much of value in the hut, though probably Cornelia had some mementoes she wanted to keep.

Jan helped Cornelia pack some things into a bundle, including her supply of herbs and some bottles of mysterious liquids. Anna rolled up the bearskins; they might need those. There was one loaf of the hard, brown bread left, and some ale, which Anna gave to Jan to carry.

A short time later, the three bedraggled and gaunt-looking figures moved steadily through the forest. They sloshed through slush and snow as gratefully as children dismissed from school early. Jan dragged the sled behind him, the rolled bearskins knotted securely in place with rope.

Cornelia led the way with brisk strides, and Anna hoped she knew the way out, but she need not have worried. Cornelia was a wily old woman, and definitely not a witch. Jan whistled a merry tune as if he were a bird escaped from his cage.

"How far is it?" Anna asked, not caring that she sounded like a child.

"It shouldn't take long until we're out of the woods," Cornelia said. They trudged for hours through the trees, or so it seemed.

When they finally emerged from the forest and saw Amsterdam, it was like the heavenly city of gold to their eyes. Its ragged rooftops and smoking chimneys were a beacon of hope as they sat on the sled and rested, catching their breath before trudging on.

Anna did not know many people in Amsterdam, and she had no idea whom she could trust. Anybody who saw her could betray her to the authorities, and the gossiping housewives would probably do so if they got the chance, especially those who had taunted her before. She also hoped to avoid the sly little servant who seemed to turn up everywhere like rain at a parade.

"I'm hungry," Anna said. "Let's eat the rest of our bread." They ate it slowly, to make it seem like more than there actually was. How would they eat later?

Remembering that she had a few coins back at the house, Anna reminded herself to check for the money. Although she had accepted days ago that the house was sure to be empty, of both money and little children. She had not forgotten how Elizabeth's house had looked after the officers went through it.

They slipped through the city gates unnoticed. Anna's stomach churned now that she walked down the familiar street, and she couldn't help glancing at each window of the houses she passed. She watched and yearned for a glimpse of fair-haired, childish faces.

"Can you two just wait behind this cedar tree for a

minute?" Anna said. "Only one of us should go to the house, lest we attract attention. I'll take a quick look around to confirm the children are not there, and I also want to see if my money is still at the house."

"Uh...do you think that's a good idea?" Jan asked. "If something happened to you, I'd never forgive myself. Somebody could still be lurking about waiting for you to come back. I'll gladly go with you. And don't worry about the money. I do have a few coins that I'm happy to spend on food."

"I'll be fine," Anna called over her shoulder. She could handle this herself. She circled around to the back of the house first; maybe she could climb in the window like Adriaen had. One shutter hung lopsided on one hinge, and she peeked inside. Nothing seemed to be out of place, but there was no way she could climb in there with her long skirts hindering her. So she crept around to the front, peering up and down the street. A few people walked about but paid her no mind. She tried the latch, and the door opened.

Anna stepped inside, and blinked. After a few moments, her eyes adjusted to the dim interior after being out in the bright sunlight. Everything appeared to be intact, although it was much too eerie and still, with no children's voices chattering in the kitchen. It was also freezing cold. The logs she had dragged inside were still lying beside the fireplace, and water was frozen in the wash bowl.

She combed through the house, trying to shake the chill from her back. No trace of the children remained, not even one article of clothing. It was as if their happy chatter, and the patter of their footsteps, had never dwelled there. Crushing grief turned Anna's feet to stone, and now that the evidence of the children's disappearance was in front of her eyes, she found it almost impossible to accept. The tears that should have flowed down her cheeks stuck in her throat. She stood in Simon's bedroom, her feet frozen to the floor.

Where were the children?

Forcing herself to keep moving, she tiptoed behind the bed frame and stuck her hand beneath the loose floorboard. Nothing. In that heart-stopping moment she remembered the little booklet Adriaen had given her, the one with an explanation of his faith, the 'Concerning a True Soldier of Christ', which fitted Adriaen so well. She reached a trembling hand under her mattress near the fireplace. It was gone. The officers hadn't turned the house upside down because they found what they were looking for right away, under the mattress where she had left it.

The skin of Anna's neck prickled as cold sweat ran down her back. Now she was in truth a real heretic. The authorities had found forbidden writings in her house; it was all they needed to arrest and condemn her.

The line had been crossed a while ago, but now there was no going back to being a loyal Catholic subject. She could recant, and promise to be faithful to the Church, but that would not necessarily save her life. The best she could hope for in that scenario was an easier death. She might as well cast her heart and her lot with the Anabaptists and hope to understand their faith some day. But could she ever become a 'true soldier of Christ'? The only one she was fighting for was herself, and she feared she could never surrender her will to Christ.

On her way back outside, she spotted a few wrinkled apples in a basket on the table, and she snatched them up. She hurried back to Jan and Cornelia, waiting behind the tree where she had left them. Two pairs of worried eyes betrayed their relief at her safety, though their countenances fell when they saw Anna's face. The answer to the anxious question didn't need to be said in words. Anna handed out her half-frozen apples, and they chewed on them, though poor Cornelia could do no more than suck at hers with her toothless gums.

Now what? Anna didn't know of any more Anabaptists who might help them out.

Just because thousands of them were said to live in Amsterdam, didn't mean they walked around with signs on their heads announcing who they were. Rather, they were as unobtrusive as possible, slipping around at night or hiding in crowds. Finding one of them without a clue where they lived would be risky and difficult. They couldn't just enter an inn and start asking questions. The baker she had known, but he had been arrested.

"Let me go and ask around," Jan suggested. "These people don't know me so maybe they won't be suspicious."

"But your red hair! It's so easy to remember."

He pulled his hat down as far as he could. "Better?"

"You can't hide your beard."

"Well then, I will put my life into the loving hands of God." Anna watched him go and clenched her jaw. He *must* come back safely, and hopefully with news of the children.

"You would do well to marry that boy," Cornelia said, with a twinkle in her dark eyes. "He has a heart of gold."

Anna nodded. "That he does, but he seems more like a brother to me. Besides, he would never look at me. Men never do." She looked up at the graying sky, desperate to hide her pain from Cornelia. The sun had slipped behind a cloud, a dark cloud that threatened more snow or freezing rain.

"That's nonsense. He looked at you quite a lot back at the

hut."

Anna blushed. This she could not believe, though Jan would be a good catch for some lucky girl. "He could hardly avoid it in such close quarters." She peeked from behind the tree, although she knew Jan could not possibly be on his way back yet.

"The servant, Pieter! He's in front of my house!" Anna gasped.

"It's a good thing you're not in there anymore."

"It seems he turns up wherever I go. I don't trust him. I wonder where Jan is?"

When Jan finally returned to their sheltering cedar tree, Anna's heart sank at the look on his face. His head hung, and his shoulders drooped. Grief filled his murky green eyes, and Anna's world spun dizzily as she prepared herself for ill tidings.

"Anna, I don't know how to say this," Jan said, hoarsely.

"Just say it."

"I met a man on the street who asked me if I'm looking for someone. I don't know what made him think I might be, but I did ask him where the family went that used to live beside Simon. Anna..."

"I want to know."

"He said they all died of fever, and the father is in a dungeon awaiting trial for heresy, and certain execution. I'm so sorry."

Anna sank down on the sled, no longer able to stand. She buried her head in her hands and shook with uncontrollable sobs. It couldn't be true! How could three lovely children all die in such a short time? In her heart she knew it was only too possible. Children got sick and died all the time. They were so fragile. But not her children. Other people's children died, and that was just a fact of life. But not beautiful little Trijntgen and Bettke and sweet little Dirk. She felt like a huge piece of her heart had just been ripped out.

Jan patted her shoulder awkwardly and Cornelia sniffled. "I guess God needed more little angels up in Heaven."

"I needed them too! And Adriaen! I wonder in which dungeon he is?"

"The man I met didn't say. Probably he didn't know."

"What shall we do now?" Anna said, though she didn't feel like doing anything. Not only because the children were gone, and she would miss them dreadfully, but also because she had failed to keep her promise to Adriaen, and she had failed Maeyken by not keeping her children alive.

"I know." Anna answered her own question, her voice watery. She got up from the sled, and even though the tears trickled down, she lifted her chin. "We shall look for Anneken and Elizabeth and Claes. If at least one of the children is still alive, the pain in my heart might ease a little."

"Yes," Jan agreed, and Cornelia nodded. "That would give us some direction. Shall we pray and ask God to show us what to do?"

"You pray," Anna said. "I can't."

Chapter Sixteen

On the Road, February 1532

Danger from my own people, danger in the wilderness, danger at sea, danger from false brethren, in toil and hardship, through many a sleepless night, in hunger and thirst, often without food, in cold and exposure...2 Cor 11:26

"Why don't we head for Moravia?" Jan suggested. "Anabaptists are safer with the Hutterites than any other place in Christendom. They live communally, with everyone sharing their goods. Cornelia, you would have a tight roof over your head, and you'd never go hungry either."

"That sounds like my kind of home," Cornelia said. "Where is Moravia?"

"Far away to the west," Anna said, not feeling the least bit excited about this idea. So many long miles to travel before they could rest, and with an elderly woman to think of. And what if they didn't like it once they got there? She didn't dwell on the real reason. Adriaen was not there. He preached in dangerous places, and whatever dungeon they had stuck him into, it wasn't in Moravia.

"We could wind our way through the Netherlands, keeping an eye open for Claes and Elizabeth, pass through Germany, and on to Moravia," Jan said.

Cornelia nodded, but Anna didn't say anything. Jan gazed at her, an inscrutable expression on his pale face. "Or where would you like to go?"

"Home. I just want to go home, back to the life I had before this horrible Reformation."

Jan sighed. "I wish from my heart that it lay within my powers to grant you this wish, but alas, I am a mere mortal. These are hard days, I know. But remember, after the storm comes the rainbow. We have to keep reaching for the hope that things will get better—better than we can imagine." He stroked his fiery beard thoughtfully. "For now, we must make a decision. I know of one or two houses near Amsterdam where I have found shelter in the past, but there is always the possibility they have been discovered by now. And who knows, maybe those Brethren have recanted and no longer shelter fugitives."

"We must go somewhere," Anna said slowly. "And one place is as good as another, I suppose. If the two of you want to head to Germany, I will go with you, as long as we stay far away from Mantelhof." No need to travel back to that scene of terror where she could be recognized.

"Of course." Jan looked at her searchingly. "I'm sorry you have had to suffer through so many painful ordeals. Please tell me if I can help in any way."

She nodded. His kindness brought a fresh wave of tears to her eyes. "Let us go, then."

"I know some Brethren who live in Strasburg, where the authorities may be more sympathetic," Jan said. "We could go there."

Abandoning the sled, being of little use since the snow was melting, they turned to the trade route leading towards Germany, carrying the bearskin and their few belongings.

There was no money for inns, so they avoided them as they travelled through the countryside. They had to be alert for highwaymen and robbers as well as *Tauferjagers*. Though they owned little, there were those who would steal even that. Even the clothes on their back had some value.

The late February snow had mostly melted, and only dirty, grayish patches remained on the leeward side of hills and ditches. Cornelia had a surprising amount of energy, and cheerfully tramped for hours, unfazed by the many miles and the uncertain destination ahead of them, calling it a great adventure.

"God will lead the way," she said, as she scurried along, her wiry body bent against the wind and her gray hair blowing around her wizened face. "The first friendly village I see, there I will stay." She taught Anna and Jan how to dig early spring roots--which ones were edible, and which ones were used for medicinal purposes.

They sheltered in a vacant barn that first night, and their supper consisted of a crust of dried bread each, washed down with icy, but muddy, water from a nearby creek. Anna and Jan insisted Cornelia use the bearskin to wrap herself in for the night, a privilege she protested. After gathering some forgotten wisps of old straw for Anna and Jan's beds, they all made themselves as comfortable as possible. Anna tried to ignore the rustlings of the night creatures, and felt grateful they had found a roof at least.

The following day, they reached the little town of Muiden on IJmeer Lake, and in order to pay the fare of a boat to travel onwards, Jan worked on the docks for the day. By nighttime; his soft schoolmaster's hands were blistered, and his back must surely ache from carrying heavy cargo. When darkness relieved him of his duties, he fell in a heap in the corner of an empty boathouse, where the three of them spent the night. In the morning, a large shadow filled the doorway as Anna awoke.

"River rats!"

Anna jumped to her feet in an instant, shielding Cornelia with her body. Jan rose stiffly and positioned himself beside her. Two more men were poking their heads through the doorway. Their dirty clothes, scarred faces and weathered appearance marked them as veteran sailors. One of them had terrible raw looking scars on both cheeks and two missing fingers. Shards of ice raced up and down Anna's spine. Jan rubbed his eyes and blinked.

"Hans? Hans Vissler? Is that you?"

"*Das ist mein Name, Rotschopf.* Where have I met you before?"

"You don't remember the runt of the neighbourhood back in Zurich? Fancy meeting my fellow countryman here." Jan was smiling. Apparently he didn't minding being called Redhead.

"You!" The scarred man took a few steps into the interior of the boathouse. "You mean you survived childhood? I thought you'd be long gone by now, the way you were always sick and mewling."

"Seems I'm stronger than we knew, doesn't it? Say, do you know of a boat we could use to cross the river?"

Anna's shoulders relaxed in relief. If Jan knew these rough-looking men and dared ask for a boat, they were probably kinder than they seemed. Cornelia was sitting up, her beady eyes daring anyone to cross her, or harm her newfound friends. At that moment, she looked quite capable of casting a spell on someone.

The big sailor, introduced as Captain Clement, peered into the dim interior. "We kin take you but we ain't taking no women."

Anna put both hands on her hips. Her sizzling look could

have fried him. “Pray tell, why not? Why would you make such a ridiculous rule?” Some men could be so arrogant.

“This is a men-only ship, a cargo ship, that’s why. We take only working passengers.” He looked disparagingly at her, not impressed by her boldness, then to Cornelia sitting on the floor in a tangle of shawls and wiry gray hair. “We can’t be responsible for the safety of women on my ship. Besides, women on a ship are bad luck.”

“I can work! And so can Cornelia! She can chop wood as well as any man, isn’t that so, Jan?” She glared at Jan, daring him to admit that *he* could not chop wood very well.

“I’ll give you my word that both these women can do as much work as I can, or more.” Clement stared at Jan, noting his pale face, his narrow shoulders, his soft white hands which were blistered from one day’s work.

“I can see that you are no stronger than a woman,” the captain said, frowning. “But you *are* no woman. That makes all the difference, see?”

Jan nodded. “We will find another ship.”

“There is no other ship heading to Germany that will take Anabaptists,” Clement said. Anna started. How did he know? Was the word ‘fugitive Anabaptist’ written on their foreheads?

Jan stared at Hans, at the raw cheeks with pus oozing from them, and at his bandaged hand with the empty space where two fingers should have been. “What happened to you?”

Hans shrugged. “The government don’t like those who read the Bible and follow it, didn’t you know? When I committed every debauchery under the sun and drank myself stupid, they didn’t care. But then I cleaned up my life after reading the Bible and spread the Word, so they decided to teach me a lesson."

Jan drew in a long breath. "Well, don't let us keep you. We will find another way to go."

"Wait!" Captain Clement said gruffly. "We can take you as far as Harlingen, that's all. And you have to pay double fare because of the women."

Anna gasped, feeling as angry as a thunderstorm. "That's not fair. We pay double *and* work? I refuse to go on those terms." It was not only that she disliked his terms, but they didn't have that much money between them. Jan's labor the previous day might have earned enough fare for him, but not for all three of them.

"Ahem..." They all turned when Cornelia spoke up, though she was still huddling on the floor. "I will make a fair offer... You will take us on your ship and we will not pay a penny. In return I promise to heal friend Hans' cheeks by the time we arrive at our destination. We will all help on ship duty as well as we are able. You agree to these terms or I put a curse on your ship. I am a witch you know." She cackled her worst and shook a crooked finger to prove her point.

Anna smiled inwardly. Good old Cornelia. If these sailors only knew how harmless she was! Her rough exterior hid a heart as soft as butter. Anna was a little surprised that Cornelia kept up the charade of being a witch, though. What if they just tossed her overboard?

Clement waved his arms frantically at those words. "No, no, no! You cannot put a curse on my ship! This is a new ship and I'm taking her out on her maiden voyage. My aging father financed the *Vrijheid,* and he will disown me if anything happens to her." Heaving a big sigh, and drawing his bushy black brows together over his dark eyes, he finally said, "Very well, then. You may travel with us, though I will not guarantee your safety, nor can I offer you a very comfortable bunk. If Hans' cheek is not healed when we arrive, I report you to the authorities as a witch, which you just admitted to being."

Smiling in triumph, Cornelia nodded. "Agreed. Isn't that so? Anna? Jan?" It seemed to Anna that Cornelia was taking by far the biggest risk; how could she heal a festering sore in less than one week? It seemed typical of her to sacrifice herself in this way, and Anna could only hope it would all work out.

In under an hour they sailed out of port, with Anna's back aching from all the heavy boxes she had carried down to the hold. She dared not think what they contained. Jan also looked ready to drop. His fair skin was sunburned and his poor hands were bleeding from broken blisters rubbed raw. Cornelia had better heal them too.

Only Cornelia seemed to have any energy left when they set sail. Serenely, she sat on deck on a pile of ropes and gazed out over the water, as if she was part of the sea. Her black old eyes sparkled like chips of coal in the sunlight. Curiously, she seemed to belong on the water and loved it.

Anna was kept busy scrubbing the floor of the ship's galley, washing dishes, preparing food and was at the beck and call of the sailors whenever they wanted their clothes mended or washed. She put in long days and fell exhausted onto her narrow bunk at night. Surprisingly, she did not become seasick, unlike Jan. It looked as if he had the hardest time being worth his fare.

Anna saw Jan a couple of times when she went below to fetch ale from the barrels. His usually white face was tinged with green, and he smiled weakly when she brought him some tea one morning.

"I fear I'm not doing a good job of protecting you, Anna. But if you run into trouble, you come to me immediately." Anna agreed although she wasn't sure what he would do in such a case. "I am constantly praying for your safety, Anna. I could never forgive myself if anything happened to you." He looked deeply into her face with those compelling green eyes.

"You have come to mean very much to me," he continued. "I don't think I want to ever part from you."

Anna stood back, amazed. "Wha…what do you mean?"

"I apologize for not making myself clear. I'm not very adept at proposing. I know I am a sorry specimen right now, but I've been thinking. And I am asking you; would you consider sharing the future with me? As my wife?"

Anna nearly dropped the cup of tea. "But why?" she gasped. Jan proposing? She had come to love him as a brother, but it had hardly crossed her mind to think of him as anything more. She handed Jan the tea and looked at him with concern. He had been quite seasick. Was he feverish, perhaps? His pale face said otherwise, but maybe he drank too much wine. She detected no sign of drunkenness, but what other reasonable explanation could there be for this startling declaration?

"Anna, I know this is sudden," Jan said. "But believe me, I do not ask this question lightly. I have come to admire your spirit, and I find myself wanting to be with you always." Jan paused, drawing his reddish eyebrows together in a frown. "I don't have much to offer you, since the family home in Switzerland has been confiscated, therefore I will understand if you decline on those grounds. All I can offer you is my undying admiration, deep respect and as much protection as I am able. This I give you freely, regardless of what your answer will be."

"Jan, you are too good. This is an honor I never expected, and I will have to give this some thought." Ever since she'd become a teen, Anna had felt the pressure from her parents, and society in general, to find someone to marry. Her poor success on that score had convinced her there must be something wrong with her. But now, here was a lovable, generous, honorable man proposing marriage, and she could not believe it. Or accept it. She wanted to say yes. YES, she would marry him, even though he seemed like a brother to her rather than a lover.

Jan was kindness itself, selfless to a fault and she knew he would be true and loyal unto death. What was wrong with her? This is what she had been wishing for, for years. But Jan? In the deepest recesses of her mind, she knew what was wrong with her. There was a man, in a dungeon somewhere, who held her heart captive. A man she might never see again, but as long as he lived, she could not think of marrying another. Not unless he married someone else, then she would have to give him up. A twinge of pain shot through her at this reminder.

Perhaps she should just forget Adriaen and consider this man, the first who ever admitted to admiring her, flaws and all. There was no way of knowing whether she would ever hear anything of Adriaen again, and even if she did, would he marry the woman who had abandoned his children? Besides letting his wife die while she slept. Anna flinched.

Jan was here now and available. Letting her thoughts wander, she wondered what her life would be like if she forgot about Adriaen and settled down somewhere peaceful with Jan. Perhaps a little cottage in a country village with little red-headed boys and girls running around. Children! How she longed for children of her own. It was tempting to accept. Very tempting. Then she sobered. She hadn't proved capable of being responsible for children, and it was remarkable that anyone was even willing to take a chance on her. Still, Jan had been the one to get her in that mess. Maybe it was him that wasn't capable. What if, contrary to his words, he left her in the lurch the next time danger threatened?

"Anna, don't decide now." Jan's green gaze seemed to penetrate her very thoughts. "Think about it and pray about it. I will continue to do the same. The Lord's will be done."

That was another thing. She didn't know yet if she ever wanted to be baptized in his faith. It was beginning to make more sense and she was fast losing faith in the Catholic church, the more she heard about their cruel persecutions of innocent people. But become a hated Anabaptist? Live every day in fear? She was in danger now, but the danger would increase tenfold if she were baptized. Even the ones who recanted were still beheaded. She could not do it, not yet.

Yet this was also the problem with waiting for Adriaen. Even if she did miraculously see him again in this life, she had no reason to believe he would see her as someone he could marry. Anna was afraid she was as far from his mind, as he was close to hers. In her impracticable dreams, he would come back, the country would settle down and agree on their religion, and Adriaen would propose to her. They would live somewhere safe where Adriaen could work at his trade of goldsmithing, and she could make his home a loving, welcoming place, and have children of her own. A woman's life could be a good thing with a good man.

Dreams! That's all it was. She could not live forever on dreams.

"I will think about it," she promised as she picked up

the empty teacup and headed back up to the galley to more drudgery. Jan would be a man who could make a woman happy. She felt like shaking herself that the idea did not appeal more to her innermost heart.

In the galley, Hans was sitting beside a table, with Cornelia bending over him smearing some strong-smelling concoction on his cheeks. The wounds were no longer runny with fluids, and it looked like Cornelia at least was keeping her end of the bargain.

"So you were baptized a year ago?" she was saying.

"Yes, by Jacob van Campen."

"I wish it too for myself as soon as possible. Is there anyone in Friesland?"

"Melchior Hoffman might be there. He has baptized hundreds of people. I am sure the Brethren can help you if that is what you desire."

"I do desire it. Jan has spent many days instructing me, and I am ready to accept the outward confession of the faith."

"God bless you and give you His peace. I will bear the scars on my cheeks forever, and my two fingers are gone, yet I can feel no shame or regret for taking up the cross of Christ."

"Is this common, that they brand heretics?"

"In some places, yes. The local government doesn't want to kill the Anabaptists, but the higher ruling powers force them to do something to protect the land from this 'heresy', so they brand us and chop off fingers instead of executing."

"Will that keep the Emperor happy, though?"

"He decreed execution without trial, but as long as I don't get caught again, I should be fine. Many magistrates disagree with Charles, but they want to keep their well-paying jobs, so they make it appear like they're doing their duty. If I'm called on to suffer death for the sake of Christ, I hope to do so joyfully with the crown of Heaven in view, and leave a faithful witness."

Anna felt a little awkward listening to this conversation. Like she somehow didn't belong. Lord knew she had heard enough about the Anabaptist faith through the long winter days in Cornelia's hut. All the words seemed to collect only in her mind, instead of passing on down into her heart. She was interested in the views and angles of the controversy, but could not commit her heart and soul to this faith until she was certain it was the true one. She wanted to become a True Soldier of Christ, but where was the True Army?

She wanted to belong to everybody. She wanted everyone to just come to some solution and agree. Why did one denomination feel the need to kill another just because they interpreted the Bible differently? From what Jan had taught, she believed in 'Thou should not kill.' That was something she could agree with, even though it made the Catholics and the Lutherans both wrong. They insisted that they had to keep order in their realms, and wars were necessary to prevent other countries from invading their lands.

What would a world be like where no one killed? It was beyond comprehension. The Old Testament was full of wars and killings, but the Anabaptists believed in the New Testament more than in the old, because Jesus came and showed a better way, the way of love. "Love your enemies and do good to those who hate you," Jesus said.

Anna wondered how one could do that. In some of the booklets the Anabaptists distributed, they even called their persecutors names; the whore of Babylon or the Antichrist. Was that loving your enemies?

Chapter Seventeen

On the Ship, February-March 1532

Let each of you not look only to his own interests...Philippians 2:4

The swaying ship set anchor in Harlingen after six days of smooth sailing. The sailors had not done them any harm, contrary to what Clement had led them to believe. In fact, once Anna even caught the burly captain on his knees, praying. His gruffness and roughness were only a ruse. But why?

Two of the sailors went ashore, presumably to arrange for the unloading of the cargo. Anna wondered if she was expected to help unload, and her back ached just thinking of lugging those heavy crates up the ladder.

She was standing on the deck, gazing across the blue waters of the sea, loving to watch the waves ripple ever onward to the ocean. If she were a man, she decided she would become a sailor and sail the high seas to foreign lands. But she would never dare say it out loud. No decent woman would admit to such a thing. A woman's place was in the home, caring for her man. If she had no man, her duty was to go around helping those in need; old widows, orphans, the poor. Anna had no objection to doing this; however, it seemed unjust that if she made her true desires known, she would be held in contempt.

Of course, women were more evil than men, a fact proven ages ago in the garden of Eden when Eve tempted

Adam with the forbidden fruit. Ever since, women needed to be watched and restricted, preventing them from leading men into temptation and evil. God had made them weaker and more prone to falling into sin, and this is how it would be for all time.

Anna sighed. She must learn to be content with her lot in life, and if she was foolish enough to decline her first offer of marriage, she ought to stop complaining. Father Hendricks had pointed out her sin of discontent many times, and she had done countless penances on her knees for her unnatural desires. All the times she had spent in self-pity because she had no man, and now that a wonderful, kind man had proposed, she couldn't accept. It was beyond ridiculous.

A commotion on the dock shook her out of her reverie. Her breath was snatched away when she saw the half dozen armoured soldiers on horseback. The flash of unsheathed swords glittered in the sunlight and reflected on the water. The two sailors from the ship were surrounded and cornered, though surprisingly they didn't struggle or protest at their treatment. With shouts and jeers from the gathering crowd they were shackled and chained before Anna's very eyes.

Now what? she thought in desperation. She might have known that criminals were running this ship. The captain praying was obviously a cover-up for some dishonest enterprise. She didn't know if she should warn the captain or let events run their course. What was it to her if the whole gang was stuck into a dungeon?

But Hans! Hans who had already suffered torture! His poor branded cheeks were finally on the mend thanks to Cornelia's skill with herbs. As soon as they caught sight of him, they would know he was a former criminal and his life would be ended with as little feeling as if he were a fly.

Anna rushed down to the hold where Hans was working with the cargo, getting the crates organized for lifting to the deck. “Hans! Hans!”

He looked up startled, his tranquil blue eyes questioning.

“Caspar and Franz have been arrested! You must hide!”

“Hide?” He looked at her blankly, unmoving, holding a crate in his beefy arms. “Where would I hide? If the dock police are suspicious of our boat, they will search it from top to bottom.”

Anna looked around wildly for a hiding place, but there was none. Suddenly Cornelia came careening down to the hold, her shawls in disarray and her skirts flapping.

“Get that crate emptied. NOW! You’re getting inside, and Anna and I will carry you to shore.”

Trust Cornelia to think of something, Anna thought.

“No, I can’t do that. This is secret cargo. If they see it, we’re all condemned.”

“Secret cargo! What kind of excuse is that? What is it, guns?”

Hans sighed. “I suppose I may as well tell you. These are crates of Bibles that we’re smuggling in for the Anabaptists. We are all Anabaptists on this ship.” Anna took a step back, astounded. No wonder Captain Clement had hesitated to take them on board. He had good reason to be selective about who he allowed on his ship. Something must have told him that they were Brethren, or at least sympathetic. Charles V could have no idea how many of these people were operating under his very nose.

“Get this crate up on the deck! These Bibles are going overboard, and you are getting in there,” Cornelia shrieked, pointing a bony finger at Hans.

"Cornelia, I am ready to meet my Master if I'm caught. They can do no more than God allows," he said piously, already resigned to his awful fate.

"God may allow it, but I won't." Cornelia grabbed a hammer and began prying the wooden slats off the crate. "I have invested a lot of time and my whole store of yarrow root in you, and now you listen to me or I shall cast a spell on you."

Anna smiled. "I thought you'd become an Anabaptist. I don't think they use spells."

Cornelia glared. "This is not the time for jesting. Help me get this off."

Hans emerged from his trance, and gently pushed Cornelia aside as he hefted the heavy crate onto a muscular shoulder. "You win. It probably won't work and I'm not sure you two can carry me, but we'll try. Heaven help us if they pry open this crate."

"They won't." Cornelia said, and Anna believed her. The woman had some powers which were unexplainable.

They were stuffing the last Bible in a sack as the first constable stepped onboard. Cornelia blocked his path as Anna tossed the sack overboard and Hans crawled into the crate. Jan came blinking and stumbling from his cabin, his eyes still heavy with sleep, just in time to see the constable shove Cornelia aside, causing her to fall onto the deck with a thump. The captain, hearing the disturbance, also came running from his cabin and stopped short when he saw the constable.

"Are you the captain of this ship?" the constable asked. Clement nodded.

"In the name of the Holy Roman Emperor, I shall hereby proceed to search this ship, from bow to stern. What is in that crate?" He pointed an imperious finger at the crate on the floor. Anna hardly dared to breathe as he stepped towards it. Other armed, hard-faced men were marching up the gangplank, dragging long chains.

"Leave my things alone, you miserable meddlers!" Cornelia scolded. She scrambled onto her feet and parked herself on the crate with a demented look on her face. The constable hesitated. Some of his men had already swarmed down below.

"Chief, come and behold this treasure!" they called jubilantly. "You won't believe this."

Reluctantly, he turned and headed for the hold. "Anna, hurry up!" Cornelia hissed. She picked up one end of the crate with the strength of two men and Anna grabbed the other end.

"Jan!" Anna gasped. "Come with us!"

"No. I will stay here and distract the soldiers if they come back up here. Run!"

Anna would have delayed, torn between distress at leaving Jan behind, and the urgency to escape with Hans while they could. Cornelia had no such qualms and tugged at her end of the crate until Anna was forced to follow. They half ran down the gangplank with their prize. The shouting crowd gaped at the sight of two women carrying cargo, but didn't stop them.

"Make way! Make way!" Cornelia commanded, "Where is the town hall? This is an important order for the bailiff. Someone show us the way." Half a dozen men stepped forth, offering to carry the crate, but Cornelia wouldn't hear of it.

"I promised I'd deliver it myself. No, no I don't need an escort. Only directions." Someone pointed vaguely towards a street on the left, and they hurried towards it. Evidently,

Cornelia's face was hag-like enough that they didn't try to cross her, and Anna was thankful for that. Everyone was more interested in seeing the ship's crew arrested. Anna and Cornelia staggered down the first alley they came to, breathless and aching, and set down the awkward crate. Anna rubbed her back. Cornelia ripped off the loosely fastened cover and a battered Hans scuttled out.

"Now run!" Cornelia ordered. Hans got up, a little dazed, and looked to left and to right. Where in this strange city should he run to?

"The Lord will lead you. You believe that, don't you?" Cornelia said. He stumbled away down the alley, and Anna and Cornelia watched him go. "May we meet again," Anna called after him.

"I'll find you somehow," he tossed over his shoulder as he picked up speed. The farther away he got, the better.

"Now, let us go and see what we can do for the others." Cornelia led the way back to the crowded dock and shoved her way through until they stood at water's edge. Anna gulped when she saw the captain and his crew being led down the gangplank shackled two by two in chains. She couldn't see Jan. Why hadn't he followed them out of there?

She blanched when she spotted him at the rear of the line of prisoners, dragging a chain around his ankles. Her hands flew to her mouth, stifling the scream that nearly escaped. Cornelia grabbed Anna's arm like a vise, but Anna barely noticed. Guilt settled in her gut and she felt sick, more so than she ever had on the ship. Jan would never survive long if they stuck him in one of their dank and dark dungeons. His face already looked appallingly white compared to the weathered faces of the seamen.

"Looks like Ole Dieter found himself some hearty galley

slaves to sell to Spain." A man chuckled cruelly from behind her in the shifting crowd. Anna stiffened in shock. She hadn't thought of this possibility. Poor Jan. And poor sailors. Anna prayed they would spare Jan, since he obviously wouldn't last more than a day on a galley ship. Cornelia had strengthened him with her potions, but he was not a robust man.

Cornelia turned to look at Anna, a fierce blaze in her black eyes. She tugged at Anna's arm with a bony hand. "Let's go," she hissed.

"No!" Anna refused to budge. Jan was not going to disappear without her finding out where they were taking him. It was bad enough that they had abandoned him on the ship, without leaving him to an unknown fate. She had abandoned enough people, and she must free Jan somehow, and soon. She hadn't even given him her answer to his proposal yet, and she hoped he wouldn't be heartbroken when she refused. It seemed unlikely.

The authorities would be pleased when they discovered they had caught an Anabaptist teacher. If they had any mercy at all they would not torture an unhealthy man, but Anna realized this was clutching at straws. Of course they would question him closely, as well as the others. Anna wondered about the ship and its crew, curious to know if they were truly all Anabaptists. She supposed the authorities would sort them out, but that didn't mean any of them would go free.

Captures. Questioning. Betrayal. Sentencing. Executing by fire, by the sword, by drowning, by languishing on cold dungeon floors with no food. Burning people along with their homes. She was sick and tired of it all. She wished she could go back to her family in Germany, back to her parents, her brothers and sister. Even now, she couldn't bear to dwell on them and their horrific deaths for long. Or back to Simon the shopkeeper's little house, back to her unexciting life, with Maeyken and Adriaen and their children living happily next door. Would she ever be able to settle down to a normal, peaceful life again?

She lifted her apron to wipe her eyes. The crowd shifted as the prisoners were hustled along towards the centre of town. Like a herd of dumb sheep, the horde followed the spectacle right up to the double oak doors of the Town Hall. How did so many people have time to gawk at these unfortunate souls? Some called out taunts and made fun of the captives, and others murmured sympathetic words. Shouldn't everyone be at their work, instead of seeking entertainment in such bloodthirsty ways?

Anna watched as Jan disappeared from view, and into the clutches of men who would not listen to any opinion that disagreed with their own. They would pry and prod and wear down the defenders until their heads swam, then bring in a fresh batch of interrogators and question some more for hours on end until they managed to squeeze out the information they sought.

If they weren't satisfied with the answers they were getting they would move their hapless prisoner to another room and rattle their terrifying equipment, trying to frighten a confession out of them. If the captives still wouldn't talk, or if they had nothing to confess, they would be stripped and laid on the unrelenting table which had brought unspeakable pain to many souls before them. Their limbs would be stretched to ever increasing degrees, legs and arms pulled out of their sockets, causing terrible anguish until they released the words their captors sought.

Into mouths open and panting in agony, they would pour

copious amounts of water in mock drownings, stopping on the verge of the sweet release of death, letting their victim recover to suffer all over again, if not today, then another day. Oh yes, Anna knew all this. The authorities back in Germany had made certain everyone understood what happened to heretics, as a grim warning to their subjects. Disloyalty and disobedience were not tolerated at all.

"Jan! Jan!" Anna called through the crowd, but nobody answered. She shoved and scrambled through the crowd, desperate now to get away, not caring where she went, so long as it was away from that wretched scene of the chained prisoners. Cornelia was left behind somewhere, but with her powers she would find Anna again. Anna ran, her long skirts hindering her until she grabbed them and pulled them up out of the way, not caring about the scandal she would cause if she was seen with uncovered ankles.

"Jan! Jan!" she sobbed silently, pushing her way headlong through the gaping crowd. "No! No! Not Jan!" She had to go somewhere quiet to plan for Jan's release. But how?

Somehow, she found herself back at the docks, where the ship still swayed out in the water. She spotted a pile of sacks filled with wheat behind a warehouse, probably waiting to be shipped out. Crawling between two of them, she sank down in a miserable heap. She pulled up her knees, wrapped her arms around them, laid down her head, and wept like a baby.

Chapter Eighteen

Harlingen, March 1532

I can do all things in Him who strengthens me...Philippians 4:13

A shadow crossed her line of vision. She jumped up, ready to race for her life, but when she saw the man, she nearly fell backwards onto the pile of wheat. This must be a dream.

"Surprised to see me?" Adriaen grinned.

Anna was struck wordless. It was not at all like she had imagined it if she ever saw him again. For one thing, she could not comprehend that he was standing there instead of wasting away in a prison tower or dungeon, waiting for the end. She was bedraggled and tear-swept, her cap askew, her nose running. She was homeless, scared and guilty, and hiding in a strange place many miles from home without a farthing to her name.

"Adriaen," she finally whispered, her fingers tangling in her straggly hair as she tried to tame the mess. Giving up the attempt to make herself presentable, she straightened her cap, and realized it didn't matter. What mattered was that Adriaen was there, alive and well. Her heart rejoiced, and she couldn't stop herself from glowing like a sunbeam. "I thought you were in prison."

Adriaen shook his head. "We need to talk. Come with me, I know a place where we should be safe."

Anna hesitated. Talk? About what? That she had lost his children? All of a sudden, she wasn't sure this was a good idea. She couldn't bear to think of his friendliness turning to anger and sorrow when she confessed what had happened.

"I have to find Cornelia."

"Cornelia? Who is she?"

"A very good friend of mine, to whom I owe my life. You must meet her; I'm certain you would adore her."

He held out a hand, which she hardly trusted herself to touch. Slowly, she reached out, and the warmth and strength of his fingers closing around hers was a tonic to her soul.

"Let's go find her then," he said.

"And Jan. We have to rescue Jan." They had the street to themselves, everyone else must have joined the mob at the Town Hall. Anna let go of Adriaen's hand, taking care to keep some space between them as they walked.

"Is that, by any chance, the young prisoner with a face like oatmeal and hair the color of a carrot you were staring at?" Adriaen teased her.

Anna blushed, embarrassed at his insinuation. "Jan is quite pale and has red hair. If I was staring, it's because I'm worried about him, and every one of the captured ones."

Adriaen sobered. "Yes, it is most unfortunate. And there is already a big fire burning on the shore, with the Bibles and tracts we were waiting on, serving as the fuel."

"That's a terrible loss. Why does the government object to the populace reading the Bible?"

Adriaen peered over his shoulder before whispering, "They don't want people to find out what the Bible really says. They know they have been teaching their subjects lies, the better to control them."

"What kind of lies?"

"Mostly striking fear into their hearts by telling them the prince-bishops are passing messages to them directly from God, forcing their vassals to serve them, and somehow ending up with most of their money and assets. The money is used for buying every kind of expensive adornment for their castles and their cathedrals, disregarding the hunger and poverty of the people. The clergy convince them that God wants them to sacrifice every earthly comfort, and honor and obey those who are so nearly like God, if they want to go to Heaven. Now when the commoners read the Bible, they find out it's just not true."

Anna frowned. What possessed these rulers? Weren't they afraid for their own souls? Or did they believe they were above reproach from ordinary mortals, and even above the judgment of God?

"I must say I was pleased to see you in the crowd, and I hoped you'd see me wave. When you ran away, I had to follow you."

"You waved?" Anna said. "I had no idea you were in the country. I didn't know whether you even lived, since the last I heard you were cast into some dark dungeon."

"You didn't get my letter? And the money?"

Anna seethed with rage and disappointment all over again at his question. "Willem lost it," she said through her teeth. "And he never said anything about money." It was dreadful of her to think so badly of Willem, but still, losing something so important really was unforgivable. "He and Jan, the young man you saw, came to my house nearly frozen to death one night, and he had lost it somewhere in the storm."

Adriaen's face wrinkled in concern. "I hope it didn't fall into the wrong hands. I tried not to write anything condemning, but it might condemn you because your name was on it."

"Oh, Adriaen, there's more bad news, something I must tell you before we take another step." She turned to face him. Must she once again be the one to inflict pain into those trustful brown eyes?

"Adriaen, the children are gone." She looked at the ground, not daring and not wishing to see the anger in his face.

"Gone where? I assumed they would be here in Harlingen with you."

Anna related the tale with anguish in her voice and eyes; how she had fled with Jan to the bush, leaving the children at home alone, how they had nearly frozen by the time Cornelia found them, the long weeks in the hut and finally going back to Amsterdam only to hear the shocking news of the children's deaths.

Slowly, Adriaen's eyes grew dull as baked mud. "I see," he said, swallowing hard. He continued walking in silence, but his shoulders seemed to droop, and his face had turned a grayish hue. "And did you find out where they..." he gulped and finished on a hoarse sob, "buried them?"

"No, Adriaen, I'm sorry. Unfortunately, we were not given that information. I cannot believe they are gone, and I will never forgive myself for abandoning them." Anna's eyes blurred with tears, but she must not break down in front of Adriaen. He was the one in need of sympathy, not her. He had lost too much—his wife, his home, his livelihood, and now his children.

"But you must forgive yourself. I don't deny this is hard news to stomach, but it is the price to pay for becoming a True Soldier of Christ. I pray they didn't suffer for long. I believe they are with their mother now, in a happier place than this sad world. If I cling to that hope, I can not wish them back."

Anna puzzled over this, and finally concluded that Adriaen's position was a selfless way to view the loss. Apart from what they may have suffered, the innocent little ones were now in Heaven with Jesus, where suffering and pain are no more. This observation made the children's demise a trifle more tolerable. She also comforted her still-partly-Catholic heart with the knowledge that they had been baptized, not that Adriaen would count that as any gain. And unbeknownst to him, his only possible remaining child, Anneken, had been secretly baptized by her. And it certainly could do no harm, she thought.

"If Claes and Elizabeth could be found, you may still have Anneken. I heard they are in Harlingen."

"I haven't heard anything about them for some time, but yes, let us pray Anneken still lives." Adriaen said. "As soon as I can get away, I will try to find her." He paused, then turned to look at Anna. He lifted his flat cap off his dark hair, then settled it again on his head. "If you didn't get the letter, how did you happen to come to Harlingen? I mentioned in my letter that I'll be here by March, but I was astonished to see you."

"I guess God must have led us here then. But why would He lead us here, only to have Jan arrested?" Anna shivered. "He doesn't deserve to be in a dungeon. I really should be searching for Cornelia, and thinking of a way to free Jan."

"Oh yes. Cornelia. Where did you last see her?"

"I lost her in the crowd of vultures over by the Town Hall. We were unaware that the ship was smuggling Bibles until we got here. I even helped load them in Amsterdam."

"I must say I'm amazed Captain Clement let you on the ship. He doesn't usually take passengers, especially not women. It's a dangerous thing he was doing, and he will probably have to answer with his life now. But he and his crew would have been arrested, regardless whether or not he had any women on board."

"He did say women on board were bad luck, and it must be true. Cornelia managed to get us on there, and without paying a penny."

Adriaen whistled. "I didn't think Clement would fall for the charms of a pretty woman. I must meet the beautiful Cornelia." Anna smiled to herself. He was in for quite a surprise, although it irked her that he was so eager to meet a pretty woman.

"Do you want to go now?" Adriaen asked.

"I really would, if you don't mind. I am concerned about Cornelia, even if she is self-sufficient. I'd hate to see her harmed."

Changing direction, they headed back to the centre of town. The square in front of the Town Hall was unoccupied now, except for some pigeons on the ground pecking at kernels of grain. Down by the shore, there was an uproar from the crowd, while the fire raged high. The air was filled with smoke. Officers on horseback rode around the area, their swords at the ready in case the mob turned ugly. As Anna and Adriaen watched, people grabbed books out of the flames and tossed them into the crowd. Not everyone wanted these books burned!

Cornelia was nowhere in sight. Adriaen led Anna down a narrow street with tall buildings crowded together shoulder to shoulder. A woman in an upstairs room of one house was chatting with a woman in the upstairs room of the house across the way.

"Watch out!" Anna leaped aside just in time as a pail of

slop emptied above her head. It splattered down into the street, and the hem of her long skirt was splashed with some of the vile smelling liquid. She choked back the furious words that rose to her throat. Women must not display unseemly temper, but it was hard.

They continued surveying some back streets, hoping for a glimpse of Cornelia, then came out through a narrow alley to the place where the weavers lived and had their shops. Anna could hear the hum of their looms as they passed dim doorways.

"Would you mind coming with me to my sister's house?" Adriaen asked. "We'll get some refreshment and search again afterwards."

"I didn't know you have a sister. Certainly, I would like to meet her." Adriaen led her to the last house in the row, a modest slate-roofed stone house with a clean look about it. The small yard was swept spotless and some early red and yellow tulips grew in a patch beside the packed earth path leading up to the doorway.

A plump, smiling woman came bustling to the door, bringing with her the wonderful aroma of baking bread. She wiped pudgy hands on her apron and bade them come inside. Two little boys tussled with a mangy looking dog on the floor, laughing and squealing. Anna felt tears rising and quickly looked away. It seemed like a long time since she'd smelled the comfort of baking bread or had the pleasure of watching children at their happy play.

"I have a visitor for you, Susanna." He turned to Anna. "This is Anna, the woman who took care of my poor motherless children when I had to leave so unexpectedly."

Anna smiled. She knew she was going to love Susanna, a woman with the same dark hair and brown eyes as Adriaen.

"Come on in," Susanna welcomed them. "You're just in time for some warm bread and butter." Anna's stomach rumbled in pleasure. Susanna made them sit by the table while she swiftly cut generous slices of bread and slathered them with butter, serving it on a platter along with foaming cups of buttermilk.

"Anything new in town today?" Susanna asked.

Adriaen set down his slice of bread, and Anna held hers halfway to her mouth, unable to take a bite.

"As a matter of fact," Adriaen said. "There are a few things, but aside from finding Anna, it is unhappy news." He bent his head, and Anna noticed moisture glistening in his eyes. For a few minutes there was silence, even the little boys scrabbling on the floor stopped their play, sensing some sorrowful news to come.

"Did the *Vrijheid* come in today, with the precious cargo?" Susanna prompted.

"She did," Adriaen said, "and immediately the ship was swarmed by officers of the Court. All the crew has been arrested, and the cargo is warming the shore."

"Oh!" Susanna clapped a hand to her mouth, her eyes round with dismay. "This is terrible! Surely not more prisoners! And so many Brethren were looking forward to that shipment."

"I know, but it appears it wasn't meant to be."

"There's worse." Anna wanted to hide under the table. Adriaen was too good a man to blame her about the children, but she had seriously betrayed his trust. And now they were gone. She should be the one who had perished, not them. Adriaen needed the children after having lost his wife, but he didn't need her.

Adriaen told his sister in as few words as possible, and

she plunked down on a chair with a dazed expression on her face. "Gone! Trijntgen and Bettke and Dirk. And the baby, you have no idea where she is either. Adriaen, this is grievous news indeed. Is there anything I can do to help?"

"You can shelter Anna and keep her safe if possible. Other than that, everything is in God's hands. He is my comfort, a comfort which can never be taken away."

"I don't know exactly what happened to the children, not even where they are buried." Anna turned tragic eyes to Susanna.

"Oh, this is heartbreaking news indeed. But, Anna, I'm not blaming you." Susanna said. "I know you only did what you had to do. God needed more angels, I presume, and the children are perhaps fortunate they don't have to be here to see all the misery that may be coming to us."

A cloud crossed Adriaen's handsome features, his brown eyes darkening in pain. "Yes, I have faith that God looked after them here on earth, and now they reside with Him in Heaven. It's not your fault, Anna. These are turbulent times and there is no safe place for the likes of us. The only safe place is in Christ the Lord, and He will not forsake us. You do believe that, Anna?"

Anna shrugged and looked down at the smoothly sanded oak floorboards. "I see no sense in this constant turmoil. I don't know what to believe."

"I will pray for you. As will you, my sister, is that not so?"

Susanna nodded. "Of course. That goes without saying."

They talked a little longer, until Susanna motioned to the narrow stairway at the end of the room. "Come, you must be exhausted." She inspected Anna's rather tall frame with kindly eyes. "I'm afraid I have no dress to offer you that will fall below your knees. But there is water up there if you want to clean up a bit."

"I would love to, but I have to find Cornelia."

"I can ask around if you will trust me," Adriaen offered.

It was very tempting to lay her weary body down. But Adriaen did not know whom he was looking for, not if he was on the lookout for a beautiful young woman.

"I feel like I should go myself."

"You won't do anyone any good if you collapse. I can make a few inquiries while you rest. You have been through quite an ordeal," Adriaen said, setting down his empty cup.

"Your offer is too inviting. I suppose you can't miss Cornelia. She will probably be somewhere casting her spells." Anna looked at Adriaen and pleaded, "Can you also try to find out what is happening with Jan? He is not very strong, and I'm afraid he won't last long in prison."

Adriaen looked at her keenly. "You care a lot for this man, don't you?"

"We endured much together for a few weeks this past winter, so yes. I do care for him very much."

She didn't tell Adriaen that she loved Jan like a brother, nothing more, that she'd had the opportunity to become more, and still hadn't given Jan her negative answer. It was better if Adriaen thought her interests lay with Jan. That way he might somehow miss the fact that she loved *him*. There was no sense in him figuring that out, since it could come to nothing. Before, there was only her appearance to disgust him, now there was so much more.

Anna was so tired. She forced herself to quit thinking these unprofitable thoughts. She lay down on the straw mattress, murmured a few scattered prayers, relaxed her weary body, and soon sleep overtook her.

She was awakened by the sound of excited voices downstairs. Surely not another capture, she thought. This had to stop. It was difficult to be alert all the time and to constantly fear the authorities, whose job it was to protect its citizens, instead of pursuing them unto death.

She jerked upright when she heard Cornelia's cackling voice downstairs. Throwing the covers aside, she took to the stairs in joyful bounds. If the police were there, Cornelia would tell them a thing or two about the way the country was being run.

Cornelia was safe and sound, wrapped in her shawls and an extra blanket, sipping some hot tea by the glowing fire, regaling the family with the retelling of her escapades.

"...and I told the officer if he didn't let go of me, I would cast a spell on his cattle so they'd all run into the sea and drown." Adriaen looked amused.

"I'm surprised he didn't drown you then and there. You admitted to being a witch, after all."

"An escaped witch is a very terrible thing, you know. They have twice the power of other witches. He decided not to take the risk."

Anna chuckled. "Cornelia, I don't think you're going to be a very good Anabaptist. They don't believe in the power of witches, so your spells will get you nowhere."

Cornelia glared at Anna. "I can tell you know nothing about Anabaptists. They are not cruel, but serve God only, with love and mercy. There is no need to frighten them with threats of spells."

Anna sobered. It was the truth. As a people, she couldn't fault them for their honesty, charity and love to others. The problem was their refusal to give in to the authorities, yet they also refused to fight for their beliefs, but chose rather to flee, since Jesus said, 'If they persecute you in one city, flee to another.' But if they refused to fight, what made them so dangerous?

Did God want so many of them to die for what they believed to be true? Was it the only way for them to get their point across? To be driven to their deaths by the hundreds? Did there have to be so much bloodshed? How long would this struggle last and how many more lives would it cost?

"Did you hear any news about the sailors they captured today?" Anna asked.

They all turned to look at her. Adriaen gazed at her thoughtfully.

"The inquisitors have been summoned. I hear they will arrive tomorrow," he said.

"Oh no!" Anna protested. "That means they have to escape tonight. Who will help me?" She held out both hands in supplication.

"Anna, I don't think there's anything you can do, except pray to God to be content with His divine will."

"I can do more than that. I am going out there and praying to God that He will show me how to get Jan and the others out of the tower."

Adriaen's eyebrows rose. "You can't be serious." *How could a lone woman free anyone from a guarded prison*, his voice implied.

"Where is your faith in God?" Anna challenged him. "I believe He can do this. I thought the Anabaptists believe that faith can move mountains?"

She headed for the door, grabbing her cloak on her way out and swinging it around her shoulders. She was so tired of adding guilt onto guilt. It was time to do something about it, and she would start by rescuing Jan.

Chapter Nineteen

Harlingen, March 1532

Why am I in peril every hour?... 1 Cor 15:30

"Anna, wait!"

She kept on going. Nobody was going to stop her now.

She didn't want to listen to anyone who'd prevent her from doing what she knew she had to do. Darkness was falling, but she felt no fear. Once again, she was heading recklessly to a prison to rescue someone she cared about. She had no idea how to proceed, and she had no money to bargain with this time. The God of the Anabaptists would show her what to do.

Nearly tripping over her long skirts in her haste, she raced down the road in the direction she thought the Town Hall was located. She hadn't stopped to think about the danger she might be in, alone in the streets in the gathering darkness. Not until she heard running footsteps behind her. She panicked. Where could she go?

Gloomy, sinister-looking buildings rose on either side of her. Their windows, like devilish eyes, caught the last diminishing rays of the sun in a reddish glow. The deep recessed doorways threatened to eject clawing, grasping night villains as she darted by them. She slid and dodged over and around pools of congealed, reeking waste gathered around the gutters in her mad rush to escape...what?

Crouching in a shadowed doorway she listened, her heart thudding, drowning out the sound of her pursuer. Her breath came in sharp, painful gasps. Somebody was rattling at the bolt of the door behind her. Gathering her skirts with both hands, she rushed madly out into the street, bounding heedlessly over gutters. She tripped over a dog dozing in front of a door, and he snapped at her ankles as she caught her balance precariously.

She caught the smell of the sea as she ran, and realized she was unthinkingly heading there once more. The sea beckoned her, as if she belonged there.

Raucous laughter filled the air as she scurried past an inn, where light streamed out of the open doorway, and women laughed shrilly. A furtive figure hurried down a dark alley as soon as he spotted her. At least he didn't come charging towards her, but he must have some reason to be slinking about secretly in the dark. She no longer heard her pursuer, and she slowed down, gasping for air.

Two sailors were weaving down the street ahead of her, carrying a large basket between them.

"Yesh, I agree with you. He ought to be reshcued," one of the sailors giggled drunkenly.

"Can you imagine? Our good brudder converting over to those baptizers." He shook his bushy head, "Even so, sheems right unbrotherly to let 'im rot there."

Anna listened, a plan forming in her mind. Did she dare? She crept closer, unnoticed by them, with her soft leather shoes now padding noiselessly behind the two conspirators.

"Which winder do we throw the rope? Can you throw shtraight, you think?"

"Oh yesh, oh yesh. I got right good aim, always had."

Anna swallowed, then produced a fake cough. They snapped around, swords drawn instantly and pointed at her heart.

"A gurrll..." They dropped their swords sheepishly.

"Dontcha know enough not to creep up on one like so? I mighta thrusht ya through." The whites of his eyes shone blurrily, about the only feature Anna could see in the dark, although she could smell the mixed odor of sweat and sour drink rather too well.

"Are ya losht? The inn's over there." The dark blur of his arm waved in the direction she had come from. Anna lifted her shoulders and straightened her back.

"I don't want the inn. I need someone to rescue my brother from the tower over there." She stared them in the eyes as best she could in the darkness, pointing vaguely in the direction she hoped the prison was located.

They both threw back their huge heads and laughed hysterically, then hiccupped as they bent forwards then backwards in mirth.

"Well, Mishy, you've found the right men for the job. How much ya gonna pay us?"

Anna was taken aback. Of course. She should have thought of that. She hung her head as they laughed some more.

"What? Ye hirin' but ya got no money? That's a shame, ain't it now?" Anna turned on her heel and began running in the opposite direction. What had she been thinking, trying to hire two thugs to help her? She guessed she would never be going back to Father Hendricks again. If she did, she would be doing penance till kingdom come.

A rough hand grabbed her arm, and she yelped. "Not sho fasht, Mishy. Mebbe we can help ya." She shoved her terror out of the way, wanting only to disappear from the sight of the hysterical pair.

"No, no. You're right. I have no money. I can't pay you. Now let go of my arm." She talked as severely as she was able, trying in vain to pull herself free.

"But what about your brudder in prison? You don't want him out?" He shook her arm. "Now tell me, what'd he do? We ain't freein' no murderer nor no robber. Them kind belongs in there till the executioner takes care of dem." He leaned closer, his foul breath overpowering as he spoke into her face.

"No, he is certainly no murderer. What did *your* brother do?" Anna asked defiantly. The two sailors found this question hilarious.

"Why, he started prayin' an the like, cleaned his life up real good-like, ya know? Well, there's some in this town who don't take kindly to sich goin's on." They looked up and down the street cautiously before speaking again. "It's not the magistrates in this city what's the problem, deary. Them big heads in the Court o' Holland gives the orders, and the local gover'ments got to obey or lose their jobs. So they meekly go about catchin' the pious people and get rewarded with a third of their property. Dirty way to make a livin', don't ya say, Mishy?"

She tried to take a step back, but the sailors had blocked her escape.

"How about you help us, Mishy?" She shook her arm, trying to break free, but it was caught in a vise-like grip.

"What can I do? I told you I have no money."

"You distract the constables on the other shide of the tower while we throws up a rope to the winder where our brudder is. There's more good people like him in der, and like as not, they all want out. It will take time."

"Yes, but what about *my* brother? If I do this, I want him out too."

"It's a chance you gots to take, Mishy." He peered closely into her face. "Is he one of them people too?"

Anna nodded, unsure if she really ought to tell them.

"Just as I thought. Murderers don't have pretty gurrlls come lookin' for dem." Pretty girl, indeed. Thank goodness it was dark.

"He's a sickly young man, pale, with red hair. I want your brother to find him and bring him out."

The sailor laughed incredulously.

"Mishy, either he gets out or he don't. There won't be time to get them all out." Anna shrank at the harsh true words. She didn't like it but she'd have to accept it.

"I will do what I can." The sailor nodded.

He turned to his fellow conspirator. "Ya think the guard is shleepy enough by now?"

"Ya, ya. Let'sh get the thing over wish."

Anna wondered what she could do to keep the attention of the guards at the front of the building. The bells began to toll the midnight hour as she trudged around the block, thinking she was about to carry out the unwisest plan she ever had in her life. What would they do to *her* if the plan failed?

And what would Adriaen think if he knew? She wished fervently he would never find out. She was acting in a most unbecoming and unmaidenly way. The chances of obtaining him as a prize after this night were severely diminished. For one, she had dashed out of the house where he had taken her to safety, and instead of being grateful for his care, she had left on a wild impulse to rescue a man from prison—a man's responsibility in a man's world.

Adriaen must be hurt that she hadn't taken his advice of praying to God to be satisfied with His will. There had been numerous miraculous escapes from prison which had been God's will, and she wondered if He would bless this attempt tonight.

Then another thought occurred to her. Maybe Jan didn't want to be free. Maybe he wanted to die and be in Heaven with Jesus rather than live any longer in tribulation in this suffering world. Many of the Anabaptists were overjoyed when they were martyred, and honored that they were found worthy by God to wear the crown of suffering for Him. Anna did not understand why they chose this, yet she knew it was so.

She tried to keep out of sight until she reached the front of the Town Hall. Now what? Should she just scream away as if she was being murdered and hope the guards come running? She would feel unspeakably foolish standing there screaming for no good reason.

When the figure of a man leaped out of the hedge beside her, she no longer needed to pretend. Before he could finish clamping his hand over her mouth, she let out a blood-curdling scream which could be heard all over the city.

"Anna, shhh...It's only me, Adriaen!"

She was no less shocked, though the terror subsided immediately, followed by embarrassment to match.

"Adriaen! What are you doing here?" She rubbed her eyes. "Is it really you?" He released her gently, and whispered, "I guess you could say the Lord led me here to you. Now, may I ask what *you* are doing here?"

"Trying to attract attention. Look, here come the guards!" Two alarmed guards came sprinting around the corner of the building, waving their swords.

"Let's run!" Anna hissed. Adriaen grabbed her right hand, she gathered her voluminous skirts with the left, and they took off. She must have gone miles this night. Her feet were sore and tired. But still she ran. Adriaen led her through some shrubbery and across someone's yard, around the house and a stable where chickens fluttered at the disturbance. The guards came crashing after them, shouting authoritatively.

"Stop! Stop!"

Anna was so tired but Adriaen kept dragging her along. Finally, they stopped running, long after Anna thought she couldn't run another step. They ended up in a small shack beside a river. It smelled like rotten fish and indeed was probably someone's fishing hut. Adriaen must have been here before. It would be a perfect hideaway for Anabaptist meetings.

While Anna sat on the floor of the shack, gasping for breath, and wondered if they had managed to elude the guards. And, more importantly, had Jan escaped?

"Anna, I'm sorry I made you run so hard," Adriaen said. "That was plenty close."

"Are we safe here?"

"I hope so. Anna, I was so worried about you out in the town by yourself at night. I was coming right after you, but you kept getting out of my sight. Didn't you hear me calling you?"

"You called me?" she echoed stupidly. Had those footsteps she had been running away from so desperately belonged to Adriaen? Why would he do that? Because he felt responsible for her? She supposed it was the gentlemanly thing to do, to rescue the damsel in distress.

"I had to rescue Jan," she said. "He is too frail to withstand the rigours of prison."

"You must care for Jan a lot, to run after him in a strange city when it's nearly dark outside," Adriaen said, almost wistfully. Anna wondered if it mattered to him. Would he care if she said she did love Jan?

"I do. I love him like a brother."

"I see." He went and stood in the opening of the door-less shack. He gazed out over the darkly flowing river, listening for any sign that they were being followed.

"I've thought about you a lot this past winter, Anna, and I've missed you." He turned around facing her, although it was too dark to make out his features. Anna stood still, hardly daring to breathe.

"I'm so sorry about the children," she managed. "You must miss them terribly. As soon as possible, I want to go back and find out what happened to them. And little Anneken. I wonder where she is?"

"Anna, please believe me when I say I am not blaming you for them. I know you didn't leave them lightly." He took a step towards her. "If you hadn't run away, you would be in prison, and the outcome for the children would have been the same. You did what made sense. We will try to find Anneken as soon possible. Right now, I would have no safe place to keep her, so I trust God to do what is best for her, and for us all."

We? He had said *we*. It sounded good. Even though he probably hadn't meant it that way.

"I still can't forgive myself that they came to harm because I left."

"You must forgive yourself. God could have prevented it, but He didn't, so it was His will." Adriaen cleared his throat. "How do you feel about the Brethren by now, Anna? Is there any hope that you will ever join us?"

So he was hoping, was he? She was touched that he cared, but how could she explain? There were so many things she didn't understand. For example, how could the Anabaptists justify their disregard of the decrees of the rulers? Did God really want them to lay down their lives without lifting a finger to defend themselves? The only course they took to escape death was hiding and fleeing, but what good could these people do if they were all killed?

"Why do the Anabaptists not obey the government?"

Adriaen screwed up his face, as if in pain. "We do obey the government, unless they want us to go against Scripture. For example, Jesus said, 'Do not swear at all, either by Heaven, for it is the throne of God, or by the earth, for it is His footstool, or by Jerusalem, for it is the city of the great King. And do not swear by your head, for you cannot make one hair black or white. Let what you say be simply Yea, or Nay, anything more than this comes from evil.'"

"So that is why you won't take an oath," Anna said. If this is what the Scriptures said, she wondered why anyone objected.

"Yes, it angers the authorities when we refuse to pledge allegiance to them by using the oath, and they accuse us of disloyalty because of that. Nothing could be further from the truth. They also need soldiers to fight their wars, but we cannot kill anyone. When the rich young ruler came to Jesus, asking what good deed he must do to have eternal life, Jesus told him to keep the commandments, 'You shall not kill, You shall not commit adultery, You shall not steal, You shall not bear false witness, Honor your father and mother, and, You shall love your neighbor as yourself.' So you see, it is impossible for us, as disciples of Christ, to fight in wars."

"Martin Luther and Zwingli go to war."

"That is another reason why we had to split from them. A True Soldier of Christ cannot kill."

"But what about the Turks? Wouldn't they just take over the country if nobody fought them?"

"It would be better to let them kill us than for us to kill them."

“That would be horrible. I think the rulers should keep the heathen out of the country, even if they must use the sword. And it may be wrong to kill their subjects for following the Scriptures, but the state needs to keep law and order somehow, doesn’t it? How can they rule if everyone does what they like? A ruler’s subjects have to pledge allegiance to him, otherwise he won’t know who is loyal and who is against him.”

“The word of the Scriptures comes before the word of man.”

“So you don’t believe the Church follows the Bible? The Pope is only one step lower than Christ, is he not, and then the bishops, the priests, the tradesmen, then the peasants? Isn’t that the way it should be?”

They had wandered outside the hut while they were talking, sitting down on a huge rock, being careful not to touch each other. The moon provided some weak light, enough that Anna could admire Adriaen’s handsome profile silhouetted against the shadowy sky.

“That is not what the Scriptures tell us. All men are born equal, and everyone has an equal chance of eternal life, regardless of their birth. The Pope is not promised Heaven any more than the lowliest beggar. The Pope is only human, after all,” Adraien explained patiently. “We should still give to Caesar what is Caesar’s, as it is written, meaning we are duty bound to pay taxes to the government.”

“Don’t we need the government to protect our country and fight off intruders?”

“The true Christian cannot kill another person.”

“Well then, how will our country stay safe? What if everyone decided to join the Anabaptists? There would be nobody left to fight the wars. Other rulers could invade the country and take it over."

"A Christian's protection is in the Lord God. We should turn our swords into plowshares and conquer with the sword of peace. Love your enemies and do good to those who hate you."

Anna got up. It was so confusing. She yearned for such a faith, yet it seemed impossible to grasp. And life seemed too precious to throw away in such a manner.

"I think we should go back now and see if those drunken sailors managed to rescue anyone." Anna began walking back towards the town.

"Ah, you're thinking of Jan. Pardon me for keeping you so long." He rose stiffly. It had been a long night. "I hope you were not annoyed by my talking."

"Annoyed? No, I'm not annoyed. I need time to think, that's all."

"Don't think too much. Just give your heart to God, repent of your sins through Jesus Christ, and follow Him." If only it were that simple.

"Would you go to another meeting with me?" She remembered the last time she had gone to a meeting with him, when the night had ended with Adriaen becoming a preacher instead of sailing away on a ship. Either way, it put him out of her reach.

"I don't know." Anna took a deep breath. She felt like she was being asked to jump off a cliff. Flying might be exhilarating, but the fall would be painful and final. "I'll have to think about that as well."

Any time spent with him was precious, and if she could prolong it by going to a meeting, it might be worth the risk. She did not want to think of Adriaen disappearing again, with the uncertainty that lay over his life. It would suit her just fine if he never went out of her sight again. She still couldn't believe how miraculously he had found her, when she thought he was languishing in some damp, cold dungeon.

"Are the persecutions very bad here in Harlingen?"

"Actually, no. Not compared to Antwerp or some places in Germany. The council here has been reluctant to do anything about the Brethren; and they would tolerate us if the Court did not interfere and order them to execute us. But then, there are always the scoundrels who think it's easy money to spy on and betray us. In that case, the local magistrates have no choice but to arrest us. The generous rewards the Court offers have tempted many a poor beggar."

They entered through the city gates and all seemed quiet in the town. They headed to the place where Anna had met the sailors, but nobody was in sight. Where would they have taken Jan? She wished she had asked the sailors about it, but then, it was sometimes safer for everyone not to ask too many questions. They tramped the streets of Harlingen for a time, but soon admitted the uselessness of their task, finally deciding to try again in the morning.

Adriaen and Anna returned to his sister's house at cock's crow. They were exhausted and hungry as a baited bear. Susanna greeted them, relief flooding her voice. The lines in her face seemed to have deepened through the night. "Here you are at last! I have been bothering Andrew to go search for you. He got up early to do his barn chores so he could leave afterwards. What have you two been up to?"

"Feed us first, then we'll talk, Sister. We are nearly dropping from hunger."

"Of course! How thoughtless of me." Susanna bustled around her little kitchen and found some food for them. Adriaen and Anna ate leftover stew and bread while they took turns relating their adventure.

"And we still don't know if the sailors were successful. As soon as we've eaten, we must try to find out." Anna said, trying not to gulp her food.

"Not before you've had a good rest. You won't be doing anyone any good if you faint from weariness."

"Nonsense. I never faint, and I'm resting now."

"At least lie down for an hour or so before you go out again," Susanna coaxed.

Just then, Cornelia came scurrying down the stairs, her skirts and shawls trailing after her. "So you two decided to come back after all!" she exclaimed. "I thought you'd been caught for sure. Well, I spent most of the night on my knees, and this proves God answers prayers." She squinted at the two people sitting at the table, and to Anna, the wrinkled old face had never looked more beautiful. If Cornelia declared she had prayed them home safely, Anna believed her.

"We've just been trying to persuade Anna to take a wee nap before she goes searching again, but the dear girl is loath to listen to our advice. What think you?" Susanna said.

"I think both of them ought to lie down, Adriaen too."

Anna doubted she could relax before she found out whether Jan was safe.

"One more hour won't make a difference," Susanna insisted. "Andrew can try to find him after he's done with his chores."

"Well, Anna. Methinks we have no choice," Adriaen said, grinning. "Susanna alone is formidable, and I don't want to tangle with both her and Cornelia." Anna watched him stroll out to the stable for a nap in the hay, then resigned herself and climbed the stairs. The straw tick bed actually felt very good once she laid on it. Despite her worries about Jan, she fell asleep within minutes.

When Anna awoke it was high noon, and the family was just getting ready to eat. She was anxious to get the meal over with and go looking for Jan. Andrew's mission in the morning had brought no results, and Cornelia had not returned. Between the old woman's powerful prayers and her wiliness, Anna had no doubt she was safe, wherever she was. Afterwards, the men wanted Anna to stay home while they went looking for more information. They hinted it would be safer if only the two men went, since the officers would be on the lookout for the escaped prisoners, if in fact they did escape. So with a small stamping of her feet, and a gritting of teeth, Anna acquiesced to the uninvolved woman's place.

Biting her tongue lest she take out her complaints on Susanna, she helped with household duties; gathering the eggs, pressing the cheese, churning the butter and then winding the endless wool, and she chafed at her forced idleness. This was not for her, sitting demurely in the house while others went searching for the answers she sought.

She had to know whether Jan was free. And she needed to know where Hans had gone. And Captain Clement and his crew. She threw down her wool.

"Susanna, I'm going crazy. Would you have some errand for me to do in town?"

Susanna shook her head, smiling ruefully. "You have a hard time sitting still, don't you?" She found a very worn-looking pair of boots in a corner somewhere and handed them to Anna. "You might ask the cobbler if he is able to repair these boots, or if he thinks I ought to buy a new pair."

Anna thought she knew the answer she would give if she were the cobbler, but at least she had an excuse to get out of the house.

Chapter Twenty

Harlingen, March 1532

For by grace you have been saved through faith, and this is not your own doing, it is the gift of God...Eph 2:8

Anna walked briskly down the street, elated to be out and about instead of being tied to a chair all day. She passed through the marketplace, and it brought a sharp pang to her heart. It reminded her too much of Simon, her former employer, who had died in prison, feeble and alone. How she longed to return to those simple, happy days when her biggest concern was whether the bread would rise or whether the butter would clabber, but those days could come no more. Simon and his house were gone.

The marketplace was noisy and crowded, and smelled of fish, freshly butchered pork, onions, and cheese. Shoppers haggled for lower prices and peasant wives whined for more money. The coppersmiths clanged their pots and pans together for attention to their wares; at the goldsmith's booth, a foppishly dressed young man with a tall powdered wig and a flourishing mustache was berating the inferior quality of the golden chains, claiming his bride would scorn such slapdash workmanship.

An escaped pig ran helter-skelter, with two screaming boys racing along behind it, as it jumped over baskets of eggs, overturning one and leaving the other tottering precariously, leaving the farmer's daughter screeching in high indignation, half her day's wages lost. Some withered apples in a battered basket were wilting further in the sun beside a woven, wooden cage where three speckled hens and a bantam rooster pecked disappointedly at the ground underneath.

Anna pushed through the pack, trying to figure out where the cobbler had his stall. She longed to see a familiar face, though the busy marketplace was the last place a fugitive was likely to go. Finally, she found the cobbler, a long, thin man with a straggly gray beard and a dirty, ragged coat, standing in his stall between those of the tinsmith and the cooper. His faded blue eyes watched half a dozen tattered young boys playing an exuberant game on the ground. They all looked the same except for their size. No wonder he looked so tired.

Anna handed him the boots and he looked at them sadly. "I fear I cannot repair them. They have a large hole here," he turned the boot over, "and here the sole has nearly come off." He picked up the other one and repeated the same melancholy story for it.

"Can you make a new pair instead?"

The cobbler brightened perceptibly, and nearly smiled. It must be drudgery to always be looking at old boots, which people wanted him to make new for practically nothing. Anna thought it would make her sad too.

When she was done dealing with him, she left the old boots for the cobbler so he could cut the usable pieces out of them to use as patches on someone else's old boots. She struggled her way out of the milling, sweaty pack of people, determined to find at least one of her lost men. She was standing at the edge of the crowd, trying to decide which way to go, when one of the cobbler's little boys ran up to her, waving a piece of rolled-up old leather, which he thrust into her hands before dashing back through the milling crowd.

She looked at the odd piece in her hands, completely bewildered. She turned it over and unrolled it. A note! Could this be a message from Jan? Or one of the others? Excitedly she read: '*The miller's wife would like to talk to you about an important matter.*'

Anna looked around, mystified. Where and who was the miller's wife? Obviously, a miller's wife would live near a mill. All she had to do was find the mill. A mill was built by a river, so she headed in that direction. Once she reached the river, it wasn't too hard to find the mill. Beside the mill squatted a small, comfortable looking cottage with wild crocuses growing beside the path. Anna walked up to the door and knocked. A pretty young girl took her inside without asking her business. By the fireside an old woman knitted, while carrying on a conversation with someone huddled on the floor covered in blankets.

The red hair gave him away.

"Jan!" she cried, running across the small room, "Is it really you? She kneeled beside him, overjoyed to see his familiar pale face.

He smiled a warm welcome. "It's me. On the floor sleeping as usual." There were dark shadows beneath his still twinkling green eyes. Cornelia would have to fix him some strengthening potions, and the sooner the better. "Are you uninjured?"

"Oh yes. Good as new. Greta and her Grandmother have adopted me, and I've never been so spoiled in my life." He smiled his charming smile at the girl, who blushed prettily. She hovered close by, with her hands clasped at her waist and her blue eyes sparkling with anxiety.

"Are you comfortable, Jan? Would you like some more

broth?" Greta asked.

He shook his head. "It was delicious, Greta. The best I ever ate, but I can't eat any more."

She smiled, dimpling her rosy pink cheeks and her hips swayed as she took his empty bowl away. Clearly, she was a flirt. Jan was licking up the attention like a puppy with a bowl of milk, and Anna found herself inexplicably irritated at the two of them. But why did it even matter to her? She just didn't want Jan throwing himself away on a simpering miller's daughter, that's all.

Anna hadn't had a chance to decline Jan's proposal, and here he was, basking in the devotion of this miller girl. A private conversation with Jan seemed unlikely to happen in this house. She wanted to hear all about his great escape, and she supposed it would be safe to discuss it with these people, seeing that he was here. Yet she'd rather have him to herself. What was the matter with her? Jan did not belong to her and she had no right to make demands on him.

Jan was like a brother to her, she reminded herself. She cared for him like the brother she once had. A sharp pain pierced Anna's heart, as she remembered how she and Heinrich used to run in the sweet meadows, playing tag while they watched the sheep on the hills. Heinrich, a year younger than herself, had always been her playmate as a child, and became her closest friend and confidante as they grew older. And now... Anna didn't want to think about it, but now those days had turned to ashes.

She shook herself. Jan would be such a nice husband for someone, if he managed to hang on to his life. If he was content with a giddy miller's daughter, so be it. He was old enough to decide for himself. Though he had proposed to her, she had yet to find an opportunity to give her answer. Probably Jan had forgotten all about it. If Jan married someone else, she would miss his companionship, but she reminded herself it would be a lot worse for her heart if this were Adriaen falling in love with Greta.

Anna rearranged Jan's blankets and his pillow, wondering if they came off the girl's bed. "How are you feeling?"

"Sleepy." He grinned.

"How did you end up here? And where are the others? Did the sailors get their brother out?" Anna could wait no longer to hear his story, audience or not. Sleepy or not.

Jan sat up, throwing aside his covers. "You women have spoiled me long enough. I have to get my blood flowing again." He winked at Anna. "Yes, the sailors got their brother out. It's surprising they cared enough about him to pull it off. God does work in mysterious ways. They just remembered him lying in prison and decided it had gone on long enough, so they set about freeing him, without further ado. Their brother and his fellow prisoners were awakened by a rock hitting their window, followed by a length of stout rope."

"Were you in that same cell?"

"No, I was in a different part of the prison." Amusement was written on his face. "After the first man had let himself down with a rope, another rock came flying through the window. There was a note attached, with orders that a certain pale-faced redhead was to be rescued without fail. So they had to break me out of my solitary cell."

Anna was touched that the sailors had gone to so much trouble, and she could never thank them enough. In fact, she might never see them again. "How many got out?"

Jan's eyes clouded. "There were five men in the brother's cell, but one of them refused to leave, saying he is old, ready for death and ready to join his Maker." A tear slipped from beneath Jan's red-tinged eyelashes and slid down his colorless cheek. "God bless him. He gave his life for my worthless one. There was no time for another to escape. I was the last one."

He was silent for a minute.

"The guards returned as we were slinking away. They were so close we could hear them talking. What did you do to get their attention?" He looked at Anna curiously.

She blushed. "Why do you ask? I got their attention; isn't that all that matters?"

"It's just that they said there was some lover's quarrel, and the woman screamed like she was insane. Then the man and woman ran away holding hands. This wasn't you, was it?"

Anna's face grew as hot as a blacksmith's tongs. Is that what it had looked like? It was scandalous. She found she could not answer the question honestly. If she were an Anabaptist, she would tell the truth unflinchingly, but it embarrassed her to hear what the guards thought was happening. Lover's quarrel indeed!

"I heard a woman scream, saving me from having to do it." Anna was ashamed of her bare-faced lie, yet there was no way she was going to disclose Adriaen's part in this. She wasn't ready to relate the incident to anyone. She could never do so without revealing how she felt about Adriaen, and it would be unthinkable to relate it to others before she had the smallest hope of winning his heart.

"Where are the others who escaped? Has anyone come looking for them? Are you far enough away? Your red hair is a dead giveaway. I'm afraid you're not safe here." Anna peppered him with questions, anything to distract him from that screaming woman.

"Hold on, hold on! One question at a time." Jan held up

a long white hand. "First of all, I do not know where the others went, but they are far away from Harlingen by now, I believe. The authorities may come searching for me, but they were hot on the trail of the others, so by the time they start searching closer to home, I'll be long gone."

"Oh, I hope they all got away safely!"

"I expect they did. The Brethren know of hideouts where they won't be easily found, Lord willing."

"But where will *you* go? Will you always have to keep running and hiding?" Anna's eyes were full of concern. What an unstable life.

Jan gazed at her gently. "Anna, the Lord will take care of me. I will go wherever He leads me until He finds me worthy to die. Can you not trust God to know what is best for me? If I die, I hope to win the crown of eternal life, so why should I fear death?"

"But Jan, you are not strong enough to go on the rack. I couldn't bear it."

"My strength is in the Lord. He forsakes not the smallest creature, and He will not forsake me, whatever comes."

"But are you not afraid of the pain?"

"Fear not, sayeth the Lord. For though ye walk through the valley of death, thou art not alone. I will never leave thee nor forsake thee," he quoted.

Anna felt the words cover her soul like balm on a wound. The words comforted and soothed. She relaxed her stiff shoulders. Jan was not afraid because he knew the Comforter. Death would not be a horrible thing to him, like it would be to her. Was it possible that death had not been as horrible for her family as she had always imagined? If they had the same sense of peace as Jan did, they would have found comfort in the hope of eternal peace in Heaven instead of fighting their imminent deaths. She longed to have that same comfort and peace in her soul, to trust God to be her Comforter, in any kind of suffering and hardship.

"Jan, if you were being executed by fire, would your comfort in God's presence be sufficient to take away the pain?" Anna asked.

"I have not been tested, but if God grants me faith like the Brethren who have been martyred, singing with joy and anticipation at the stake, I fully believe this is possible. Is there anything troubling you?"

Through all the days huddled in Cornelia's hut, Anna had never trusted herself to talk about her parents and siblings. But now, a torrent of pent-up grief and guilt poured out into Jan's sympathetic ears, cleansing her heart and soul of all the turmoil she had carried for so long.

"Anna, I am so sorry. I did not know you have suffered so much." Jan touched her arm. "You do not need to bear this burden alone any longer. Accept Jesus into your heart. He will be with you always, and never ever forsake thee. And from what you have just told me, I am certain your family believed this too, and clung to Him in their last moments. The short time they may have suffered was worth it, in exchange for a crown in heaven."

Finally, Anna accepted there was no need to torment herself, or dwell on what her loved ones had suffered. God was already taking care of them, so much better than she ever could, and He always had been. Anna had been spared for a reason, and could the reason be that she hadn't been ready to meet her Maker, and thus she was given more time?

Jan watched her, all the love in his heart reflected in the deep green pools of his eyes. Anna's aching soul filled with a love more profound than anything she had ever known.

Not a romantic kind of love, but a heavenly love with a tiny glimpse of a golden eternity. Finally, she could begin to see how the Anabaptists faced cruel deaths with hearts full of joy and a song on their lips. Heaven would be worth it all, and God would never forsake them.

Greta and the old grandmother went quietly about their chores, caught up in the wonder of a soul wavering on the brink of a great new truth.

Anna whispered, "Jan, I need to pray to God for forgiveness for my many sins, but I don't know how. Will you help me?"

"Gladly." He bowed his head and so did Anna. "Dear God, humbly we come before Thee to ask forgiveness for all our sins, and we thank Thee for sending your Son to die on the cross, so that henceforth, we may be washed clean by Thy blood. Amen."

Anna's tears fell unheeded down her cheeks, washing away all the despair, all the worry, and all the fear; the love of God taking it all away and replacing it with a peace and comfort found nowhere else.

Chapter Twenty-One

Harlingen, March 1532

Put on love, which binds everything together in perfect harmony...
Col 3:14

Anna wended her way back to Susanna's house in a trance. She barely noticed when Adriaen left a house she was passing and fell into step beside her. After glancing at her face, he stayed silent, maybe sensing the mantle of deep spirituality surrounding her.

The day was nearly spent, and a fog was rolling in from the water. In the dwindling daylight and the enveloping mist, the rest of the world shrank away into a white veil. No curious eyes could intrude on the pocket of togetherness of the man and woman meandering through it.

When Adriaen reached for her hand, Anna clasped it as naturally as breathing, a further extension of the light of love that had lit her heart. On a lane where the spring grasses whispered, and early crocuses nodded knowingly and secretly, they turned to face each other.

"Anna," Adriaen said. "Your face tells me you have accepted the Truth. You seem more at peace."

Anna nodded, and Adriaen's tender smile reflected her own. Gray eyes met honey-kissed brown, and their gazes locked. He opened his arms, like a rose unfolding, and she floated into them like a dewdrop in a dream. As his lips came down on hers, she responded to his gentle kiss. It was a long time before they remembered where they were.

"Anna," he whispered, the sweet moment obliterating every heartache and every fear she had ever had. Safe. She felt so safe. It must be because she first found her haven and her refuge in God, and Adriaen was the mortal embodiment of her great love and peace. It was all that and more.

Heavenly love and love for this man mingled until they became as one. She could not have one without the other. When his lips sought hers again, it sealed the great longings of a lifetime forever into the past. Anna floated on air the rest of the way home and there he led her to a seat beside the bed of tulips and sat down beside her. His arm went around her, and she revelled in the sensation of being protected and shielded by this man.

"Let's start at the beginning," Adriaen said. "I didn't find Jan or any of the sailors who were captured, and I was getting worried about you. I was standing in front of a house when you suddenly came gliding out of the mist, and I could no longer resist you."

"Really?" Anna blushed. "I found Jan at the miller's house, recovering from his ordeal. He seems to enjoy the company of the miller's daughter, which should help him heal fast." She smiled.

Adriaen gave her shoulders an affectionate squeeze. "So, you're not too jealous?"

"Jan will always be dear to my heart, as a brother. Nothing more." Anna shuffled her feet in the dewy grass. "I had two brothers back in Germany, you see. And a sister."

"Had?" Adriaen said sympathetically. "You must miss them."

Tears welled in Anna's eyes in spite of herself. "I do. My parents, my siblings and a few of the neighbors, seventeen people in all, were burned along with our house."

Adraien pulled her close. "Oh, Anna! That's dreadful!"

"I still have nightmares," she admitted. "And there is something else, which I never could accept until tonight." Adriaen waited patiently as she searched for the words to express what was in her swelling heart and clogging her throat. "They ... were Anabaptists. I ... I had a burning anger in my heart against their beliefs. If they had only gone to the state church, they might still be alive." She ended on a little sob.

"I see. That's certainly understandable." Adriaen leaned towards her, his warm breath brushing her ear as he spoke. "What changed your mind? You did change your mind, didn't you?"

"I was so anxious about them. It was intolerable to think of them being tormented in purgatory because of their misguided faith. They didn't have last rites done by any priest, which I believed was so important. Heinrich had always been my companion, and I couldn't bear the thought of him or the others suffering forever." She paused, basking in the pleasure of Adriaen's body so close. "I could not understand how the Anabaptists could go singing to their deaths. I always pictured my family desperately trying to escape the fiery flames as the house burned, but tonight I realized I must have been mistaken. As Anabaptists, they probably went joyfully to their deaths, eager to meet their Savior."

"And you?" Adriaen asked. "Could you now die in peace with the happy hope of a home in Heaven?"

"I cannot believe I deserve so rich a reward after all my sins and mistakes, yet Jesus died for me so I could be free of sin."

"Exactly. Anna, you cannot know what this means to

me. I have missed you more every day and prayed that you would find peace for your soul." For a time, they needed no conversation as they digested all they had discovered about each other.

Anna broke from her reverie when she heard a rustling in the bushes behind them. She stiffened. Adriaen didn't seem alarmed, and she told herself there must be some wild animal, or perhaps a stray cat, hunting in the night.

"It's getting late," Adriaen said. "I should let you go inside now."

Anna yawned. "I'm tired, yes, but a happy kind of tired."

"I'm glad you're happy. Could it make you even happier to become my wife?"

It was well that Adriaen was holding on to her, or Anna would have fallen off the bench. A proposal? From Adriaen? She had gathered that he might be thinking along those lines eventually, but so soon?

"Are you serious? I mean, are you sure?" Anna felt hot all over as her tongue tangled, and she hoped he wouldn't withdraw the proposal because of her nonsensical questions.

"I am sure, and I am serious." Falling to his knees, he proclaimed his love for her. "Anna, *mijn liefde*. Will you do me the honor of accepting the love of a poor homeless man and share his life? I have nothing to offer you except my heart, which is brimming with love for you that will last from now to eternity." He spoke as tenderly as an angel's whisper.

Anna lived on a dream cloud, floating above the realm of mere mortals. Her eyes searched the mist, catching sight of the dew-covered tulips at her feet. "Adriaen, I accept with all my heart," she finally said, "Nothing could bring me more joy than living the rest of my days with you, as well as in eternity." She sighed in bliss as Adriaen rose and seated himself beside her, a protecting arm encircling her waist as he leaned in for another sweet kiss.

The village clock announced the midnight hour with its measured tone when at last the two of them were able to part. Adriaen opened the door for her, and the soft glow of a lighted candle greeted her. With another long, sweet look Adriaen went back outside to sleep a peaceful slumber in a pile of straw in the stable.

At cock's crow the next morning, the city was already stirring to life as the farmers got up from their straw filled mattresses, climbing into their tattered and mended hose, getting ready to tackle another day. Their raggedy children still snored softly in their shared beds, piled up like puppies with arms and legs entangled.

The craftsmen slept a little longer until they too rolled out of their rope beds, expecting their servants to have built up the fire and their apprentices to be alert and ready for the day's tasks. They all ate their humble but adequate meal after saying their prayers, then arranged their wares enticingly to lure the shopper to his stall.

The bailiffs rested in their four poster beds until their breakfast arrived on trays to their room, then inspecting it for any deficiencies, they condescended to start eating it. Their lackeys suppressed yawns as they laid out fresh linen underclothing, doublets and hose.

By the time the nobles climbed from their featherbeds, the sun had risen halfway up the horizon. Their well-brushed mounts waited in the stables for their saddles as the grooms listened for orders. The stalls had been well mucked out and freshly strewn with straw at break of day, and now idle grooms lounged about prepared at any moment to spring to life whenever one of their superiors appeared.

And in hidden hideaways in narrow alleys the lowlifes of the city had just laid down to snatch a few hours of sleep on a pile of straw and rubbish, their work done for the night, and their consciences keeping them awake no more than a minute.

One of them could be seen to smile in his sleep. Perhaps he dreamed of a better bed in a better place by nightfall. His doublet hung loosely over his bony shoulders and was roughly stitched together in places where it had ripped. The stained hose sagged on his thin legs and were riddled with holes. His leather shoes had fallen on tough times along with the owner, and were tied on with strips of filthy cloth. He snored with his mouth wide open, the yellowed teeth broken or missing. His long, tangled beard was as dirty as the sparse black hair on his head. Two fingers had been chopped off on his right hand, the proof of a convicted thief.

Once, long ago, he had been a husband and father, but after the plague robbed him of all those he loved, despair overtook him and he turned to drink and crime. Now, the secret he had discovered should provide him with enough money to live comfortably once more, for a little while at least. And new clothes. He sighed in his sleep as he dreamt of the pleasure of wearing unworn, untorn clothing. And food. His cracked lips opened and closed in his sleep as he dreamed of eating meat once more.

When the sun reached into the crevice in the wall where he had been sleeping, he knew that now it was time. He couldn't read but that didn't matter. He had previously reaped the benefits of selling secrets, and there was no easier way to make money if one's eyes and ears stayed open. The rewards that were offered were generous and should have kept him in decent style for some time, if he hadn't gambled it away. No danger attended this assignment, and it raised his self-esteem considerably to have Governor Joris smile at him in that brotherly way.

"Good job, Joost. Here's your reward. Now go find me some more. Then you won't have to hang for that murder."

Never mind that he had never murdered anyone. Someone wanted him to hang so they wouldn't have to. Somehow, ten guilders did not last long in the gambling houses. Every time, he meant to use only half of his reward to gamble, and every time it would all disappear. No matter, he was a sly man and soon he would earn more. Yes, it was surprising what one could learn by listening at cracks in the doorways or crouching under windows.

He chuckled. The heretics never found out who betrayed them; the secret would go with him to the grave. It was a good thing, this reward business, using only his ears to earn his keep. Still, he lay in a gutter, unable to rise above the mire of his life. Today it would all change; today he would not go near the gambling house or the tavern. He would order a new suit of clothes, then head to the inn and order every sort of meat in the place. Pheasant, beef, veal, pork, duck, new lamb, goose, all of it.

No more would he exist on the bottom crust of the bread which the gentry threw outside onto the ground for the beggar or the stray dog to scrabble for in the dirt, they hardly cared which. Encouraged by his thoughts he rose stiffly; he was becoming an old man. He shook his shaggy head to clear the fuzz from his brain, then smiling crookedly, he headed for the government office.

Anna had trouble believing that the previous night had really happened. She walked about in a daze, a silly smile on her face, unmistakably in love. Was this how everyone felt after they had been proposed to, or was she just a foolish spinster who didn't know how to act? She suspected the latter. She had never felt so alive, so eager to carry on with her day.

The mist still lingered, bathing the morning sunshine in translucent light. Anna nearly skipped through the green grass, wet with dew, on her way to the garden to gather some of the beautiful red and yellow tulips to brighten the table. Birds chattered and trilled their morning songs, fluttering out of the branches of blossom-laden boughs when Anna appeared.

Absently she picked a handful of the brilliant blooms and tucked them into her apron, holding the blue cotton material in a bunch with one hand. Wet branches of a willow tree brushed her shoulders and dampened the cap confining her curly hair. The clear, fragrant air of a country morning filled Anna's heart with new hope for her life. She stood still, listening to the sounds of the early dawn. A cow mooed nearby, probably coaxing her baby calf closer to her side. The plaintive voice of a milkmaid calling from the hills echoed from afar.

When she heard approaching footsteps, she smiled.

"Good morning," Adriaen emerged from the mist with a radiant smile. "Is this where I have to go to find the love of my life?" It still felt strange to be called the love of someone's life. It seemed too good to be true, in fact. All the accumulated pining for love over the years at last materialized into something real. It was like finding the long lost missing half of a pair of gloves, only much more thrilling. Anna's eyes glowed with pleasure and it turned her plain face into a beautiful one.

With a sudden pang, she wondered what Maeyken would say if she knew. Would she be pleased? Did Adriaen expect Anna to be as loving and docile as Maeyken used to be? Anna didn't think she could manage that. "Adriaen..."

"What's troubling you now, my friend?" He reached for Anna's hand as they walked around the garden.

"I just thought of Maeyken. I'm ... I'm not nearly as perfect as she was, and what if you get tired of me?"

"Tire of you? Never. Maeyken was a wonderful, loving, faithful wife to me, and a part of me will always miss her and love her. But that does not take away one bit of the love I now have for you. Ever since you moved to Amsterdam, I admired you from afar, never thinking you could one day be my wife. Who would have thought of such a possibility then?"

"What will people think if you marry again so soon?"

"If you are uncomfortable with it, I will not insist," Adriaen said. "But I'll tell you what is in my heart, and I know the Brethren would agree. There was a time when such a thing would have been unthinkable. But everything is different now. There is no sense in mourning for a whole year when our lives are so unstable. Life could prove to be very short, and circumstances could place us hundreds of miles apart. As my wife, I have the right to protect you as far as I am able. Besides," he gave her hand a squeeze, "I love you too much to wait six more months to marry you."

The last argument convinced Anna. She didn't need to wait either.

"Nobody could ask for a better friend than you were to Maeyken and me, and I know you have a loyal heart. If you can love me and accept me, though I have nothing to offer except my love and protection, as far as I am able, I will be very much honored."

"Of course, that I can do gladly. There is one more thing," Anna said. "You say I have a loyal heart, when you know I abandoned your children, leading to their deaths. How can you trust me? And your brother, whom I betrayed. I wasn't loyal then, either."

"Anna, stop blaming yourself. Of course, losing them was heartbreaking, and I did struggle, while I tried to accept that God knows best. Yet He was there beside me all the time to comfort me. You had little choice with what you did, and I would trust you with my life." He pressed her hand reassuringly, and smiled. "Now, would you be up to discussing our wedding?" Adriaen asked, his eyes sparkling like a gold coin in the sunlight.

Anna blushed. Yes, the wedding. She would be more than happy to discuss it.

"Come, let us sit in the garden again." He took her free hand and led her to the seat they'd sat on the night before. The tulips swayed gently, their red and yellow buds beckoning them.

"You look radiant this morning, Anna. Being in love suits you, and the peace you have found has made you more beautiful than ever."

Anna waved away his compliments, but she did feel like a new and happier person, as if everything had fallen into place, and a great mystery solved. She still had many questions, but it was wonderful to think that her spinster days were over. Love filled her soul, and it was a relief that she'd never have to confess on her knees to Father Hendricks again, then do whatever penance he decided on. Holding God's hand, she would follow wherever He led, whether in joy and peace, or in suffering.

"I do feel the peace in my soul," she replied. "There's

still much I do not understand, but I do desire to live by the Scriptures."

"That is well." He paused, rubbing his chin with his hand. "Do you desire baptism?"

Anna took a deep breath. "I do, though I feel unworthy."

"Would you care to come with me to a meeting tonight, and be baptized if the Lord so leads you?"

Of course. As a preacher he would desire a wife who was also of the faith and must have been waiting for her to find her peace before he was able to propose.

"If the Lord so leads me, I am willing."

"I know you have been around us long enough that you realize the danger we are in constantly from the government and those who would betray us."

Anna knew it very well, and it was beyond her to know how anyone's heart could be cruel enough to betray someone, knowing what suffering they would have to endure. Especially when they knew the person to be honest, having committed no crime except wishing to worship God in their own way. She was not treading lightly into this future.

"I am ready to place my life in God's hands, come what may. It will help knowing you are there to be my protector."

"But that is just the thing, Anna! I will do my utmost to protect you, but I may not always be able to be at your side. In fact, I feel selfish in asking you to marry me. It may be a very unsettled, dangerous life and I would not force you into it."

"Oh, Adriaen, do not speak so! It is my heart's desire, believe me. I know what your life is like, but I will try to appreciate, and thank God, for whatever time we have."

"Bless you. The other thing is, who will marry us? We will have to find out where one of the bishops is, and go to him.

Only a few of them are willing to take it upon themselves to hold a wedding service. There can be no fancy wedding, only a simple ceremony as we are pronounced man and wife. In our eyes and in God's eyes it will be a true marriage. The magistrates do not recognize it as such and will deny it. If we have children, they cannot inherit." He smiled ruefully. "Not that there is anything to inherit at this time."

Anna stared at him, her eyes round in shock. "Not a true marriage?" She felt like a gasping fish, her mouth open and round and sucking air. "Do the Anabaptists keep marrying, knowing this?"

"Yes, Anna, all the time. In God's eyes, it is a true marriage, even though the government doesn't think so."

Anna stared at the tulips that she still held in her apron. She did not fancy the idea of not being legally married. It seemed there was always something new to learn with this group. Wouldn't it be a sin? She wanted to be properly married or not at all.

Adriaen reached over and selected a red tulip from her bunched-up apron and held it up. "Look at this tulip. We all know it is a tulip, isn't that so?" Anna nodded. "Will it stop being a tulip if someone calls it a rose? No. In the same way, we know that calling our marriages illegal does not make them so in God's eyes."

"I understand what you mean. But they sure make it difficult in every way they can." It did not change her love for Adriaen, but it was a foreshadowing of what it would mean to join the Anabaptists. With that cup of water poured on her head, every freedom and every right would be snatched away. As an unbaptized woman who had up until recently attended the Catholic church, she was not in half the danger she would be as a baptized woman who attended Anabaptist meetings and was married to an Anabaptist preacher. They would not join her name with Adriaen's in the big black record book in the cathedral and write their children's names underneath. To them she would be living in sin and her children illegitimate. It was a difficult thing to swallow.

Adriaen studied her face; he was not going to brush over the reality of what their life would be like after they married. I know it will be hard, and I release you if you decide this life is not for you."

"There is much to consider, that is true." Finally, her dream of becoming Adriaen's wife was becoming real. It was just not like she'd pictured it. Nothing was the same anymore since the upheaval began in Europe. It was not possible to settle down anywhere and live in peace with an Anabaptist preacher for a husband. Anna reminded herself of all the difficulties, but her heart refused to listen.

"Whatever happens, I will do my best to accept as God's will. If you or I or both of us must sacrifice this life, we will meet again in Heaven, is that not so?"

Adriaen's eyes shone with tender feeling, and softly he replied, "Thank God, you do understand. I love you, and it would break my heart to part from you, but it's only fair that we discuss these things." He took her hand and caressed it gently. Shivers of pleasure tingled her spine when his lips descended on hers, and moments fled by, unnoticed by either of them.

Chapter Twenty-Two

Harlingen, March 1532

That each one know how to take a wife for himself in holiness and honor…1 Thess 4:

The next morning, they set out at daybreak to make inquiries.

"Do you know where to find one of the Brethren who can marry us?" Anna asked. They were strolling along a cobbled street still damp with dew. Susanna had been excited, though a little concerned when she heard about their plans to marry.

"I'm happy for you both and I will pray every day that God keeps you safe," she had said.

Cornelia had beamed happily and wished them a long and fruitful life.

"God will be with us wherever we go." Adriaen had reminded them.

Anna and Adriaen walked several blocks before they saw anyone else about. A couple of early farmers trundled along with their tired old mules, pulling awkward wooden carts laden with piles of onions, live chickens, whole butchered piglets, woven baskets of eggs and other farm goods. Bits of straw and dirt sprinkled the road behind them, and a whiff of animal waste hung in the still air after they had passed by.

The morning was bright, but rather cool, and the odors of the gutters and the rotting rubbish heaps were not too bothersome at the moment, though when the sun shone hot later, the stench would become overwhelming.

They passed the cobbler's shop, where the cobbler was busily arranging his new pairs of leather shoes in an enticing way. The happy couple smiled and nodded at his long, mournful face, and he waved back languidly. Anna was still curious how he had known about Jan, and how he knew her. But these days it was better not to ask these things.

Down the street of the printers they strolled, where a jangle and clatter resounded from within the shops. Here were printed all manner of pamphlets, tracts and mandates, important papers that changed men's opinions or strengthened them. Through the open doors, Anna spotted apprentices bent over their letters in deep concentration. A mistake could mean a severe tongue lashing — or worse.

With pleasure, Anna sniffed the sea in the breeze, while it teased the escaped strands of her hair, and caressed her cheeks. The couple passed the docks and continued down the street of the weavers where the looms were busily whirring, and slowly the threads of red, yellow, brown and blue were being woven into rich tapestries depicting scenes of pagan gods and goddesses or men and women of the Bible.

Anna thought she could walk forever this way, taking in all the scenes of the city with Adriaen for a companion. Yet in the back of her mind, there was the constant, niggling fear of being discovered by the wrong person. She looked away nervously whenever anyone gave them more than a passing look. Friend or foe? They all looked the same on the outside.

Adriaen pointed out to her all the old architecture of the city. The grand home of Count Enno featured a long stone walkway, leading up to the massive double oak doors, which was bordered by greenery and colorful flowers of every kind. There was a pond with a bench invitingly set out beside it beneath a spreading chestnut tree. Swans swam majestically, fluffing their pure white feathers and ducking occasionally beneath the surface of the water to catch their breakfast.

To Anna's surprise, Adriaen led the way behind the stately mansion to the stables. He grinned, enjoying her astonishment.

"One of the grooms is the son of a preacher. Count Enno is sympathetic to the Brethren and turns a blind eye to their doings." Anna followed Adriaen inside the stable, and a sturdy fair-haired boy sauntered towards them.

"What can I do for you today?" The lad's blue eye twinkled with a hint of mischief. "You found yourself a woman?"

Anna blushed.

"This is my fiancée, Anna. Where's the preacher?"

The groom's eyes grew round as silver coins. He stared at Anna with new respect. Probably he thought Adriaen could have found himself a more beautiful wife. Anna didn't care about that anymore. She only cared about Adriaen's love, and if he was satisfied with her appearance, why would she complain? God had brought them together, and now they needed only the blessing of a preacher to make it real, if not legal according to the law.

"So, may we all come to the wedding?"

"You know we're not allowed to have crowds. I would love to have everyone come, but I fear we must keep it down to twenty people and hope to attract no attention."

The groom's face fell. "I know. A wedding should be an occasion for all of us to gather, like it used to be." He shrugged. "I wish you happiness, Preacher."

"Is Melchior in town?"

"I believe he is." He looked around, checking who else was within earshot before replying. "He got to bed late last night because he led a meeting, you see. He's catching up on sleep at Widow Jennken's house."

Adriaen thanked him and they headed down the street once more.

The delicious smell of freshly baked bread wafted from the bakery shop and Adriaen searched the leather purse at his waist for a loose coin or two. Coming up with a few farthings, they entered the shop and Anna looked around hungrily.

Adriaen handed her a crusty loaf of dark brown bread, still warm from the oven. She carried it outside, where they found a seat under a willow tree to eat it, washed it down with ale from Adriaen's pack. Though simple, it was the best meal she had ever eaten. Afterwards, they relaxed, sitting side by side, their heads resting against the tree trunk. Anna could have been content this way all day, but they had other things to see to.

They found the preacher, Melchior Hoffman, in a stuffy attic room sitting at an old paper-strewn desk reading his Bible. Widow Jennken had pointed them up the steep stairway and went back to her kitchen.

"Come on up and have a seat," Melchior greeted Anna and Adriaen. "I was just hankering for some company, and here you are." He pointed to a couple of wooden chairs. "What can I do for you?" He shifted a pile of papers to one side of his desk, then clasped his freckled hands on the desk in front of him. His large, dark eyes were intent, and the rest of his face was partly hidden by his forked beard.

Adriaen shifted on the hard chair and cleared his throat, a little nervous now that he had to announce his errand. Anna gazed demurely at the rough wooden floor, feeling flushed.

"We have come to ask you to marry us."

Melchior cleared his throat, and straightened the stiffly-starched, white ruff around his neck. "That's what I thought." He grew serious and peered intently into Anna's face, as if trying to gauge whether she was prepared for this step. "You do realize that it will be impossible for you to settle down in one place? That you will be constantly on the move, following your husband wherever the Lord leads him, without in any way trying to prevent him from entering places where he will be in danger as he spreads the word of the Gospel?"

"I do." Anna said. The seriousness of the situation registered in her mind--still, she knew she wanted Adriaen as a husband. But she couldn't deny that she dreaded the life they would have to lead, never knowing from one day to the next whether it would be their last on this earth.

"Also, there may be times when you will need to stay somewhere without him, for lengthy periods of time. While I have no doubt that he loves you dearly, yet his first obedience is to God. Do you understand?"

Anna took a deep breath. "Yes. I am aware of the risks, but I am willing to go where he goes or stay by myself if the need arises. I know our time could be short, but if it is only one hour, I shall feel myself blessed."

It was the truth. She did not want to let him go now that the Lord had brought them this far. She believed that God meant for them to be together, and she didn't appreciate everyone's efforts to show her the dangers of being married to Adriaen. She had mulled it over enough on her own.

"Have you been baptized?"

So many questions! "No, not yet, but it is my desire to do so at the next meeting of the Brethren, as the Lord leads me."

"*Gut, gut.* I would not like to yoke Adriaen, or any of the Brethren, to an unbeliever."

"I do believe, but there are many things I do not know or comprehend."

"That is understandable." He turned to Adriaen. "You will take the time to instruct her before your marriage, so that if she is ever questioned, she is able to give a good witness?"

"Absolutely." Adriaen turned to gaze deeply into her eyes, as if trying to see into her very soul and the condition it was in. She felt as if she was lacking something vital which she hoped would be fulfilled by the baptism. Or marriage to Adriaen.

"When did you want to have the wedding? I am thinking of staying here in the city for another week, Lord willing, if you want it before then. After that I will be travelling again, and it's unpredictable where I will be." He looked at Adriaen, then at Anna.

One week! In one week, she might be a married woman. Unbelievable.

And a baptized one. She sobered. She prayed that she and Adriaen would have enough time together for him to instruct her in the Scriptures. The last thing she wanted to do was betray anyone ever again, yet she feared what the authorities might do to her to drag names out of her unwilling lips. She sighed. Here she was trying to do things on her own again. When would she learn to trust God?

The days when she could go to Father Hendricks to have her petty sins forgiven seemed very far away and in the past. It had been an easy way out, but now she knew that there could be no middleman between her and God. She needed to go directly to God for forgiveness and believe that Christ died for her sins on the cross.

It seemed like a lifetime ago when she had watched Maeyken die, then gave away her baby. Where were they now; Elizabeth, Claes, their baby boy, and Little Anneken? And the other children?

Would peace ever come to the world? The kings and lords of the land were constantly in conflict, causing huge loss of life to their subjects, and grief and sorrow to the families of the slain. Couldn't there be a better way to make peace? Like discussions, agreements and just planning to get along? She supposed this was only the view of a weak and silly woman. The men of the world knew better how things should be run.

If it were up to women, Anna thought, very little blood would flow. Or if it were up to men like Adriaen and Melchior, there would be no bloodshed either. In fact, the men of the Brethren would rather die than use weapons on any human being, even in self-defense, and many had already paid with their lives for sticking to this view.

The kings and emperors could not tolerate this belief. They could not have the whole country's men turning to pacifism to escape their duties to their rulers by refusing to go to war. For them, war was a part of life, and men had to fight. It was their duty as subjects.

Adriaen beamed at her, his eyes filled with love. "Are you ready to be married within a week?"

"I am ready to be married whenever you are," she replied simply, her gray eyes shining back in adoration.

Melchior nodded. "We can plan on having the wedding on Thursday, six days from now, if that suits you."

Anna couldn't believe her dreams were coming true at last, that finally she was on the way to becoming a married woman, Adriaen's wife. Before she went to sleep that night, she sent a heartfelt prayer of gratitude to God, without once thinking of, or asking the intercession of the saints.

Chapter Twenty-Three

Harlingen, March 1532

One Lord, one faith, one baptism, one God and Father of us all, who is above all, and through all, and in all... Eph 4:5

Anna and Adriaen invited a small group of friends to their wedding on the way home. They went from house to house, inviting the baker who smilingly offered to bring fresh loaves of his best bread, the tall cobbler who cracked a small smile and offered to bring a pair of new leather shoes for the bride. The miller laughed jovially, telling Adriaen it was high time there was a wedding in these parts. Everyone they met with their news offered something.

The weaver handed her a piece of fine blue wool to make a new dress, and the seamstress hired an extra girl to finish it on time. It was a beautiful sky-blue material, and the dress was fashioned modestly, as befit an aspiring Anabaptist bride. The skirt draped gracefully over her hips, trailing nearly to the floor. Long loose sleeves ended in a simple cuff and the bodice laced up modestly up to the throat. A soft blue silk apron covered it smoothly, and a new headdress completed her outfit. Anna felt like a queen, yet humbled by everyone's generosity.

Social gatherings were nearly non-existent in these troublesome times for the Anabaptists, and even a wedding would have to be somewhat disguised. Anna was warmly surrounded by welcomes from the women who took her under their wing and give her all the advice they could muster about being a married woman. Anna blushed and thanked them, appreciating this generous sisterhood.

Wedding preparations began at Susanna's house and Anna was swept into a haze of cooking, frantic cleaning and gardening and churning and moving of furniture. She hadn't realized there would be such a to-do, just for her benefit, and she moved through it with her head in the clouds and her feet barely touching the floor. She felt bad not to contribute, but she was not allowed to speak of it. The good ladies were all overjoyed to be involved in a wedding and laughed and joked as they worked.

Their loving togetherness and busy industry was certainly inspiring. Even the stable boy had a spring in his step these days and mucked the horse stalls with extra care, and cleaned out long neglected corners.

The weather cooperated as well, and the days sparkled by. Adriaen dropped in nearly every day to say *goede dag*, then hurried back to his job at the goldsmith's, earning as much as he could, so they could eat after they married.

One evening three days before the wedding, Adriaen came by, his gray doublet and hose freshly washed and ironed, and his face gleaming with unbridled joy.

"Ready to go to meeting tonight?"

Anna fingered her apron and tucked some stray curls behind her ears. She was ready and yet not ready. How could one become ready to join a persecuted people? She knew she must trust God in this, and with Adriaen to guide her she hoped to become worthy of these people, and of God's grace.

They walked side by side, close but not touching. The meeting would be held in an Anabaptist house, half an hour's walk away. The sunset was beautiful, with the flat horizon streaked in fiery flames of red and orange. Few people were on the street this late in the day, and outwardly the town appeared to be quiet. They could only hope that nobody was suspicious and follow them to the meeting. A young couple on an evening stroll should be no cause for suspicion, after all.

"Tell me about Melchior Hoffman," Anna said. "Has he always lived here?"

"No, he was born in Germany, and used to be a furrier. He became interested in the mystics, and thoroughly read the Bible and Luther's writings. His furrier business took him to Livland, where he ended up preaching for the Protestants, until he was imprisoned and expelled. He went to Dorpat and preached against images, and you know what happened after that."

Anna nodded. "Oh, is that when mobs of people destroyed all the images and idols in the churches?"

"Yes, but Hoffman never intended for this to happen, nor did he help with the destruction. The church authorities were going to arrest him, but were prevented by the populace."

"That means many people must have supported him. When did he come here?"

"Several years ago, in May 1530, he came to Harlingen for the first time as an Anabaptist evangelist, and found the soil well prepared for his message by the Reformers. He was even allowed to use the Grosse Kirche, and was able to baptize around 300 people right in the church. He baptized both burgher and peasant, lord and servant. Count Enno—remember, we talked to his stable boy—was moved to tears by Hoffman's message."

"So he had support from the nobles. I guess that's why he was so successful."

"Yes. Unfortunately, he left without leaving an able leader behind. Later, Jan Trypmaker led the congregation, before he went to Amsterdam."

"Trypmaker? The man whose head was displayed on a pole in Amsterdam?" Anna shuddered.

"Yes. Well, here we are at our destination." They entered a tall, narrow house with stepped gables, and were taken to a large back room, already crowded with people talking quietly. Melchior Hoffman was there, surrounded by a cluster of men talking earnestly. Adriaen joined them and Anna walked over to a group of young women, who happily pulled her into their circle.

"We are so envious of your husband-to-be, Anna. We've all tried to reel him in, but he just wasn't interested. He was waiting on you I guess." A lively-looking girl grinned at her, smoothing black hair done up in braids around her head. Anna looked at the floor, suddenly shy. Of course, Adriaen would have had other caps set for him. It was a wonder he hadn't succumbed to the wiles of one of these charming girls, so much prettier than she.

The meeting began, with the women sitting on benches on one side of the room, and the men on the other. Anna shifted nervously. Would tonight really be the night she let herself be baptized? She desired it, yet also felt the heavy responsibility of joining with these Brethren. She hoped she'd never be caught or put to the test of standing up for her faith. Anna shivered. Only by hanging on to God's hand could she hope to become a True Soldier of Christ.

Adriaen sat beside Melchior at the front of the room, and when everyone had grown respectfully quiet and still, Adriaen stood, holding an open Bible in his hands. While her beloved read in his deep, reverent voice, Anna found it easy to let the words flow into her soul, soothing and healing.

When the chapter was finished, Melchior Hoffman stood and praised the Lord that everyone was able to gather here tonight. He stressed the importance of living peacefully, in obedience to the government as far as their consciences allowed.

"And prepare yourselves, for the Kingdom of God is at hand," he said, with a zealous light in his eyes. "Christ will be returning soon, and He has sent me as His prophet to testify to the people, and stir them to repentance. It is not enough to be justified by faith. We must be sanctified, and live our lives in the imitation of Christ." The gathered believers listened intently, and leaned forward to absorb every word. Anna shifted on the hard, wooden bench.

"Baptism," he continued, looking straight at Anna, "should be the symbol of the covenant with God and the Lord Jesus Christ, administered only to adults who can understand the Lord's teaching." After continuing with his sermon for an hour, Melchior offered a prayer, then everyone joined in singing a long, slow hymn with praise sent heavenwards, and asked for strength from above. Anna was caught up in the spell of love in the little room, which seemed thick enough to hold with the hands. Here, one was safe in the love of Jesus and He seemed very near. She could almost believe that angels were present.

When Melchior asked anyone desiring baptism to come forward, Anna found herself rising, seemingly not of her own volition. Two young men, aged about eighteen, also followed her to the front, and they all kneeled before Melchior Hoffman. Anna was reassured by the quiet presence of Adriaen nearby, while the three of them were asked some questions.

"Do you repent of your sins and desire to amend your

life?" Melchior asked the three of them. They all said '*Ja*'. "Do you believe truly that your sins have been taken away by Christ, and from everyone who walks in the resurrection of Jesus Christ, and do you wish to be buried with Him in death, so that you may be resurrected with Him?" Again, they answered '*Ja*'. Dipping one hand into a dipper of water held by Adriaen, Hoffman cupped some water in his hand and sprinkled it on the first young man's head, then placed both hands on the man's head, saying, "Upon confession of your faith, I baptize you in the name of the Father, of the the Son, and of the Holy Spirit. Amen." He repeated the procedure with the other man, then it was Anna's turn. She had never felt so calm in her life, nor so close to Jesus Christ. One of the women came forward and removed Anna's cap from her bowed head. Cool water dripped onto her hair and trickled down her forehead. Gentle hands were placed on her head as Melchior repeated the blessing.

Next, Hoffman offered his hand to the first young man, saying, "In the name of the *Gemeente*, I offer you my hand," and here the young man took the proffered hand and rose to his feet, standing before the preacher with his head bowed, "*Stel jezelf in op nieuw begin*, and you are welcomed as a brother in the *Gemeente.*" Melchior kissed the young man with the Holy Kiss of peace.

In the meantime, the woman holding Anna's cap replaced it on her head, smoothing back the stray curls. When Anna's turn came to rise, the same words were used, except she was welcomed as a sister to the *Gemeente*, and the woman gave her the Holy Kiss. Anna's doubts were washed away with the water sprinkled on her head, athough Melchior had admonished that all the waters of the sea could not wash away their sins. Only the blood of Jesus and a renewal of one's life could do that.

On their homeward way, Adriaen held Anna's hand tenderly, his strength passing from his heart to hers. No words were needed to express their closeness to each other and to Christ.

When they were almost home, Adriaen spoke softly, "Anna, this night is more special than you can ever know. My cup of blessings is running over." He squeezed her hand. "Have I told you how much I love you? Never forget that, no matter what happens."

A small shiver of apprehension shook her body. She didn't want to think about anything happening. She wanted to keep this moment forever in her heart without the foreshadowing of a tragedy that would tear them apart. She didn't want to think about the ever-present danger they were in. For now, she wanted to pretend that their happiness would last forever, that there was no persecution just around the corner.

"Yes, Adriaen, you have." Anna smiled, "but you may tell me again, even though I won't forget. I love you, too, with all my heart and have for a long time."

She wished she could walk on forever in this star-sprinkled world with Adriaen. Tonight, she refused to think about anything except the pleasure she felt in his company. Not for a moment did she doubt he would do all in his power to make her life happy and safe. She trusted him as much as it was possible for one human being to trust another, and she wouldn't think about the things over which he had no power. What mattered was that he loved her, and she loved him, and they both loved God.

Every evening, for the remaining days leading up to the wedding, Adriaen would come to see Anna after his day's work was done, and the two of them would sit on the bench in the garden, while Adriaen instructed her further in the Anabaptist doctrine. This was not only for the purpose of her own salvation, but so that in the event of her being arrested, she could hold her own against the inquisitors, and answer each question as befitted a True Soldier of Christ. The inquisitors were notorious for trying every obscure argument under the sun to trick their victims into denying their faith.

"Usually, you would have this instruction before baptism," Adriaen began, "but because Hoffman is leaving soon, and because he trusts me as a *Diener am Wort*, he has gone ahead with your baptism, believing that you do repent of your sins, and wish to have a new life in Jesus." Adriaen brought forth a small tract written in German, and showed Anna the title: '*Bruderlich vereinigung etlicher Kinder Gottes/ Sieben artickel betreffend*'.

"This Confession of Faith was drawn up in Schleitheim, Germany by Michael Sattler and others," Adriaen continued, "attempting to unite the scattered brethren, for guidance in our faith, and to give a cohesive message to the government. So, the first of these seven Articles is about baptism, how it is the seal of the covenant made with Jesus Christ, that you will henceforth take up your cross and follow Him. You will shed the old man and put on the new, and be dead to sin."

Anna truly wanted this, but what if she failed? No more could she hide her shame by asking the saints to pray to God for her, she would have to face the Lord herself when she sinned.

"The second Article is about excommunication. Those who have twice been admonished by their brothers for their sins, and repent not, will on the third occasion be excommunicated because of their sinful life. Anna," Adriaen said, looking at her, "I hope neither of us will ever need to be reminded more than once."

"I don't want to think about it," Anna said. Excommunication was about the worst thing that could happen, since it would mean one had denied Jesus, and was unrepentant. The Catholics also practiced excommunication, and even kings could face this chastisement, so this concept was not new to Anna.

"The third Article speaks of communion with Christ. Only those who have been united by Christian baptism and separation from sin, may be admitted to the Lord's table for communion. Jesus Christ asked us to hold communion with like-minded brethren, as a remembrance of His dying on the cross for our sins. The bread is a *symbol*, not the actual body of Christ, and the wine is a *symbol* of his blood.

"The fourth Article tells us to separate ourselves from the world, for the child of God is called upon to withdraw from every institution and person which is not truly Christian, or is not a True Soldier of Christ, we might say.

"The fifth Article concerns shepherds, or pastors, of the flock of Jesus Christ. Their duties are to read, admonish, teach, warn, discipline, excommunicate, to lead in prayer, to administer the Lord's supper, and undertake the general oversight of the congregation. You may think that because you are a woman, this does not concern you, but your part in this is to support your husband if he is ordained as a shepherd of a flock, and be not a stumbling block to him."

"Oh, Adriaen, I don't want to be a stumbling block to you, though I have been a stumbling block for you and your brother."

"Don't be so worried," Adriaen assured her, "You are forgiven. Just hold on to the hand of Jesus, and you will be fine. Now, the sixth Article deals with taking up the sword. In other words, using a weapon with the intention of killing someone, even in war. The child of God is to follow the law of love as taught by the New Testament, and leave the sword to the officers of the state as ordained by God. Article seven forbids the Christian from swearing of the oath, since it is forbidden by the express commands of Scripture. That's it. Now, all you need to do, is say with '*Ja*' that you agree with these Articles, for you to be a true Sister in Christ."

"*Ja*," Anna said in a quiet and subdued voice. *This is no child's play*, she thought. *This is serious.*

Chapter Twenty-Four

Harlingen, April 1532

But God had mercy... lest I should have sorrow upon sorrow...
Philippians 2:27

The day of the wedding dawned in a glow of orange sun, fluffy clouds and an air of anticipation. Soon after cock's crow people began arriving in pairs or individually, dressed in their best finery. Cornelia was warmly greeted and adored by everyone, as she sat in the best chair and cackled happily at each new arrival. She soon recovered from her initial disappointment that Anna wasn't marrying Jan, and had joined in wholeheartedly with the flurry of wedding preparations.

Anna's only wish was that they could have invited all Adriaen's friends. It wasn't safe, although she had a feeling that come darkness, more merrymakers might join them. But Jan was there with the miller's daughter, and Captain Clemens had been found in an Anabaptist home and accepted the invitation.

Jan looked well, and Greta looked even better. Anna greeted the two of them with genuine pleasure. "I'm so glad you were able to come!"

"So am I," Jan said, grinning. "I wouldn't miss your wedding for anything." Anna was relieved that no awkwardness remained between them because of his one-time proposal. It was as if it had never been. She still needed Jan as a friend.

Susanna hurried about the house, checking the roast pig

someone had selflessly provided, as well as some chickens and geese. The fresh loaves of the baker's bread sat invitingly on the windowsill, and a bowl of well-polished apples gleamed beside it. The cellar held well-mellowed sweating barrels of red wine and ale, and great rounds of golden cheese filled the shelves.

The guests greeted each other with handshakes and 'peace-be-with-you's' then wandered about with shining eyes beholding all the treats in store. Not to be missed was Susanna's bountiful garden, brimming with red and yellow tulips, yellow jonquils and emerging vegetables.

In front of the stable, men were standing, relaxed and chatting, now serious, then a minute later bursting out in laughter. The stable boys, having done their chores before daylight, appeared with freshly scrubbed faces and clean clothes, clearly looking forward to a day off. Melchior Hoffman arrived, with his ruff newly pressed and large beard neatly combed. He looked around with large, solemn eyes, and people put on their best behavior.

The service began shortly after, and for Anna, it passed by in a dream. A year ago, she had just arrived in the Netherlands—alone, broken with grief, and angry at God. She had soon found employment with Simon den Kramer, and met Maeyken and Adriaen, who had welcomed her openheartedly. The little family had helped to lessen her sorrow, and now, after unimaginable and tragic circumstances, they had also given her new faith, new hope, new peace, and a husband. Although much had been lost, and the bittersweet memories would always dwell in her heart, Anna had much to be thankful for, and on this special day, she thanked God for all her blessings.

The guests assembled in Susanna's spare room, the men,

as usual, sitting on one side of the room and the women on the other. Adriaen and Anna sat together at the front of the room, opposite Melchior Hoffman and a few other *Diener am Wort.* Adriaen handed his wide-brimmed black hat to an attendant, and smoothed the fringe of his brown, chin-length hair with a wide hand. Anna admired him in an impeccable black frock coat and trousers, worn over a snowy white shirt with a starched collar. His brown leather boots had been polished to a fine sheen. She swallowed. He was a handsome bridegroom, indeed.

After opening the ceremony, Melchior read the seventh chapter of Corinthians, then retold the story of Abraham and Sarah from the Old Testament, as well as that of Isaac and Rebecca, and Jacob and Rachel. Finally, it was time for Adriaen and Anna to exchange their vows. Standing side by side with bowed heads, they answered 'Ja' to the questions Melchior asked; about believing in the one True God; acknowledging each other as a baptized member of the *Gemeente*--being free of any other man or woman which would affect their union; promising to live in love, peace, and harmony; and not to forsake each other for as long as God granted them life.

Then, the bridal couple was asked to hold each other's right hand, and Melchior prayed, "May the God of Abraham, the God of Isaac, and the God of Jacob, bless this union. May you bring forth fruit of the spirit, fear God, and keep His Commandments. Amen."

When they resumed their seats, there were few dry eyes in the room. Adriaen and Anna were now husband and wife before God, if not legally. After a few more words of admonishment, everyone knelt to pray, and a hymn was sung. After a closing prayer, the ceremony was over. Anna could hardly believe this was happening to her. She had gone from being a devout Catholic only a year ago, to joining the Anabaptists, to marrying an Anabaptist preacher. What was next?

Board tables were set up in the kitchen and the wedding feast was spread. Everyone was seated around the tables on benches and chairs. Adriaen and Anna sat together at the head of the table, and Anna couldn't believe the abundance of delicacies the guests had provided. With a twinge, Anna remembered that the Catholic world would be observing Lent right now, and therefore were not allowed to eat meat. At first, it seemed strange to Anna to just eat away, even though it was her wedding. Adriaen had assured her that the New Testament did not require fasting, and it was written, 'Therefore let no one pass judgment on you in questions of food and drink or with regard to a festival or a new moon or a sabbath.'

The Dutch did love to eat well. Besides the stuffed roast pig, the ducks, and the geese, there were dishes of herring and onions, platters heaped with vegetables, a variety of cheeses, butter molded into hearts and flower shapes, braided breads, crunchy and sweet *krakelingen*, the flat *poffertjes*, and fruity *vlaaien*, all special foods reserved only for weddings. Sweet red wine was served with the meal, a treat for everyone.

Adriaen encouraged Anna to taste everything, and by the time the meal was over, she felt as stuffed as the pig. The women cleaned up together afterwards, except they wouldn't allow Anna to help. They sent her outside to the garden with Cornelia, where the apple trees were budding, and every tree and shrub shimmered with fresh, green springtime color. The men had been banished to the barn with more wine, until the house was in order again.

"So, what is it like to be a married woman?" Cornelia asked, smiling.

"Cornelia, it hasn't soaked in yet. Is this truly my wedding day, or is this a beautiful dream that will disappear by morning?"

"Seems real enough to me. Anna, you're glowing today, and I'm so happy for you and Adriaen. My wish for you is courage and faith in God when the trials come. May you live in peace here below, and in Heaven." They were sitting beneath an apple tree, and Cornelia looked angelic with the budding branches surrounding her.

"Thank you, Cornelia. I wish the same, and God's will be done."

The rest of the guests soon joined them in the garden, and the rest of the day was spent chatting beneath the trees. The bride and bridegroom were given a comfortable bench and sat together as their guests' voices hummed around them. Anna wondered if Adriaen was thinking about his first wedding day. Of course, it would have been a much livelier affair, with dancing and plays and musicians. Maeyken would have been a lovely bride.

"What are you thinking about?" Adriaen asked, smiling.

"Me? Oh, honestly, I was wondering about your first wedding, and thinking what a beautiful bride Maeyken must have been."

"She was, but no more beautiful than you are." Anna shook her head, finding this hard to believe, but she was glad Adriaen thought so. "The wedding was a rather wild affair," Adriaen said, "and truth be told, I was glad when the last drunken guest had left. This wedding is small, but so very warm, friendly, and respectable. God must be smiling, whereas my other wedding celebration was rife with dissolution and debauchery, and must have made God weep."

Later in the day, dusk was creeping up on the wedding party. The guests sighed in satisfaction at the end of a wonderful day filled with brotherly love, and their often-hungry stomachs were filled with delicious food. Just as the guests were preparing to leave, and parting words were being spoken, a dog barked in sudden alarm.

"What's that?" Anna gasped, holding a cup of wine halfway to her mouth.

"The bailiff! Everybody run!"

In an instant, everyone stopped what they were doing and stared at each other in dumbfounded alarm. Galloping hoofs clattered along the street in their direction, and in a snap of the fingers, the wedding guests scattered. By long practice they had already formed a plan in their minds, and knew exactly where they would run to if the worst happened.

Anna groaned as she ran, not sure where Adriaen was now. He had been in a conversation with the other preachers, but she prayed he'd see her and follow. She looked desperately to the left and the right; which way should she go? She spied a pile of wood. Could she hide there? No, too obvious. Already the soldiers were dismounting and shouting when they saw people running everywhere. Anna saw the baker racing into the woods and decided it was her best bet as well. Lifting the floor-length wedding dress off the ground, she ran like the devil was after her. Her feet in the new leather shoes slapped the ground in a frenzied beat.

Over her shoulder, she saw two of the soldiers remounting as they watched their prey fleeing to the woods. Anna gasped, terror closing in like a steel fist around her heart. Oh Lord, not on her wedding day! Could the little glimpse of paradise disappear so soon? She scrambled beneath low hanging branches and clawed her way through undergrowth, branches tearing at her wedding cap and her new gown. Anywhere to get away. She could no longer see the baker, and she headed for the thickest corner of the woods where the trees stood close together and certainly no horseman could follow.

At least if they followed her on foot, she had a better chance of evading capture. Her breath came in short, terrified gasps as she ploughed deeper into the forest. The tears coursing down her cheeks came from terror and despair, but most of all anger. Couldn't they leave a woman in peace on her wedding day? Now the bride was running through the forest and the groom was nowhere in sight. But perhaps better to be nowhere in sight than to be captured.

It seemed like ages until she no longer heard her pursuers, but she was hopelessly lost. The sun slowly withdrew into the hills for the night, and dark shadows surrounded her. She collapsed onto the floor of the forest, exhausted and gasping for breath. Hatred for those who hunted innocent people filled her soul with bitter sorrow. She almost hated God for not saving her from this trial, but then quickly fought down the thought. He had the power to smite her dead right here if He chose, and then what? She already felt the flames licking at her feet; and she dared not continue with such unholy thoughts.

She was newly married and newly baptized, and no evil should dwell within her. As a disciple of the Lord, she should be praying instead, even if screaming in frustration would be easier. The only thing she desired was to escape this dark forest and go somewhere safe with Adriaen. Except there was no safe place for an Anabaptist in the Netherlands or anywhere else.

She sat on a mossy piece of ground with tangled bushes all around her, feeling like a rabbit hiding in the brambles to escape a fox. It was a quiet spot with only some chirping insects and twittering birds intruding on the solitude. The sweet, clean fragrance of earth and pine was soothing, and she felt no real fear from the forest. She supposed this spot was as good as any other to spend the night.

As she kneeled on the damp earth, she tried her best to pray, and though it wasn't skilled or practiced, her prayer came from her heart.

"Dear God in Heaven, can you see me? Do you care that I am alone in the forest with darkness coming? You must know how much I want my bridegroom, whom I love so dearly and have waited for so long. I know I am unworthy, but if it is Thy will, please return him to me. Thy will be done. Amen." Feeling better already, she remembered the Anabaptists saying that God is everywhere. That meant He was here in the deep forest with her. On the soft, mossy forest floor, she slept.

She awoke in the pitch dark of midnight to the sound of someone crashing through the bushes accompanied by lights flashing. Rescue? Or pursuers? Who would be out searching at night?

'Please God, let it be Adriaen.'

"Aaannnaaa!" A man's voice echoed eerily through the forest. It wasn't Adriaen, but any rescuer was welcome right now. She felt damp and chilled, hungry and thirsty. What a way to spend one's wedding night.

"Hellooo!" she called out, her voice coming out in a croak. She tried again, "Hellooo!"

The snuffling dog found her first and commenced to lick

her face eagerly. Following closely behind was the baker and the long cobbler; the wedding guests on a search party for the bride. It was beyond disappointing that the bailiff ruined her wedding night like this. Why oh why?

"Where is Adriaen?"

"He is safe for the moment in an empty farmhouse. He twisted his ankle when he was trying to escape so he's waiting there and howling for his bride." The baker chuckled, though the cobbler managed to keep his face straight. "He tried to come on the search party and ended up flat on the ground again, so he admitted defeat. He was frantic and gave us no peace until we agreed to search until we found you, regardless of how long it took."

"Did the bailiff arrest anyone?"

Their faces saddened, and the cobbler's face became even longer than usual. "Susanna was caught, and Captain Clemens and the neighbor couple and their son, a stable boy."

"Oh no! Not Susanna!" This was a heavy blow. After all the work, and the risk she had taken to have the wedding at her house. And the Captain. He had stayed around so he could attend the wedding. If only he had left for the sea instead.

"Is Cornelia safe? And Jan?"

"They are both safe." Anna was glad for that, but her heart ached for those arrested. She sent another prayer heavenward, asking for strength for her friends to stay true to the end.

The men led the way out of the forest and within an hour they were walking up to the door of a small house nearly hidden in the forest. Adriaen came hobbling to the door, supporting himself with a stick.

"Anna, my wife!" he exclaimed joyfully, "I died a thousand

deaths waiting here for you! To be stuck back here waiting was the worst agony I have ever known." His wife, he said. So it was still, incredibly, true. He let the stick fall and held out his arms.

She rushed into them, careful not to knock him over, then became oblivious to her rescuers as she rejoiced at finding Adriaen safe and whole. The two men slipped quietly away, shaking their heads and chuckling.

Chapter Twenty-Five

Amsterdam, June 1533

Striving side by side for the faith of the Gospel...Philippians 1:27

The newlyweds moved to a tiny house in Emden, a seaport town in Lower Saxony, on the river Ems. Because the town had an independent government and was rarely raided by the Council of Holland, Emden was a kind of refuge for the Brethren. There was security enough for new preachers to be trained by those more experienced in the doctrine. When other cities and towns were deprived of their Anabaptist preachers because of execution, they would send to Emden for one of the Brethren to lead their congregation.

For the year after their marriage, Anna frequently accompanied Adriaen to meetings, in comparative safety and openness. She helped him with the female baptisms, removing their caps, replacing the caps after the water had been sprinkled, then offering the Holy Kiss as a welcome to the *Gemeente.* Her former life seemed far away, and she rarely missed her former church and its traditions and magnificence. Here, she could not remain friendless; the people were just too welcoming for that.

She did often think of Maeyken, and the children, especially Anneken. Maybe she would never hear of the baby again, a thought which tore at her heart. On the other hand, what if one day, she would chance to find her? She had asked around wherever they went, and sympathetic though the Brethren and sisters of the faith were, they could give her no clues. Nobody had seen a couple of Claes and Elizabeth's description, with two babies, even though there was a continuous trickle of refugees coming from the Netherlands and Germany. Only God knew where they were, and Anna prayed every day that they were safe, and stood strong in their faith.

In Emden, she met Dirk Philips, a former Franciscan, who had left his orders and become a disciple of Melchior Hoffman. He was a well-organized man of strict, unwavering beliefs who set many a man on a sure, straight path. Some of her new friends confided they thought him a little *too* strict, but his vision for the *Gemeente* was a pure church, without spot or wrinkle, and he stuck firmly to his principles. Melchior's favorite topic was the last days, and Dirk's favorite topic was building this pure church of believers only.

Adriaen spent much of his time reading and studying the Bible and religious tracts written by the Brethren, especially those of Dirk Philips and Melchior Hoffman. Sometimes he got letters from Brethren elsewhere, usually well-handled ones which had been passed from brother to brother across various borders.

One early June evening, Adriaen looked up from reading a letter he had received that day. "Anna, what do you think of this?" he asked, holding up a wrinkled piece of paper. "Jacob van Campen has sent this letter, asking me to return to Amsterdam to help lead the congregations there. Would you be willing to move back to Amsterdam?"

Anna stopped in the middle of chopping onions and stared at her husband. "You mean we can't stay here, where we are safe?"

"We can say no, but if this is the Lord's will, I am willing to go, if you don't object." He looked at her sympathetically. "I know you have made friends here whom you would miss, but I would introduce you to other women of the faith in Amsterdam, so you wouldn't be too lonely."

Anna sighed. "I cannot object if you are called to go there, but you are right. I have felt so welcome here. The women are friendly, and since I do not have the gift of making friends easily, I wonder how it will be back in Amsterdam."

"Now that you are my wife and baptized, I think they will open up more to you. We will pray about this, and listen to what God puts in our hearts. Do you agree?"

"Yes, you are right." So much had happened while she lived in Amsterdam previously, and now she might have to go back into the middle of the fray; this time as a baptized member of the Brethren, married to a preacher.

Adriaen and Anna said their good-byes one fine day in June, with visits to all their friends. In these unstable times, any departure of dear friends was worth a tear, and for the newlywed preacher and his wife, there were plenty. Cornelia had moved to Emden to be near Anna and was living with another Anabaptist family. She decided that she would stay there. Cornelia had won the hearts of the congregation, and Anna knew she would be loved and cared for as long as she lived.

They arrived in Amsterdam by boat at the end of June without incident and moved into a sparsely-furnished apartment above a shop which the Brethren had found for them. There was a bed-in-the-wall, a table and a couple of rickety chairs, and not much else.

"The place needs a woman's touch," Adriaen said, looking

around the single room.

"That may be, but I could live anywhere with you as my husband." Husband. The word still felt delightful coming from her lips. It was more than she deserved, to have won his love and his heart—except she hadn't really won him. God had put love in both their hearts as a gift, as a reminder that prayers do come true, even those from inexperienced believers.

Adriaen knelt in front of the fireplace to get a fire started, and Anna found a bucket and headed down the steep stairs to find some water. The apartment needed a good cleaning, but it would be home.

A couple of hours later, with a fire burning cheerfully, and everything scrubbed clean, it began to feel more livable. Adriaen took his New Testament out of his pack and set it on the mantel, and they hung their few extra articles of clothing on some pegs in the wall.

Jacob van Campen had invited them to his house for supper, which took care of food for today. They finished cleaning just in time to straighten themselves up and head out. After a short walk of two blocks, they arrived at a tall, narrow house which backed onto the water. Anna could see a small boat bobbing behind it.

"Welcome in," Jacob greeted them warmly, "It's good to have you back with us." A shadow crossed his face. "So many have been imprisoned now, but the Lord keeps sending new men to help spread His word."

Jacob's wife, Aeff, came bustling in from working in her garden to meet them.

"So, you're the young woman that captured Adriaen's heart?" she smiled, and clasped Anna's hand warmly, then Adriaen's. "I'm sure we shall all become good friends." She shooed the men to the back room and allowed Anna to help prepare the meal.

Anna immediately felt at home with the friendly, plump little woman. Her house was clean and organized, and fragrant with simmering beef stew. Aeff tossed in the herbs she had brought from the garden, and bent to remove a crusty apple tart from the oven. Anna's mouth watered. She hadn't seen such a wonderful dessert for a long time.

While they ate, the conversation soon turned to their church.

"We have a meeting tomorrow night, and I hope you can both come," Jacob invited them. "We are gaining more followers all the time, some say there are thousands, though I don't know who is counting. We're fortunate that the authorities have settled down for the time being. If the officers from the Court of Holland don't come around, we're usually unmolested."

"Do you know where Melchior Hoffman is now?" Adriaen asked.

"He is now travelling throughout the Roman Empire, gathering the 144,000 chosen ones for the return of the Lord." Jacob said. "An elderly friend of his had a vision that Melchior is a prophet, and he will be the head of these people. He is calling on all believers to meet him in Strasbourg, which is to be the New Jerusalem."

Anna shivered. She had to remind herself that as a believer, she had nothing to fear at Christ's return. Only joy awaited those who believed in Him, and suffered for His sake. But still...she dreaded that day, and it wasn't far distant.

"He says that according to Revelations 14:1 the chosen city will suffer a bloody siege, then recover its strength and destroy the ungodly," Jacob said.

"Do you believe this?" Anna asked.

"Believe it? The Old Testament foretells this, and it has been revealed to Hoffman that he is the new Elijah, calling sinners to repentance and warning them of the great day to come. I believe this to be true, yes."

The beautiful apple tart that Aeff had made nearly refused to go down Anna's throat, and she barely tasted it.

After the meal, Jacob showed them his shop where he sheared cloth, and Anna watched half-heartedly as he demonstrated how he snipped all the fuzz and little bits sticking up in the wool. At Jacob's urging, she ran her hand over the sheared cloth, and remarked how much smoother the cloth was afterwards.

"It has to be perfect before we ship it out to other lands," he said. "It serves as a reminder of how our sins have to be perfectly forgiven by God before we can ship out to Heaven. We must trust Him perfectly."

Later, the men went out to some of the other *Diener* to discuss business, and Aeff showed Anna her garden, and chattered away until Anna felt completely at ease with this woman.

"I must take you to meet some of the other young women in our congregation. The more you get out and about, the sooner you will get to know more people," Aeff said. "We're all one big family in Amsterdam, and there's lots to do. Refugees come in almost every day from places worse off than us, and you wouldn't believe how poor most of them are. They've had to leave everything behind; their homes, their animals, their friends and family...everything."

Anna nodded, gulping to prevent the tears from flowing. "I know, I used to live in Germany. I saw so many terrible things there." Somehow, kindly Aeff seemed like the very person to pour out her grief to. She would understand. Only, Anna had been trying so hard to put it all out of her mind; the burning of her home with her loved ones still inside, and the cruelty of the provost, Aichelen. He had led the other horsemen to Mantelhof where they whooped and shouted as they rounded up human beings as if they were merely wild animals. The insane laughter still poisoned her memories. It all came pouring out into Aeff's sympathetic ears, like an avalanche that had been held back too long.

"Oh, I feel so badly for you," Aeff said. "We have had times of severe persecution here in Amsterdam as well, but remember… it is written in the Scriptures that the true church is a suffering church. Men reviled Jesus while He walked on earth, and so shall we also be reviled. Only for a short while longer, my friend. When Christ returns, he will gather those who love Him and take them to Heaven with him. There we shall have our crown at last."

"Thank you, Aeff, for reminding me. This is something I need to remember and talking about my terrors does seem to lighten the burden." Anna had never unburdened herself like this to Maeyken, though she had been a loyal friend. Maybe the subtle differences in faith, though not spoken of, had been present then, though hidden from view. Many times, she regretted the harsh words she had said to Maeyken about the Anabaptist faith, and wished she could ask for her forgiveness. Now, she could only pray to Christ to be forgiven, in private, thankfully without kneeling at Father Hendrick's feet.

Later that night, as they lay in their lumpy bed, Anna turned to Adriaen. "Do you believe in what Hoffman is saying?"

"I cannot do otherwise, since he has had visions and revelations. Don't worry too much about it," he said, pulling her close to him. "You, as a believer and beloved of God, have the hope of a crown in Heaven. The ungodly who persecute the chosen ones, are the ones who will suffer eternal damnation."

"I'm so glad I have you to turn to for advice and comfort, because so often I doubt the strength of my faith, even when I really want to believe."

"That is natural, my dear wife. We are weak, but the Lord is strong, and He will carry us through."

The following night, the young couple tidied themselves, descended the steep stairway and let themselves out onto the cobbled street. They lived in a different part of the city than before, but the narrow streets and tall buildings were the same. As they passed the deep doorway of a weaver's shop, Anna heard a childish voice, and out of the corner of her eye, she caught the flash of a little girl's skirt.

Anna gasped. "Trijntgen!"

Adriaen looked at her oddly. "Anna, what is wrong? Trijntgen is..." He hesitated, not quite able to say the word.

"Nothing. Just when I saw the little girl in there, something reminded me so much of Trijntgen." She swiped at her eyes with her sleeve.

Adriaen cleared his throat. "It doesn't get any easier, does it? I find myself watching out for the children all the time, then I remember that they are gone."

"I do wonder where their little graves are, and how they died."

"Who told you about their deaths?"

"Jan went out making inquiries and met a man on the

street who told him they're gone, but he didn't say more. He also said you were in a dungeon and would be executed. Thank goodness that wasn't true."

Adriaen frowned. "Why would he tell you that? Did you know this man?"

"I didn't see who Jan talked with, because Cornelia and I were hiding behind a tree. We didn't want anyone on our street to recognize me."

"Good idea. Well, false information goes around all the time. I had a few narrow escapes, but the Lord has watched over me thus far. We both know my luck will not last forever, so we can only thank God for every day we can be together."

"Yes, and I do thank God for every hour that you are free. We have been blessed, and maybe you will live to a be an old man with grandchildren."

A pained look crossed Adriaen's face. "Even if Melchior is wrong, and the Lord hasn't returned by then, you must know it will not come to be. It is very unlikely I will escape capture that long and live to see my grandchildren, dear Anna. Much as I would like to have it so."

Other people were walking in the same direction they were, and as they crossed the bridge, the swish of oars could be heard in the water as several boats slid by.

"Do you know what I would like?" Anna asked.

"A kiss?"

"Certainly, my husband," she grinned, "just not in public. I was thinking of riding a boat." She watched the boats as they swept smoothly along the Amstel river, the passengers manning the oars with muscular arms.

"That might be managed. I know a man or two who owns a boat, and I'm certain they wouldn't mind us borrowing it. I'll see what I can arrange." Adriaen smiled at her as if he were a knight bowing to his lady's wishes.

"You are too good to me." Anna loved him more with each passing day, it seemed.

"I can never be too good. There is always room for improvement."

The meeting was being held in an open space near a tower, which cast its long shadow on the assembly. Several hundred people must be gathered there, something that wouldn't have been possible a year ago, when the Court officers were lurking about. On a raised platform near the tower wall, Jacob van Campen stood beside a man Anna had never seen before; tall, dressed in a black robe knotted at his waist with a leather rope belt, he looked around with the imperious air of a king. Jacob's meek and mild demeanor was in sharp contrast to this rather arrogant man.

"Who is that?" Anna whispered to Adriaen, who stood protectively at her side.

Adriaen's brows drew together in a frown. "That is Jan Matthys of Haarlem. He used to be a baker, but now he is one of the leaders of the Brethren, ever since Melchior has left for Strasbourg. Melchior was going to put a hold on baptizing people for two years, after Trypmaker and the others were executed, just to keep a low profile here in Amsterdam. Matthys would have none of that, and kept on baptizing."

Anna stared at the gaunt, stooped figure; he was no longer young, perhaps in his fifties, with a huge, nearly bald head, and he looked around with black, piercing eyes. She gripped Adriaen's sleeve and whispered, "I don't like him."

Chapter Twenty-Six

Amsterdam, June 1533

See that none makes a prey of you by philosophy and empty deceit...Col 2:8

"There was something different about Jan Matthys," Anna said, as they walked home in the velvet mantle of midnight. "He seems a bit...wild? Or like he is straining to hold back violence. And those eyes! They were like black fire."

"He is just worked up because of the imminent coming of the Lord. Melchior Hoffman claims to be the new prophet, Elijah, from the Old Testament; and Jan Matthys believes himself to be Enoch. We need to listen, and help them to call the whole world to repentance, so that when the Lord returns we are ready to meet Him."

Adriaen seemed a bit distant, and Anna swallowed her panic. She prayed he was not being misled by this fanatical man. Anna had met many God-loving, pious people who were ready to sacrifice their life rather than fight, or kill anyone, but Matthys seemed prepared to push his agenda no matter what the cost.

"What does Jacob van Campen think of this idea?" Anna plucked at Adriaen's sleeve, trying to break past her husband's preoccupation.

"Hmmm? Oh, Jacob. Tomorrow, some of the leaders are going to meet at his house to discuss what position we are going to take, and how we may best prepare our congregations for the coming of the Lord."

"Can I come?"

"No, this is a meeting for the leaders only. No women will be present."

Only by a hair did Anna stop herself from stamping her foot. Women were always left out of the most important decisions, and had to abide by whatever the men thought best. All because Eve, in the garden of Eden, broke off an apple and gave it to Adam, proving herself incapable of resisting evil.

The next day, she tried to hide her irritation when Adriaen left. What was she going to do while he was gone? She hadn't met anyone yet except Jacob's wife, so she decided she might as well pay her a visit. Smoldering inside and smiling outside, she entered the van Campen's house.

"Here you are!" Aeff greeted her. "I was just ready to come and get you, and take you on a round of visits to the sick. This is a good time for you to meet some of our congregation." She packed a woven straw basket with herbs, and liquids in dark bottles, along with some food. *Cornelia should be here,* Anna thought. *She would have lots of healing to do here, with thousands of members.*

As the two women passed the weaver's shop, Anna happened to glance up to a window on the top floor of the building. Some movement had caught her eye; only the fragmented glimpse of a child with blonde hair, then a heavy curtain quickly pulled in place.

"Aeff, who lives here?" Anna's heart beat faster. Was she going insane, expecting to see Trijntgen at every turn? If she did exist anywhere, it would be as a ghost. But still, it was odd that she couldn't shake the feeling of the child's presence nearby. She had better not tell anyone, or she'd be accused of being a witch herself.

"Just an older childless couple, who are Catholics. Why do you ask?"

"I fancied I saw a child at the upper window just now."

"I've seen Maria with a fair-haired girl at the market. I think she adopted her niece a year ago or so. The little girl's parents are dead, I believe." Aeff shifted her basket and kept walking.

Anna wanted to stop right there and investigate the child who lived with the weavers, but she feared it was nothing but a foolish, ungrounded notion. The woman's story about a niece might be true, just as well as not, but Anna would dearly love to see the child up close.

They reached the end of the cobbled street and Aeff turned into a muddy lane, where the rundown houses sagged in despair. Barefoot, raggedy children quarreled in the yards, while starving dogs wandered about aimlessly with noses to the ground. Through one of the leaning doorways, half covered in tangled vines, Aeff entered, and Anna followed warily.

"Here comes our angel of mercy!" a scrawny, dark-haired woman cried from a seat near the window. "Come in, come in, welcome to my humble abode." Her dress was too faded and patched to have any particular color, and dirty bare feet peeked from beneath the hem. She stooped over a piece of rich, gold cloth in her lap, working on some fine stitching.

"How are you feeling today?" Aeff asked. "Is your back any better?"

"Oh, it's well enough if I keep still. I just don't see how I can care for the children, they're just looking after themselves for now."

"Where is Balthasar?"

Balthasar? Where have I heard that name before?

"He's gone to look for some errands to do, trying to earn a few farthings to keep bread on the table. He's a good boy, and does what he can."

"Just like his poor, dead father did, then. I brought you a nice loaf of bread and some apples too, so you need not worry about feeding your children today." She rummaged in the basket and laid her offerings on the table. "And I brought you this concoction to rub on your poor back."

When Anna and Aeff turned to leave a short time later, a gangly young boy, possibly twelve years of age, came whistling up the walk. By the looks of it, he had grown out of his carefully-mended gray tunic and hose faster than they could be replaced. To Anna, he seemed vaguely familiar. The whistle stopped in mid-note as the boy stared at her, his eyes wide.

"Say, Anna! That is your name, isn't it? You used to work for Simon den Kramer, and you cared for Adriaen's children after Maeyken died, isn't that so?" He lifted his flat cap off his dark head, smoothed his hair, then settled it down again securely.

"Yes," Anna said. "But...how do you *know*?" Where had she seen this boy's face before?

"Don't you remember when I found Janneken for you? And you gave me a nut cake by the ice just before Christ's Mass day?"

"You!" Anna exclaimed. "Now I remember. I didn't think I would ever lay eyes on you again."

The mother by the window looked up in surprise. "So you were the one who was the answer to our prayers at Christmas last. I told the children that God never fails to care for His own, though we didn't know where our next meal would come from. Then Gerritt came home with this most wonderful nut cake, and I must say, I've never tasted anything quite so delicious."

Anna blushed. "I'm glad you enjoyed it."

"Did you ever meet up with Adriaen?" Gerritt asked, "That mean little servant who spoke to you on the ice that day is a spy for the Council of Holland; and besides spying, he makes people as miserable as possible by spreading lies. Did he tell you Adriaen is dead or in a deep, terrible dungeon?"

"He told me he was in a dungeon and would be executed. Thankfully, it wasn't true. But Gerritt, you won't believe this. I have been married to Adriaen for an entire year now!" She smiled at his astonishment. "And now we're your neighbors."

There was a general rejoicing all around and promises given to visit each other often. Anna and Aeff spent the rest of the day ministering to more of the poor and the sick, and by evening, Anna thought the soles of her feet must be half worn through. Wearily she climbed the long stairs to the apartment, collapsed onto the hard, little bed, falling asleep on top of the covers.

She awoke several hours later, to the tantalizing smell of hot meat pies, which Adriaen had purchased at the market.

"A special treat for my tired wife," he smiled, as he offered her one.

"I certainly am tired, and this smells wonderful."

They sat side by side on the bed and devoured the pies to the last crumb, licking their fingers clean.

"So, am I allowed to know what you men talked about today, or will it be too much for my feeble brain?"

Adriaen chuckled. "I wouldn't call you feeble-minded, wife. You had enough sense to marry me."

Anna swatted him with a handful of apron. "I almost

married Jan, you know."

"I'm glad you came to your senses in time."

"So am I. Now, how did the meeting go?"

Adriaen sobered. "Jan Matthys is sending out twelve apostles, whom he selected, throughout Christendom to spread the news of the Lord's return. Instead of in Strasbourg, as Melchior Hoffman first prophesied, the New Jerusalem will be in Munster."

Anna blanched. "You are not one of these apostles, surely?"

"No, I'm not going. But Jacob van Campen is leaving next week, as soon as he takes care of some business matters, and I will lead the congregation here in Amsterdam while he's gone." Adriaen was bent forward, with his hands clasped between his knees, and his head slumped.

"When is he predicting the Lord's return?" Anna asked.

"As soon as the 144,000 chosen ones have gathered in the New Jerusalem. We are going to Munster to await his coming for as long as it takes, but probably in 1534."

"We? Did you say we? I don't know if this is a good idea."

"Anna." He turned to face her with a stern look in his dark eyes, which she had never seen before. "Isn't it time you surrendered your will to the Lord, and let Him rule your life? The Scriptures say a woman is to be obedient to her husband in all things, without complaint. I want you to be still and accept my authority in this."

Anna stared at him, as tears welled in her eyes. She hardly recognized her husband in this mood. Did it have anything to do with the meeting with Jan Matthys? The man was unsettling, but perhaps that, too, was just a foolish woman's opinion.

"What would you have me do?"

"I want you to be ready at all times for when we are summoned to Munster, and we will join the chosen ones there. This could be in a few weeks, months or even years. We will wait for the Lord's instructions through the prophets Elijah and Enoch."

This news sounded unlike anything Anna had heard from the Anabaptists. She desired to be a true believer and have a part in the Kingdom of Heaven when she died, but this idea of going to Munster seemed fantastical. Why did they need to go there to meet the Lord?

"Are you sure these men are prophets? Doesn't the Testament say to beware of false prophets?" They had barely settled down in Amsterdam, and now Adriaen was speaking of moving again. She had a hard time keeping more of her woman's opinions to herself. Even when she did speak up, no man would listen to her, including her own dear husband.

"I don't want to go."

"Anna! That is like saying you don't want to go to Heaven!"

"Jan Matthys has really got you hooked, hasn't he? she retorted. "Isn't he just a vain, self-proclaimed baker-turned-prophet?"

"Can you prove that he is not a prophet? Jesus had humble beginnings too."

"Jan Matthys doesn't look like a prophet. Nor does he act humble and loving, like Jesus did."

"I thought his words made perfect sense."

How could it be that she and Adriaen were arguing about this? Anna had always looked up to Adriaen when it came to matters of faith, and trusted him to show her the way of the Anabaptists. But this was carrying things a little too far. Call it women's intuition, or women's weakness, but she had no intention of following Jan Matthys to Muster.

Chapter Twenty-Seven

Amsterdam, December 1533

We had courage in our God to declare to you the Gospel of God in the face of great opposition...1 Thess 1:8

In December 1533, the twelve apostles ordained by Jan Matthys commenced on their preaching journeys, scattering in all directions throughout the Netherlands. They were to gather the chosen ones and have them meet in Munster, Westphalia, which was to become the New Jerusalem. In the meantime, Melchior Hoffman was arrested in Strasburg, further proof that he was the true Elijah, because it was written that the prophet would be imprisoned for a time.

Anna was sad to see Jacob van Campen go; he seemed less excitable than the others, and not prone to violence. She worried that without his influence, the rest of the Anabaptists would be swayed by the intense Jan Matthys and they'd all go on this fool's errand to Munster.

It was probably because she hadn't learned all their ways, but she couldn't shake the feeling of an undercurrent of some undefined, restless spirit at work in the congregation. With the mystical, but always peace-loving Melchior Hoffman now in prison, and Jacob van Campen gone, many of the agitated and over-zealous element remained in Amsterdam.

Adriaen's moodiness troubled her, but she didn't want to impose her unwelcome, weak woman's views on him. Did he already regret having married her because she was too vocal in her opinions? The idea broke her heart.

Upon moving to the Netherlands, she had learned that women were treated better here than elsewhere, but still, they had much less authority than men. At least women were allowed an education here, as well as to inherit. Otherwise she could never have inherited Simon's little house. Still, women were not thought strong enough to have a worthwhile opinion on spiritual life, and therefore had to defer to the man of the house. Anna's heart rebelled. This most important of matters should not be entrusted to anyone else. Who was going to suffer for her in the after-world if she refused to obey God's word?

Several months passed, until one chilly, drizzly February evening, Adriaen came home clapping his freezing hands and shaking flecks of ice crystals out of his dark hair.

"Miserable weather out there," he remarked, reaching into an inner pocket of his heavy, black overcoat. He handed her a little booklet. "Here is something for you to read," he said, "Maybe it will help you to better understand the doctrine. I feel like I have failed to make it clear to you."

"Oh, Adriaen. I'm sure that is not the case. Though it does seem like things are shifting away from the peace-loving spirit there was in the beginning." She flipped through the few pages of the pamphlet, which bore the lengthy title *'Prophezey oder weissagung uss warer heiliger götlicher schrift. Von allen wundern und zeichen bis zu der zukunft Christi Jesu unsers heilands an dem jüngsten tag und der welt end. Diese prophecey wird sich anfahen am end der weissagung (kürtzlich von mir aussgegangen in eime andern büchlin von der schweren straf Gottes über alles gotloss wesen durch den Türkischen tirannen'.*

"Is this written by one of the Brethren in Munster?" Anna asked.

"Melchior Hoffman wrote it, explaining verse by verse the twelfth chapter of Daniel, where Daniel writes of his visions of the end times." Adriaen huddled up to the fire, and droplets of melted ice dripped off his clothing, sizzling into the flames. "Would you mind reading it aloud? I'd like to hear the words once more."

"I will do it for you, if you don't mind slow reading." Anna decided she would stop reading if it became blasphemous or violent. "At that time shall arise Michael, the great prince who has charge of your people. And there shall be a time of trouble, such as never has been since there was a nation till that time; but at that time your people shall be delivered, every one whose name shall be found written in the book."

"So you see, this does tell of a time of trouble, which we certainly have," Adriaen said. "The pope is Michael, and the Brethren are the people whose names are written in the book, and shall be delivered."

"So you think that means we should go to Munster?" Anna looked at her husband, bewildered. What was wrong with staying right here?

"We will have to wait for fair weather, I would think. And first the news must be spread everywhere, and that will probably take a few months. In the meantime, we will continue to meet here in Amsterdam as usual." Adriaen lighted a candle and set it on the table, while Anna watched him from behind the booklet in her hands.

She never tired of gazing at him, and marveling at the miracle that had brought them together. They had come through so many trials; surely nothing could pry them apart, least of all the faith which had joined them. Adriaen opened his Testament and read some more from the book of Daniel, in preparation for his next sermon.

A taut silence filled the room while the wind raged outside and rattled at the window. Even so, Anna had nearly fallen asleep beside the fire when she heard the bang of the street door below, followed by the clumping of someone's footsteps coming up the stairs. Her heartbeat picked up speed until she thought it would drown out every other sound.

Knock, knock.

Adriaen opened the door, shrugging in Anna's direction as if to say, 'It is who it is.'

"Obbe! Come on in," Adriaen said, welcoming the tall, stooped man. "Nowadays you never know who stands on the other side of a closed door, friend or foe. I didn't know you were in town." Anna's shoulders lowered back to where they belonged, and her breaths returned to normal as she rose to greet him.

"Meet my wife, Anna. And this is Obbe Philips, brother of Dirk Philips, who we met in Emden."

"Aren't you the doctor who fixed up Adriaen after he was in prison?"

"That I am. He looks much better than he did that night." Obbe smiled. Anna didn't even want to think about that night. Adriaen led his visitor to the table, with Anna joining them after she set out some food and wine.

"I came by tonight in the hopes that you share my concerns about Jan Matthys and his followers." He looked at Adriaen, who fingered the pages of the Bible in front of him, but didn't answer. "I admit that I regret from my heart that I ever agreed to go on this recruiting campaign for Matthys; I'm afraid he will resort to violence if things don't go his way. I think we should always seek peaceful solutions for every problem. I doubt this idea of Matthys is going to impress the authorities favorably, although I haven't found many men who share my opinion."

Here's one woman who shares your opinion, Anna thought.

"I don't see any harm in it." Adriaen said. "It's quite possible that God has spoken to Hoffman and to Matthys, and I for one don't want to take the chance of not being in Munster when the Lord returns."

"But haven't you heard? These Brethren are buying arms to take to Munster. Will we need weapons to meet the Lord?"

"No, but we might need arms to destroy the whore of Babylon, which is the Catholic church, and that will happen before His arrival," Adriaen said.

Obbe shook his head, "It is hard to know what is right, and I weep to think of the Brethren divided like this." A few tears did indeed drip onto his sober black robe. "I had to leave Leeuwarden because my name is on the Stadtholder's bulletin, naming me as one of the 'seducers and deceivers who wander about the country, who re-baptize the people and teach bad and dangerous errors and sects.' God help me find the truth in these treacherous times."

Adriaen nodded. "That is true. All the more reason to let God speak through the prophets he has sent."

Anna clenched her teeth. Anyone could claim to be a prophet. Even she could foresee that things would not end well for the Anabaptists if they challenged the might of the government, the might of God notwithstanding.

"Where are you residing, Obbe?" she asked. "Perhaps when we've thought this through, we will contact you." She, for one, wanted to know where the peaceful ones dwelled. Not for her these talks of revenge and destroying tyrants. Adriaen sent her a withering glance, but said nothing.

Obbe gave her the name of the family he was staying with, then got up to leave, probably thinking he had wasted his time on a fruitless errand. He smiled at Anna as he left. "Remember, if there's anything you want to talk about, you may find me at Jan Peauw's house." Anna nodded.

When the door closed, Adriaen turned to face her, "So, my wise little wife, you do not believe my words?"

"I believe the words written in the Scriptures. 'Thou shalt not kill' for example. And 'vengeance is mine' says the Lord." Her voice ended on a sob and she fled to her stool beside the fire, weeping in anguish. How much pain could one endure in a lifetime? Now that she had finally accepted a faith she could believe in with all her heart, Satan was already busy ripping things apart; the fledgling church, her marriage, and even sanity, it seemed.

The following afternoon, Anna put on her warmest clothing and ventured outside for a walk, hoping to clear her mind. Adriaen maintained a disapproving silence, and it hurt too much to bear. "Oh God, show me what to do," she prayed. "I want to obey my husband, but I want to obey you more, and You have commanded us to love our enemies, and to do good to those who hate us. Please help me understand, and to do Thy will."

She walked on blindly, not caring where she went, wishing only to be alone. Her footsteps took her to the edge of the sea; in times of distress the water soothed her soul like warm milk on a cold night. Taking shelter from the biting wind behind a warehouse, she gazed across the gray waves of the *Zuiderzee*, where even in winter the tall masts of sailboats dotted the shore.

In fact, several men were working on the docks, and

boats were in the process of being loaded with provisions. Who would be going on a journey in the winter? Her heart skipped a beat. They wouldn't! At the same time as she was trying to deny it, she had a sinking feeling that the fanatics would. They *would* attempt to sail to Munster on the *Zuiderzee* in the wintertime to meet the rest of the prophesied 144,000 chosen ones.

And Adriaen! Did he know about this? Or was she building a bridge where there was no water? Slowly, she turned towards home, having gained no comfort from her walk, only more worries. Where was the house Obbe Philips was staying? It must be close by. Maybe he would know what was happening. She considered going back home and asking Adriaen whether he knew anything about it, but thought better of it. He had made his views plain enough, and she didn't feel like arguing with him. Anna asked a pedestrian for directions to the Peauw house.

The house was like any other on the street; tall, narrow, and made of stone, the usual square kitchen with its fireplace and one window inside. A cluster of people chatted in the back room, and Anna noted with some relief that a few other women were present.

"Anna! Welcome in." Obbe Philips waved her into the room, motioning to an empty spot on a bench, beside a pretty young woman. "You're just in time to catch up with all the news. Jacob van Campen is back from his journey, and we're anxious to hear everything."

Anna decided her question could wait.

"Before we go any further, I want to ask if you all have seen the new placards that the Court has sent out?" Obbe looked around the room with dismay evident in his eyes. "There is a reward of twelve guilders on some of our heads, including mine. In fact, everyone who has baptized others or is named a leader is wanted by the authorities."

Heads nodded all around. This was no surprise to them.

"The reward will be attractive to the many job-less refugees in Amsterdam. Let us all use extra caution," Jacob van Campen said. "This is probably the work of the new sheriff, a man the Court sent just this week. Too bad they got rid of Jan Hubrechts. It's dangerous when the Court replaces one of the faithful with an outsider, and we must pray earnestly to God for His protection. Barring that, let us receive strength from the Lord to stand true in our trials until the end."

"So, what's the news from Munster?"

Van Campen's brow furrowed. "I don't know what to make of it, but I heard Jan Matthys is now in Munster, and he and his followers have begun evicting non-believers from the city. I heard they threw out old people, women with newborn babies, and children, locked them outside the gates with nothing except the clothes on their backs, on a day too miserable to let a dog out." He frowned. "I don't believe we should treat people so badly."

A fiery-looking man wearing a tall hat stood up and addressed the Brethren. "I say it's high time we got rid of the godless. God has made known to us that all believers should get ready to go to the New Jerusalem, the city of saints, because he is going to punish the whole world. Flee out of Babylon and deliver every man his soul, for this is the time of the Lord's vengeance."

This must be Jan van Geelen. He had been going around gathering supporters for Matthys, as one of the twelve apostles. She wanted to leave immediately. These were not the words of love and peace that had won her to the

Anabaptist faith. The group had gone sadly astray, and she had nowhere to turn. Even her husband took the side of the fanatics. She shifted on the hard bench. Would it be too rude to just leave?

Van Geelen dug into his leather pouch and withdrew a handful of pamphlets, which he passed around to everyone. He smiled engagingly as he handed one to Anna.

"Where's Adriaen? Hope he's not ill?"

"I don't think he knew you were gathering here." Anna looked down at the booklet in her hands. *Van der Wraecke.* 'Vengeance'. Oh dear. When no one was looking, she let it drop beneath the bench, her long skirts hiding it. Adriaen didn't need to see this.

"What! How can that be? Obbe? Didn't you bring him word yesterday?"

Obbe struck his forehead with his palm. "Can it be? I must be getting old and forgetful." He peered at Anna. "So how is it that you are here?"

"By chance. Say, I was walking out by the docks and there was some action out there by the sea. Does anyone know who would be preparing for a journey in the winter?"

Some of the men looked at each other, half sheepishly. "We'll be embarking for Munster soon, so we're just getting a few things ready now. As soon as we hear a date, we're leaving. Are you coming with us?" van Geelen asked.

Anna put her shoulders back and sat up straight. "Not if there's violence involved. I will take my chances here." For a few seconds, there was complete silence in the room.

Jacob van Campen cleared his throat. "I'm staying too."

"And me." Obbe Philips said, folding his arms. More people opened their mouths to speak.

The fiery man stood up again. "Now listen, good people.

Dare you disobey the commands which God Himself revealed to the prophets? I tell you, the Kingdom of God is at hand and all the godless will be destroyed. Repent! Repent!"

Suddenly he leaped into the air, twirled around, and headed out the door onto the street with his hands in the air, shouting, "Woe! Woe! Woe to the godless!"

Several of the young men followed, and ran whooping down the street. Anna ran too, as fast as she could, to the safety of her own home. She didn't want to be caught with these people.

In the morning, she heard that a few of the young men had been arrested. But Jan van Geelen had escaped.

Chapter Twenty-Eight

Amsterdam, March 1533

Give thanks in all circumstances, for this is the will of God...Thess 5:18

After a frenzy of baptisms in February, when Jacob van Campen and another *Diener*, Pieter Houtzager baptized over one hundred believers in one day, preparations began in earnest to remove to Munster. Bags were packed and properties rented out or sold. People from the surrounding farms, villages, and towns streamed into Amsterdam to catch the boats. They were planning to leave by the twenty-second of March. Men, women, and children flooded through the city gates every day, swelling the population of Amsterdam.

The inns and boarding places were full of strangers from every walk of life, although the common people and tradesmen far outnumbered any persons of higher social standing.

The authorities did nothing to prevent this exodus; on the contrary, a few of the councillors were sympathizers, if not actual members of the Anabaptists. Those going to Munster were called the 'saints' by Matthys, and Anna thought they probably wanted to leave before the warm breezes of spring blew in the Court officers from The Hague.

"So, my dear, have you changed your mind yet?" Adriaen asked, while folding his extra hose and packing them in his bag. "Won't you come with me to the New Jerusalem?"

Anna swallowed. Was he really going, whether she went or not? She had never dreamed on their wedding day that they could ever part because of differences of opinion on the Anabaptist faith. Death by execution had always been on her mind, but not deliberate separation. Adriaen had taught her so much about love and faith during their short marriage, and how following Jesus' words was the most important object of one's life, important enough to suffer and die for rather than disobey any part of it.

Right now, forgiveness was the most difficult command to obey. How does one forgive the zealots who divide a husband from his wife? And how does one forgive one's husband for abandoning her? The Bible on her lap held the answer, and she had read it over and over, 'For if you forgive men their trespasses, your heavenly Father will also forgive you, but if you do not forgive men their trespasses, neither will your Father forgive your trespasses.' There it was, plain and simple for all to see. Easy to read about, and nearly impossible to do.

"Father, have mercy," she prayed silently, bowing her head, "and put the right words in my mouth."

Adriaen had finished packing his few things, and he reached for his own copy of the Bible on the mantel. He flipped through until he came to the passage he sought, and began to read, "'Wives, be subject to your husbands, as to the Lord. For the husband is the head of the wife as Christ is the head of the church, his body, and is himself its savior.'" He peered at Anna, his intent brown eyes searching her very soul. "Would you disobey these words?"

A bug under the heel of a boot could hardly have felt any smaller than Anna did right now. The words were there, as he showed her, and what was she to do?

"Anna, you are a chosen one of God. Please come with me

to the New Jerusalem, where we can wait with joy together for the Lord's return."

Anna shook her head, as sobs shook her body. "Adriaen! Adriaen! Do you know how much I want to be with you? But I know in my heart that seeking the Lord with violence is wrong. I cannot go."

And so he left without her.

An icy wind blew across the cold, gray waters of the Zuiderzee that March morning when they sailed. The cobbled streets of Amsterdam rang with the footsteps of many hundreds of excited men carrying swords, halberds, and pikes; and women and children with their backs bent under bundles large and small, filled with everything they could possibly carry. They had been told to bring weapons and money especially.

With shouts and cheers they piled onto the boats, unmindful of the frigid air and the icy sea. Anna watched from the safety of her window as Adriaen was swept away in a tide of exuberant pilgrims. Was she a coward after all, to stay here? The loneliness began as soon as Adriaen closed the door behind him. There was still time to go with him. All she needed to do was throw her few belongings into a bundle and leave. But she could not forsake the faith God had given her, the everlasting gift of His mercy and love. Should she try one more time to convince Adriaen to stay home? At least go as far as to the boats and watch him leave? She loved him so much, and with a jolt, she realized she had not told him that she loved him before he left. And she hadn't told him that she forgave him. And she did forgive him, from the bottom of her heart.

She hesitated only a moment longer. In a few more minutes she clattered down the stairs, half laughing and half crying. What would Adriaen say when he saw her? Would she even be able to get close enough to say anything? Surely, she could get close enough to wave to him. He must not leave, believing that she held anything against him. What if he died, and she never got a chance to tell him?

The crowd swept her along the street, past the door of the weaver. A little blonde-haired girl with large blue eyes was standing in the alcove of the doorway, watching the crowd hurrying by. Anna's heart slammed against her ribs. Could it be? She fought her way back through the swarm, grasping and pushing. Her backpack caught on something and she shrugged out of it.

"Trijntgen!"

The little girl had disappeared into the building. Anna plunged after her, determined not to let her get away. She dodged between huge looms, which were already humming with industry, weaving colorful threads into beautiful cloth. The weaver's apprentices stared at her in amazement with their flat eyes as she charged first through the workshop, then through an arched doorway and into the weaver's living quarters.

"Halt!" A startled female voice ordered. "Stop right there!" Anna skidded to a stop in front of a buxom woman, whose two hands were stuck deep in a bowl of bread dough. A pair of dark, beady eyes sent daggers through her heart. She gasped, and stood there uncertainly, embarrassed for having barged in uninvited. But she had to know whether she had seen right; if the girl wasn't Trijntgen, it must be a twin.

"I'm looking for my niece, and I just saw her run into your house," Anna explained, nervously pushing back some escaped strands of dark hair.

"There is no such person in this house, I tell you. Get out!"

Anna frowned. The woman was lying, of course. She perked her ears as she heard a scuffle on the stairway beyond the kitchen. A woman hissed a string of unintelligible, angry words.

"Aaannn…!" A child's voice was quickly muffled, probably with a hand.

Trijntgen! Anna stood paralyzed for a second, then ran across the kitchen towards the stairs.

"Oh no, you don't!" A doughy hand grabbed at her skirts, pulling her back. "Just who do you think you are, trying to kidnap my little darling? I think not, as long as Old Lysbet has breath in her body."

Anna swirled around to face the red-faced cook. "She belongs to *me*! She was kidnapped from *me*!" She tore loose from the woman's grip, splattering little bits of dough behind her as she made another mad dash for the stairs.

"Trijntgen!" she called, taking the steps two at a time. And then the little girl was flying towards her in a flurry of blue dress, blonde hair, and sobs. A loose-jowled woman ran hard on her heels, swearing, and grasping ineffectually for a handhold on the girl's dress.

"Anna!" Trijntgen cried, throwing her arms wide. Anna caught her up, turned around and pushed the cook aside as she barreled down the stairs, through the kitchen and out the door. The two elderly women were no match for her panicked race outside, and the still-surging crowd soon swallowed her up, with her precious burden clinging to her neck.

Now, to find Adriaen in this multitude would be impossible. If Anna couldn't find him here, she would just have to go as far as Bergklooster, where the prophet Jeremiah, alias Jan van Geelen, would meet them, and lead the chosen ones the rest of the way to Munster. No one could ever follow her or Trijntgen in this tightly-packed throng, and she didn't have the breath to ask the little girl any questions. That could wait. The main thing was to re-unite her with her father.

Several of the boats were already filled to the brim, and pushed slowly away from shore, their tall, white sails snapping in the wind above the spirited passengers' heads. Anna was swept along the gangplank, and then she was stepping over the sides into one of the gently swaying boats. Adriaen was nowhere to be seen.

Anna found a spot on the deck to sit, and settled Trijntgen on her lap. She smoothed back the child's beautiful blonde hair, so like her mother's, and noted the blue circles under her eyes.

"Trijntgen, you have grown so much taller!" But not bigger around the waist, Anna thought. "Are you feeling quite well?" The pale face was a little concerning.

Trijntgen nodded. "I helped Aunt Maria in the weaver's shop, cutting threads. I don't work as hard as the other 'prentices, so I eat after them, when all the vegetable bits are gone. And me gets the crusts they leave behind for the servants and the beggars. Anna, I'm glad you found me." She snuggled against Anna like she always used to do.

"I'm glad too," Anna said, "and guess what! We're going to find your *Vader* once we arrive in Bergklooster."

Trijntgen gazed at her in awe with her huge blue eyes. "*Vader*? My *Vader*?"

"Yes, *schatje*, your own *vader*."

"And Mother and Bettke and Dirk?"

"Your Mother is with God, remember? She is happy in Heaven now. Was your sister not with you at the weavers'?

And little Dirk?"

"No. Just me and the 'prentices." She frowned. "I want to find them."

"I know you do. And I will help you." Finding Trijntgen was miraculous, and she took the time to send a thankful prayer heavenwards. Finding the others would need a few more miracles, only perhaps they really had died. She did not for one moment regret stealing Trijntgen back from the weavers', and she would steal the others as well if she could find them.

She watched the other passengers intently. What if Adriaen was on this boat somewhere? There were more women and children than grown men, and looking at their hopeful faces and bright smiles, she wished she, too, could feel their happy expectation. Well, she had made her choice, come what may. Finding Trijntgen seemed like a good omen for the future.

Clouds gathered on the flat, gray horizon as the last of the thirty boats pulled anchor and pushed their way through the murky waves. Amsterdam had spit out all her restless souls, and sent them skidding across the sea by the thousands. In joyful anticipation, they set their sails for a New Jerusalem, where their bridegroom would descend from heaven and gather His chosen bride for the city of God.

If everyone threw their weapons into the sea, Anna could celebrate with them wholeheartedly. But God would show her what to do next, and she resolved to submit to His will.

For two days they sailed, and Anna had to resort to begging for food. Her pack had either been stolen, or it lay trampled back in the streets of Amsterdam. She thought she could have waited until Bergklooster, but she had the child to consider. One thing about the Anabaptists-- they didn't begrudge you anything so long as they had a crust to spare, and they would rather do without themselves than let anyone else go hungry.

On the second day out, Anna sat on the deck, gazing over the gray waters, and at the clouds billowing and taking up the whole sky. She did love the gentle rocking of the boat, although many of the women and children were already sick from the constant rolling motion. Trijntgen slept beside her, her head on Anna's lap. The thirty boats travelled together, but the one Anna and Trijntgen were on flanked the others on the sea-side, giving her an unbroken view of sea and sky.

Suddenly, she sat bolt upright, startling Trijntgen out of her nap. Was someone screaming for help? Not one, but many screams. Anna sprang to her feet, and grabbing Trijntgen's hand, she raced to the other side of the deck. She clapped her hand to her mouth. One of the boats was tipping its passengers into the frigid *Zuiderzee*, though they clung to every available handhold, panicking and screaming. The *Hollandia*, which Anna was on, raised the alarm, and edged closer to the sinking *Gouden Leeuw*, picking up her drowning passengers. Another boat, the *Brederode*, also came to the rescue, and between them, they hauled in the passengers.

Anna made herself useful, helping the icy cold victims change into dry clothing as they clambered aboard. Clothing was donated by the generous people on board the *Hollandia*, and blankets were produced. The victims' teeth chattered with cold and shock, and Anna noticed most of them were women, some were men and there were a few children. At last, the final victim climbed over the rails, a dark-haired man whose strength seemed to be nearly gone.

"*Vader*!" Trijntgen screamed, streaking to the man and throwing herself into his arms, water and all.

Anna could not move. It was him. Her husband. Finally, her feet obeyed her mind, and she made her way over to the embracing father and child. Everyone on deck turned their eyes towards the scene, though none of them could know what a true reunion this was.

Adriaen eventually noticed Anna, and his eyes widened. "Anna! You came!" He clasped her waist with his free arm, as tears rolled down his cheeks. "I don't deserve such joy! Oh my God, forgive me! Anna, Anna, can *you* forgive me?"

"Gladly!" Anna said, her heart too full to say more. A curious crowd had gathered around them, and dry clothes were passed to Adriaen. Shielding him with her body, Anna helped him into them, then led him and Trijntgen below to her berth. There was little privacy, but somehow, Anna and Adriaen managed to spill out their experiences to each other, amidst prayers of thankfulness and promises never to part again under such misunderstandings. Trijntgen's story was retold again, and Adriaen could not believe how close they had been living to his daughter, all unknown to them.

"When I was in the water," Adriaen said, "I realized what I had done by abandoning you, Anna, and God as well. I almost allowed myself to sink beneath the waters in shame. But God kept calling me through my conscience, and finally I made the effort to reach this boat. I guess that's what it took for me to realize that you were right. I promised God that if I survive, I will not go to Munster."

"Oh Adriaen. I'm so glad you did. I was going to try and see you off, and somehow get the message to you that I love you, and I forgive you. I was so afraid you would die with wrath still between us."

When Trijntgen was informed that Anna and her father had married, her joy knew no bounds. She embraced Anna tightly with her scrawny little arms, and asked, "May I call you *moeder*?"

"Of course you may." Anna's cheeks were wet, all of a sudden.

"How about we forget about going to Munster, and instead go on a search for your brother and sisters?" Adriaen asked Trijntgen. "Of course, they may be in Heaven, but we will ask God to help us find out what happened. How would you like that?"

Trijntgen's eyes brightened even more, and she clapped her hands. "I would love that, *Vader*!"

Further Reading on This Subject:

Websites-

homecomers.org/mirror

gameo.org

Books-

The Anabaptist Story by William R. Estep

The Reformation of the Sixteenth Century by Roland H. Bainton

Youtube-

Upon This Rock lectures by Dr. Thomas Fudge

The hymn 'Oh God do Thou Sustain Me' on page 97 was written by Leonhard Sommer in the 16th century and is also on YouTube.

Real historical characters-
Melchior Hoffman* Jacob van Campen* Aeff van Campen* Obbe Philips* Dirk Philips* Jan Hubrechts* Jan van Geelen* Jan Matthys*- Jan Trypmaker* Simon den Kramer (an actual person, but fictional story) * Felix Manz* George Blaurock*Conrad Grebel* Charles V* Martin Luther* Ulrich Zwingli* Johann Tetzel* Albert of Hohenburg* Count Enno
Fictional Characters-
Anna* Adriaen* Maeyken* Trijntgen*Bettke* Dirk* Anneken* Jan* Janneken* Helga* Joachim* Officer Stein* Pieter the servant* Balthasar* Elizabeth* Claes* Jorg* Cornelia*Captain Clement* Hans* Susanna* Andrew* Father Hendricks* Jan Jansen* Greta

Actual Historical Happenings:

1. The burning of the house with Anabaptists inside in Mantelhof, Germany on Jan 1, 1531
2. The heads on poles in the Amsterdam square
3. The sailors who rescued their brother from jail
4. The decree of Charles V ordering the arrest of the Anabaptists
5. Anabaptist women chained to table legs so they could continue working
6. Not recognizing Anabaptist marriages and children called illegitimate, so they couldn't inherit
7. The tauferjager were specially commissioned to hunt Anabaptists. First 300 men were hired, but they couldn't control Anabaptism. So they hired 1000. These were rough men who looted and killed without mercy.
8. The 30 boatloads of people heading to Munster from Amsterdam

Thank you to the following people for helping to make this book a reality:

Blair Thornburgh, editor

Wendy Cross, for your very helpful critique

Roseanna White, cover designer

The SPS-FOF members for all your support

Reviews on Amazon are greatly appreciated and help other readers and the author. Thank you for reading Sword of Peace.

43981016R00201

Made in the USA
Middletown, DE
04 May 2019